A Pirate

Danielle Thorne

DEDICATION

To my readers and friends who are one and the same: Thank you for your continued faith in me and for supporting my love of all things historical. Most importantly, thanks for reading my books so I can write to my heart's content. I couldn't do it without you.

MORE BOOKS BY DANIELLE THORNE

The Privateer of San Madrid
By Heart and Compass
Josette
Proper Attire
A Smuggler's Heart
A Captain's Bride
His Daughter's Prayer
Turtle Soup
Death Cheater
Cheated

A PIRATE AT PEMBROKE

CHAPTER ONE

Sophie Crestwood felt nothing could be worse than having a father who gossiped like a goose and a mother who read Gothic novels. Although it could be amusing at times, in truth she was long past her first Season and the only Crestwood at Leatherbury weathering serious reservations about her ability to find a husband.

Life at Leatherbury trotted along rather slowly compared to Town, but she liked it that way despite worrying about her lack of opportunity in the rolling hills of Higfield. Then there was Jack. He stood behind her, soaked and dripping water onto a lilac rug that protected the floorboards of her room.

She turned from her looking glass and pointed at the puddles. "Where have you been?"

"Swimming," he said without sorrow. He swiped at the copper cowlick that hung perpetually over his right eye to radiate more innocence.

Sophie was not ashamed of her youngest sibling, merely exhausted by him. In the farthest recess of her heart, he amused her, although he knew everything there was that tried her patience. Things she fancied disappeared. Things she did not fancy found their way under her bed or into the ivory armoire beside her dressing table. At her elbow rested a soft folded, cloth. She handed it to him with a flick of her wrist. "What will Papa say when he learns you've skipped your Latin again?"

Jack dried off the best a twelve-year-old boy cared to do and handed her back the damp cloth. "Mr. Lyman doesn't care if I do my

4

studies or not. He's overcome with his new volume of poetry and Margaret."

"Margaret?" Sophie's mind imagined housemaids with round cheeks and hips, and she flushed with understanding.

"Guess what I discovered?" Jack dared.

"The pond."

"No," he said, ignoring her wit. "I went over the rock wall to Pembroke and walked up to the house."

"Pembroke? Jack, you could have been shot. Someone lives there now."

"Do I look like a hare? Besides, no one was in the woods anyway." Jack cocked his head toward the door to hear if any of the servants were eavesdropping. "It's all commotion at Pembroke Hall, don't you know."

Sophie put a hand on her hip. "You ginger-haired devil."

"It's true. Mad Murdock's heir has come home. I seen the carts and wagons myself. There were heaps of strange looking things like we saw at the Bazaar."

Sophie maintained her look of severity, more at his grammar than his spying, but a morbid curiosity caused her to utter, "And?"

"Oh, I didn't see *him* as such, but the servants were there." Jack grinned with such wickedness his brown sun spots glowed. "They wore monkey jackets and tar caps and had pigtails down to their backsides."

"That doesn't make them pirates." Sophie gave a little shake of her head. "They are men who've come home to rest until the press gangs hunt them down again." A short ride from Portsmouth, Higfield was no stranger to the Navy press.

"They looked like pirates," Jack insisted in a loud whisper. His moss-colored eyes shined. "They was so fresh I could smell the salt and tar."

"You're ridiculous."

"I know what I seen."

"What you *saw*," Sophie corrected. Jack exercised a terrible grammatical habit, not to mention vocabulary when he became irritated or excited. It gave him the air of a lowly Jack Tar, an idea he relished.

"They're brown and withered like bad fruit, and one had a fishhook hanging from his ear. It's a whole band of buccaneers from the Indies. They've come to hide out at Pembroke Hall."

Sophie's breath escaped in a laugh. "You, dear brother, have been listening to rumors. Why would they come to England? The gibbets are here. The poor man living there now just happens to be a captain who's inherited, and it's about time, too. Why, I've watched Pembroke crumble to the ground my entire life. I imagine it was grand once upon a time, but—"

"Papa says—"

"Papa?" Sophie chided him, for everyone knew Mr. Crestwood's penchant for embellishment. "Go change your clothes before you catch a chill." Sophie pointed to the door.

"Pretty Sophie," Jack muttered, "you don't know nothin' at all."

"I know you shall be late for supper, and Papa will complain about it until the very last candle goes out." She shut the door behind him and finished pinning up her hair without any help. Where was Margaret when she actually needed her? "Pretty Sophie," she sniffed.

Despite her grimace, Jack's compliment pleased her. She was neither gifted with a great mind like their elder brother, Richard, nor as fearless and brave as Jack. Her music and netting were very well indeed, but any young lady could claim those accomplishments.

A bell rang for supper. Ignoring it, she frowned. Very little, Sophie worried, laid beneath the fair complexion and deep-set eyes that mirrored her movements in the looking glass as she smoothed down the pleats of her gown. "Pretty as a doe," was how Jack described them when feeling complimentary. "Dull as church," he amended when being a dog.

Sometimes Leatherbury and its occupants rubbed up against one another's nerves like harsh wool. Besides Jack's efforts, this occurred most often at the supper table while Papa mused over the latest tittle-tattle, and it began quite early this late afternoon.

"Carrots," Mr. Crestwood said with pleasure. "We haven't had a crop like this in so many years." He closed his eyes like they melted over his tongue.

"They are very good, Papa," Jack agreed, although they were from the cellar, last year's, and quite chewy.

This only encouraged Papa, who informed them his last dinner at Lady Mary's estate was no comparison when it came to the carrots at Leatherbury. Their carrots had not been half so capital, if he did say so himself, and didn't Mrs. Crestwood agree?

"Of course, you're right," murmured his wife, "I do not prefer the carrots at Oak Grove."

Sophie raised a brow and glanced at her mother because this was a perfect opening for a little teasing, but Mama had a faraway look which meant her thoughts were back in the library with her most recent novel.

"I don't remember the carrots at Oak Grove," said Sophie in a loud voice. She studied Jack and saw his mind scrambling for more conversation. He was waiting for an opportunity to speak, so he could draw away attention from the fact he'd neglected his studies, much like he had done at boarding school. She knew her brother would argue the pursuit of a naval career necessitated the skills of wading and floating more than schooling.

"How were your lessons this afternoon, Jack?" She smiled as she took another bite of carrots and decided they tasted very good indeed.

"I don't recall," Jack replied. "Papa, any news from Pembroke?"

"Ah," said their father, raising his fork in the air, "Sir Edward's heir arrived just yesterday from the Indies. They say it took four carts to bring his belongings up from Portsmouth, and there are more on the way. Can you believe it? How many things can a man possibly keep aboard a boat?"

"A ship. He's a captain, Papa," Jack reminded him. "He can use the entire hold to stow his valuables if it pleases him."

"A captain, that's right." Mrs. Crestwood's comment surprised them all. She cleared her throat, took a drink, and set the goblet back on the oblong table with a light hand. "No doubt Mr. Murdock has led an exotic life."

"*Captain* Murdock," Jack said under his breath.

Papa nodded. "Yes, and to be an heir, too. It makes no sense at all. How he came into his epaulets, one can only wonder. Sir Edward was never keen on the Navy. Speaking of the son," Papa said in a conspiratorial voice, "I understand the sins of the father have followed him home."

Sophie glanced at her father's drink with a wary eye.

"It must be he is the rightful heir," said Mama, in a vocal stream of thought, "though I'm sure news of Sir Edward taking a second wife did not reach here at all. I would have read about it."

"I've been made to understand," her stout husband insisted, "he had an eye for the ladies of the Caribbean." He gave her a scandalous grin. "Hmm? Ha-ha!"

"Papa," Sophie exclaimed, but she could not stop from smiling.

"Mr. Crestwood, please," said his wife, blinking fast, but her lips curled up with the admonition. "It's indeed a quixotic notion, but if he is the new owner of Pembroke Hall then he is most certainly worthy of it unless there has been some undiscovered intrigue." Mama leaned forward in her seat like one of them might share something to drag her thoughts away from the shadowy figures and dense fogs in her books.

Papa shared his gift for sniffing out news the way a hound tracked down a fox. "He did not need the Navy with his family name, so he must have gone to sea under some other circumstance."

"According to Mrs. Porter," offered the seldom chatty Mrs. Crestwood, "the family's holdings in the Indies were lost years ago. A violent storm or earthquake, or perhaps a horrific fire burned the plantation to the ground. It must have been tragic." She hesitated then looked down at her plate with pity in her eyes.

Papa's conversation frothed along with his wife's encouragement like a tidal wave. "I doubt it was a natural event. It's no secret Sir Edward spent the family fortune on gaming and drink, the poor devil. He always did like to sport, even before he went..."

His voice faltered, and he scowled as if recalling a memory but shook himself out of it the way a horse tossed its head. Sophie looked at her mother who frowned over her half-eaten meal. Papa carried on: "Pembroke's heir must keep up some manner of business in St. Kitts, else he lies heavily in debt."

"Pirating," offered Jack. "He is a captain after all, even if it ain't the Navy."

Mama's head jerked up, and her eyes held a curious light. "No, I could never believe it." She repositioned herself in her chair and picked up her fork. Papa, looking both pleased and aghast, declared, "We shall soon find him out." He stabbed another carrot.

"Poor Captain Murdock," Sophie said, chuckling as she did so. "He's only just arrived and already his title is questioned, his income decided, and his career open to speculation."

"The word is he is no *poor* man, my dear." Papa looked around the table and lowered his voice. "I hear tell he intends to refurbish Pembroke Hall to its original glory. It will take a great deal of money."

"Well, he could not do so on a lieutenant's pay," Jack said.

Papa's smile gleamed in agreement.

"Let us presume he is respectable," Sophie decided. "You should call on him and welcome him home, Papa. Then we shall puzzle it all out."

Her father frowned again and fell silent. In the peculiar quiet, Mama said without looking up, "He must have come into his fortune some other way."

"Buccaneering," Jack repeated, and though Sophie raised her eyes to the aging plaster ceiling, this time neither one of her parents corrected him. Her father looked both excited and appalled, while her mother's expression remained distant.

"When will Richard come again, Papa?" Sophie wondered, to change the direction of their coarse conversation. Her elder brother had been married over a year, and his visits to Leatherbury had been few and far between.

"Lavinia writes they will not be able to return in time for the assembly," said Mama. No one could deny the disappointment in her tone.

"They won't attend?" Sophie grimaced. "I do miss Lavinia. I'd hoped they would stay with us for a time."

"Yes, we need them here," her father harrumphed. "Besides," he nodded at Jack, "we could use an extra man in our fishing party."

Jack glowered at his plate. "Which Richard don't like to fish or hunt," he said, using his vulgar deckhand vernacular. "I'm twice the shot he is."

"Oh, ho!" laughed Papa, "I see a contest in our future."

"He's no match, Papa," Sophie agreed. She leaned across the table. "Jack's quite the marksman and fisherman, too, but Richard is better with accounts." Jack gave her a rueful look.

"It's true," she said with a shrug. "You're as poor at figures as your sister."

"I am not," he said, his ire rising.

"Now, boy," said Papa, for Jack's temper, was as well acknowledged as his sister's candid observations.

"My dear," their mother interrupted, eyeing her son with consolation, "you do not need to be a good shot to be a clergyman. Your living is waiting for you to come of age thanks to Lady Mary. After Oxford, you will get your inheritance and settle at Oak Grove, and there in its elegant parsonage you'll raise a lovely family with a pretty little wife who will be grateful for the situation."

"Which may well be above her own," Papa added. "It's a fine situation for you, Jack."

Sophie bit her lip as their words fluttered through the air and settled across the table like dry leaves. Jack stared down in silent exasperation. Mama's lips were pressed together in a stiff line. Margaret chose that moment to enter with another course.

"Treacle-dowdy," exclaimed Sophie with pretended delight. "I've waited all the day long!"

THE NEXT MORNING SOPHIE went to the library and pulled out the only book of maps at Leatherbury. It did not offer up a great many details, but the islands of the West Indies were carefully drawn and labeled. She wondered where their new neighbor had lived. Antigua? Tortuga, perhaps? Her mind raced. St. Kitts, Papa had said.

Someone had drawn a black flag beside a little dot. Jack, no doubt. Poor boy. Sophie knew her parents believed Jack's dreams of seamanship to be a passing fancy, but he had set his heart on a naval career before he was out of strings.

Sophie let out a heavy breath over the drawings. It was her duty to marry well. Mr. Crestwood was a country gentleman with a generous income, but it had not increased when he won his wife's consent so many years ago. If only he'd been titled. Sophie was certain that was all that was lacking in her favor. Her family was respectable. They had a good living and were settled in her father's ancestral home in Higfield, a stone's toss from Guildford, almost equally between London and Portsmouth. It was a convenient location, but none of it had made her a young bride. She had tried, really, she had and so cheerfully, but—

"Miss Crestwood?"

Sophie looked up from her contemplations. Margaret stood at the door wringing a cloth in her chubby hands. "Mr. Lyman can't find Master Jack."

"That boy!" Sophie slid off the honey-colored sofa and set the book back on its shelf. "I have a good idea where he may be found." She snatched a bonnet and shawl then strode out the back of the house beyond the kitchen garden.

Once through the gate, she forgot her urgency and slowed her pace, skipping across the greening pastures beyond Leatherbury. A silvery light shined over the land like it knew winter had kissed the world goodbye for good.

Sophie strolled through scattered groves of trees until the woods began to thicken. Uncertain of her direction, she stopped for a time and studied the landscape. She tried to recall the direction of the small lake her brother so loved. It was rather a large pond, but the family insisted on calling it a lake. She assumed this was because it sounded grander, but it was only a murky green body of water with some good fish and a few waterfowl.

Looking ahead, the view stopped her in her tracks. It was not the lake, but the crumbling grey peaks of Pembroke in the distance. Sharp, formidable chimneys stood frozen above the hills hinting at some foreboding curse. They were dark and ragged, grasping at the sky with angry fingers as if intent on pulling the heart out of heaven itself. She swallowed and took a step into a pool of light.

The sun warmed the morning pleasantly enough so there was no chill creeping through her layers. In her favorite walking dress and faded spencer, Sophie clambered over the dilapidated stile that bridged a stone wall separating one pasture from another. On one side lived Leatherbury, warm and busy, with happy animals and eager flower buds. On the other side slept Pembroke.

Sophie looked up the hill at the towering manor, trying to imagine life within or without its walls. Pembroke answered like a giant shadow challenging the day. She suspected the foundation was ever more gnarled with weeds and ivy than when she last saw it, holding itself prisoner on its very own property. It seemed forever doomed to crumble away and sink into the earth like a ship into the sea.

The rumbling sound of hoofbeats made Sophie turn her head to look. From out of a copse of trees blocking her view, appeared a rider on a dark bay mount. The gleaming horse slowed to a trot and spying her, its master veered it off toward the echelon of stone and approached her.

Sophie stepped back against the wall, leaning into the cool rocks for support. When he came to a halt within a few paces, the man removed his cocked hat, a black Naval-looking issue with a pretty blue cockade. It stood out, just as his bright eyes stood out against his tanned features. Unlike the neat bicorn, his long and wild hair looked unkempt.

She had imagined the dark silhouette would take the shape of a specter, perhaps with a sickle in its grip; instead, the man appeared to be a gentleman, although not an altogether cheerful looking one. Other than his hat, he was rather too brown and rumpled.

The horse snorted and turned its head to look. The rider studied her, too. Sophie pushed off the wall and stepped forward.

"You are from Leatherbury?" he assumed in a flat tone.

"Miss Crestwood of Leatherbury," she informed him, trying to maintain her poise. Her attempt was foiled by an examining gaze with eyes so pale she could not tell their color. She couldn't look at him without glancing away and back again.

"Then, Miss Crestwood of Leatherbury, I recommend you and your family reacquaint yourselves with the boundaries of your estate."

Her mouth dropped open at the ill-mannered admonition. Sophie stared up at the horseman from beneath the brim of her bonnet, aware she was mussed and the hem of her skirt damp with morning dew. One of her ribbons, frayed at the end, fluttered up in her face, but she did not shoo it away. "I am looking for my brother," she said, trying to gather up enough dismay to feel slighted. "I assure you I am within the boundaries of my home."

The man gazed off into the distance behind her. "I beg your pardon," he said with a slight apologetic cough, "but your boundaries are the low-lying stream several yards beyond the grove, to where I suspect I've just chased your brother from my orchard."

"Please accept my apologies then." Sophie kept her tone stiff.

She whirled away toward the stile to escape his censure, wondering why she did not debate with him that the wall had been the boundary for ages. Everyone knew it, even the cows. She was a Crestwood from Leatherbury, and she knew it. Who was he to tell her differently?

She pivoted back on her heel. "And you are?" She inclined her head and raised her chin, just like Lady Mary did when she questioned some poor, culpable soul.

The man shifted in his saddle like he might slide off the horse, and the animal whinnied and stamped its feet. "Captain Edward Murdock of St. Kitts and still you are trespassing on my property."

Sophie swallowed. Her cheeks flamed with embarrassment. Captain Murdock, Jack's imagined buccaneer, with a look of disapproval on his sun-browned face was anything but gracious. Gathering her skirts, she turned her back on him. She dared not look; she would not be angry or show any offense. He would feel awful, she just knew it, when he realized he'd made a horrible mistake. How cold and cruel and above all rudely suspicious to behave like she was intruding with some wicked scheme in mind. The poor man was misinformed.

A small flash of something round and black flew past her head. She winced, just as the horse snorted in pain. The mount squealed and reared, and Sophie watched in dismay as it forced the captain to cling desperately to the reins to keep from falling off. The look on his set jaw could have lit a match. He called down the beast, but it was no good. Taking a deep breath, she called out, "Welcome to Higfield, Captain Murdock." He was too busy to reply.

Another shot fired from the grove like a miniature cannonball and smashed into the stone wall with a crack. Sophie jerked at the explosive sound and watched the startled horse race back up the pasture hill in the direction it had come. The rider flailed as he struggled to stay astride.

Sophie's hand flew up to her mouth to stifle a laugh. She looked in the direction of the unseen attacker and made a face of furious warning less someone be hurt. Once over the stile, she strode into the woods to find Jack.

He was waiting for her underneath a giant walnut tree, with a grin on his face. "Capital aim, wouldn't you say?"

Sophie could not hide her amusement, but she tried to sound stern. "You could have killed one of us, and you spooked his poor horse!"

"I hit his mount right where I intended."

"What will Papa say," Sophie asked, "when word is sent to Leatherbury? Oh Jack, what trouble you've made for us now. This isn't boarding school. That was Captain Murdock himself." She snatched her brother's arm and forced him to escort her through the trees.

"I was defending my sister."

"Gentlemen don't hide behind trees and lob nuts. Really, Jack, if he is truly angry he might call you out."

"Me?" Jack spread his hands out in an innocent gesture. "I'm just a lad."

"No, you are a young man, and it's time you start acting the part. If you want to convince the family you are fit for a naval career you must quit running through the forest like Robin Hood."

"Mama did mention the army," Jack reminded her. "I am going to sea, but at least she's opened her mind to something other than a cassock." He led his worried sister by the hand through a maze of young saplings and tangled briars that would soon droop with fat berries.

"Leatherbury is this way, Sophie. You've no direction at all. At least look up and follow the sun."

"I have good sense, of which you have none. We best hurry and get you back to Mr. Lyman before he tells Papa."

"I'm sure he won't notice."

"He has noticed, and he's sent Margaret to find you. They've probably alerted the entire household, and now we will run into Old George if we're not careful."

"That old fool? I'm twice the gamekeeper he is."

"Just because he's losing his sight doesn't mean he can't track down the likes of you."

Jack shook his head in disagreement. "I've been dodging Old George for years now. It's the pirate next door that's the problem."

"You can't say he's a pirate, Jack. It's a vicious lie."

"Did you see the dagger at his side?"

Sophie nodded.

"Gold, covered in jewels, and glimmering in the sunlight." Jack lost himself in a slow, pensive daydream.

"You are such a romantic, silly boy. He's probably uneasy about poachers since he's just arrived. Pembroke's been deserted for years."

"I'm not romantic, Sophie. The fellow ain't been here a week, and already he guards his estate like a bull."

"Perhaps he was riding out to get a feel for it."

"He already knows the boundaries," Jack insisted.

"Yes, it's true." Sophie reflected on Captain Murdock's confident knowledge of the stream bed she had maneuvered around and then the stone wall. "I imagine he's studied Pembroke's papers."

"You mean maps. All pirates can read maps." Jack eyed her with gravity.

Sophie gave him a teasing smile back. "You sound like Mama. She was reading that *Robinson Crusoe* this morning."

"I read it ages ago."

"Then I suppose you must know everything about which you assume: Captain Murdock is indeed a pirate, the stone wall is the estate's boundaries, and you are well on your way to an infamous naval career."

Affronted, Jack let go of her arm and darted toward Leatherbury. It had come into view in the distance.

"Jack!" Sophie cried with exasperation, but he did not look back. Huffing in the warm air and put out with wandering boys and boundaries, she marched back home and up to her room to change her dirty gown and not think about Captain Edward Murdock of St. Kitts.

CHAPTER TWO

Gilded paper with small bouquets of salmon-colored flower buds adorned the breakfast parlor walls at Leatherbury. They made morning affairs pleasant and garden-like, even on damp spring days. Sophie felt a touch of affection for the room as she slipped into her seat.

Papa could not contain himself over the latest rumors from Town. He was a man of endless information, mostly the kind that had little utility, but as it was his duty to find an eligible match for his only living daughter, he had no qualms seeking out any detail that would assist him in accomplishing his design. Although sometimes to Sophie's great consternation, he was not as delicate as he was practical, she understood it had to be done.

"I hear," he said, smacking his lips over a three-minute egg, "Lady Mary will have a guest visit Oak Grove this year of whom everyone will be eager to be introduced."

When no one at the table raised their eyes in any way of hopeful interest, he continued louder than before. "The nephew, Henry Billingham, is coming to the country." He caught Sophie's eye and offered her a broad grin. "Not just to tour the estate he has inherited, I understand."

"First Sir Edward's heir, now Mr. Billingham will come. Two gentlemen of fortune," said Mama with interest.

"Yes, it's true," Papa said rather hastily because he had not thought of it before. Sophie tried to beam at them both, but she found she pressed her lips together and looked down at her plate much like Jack did when her parents showed interest in his future affairs.

At last, she managed to say, "Poor Lady Mary. How distressing, to have her home pass from her husband to another with her still dependent on its living."

"We saw him on the rare occasion when he was a boy, but it was years ago. Mr. Porter tells me Billingham finished his studies at Oxford and will have an inheritance from his father of five thousand pounds. It's unfortunate his aunt should be widowed, and that the elder cousin died suddenly, but he also inherits Oak Grove now, too."

"Two incomes. How uncomfortable he must be with his good fortune." Sophie looked at her father and smiled then glanced around the room to find something to hold her interest. Jack leered back at her, wide-eyed.

"My," said Mama, when it became obvious her husband waited for someone to respond, "that is a tidy sum indeed, at least five thousand a year, and to inherit such a great house, too." She also looked at Sophie who found the cuckoo clock to her liking. She studied the brass hands and willed them to move forward so the funny bird would waddle out. Papa leaned back in his chair and tucked his thumbs under the folds of his banyan.

"Pity all of Lady Mary's daughters are married," Sophie offered. Her father narrowed his eyes at her and grinned like they shared a secret. "It will not do to make assumptions for the poor fellow," she added at his steady gaze. She felt rather on the defensive.

"I assure you," Papa said, "Lady Mary has a great many years of life yet, and Billingham insists she remains at Oak Grove. But I have not told the best part. I have been informed Billingham has welcomed the idea of being introduced to certain ladies of his aunt's acquaintance."

Papa dropped his hand on the table with a muffled clap and drew in a sharp breath, expended from his triumphant announcement.

Mama looked at Sophie, and the corners of her mouth turned up with some small amusement. Sophie smiled back but said nothing.

"I wonder if he's very ugly," Jack mused, "with pockmarks and a nose that drips all hours of the day, no matter the weather."

"Jack." Mama scolded him with a word and her soft tone.

Sophie's nose curled up in distaste.

"I'm sure no gentleman of fortune would ever lower himself to such a description," said Mama. The idea an heir could be so repugnant was impossible in her ardent mind. "Sophie will have every opportunity to examine him herself when he arrives." She glanced at her daughter. "Lady Mary has already promised me Sophie will be his very first introduction."

Sophie blushed that she should be the topic of so intimate a conversation while absent. It appeared Mama knew just as much about Papa's announcement, if not quite a bit more.

Jack held his tongue and pretended to find the whole thing ridiculous, but Sophie knew he'd secretly become fond of country maidens. He was noticing love and attraction, although it had not affected his desire to run off to sea. He was still a boy after all, although society would soon see him different.

"Then I will look forward to his re-acquaintance," Sophie replied to her family around the table, "leaky nose and all." From the corner of her eye, she noticed her mother's grimace. "Would it please you, Mama?"

"It would," said the lady though she added with a sigh, "but let us be hopeful Henry Billingham is the most handsome gentleman ever to set boots on the grounds of Oak Grove. Oh, what a great house!"

A gentleman, mused Sophie. Another one. Captain Murdock, she realized, was all but forgotten this morning. Or so he was until Jack kicked her shin under the table and said with a cheeky grin, "No pirate there. I wager he's dull as church."

"IT WILL BE A BEAUTIFUL evening for a dance. If the clouds do not all blow off, it shan't be too cold, either. You must wear your best white muslin with the lavender ribbon in your hair."

"It's my best new dress," disagreed Sophie, the night of the country dance, but Mama would not be swayed. After complaining of the evening chill sure to come, her mother offered to loan her a beautiful shawl with colorful swirls of slate and salmon.

In fairness to herself and her family, Sophie had been introduced to several eligible bachelors in the past year, but overall, they had been homely, conceited, or shamelessly desperate. Those beneath her income were no temptation to her father. To those who had a good family and respectable inheritances, he was polite and receiving. But to no end, his proper ambition and duty to his daughter had yet to yield any results. It would be a shame, Sophie thought, as the Crestwoods rode the short distance to Guildford, to be born with agreeable looks and a suitable family for no useful purpose at all. She imagined Mama might start reading Shakespearean tragedies if her daughter did not marry soon.

Papa was in a foul mood, grumbling to Mama as the horse pulled them toward the assembly hall. It dampened Sophie's excitement, and she hoped his love of gatherings and conversation would help him forget himself.

He'd spent most of the day distraught over reports of Jack's expeditions into the woods during scheduled times with his tutor. "I shall send Jack away again," said Papa, furious a private tutor should fail in his duty to Leatherbury. "Lyman came so well recommended. I heard all about him at the Red Fox. They were so unhappy to lose him in Yorkshire."

Jack's adventures had already caused his dismissal from a reverend's boarding school in Guildford. In hiring the young clergyman, Mr. Lyman, Papa hoped to better prepare Jack for Harrow School outside of London.

Jack could have saved himself from trouble, but rather than send his tutor packing and have Margaret scolded or worse, he kept the knowledge of Mr. Lyman's distractions to himself. Following her brother's example, Sophie kept it secret, too.

Twisting a loose thread from her reticule taut around her finger, Sophie listened to her mother and father chatter about their friends until the carriage had its turn to pause at the doors that swung open into the assembly rooms. They were helped and hurried indoors melting into the throng. It seemed everyone who lived within miles of Guildford had come out, anxious to celebrate the excitement of the new Season. Candles draped each room with smoking scent, and clusters of conversation echoed off the ceilings.

Sophie abandoned her parents and skipped up a flight of narrow stairs to the open space for dancing where musicians tuned their instruments and couples had taken the floor. The long, oblong room had a pitched ceiling with exposed beams and a row of several windows that looked out over the street below. At one end, a crowd of ladies and gentlemen were complimenting one another as their gazes roamed around the mob. The cool evening air had not yet dissipated, but Sophie knew it would soon warm up with so many friends crushed together.

She made her way to a line of hard chairs and the occasional outdated settle, which provided seating for chaperones and wallflowers. Her very good friend, Katherine Blackburn, had replied to her hasty letter that she, too, would be at the dance with her older, married sister and that Sophie could indeed count on her companionship.

Sophie searched the assembly for Katherine as she rubbed her arms. She was nowhere to be seen in the mire of gowns and waistcoats.

"Here I am," she murmured under her breath. She felt a bit out of sorts like she had at her coming out; like she always did at suppers and balls, but a country assembly was not quite as unpleasant. A few girls wandered over to the uncomfortable chairs and seated themselves to wait for invitations to dance. There were always more ladies than gentlemen at such things, thanks to the villain Bonaparte. Sophie reasoned the scoundrel was yet another reason she was still single.

At the front of the line, a handsome dancer caught her eye. All the room seemed drawn to him. He moved with finesse in a flaming gold waistcoat with Pomona green embroidery. His beaming countenance radiated a happy, careless air. Sophie noticed her father standing along the set with other onlookers in his club and realized, they too, were watching the pretty fellow with high, coiffed hair take his blushing partner down the line.

Papa caught her eye across the room and dipped his head at her in a gleeful motion. Someone snatched her elbow with a warm grip, and she jumped.

Katherine giggled, putting her pert nose against Sophie's cheek in a sister-like token of affection. "You've spied him already, I see."

"Who is he? It's Billingham, isn't it?"

Linking their arms together, Katherine stood beside her, a bit shorter but shapelier, with a head of thick, dark hair that gleamed like brass. "You've not heard?"

Sophie thought. "It's not Mr. Billingham, the heir of Oak Grove? You do know Lady Mary's nephew is coming to the country." The newcomer dancing with great enthusiasm was lovely indeed.

"Yes and no." Katherine giggled. "Mr. Gregory Devlin is his name there."

"I'm shocked I did not know."

Sophie glanced back over at Papa feeling some suspicion.

"He is Mr. Porter's nephew and pursuing a career in law. He's come to spend some time with his uncle and help him with his affairs."

"Poor Mr. Porter has been ill off and on this past year. It's not a happy reason to come to Higfield, I suspect."

"He looks happy to me, and his uncle must be improved because I just saw him speaking with your father." Katherine tapped her foot and hummed under her breath.

Sophie joined her in observing Mr. Devlin's spirited steps. Her anticipation for the dance dampened. "I had hoped to dance with no concerns about my looks and charms."

Katherine looked in surprise, her eyes wide. "He has a generous inheritance for a second son, and see, Sophie, he is not some farmer or clergyman." She elbowed her, and Sophie winced and laughed.

"It's not that a dance in Guildford does not excite me, but the tiresome rote of flirtation required of us is beginning to wear on my nerves."

"Lud, Sophie, you sound like an old maid already. With a future in law or politics, he will be sure to raise his family name. His uncle is very proud. Just think, dear friend, he has come to the country, so we do not have to suffer in the crowds and filth of Town."

Sophie nodded her head in slight assent. She had to agree that suitors who came to Guildford were easier to entertain than those who waited for the ladies to come to the city.

The dance finished some minutes later, and Sophie gathered her courage. It would not do to stand at the back of the room all night long. After all, she did want to dance. Everyone who knew her smiled, and even those she was only acquainted with met her gaze with approving glances.

There would not be many years left for dancing, an unpleasant thought reminded her. She would soon be relegated to the spinsters or married women prattling on in the corners as the party raged on around them. One way or the other, she would be on the benches and chairs with them soon. For a fleeting moment, she saw in her mind's eye the back of her brother's head as he dashed away into the woods to freedom, day after day.

Gathering her gown, Sophie made a beeline for her father, dragging Katherine along with her. At the same time, the vivacious dancer happened to join her father's circle, too. She watched them make their bows and nearly diverted, but her father called for her and held out his hand.

"My daughter," he said with paternal pride, "Miss Sophie Crestwood."

A first-rate set of tawny eyes shifted to her face, and Mr. George Devlin dropped the most flattering bow that had been made to Sophie in more than a Season. She could hardly bend a knee before Katherine stepped forward, staring at Mr. Crestwood with a small smile.

"Oh," he said, somewhat flummoxed and stumbling over his words, "and her especial friend, Miss Blackburn."

Mr. Devlin made the proper respects to Katherine, too. His gaze sparkled as he looked from one to the other.

"Miss Crestwood," he said, "at long last. I have been all agog to meet the most beautiful young mistress of Leatherbury. My aunt and uncle have spoken so highly of you I had to seek out your acquaintanceship at once."

Feeling her friend wilt beside her, Sophie said with a broad smile, "You flatter me, Mr. Devlin." She did not blush, but she liked his pretty words.

"Mr. Devlin, you are indeed everything we have heard." Katherine smiled with gaiety, her fingers tapping out a tune on Sophie's arm.

"Oh, Miss Blackburn, I'm sure you have heard very little of me. I'm just a struggling law clerk with a generous uncle."

Katherine giggled, and Sophie smiled again. He was the most fetching dandy she had ever seen with his golden locks, tawny eyes, and fine cut clothes.

His enthusiasm to greet her almost made her think he would take her hand, but he did not. She saw, as others joined their merry throng, that Guildford's newest caller welcomed everyone with the same energy, and she soon realized that no favor had been shown her, although he did catch her eye on more than one occasion with a generous grin. At these interludes, her heart would give a flutter, and she would look away. Katherine, however, could not. Her eyes latched onto Mr. Devlin like a burr to a stocking.

Sophie observed Katherine's rapt attentiveness with some interest before examining the room for more friends. A movement at the last window caught her eye. Positioned with one shoulder to the frame and the other to the corner stood a gentleman in black. He did not look festive in his somber colors; only a white shirt and proper cravat kept him from appearing morose altogether. It was almost clerical, but for the face. It looked all wrong. Intelligent eyes as pale as daffodil stalks were half-disguised by heavy, lowered lids. Dark chestnut hair with streaks of copper, long, but well-groomed, was tied back in a knot behind his neck. A prickle of awareness skipped down Sophie's spine. He watched her, turning the top of a dark cane in his hand. Captain Murdock.

She looked back to Devlin and smiled at nothing because she hadn't been listening to a word that had been said. Her father and everyone around her crowed with laughter, and she beamed again. It was hunting the men were discussing, as if she had faded from the room. She tried to look interested. Everyone chuckled at Devlin's good story of being thrown from a spirited thoroughbred, and Sophie put a hand over her mouth and feigned more amusement.

The prickles returned, and she wiped a kiss of perspiration from her temples before it manifested. Holding her breath for a quick instant, she turned to see if Captain Murdock still gawked at her and he did, but this time with a studious look on his face.

She stared. He frowned. She frowned back, and he grimaced with annoyance before looking away. Her fingers scrambled for her fan, and she snapped it open to impede his view. What a bold, insolent thing. She swallowed. Heaven and earth, what a summer it would be. Not two, but three, marriageable bachelors in the country. Her throat felt dry like the captain had drained her with his stare from across the room.

The musicians struck up the next set, and just as Sophie began to feel insulted with every gentleman at the assembly, the conversation stopped, and Devlin offered his arm. "You have waited too long to dance, Miss Crestwood," he declared, "and I am horrible ashamed."

She smiled, her father beamed like the North Star, and the couple took up their places for a reel. Sophie noted that when Katherine reluctantly loosed her arm, she was approached by another gentleman, and it set her heart at peace. Katherine wanted to dance just as much as she; but Katherine had set her sights on Devlin before Sophie even knew he was there.

As they waited for other dancers to organize themselves, Devlin fastened his attention on Sophie. "I understand you enjoy the hunt?" she asked, trying her best to not shrink under his appraisal.

"I missed much of last year," he answered. "My mother wanted me to stay in London for the Season."

"You sacrificed your time for family?" Sophie smiled. "I approve of honoring a lady's wishes."

"A-ha," teased Devlin. "You mean the balls, I suspect. Yes, I made the rounds with my parents, but I am happy to be in the country for a while even if it means missing the beginning of the Season in Town."

"We are happy to have a gentleman qualified for our assemblies." Sophie glanced around the room at the lack of gentlemen, although no ladies were dancing together yet.

"I have come to help my uncle with business," Devlin confessed. "Perhaps you will be able to return in the autumn."

"I'm sure I have several reasons to now," the gentleman answered. He winked at Sophie, and she felt her cheeks warm to a low burn. She knew he was only flirting, and she should be used to such pretenses by now. As if reading her thoughts, he laughed, and that made her laugh, too. The orchestra struck the opening notes, and they met to join hands and make their circle.

Sophie's flitting gaze caught Captain Murdock watching, and whatever she was going to say next fell from her mind. Devlin's voice interrupted her surprise. "You dance well, Miss Crestwood. Who needs Town when there is no shortage of beautiful partners in Guildford?" She almost stumbled over herself as they turned to weave in and out among the other dancers.

His grip felt firm on her hand, and he flashed a look at her every time their eyes met. This breathtaking sequence of interludes would have been her most enjoyable moment of the evening if Captain Murdock had not been such a distraction.

While she could see Mr. Devlin's glances, she could feel Captain Murdock's. They pricked her in the middle of the back then crept slow and warm up her spine until it felt like hot fingers were wrapped around her neck. Her hands tingled, too. Shaking her head, she noted Murdock did not offer to dance with any of the other many ladies waiting for a partner.

Plain and spotted Mary Jennings, who always danced last if at all, stood just steps away from him, but the captain acted like she was not there. True, the sweet, mouse-mannered girl seemed happier with her nose in a book, but to see her dancing with the striking Captain Murdock would be entertaining. The thought made her grin with glee. She caught his eye and silently laughed at him while Devlin whirled her past. His gruff countenance dropped ever so slightly before she looked away.

He could almost be called handsome but for his morbid countenance, Sophie told herself. His penetrating eyes were an unusual pale shade of green. He did not sport the fashionable mutton chops but was cleanly shaven, except for a small patch of whiskers under his chin. He looked almost French she thought. He was not tempting in the least. No. He reeked of swashbuckling and sea life, as if he'd just abandoned a Portsmouth tavern for more sophisticated entertainment. It was no matter at all he had washed up and presented himself to the country as a gentleman.

Devlin turned her again, and Sophie saw the captain had noticed Mary Jennings. They were attempting some kind of conversation. She pursed her lips at the thought of Murdock pitying her enough to request a dance. She would feign fatigue if such a plan came to his mind.

At the music's conclusion, she clapped and laughed with Devlin for dancing her out of breath. He was complimentary of her gown and her papa. He asked about Leatherbury, but nothing, Sophie suspected, he did not already know. She made her curtsey and thanked him with sincerity. He said, "You will allow me another dance before the assembly is through?" She couldn't help but squeeze his hand and smile as she agreed. He was a charming dog.

Two dances with George Devlin. Wouldn't that please everyone? True, they had not had that much entertaining conversation, but that was the staring pirate's fault. Devlin was full of compliments and looked very well.

Her warmth and eagerness to dance with Devlin seemed to embolden the other gentlemen in the room, and Sophie found she did not have to sit out any more dances. Katherine had her circle of admirers, too, and when Mr. Devlin asked her to dance she blushed more than Sophie had ever seen. She felt elation for Katherine, but suspected Devlin would find herself again to capture a few more moments together. She lost him in the crowd.

SOPHIE WAS OBLIGED to take refreshment with her parents and listen to Mr. Porter talk about agricultural ideas. She felt certain such experimentations would not do for Leatherbury. It was already a fine country manor that put out at the very least, lovely carrots. She did not have long to dwell on it, for before she contemplated a second drink the dancing resumed, and Mr. Devlin was nowhere to be found.

"No matter," she told her mother, who raised her brows after Sophie confessed she had promised the newcomer another dance. "He's probably been led off to cards."

Katherine waved from across the room, partnered with an officer in a bright red coat, probably on his leave. There was not military at Guildford that often beyond the occasional naval man. Sophie fanned herself and laughed with the gentlemen who came to pass away the night in idle chatter. She had already danced with almost everyone near her age in the room, but for Captain Murdock. He had not taken his leisure to disappear to play games, nor had he been anywhere about the drinks. It seemed he fancied the shadowed corners of the room.

From her chair seated next to her mother, Sophie examined him as he watched the new dance with no expression. She could not determine if he loved or hated it. Why did he come, she wondered? Most seafaring gentlemen danced well because of their heightened sense of balance, and though the aptitude probably applied to their new neighbor, she suspected that he instead clomped about like an angry troll.

Captain Murdock did not have a pleasing air about him, certainly not like Mr. Devlin. True, he was all seriousness and civility, proving he was a gentleman of breeding despite his tirade over Pembroke's boundaries. Why had he bothered to come to England?

As if hearing her unspoken questions, Captain Murdock looked across the ballroom and caught Sophie studying him. Struck with mortification to be caught a-spying, she bolted for Katherine's side of the room. A generous fellow without a partner asked her for the next set, and though he was old and widowed, she accepted with heartfelt pleasure.

She had partners for all but the last dance, which seemed have been set aside for the girls who had not had many dances that night. As she said goodbye to Katherine and begged her to come visit, she observed Devlin on the floor with a young, flirty-looking miss far too young to be out. She sighed and shamed herself for wasting so much time catching up with her other friends. Surely Devlin had looked for her everywhere and been left with no choice but to dance with a baby.

Katherine saw him, too. "He's a fun fellow, don't you think so?"

Sophie agreed. "He's a lovely dancer, too."

"Yes," said Katherine, "and Mrs. Porter told me he will inherit their living someday since they don't have children of their own." She leaned her head close to Sophie as the crowd of weary folk began to funnel toward the door. "That's two inheritances, Sophie, and he'll probably be a barrister, too." She squeezed Sophie's arm and giggled.

Sophie bussed her cheek and motioned toward Katherine's waiting sister. "Your sister is waiting, and I can tell by the gleam in her eye she wants to hear all about your evening."

Katherine smiled. "Mark my words, dearest friend, I will be married before Michaelmas."

She floated away. Her damp tresses, streaked with honey-colored brushstrokes, were loose and tangled around her long ribbons. She looked cherubic and just as spent as Sophie felt.

Papa waved from the door, and Sophie made her own way toward her chaperone. Not that she had seen either one of her parents often that night, but it was just the town folk of Guilford after all, and she was no longer a young debutante.

"He dances very well, does he not?" Papa leaned over to whisper, but it was too loud. A few bystanders overheard and smiled in agreement. Sophie glanced at him and nodded without a reply. When they were alone in the carriage and Mama dozing on his shoulder, Sophie told him, "He danced well with me. Mr. George Devlin, if that's who you mean." She said it only because she knew it would please him. In truth, Sophie did not have the opportunity to tell Mr. Devlin farewell, and she felt disappointed.

"I think he fancied you," Papa said, with a bit of inebriated cheer, and she grimaced in the dark, knowing he was not teasing at all.

"You did not tell me the Porters had a nephew here."

"It slipped my mind, Sophie dear, with Lady Mary's Mr. Billingham on his way to Oak Grove." Nonetheless satisfied, Papa began tapping his shoes as the carriage swayed along over the rutted road toward Higfield. After a while, he cleared his throat in the quiet, rousing Sophie from her secret contemplation of Captain Murdock's conduct.

"I was introduced to our neighbor at long last." He did not sound like he approved.

Hoping the man had said nothing about Jack's walnut broadside, she tensed.

"He's not at all like his father, I must say."

"I suspect the father he knew may have been nothing like the man of Pembroke Hall."

"True, you are right," agreed Papa, "but I daresay Sir Edward would have preferred his only son to at least be a pleasant fellow."

"I confess," Sophie admitted, warming to her father's censure, "I was surprised he did not offer to dance; not with one lady. Not even Katherine or me."

"Oh, yes, well," her father explained, "you did see that hideous cane he would not release all the night long?"

"Yes. I'm sure he could have parted with it for the cotillion. Was he afraid someone would steal it?" Sophie chuckled at the ridiculousness of the idea.

"I suppose he would not have been able to manage it. He hobbled like a cripple when he excused himself for the evening."

"Oh? I did not see him leave." A finger of guilt gave Sophie a sharp poke in her center. "I did not know. He is lame then." No wonder the man acted so.

"Yes. I made note of it to Mr. Talcott, and he informed me it was not a childhood defect. There was some incident in the Indies; a violent activity that left him maimed and useless."

"The poor dear," said Sophie, before she could stop herself and wonder how Mr. Talcott, who lived on the other side of Higfield and in a much smaller home, could know what had crippled the newcomer.

She remembered how suspicious Murdock had acted. She felt terrible she'd made assumptions about the captain's ability to dance, and yet Jack's voice niggled in the back of her mind that there were pirates at Pembroke.

Her father sighed in the darkness of their bouncing horse-bound cocoon. "As I said before, dear girl, there is nothing poor about him. Not if he has returned to Pembroke to refurbish it and continue his father's legacy. The mystery, you understand, is how he has come into a fortune his father lost, and after all this time, why?"

Sophie returned nothing, choosing instead to close her eyes and wonder why Sir Edward's heir behaved so dark. So angry. So crippled. What if he had sailed the Indies with a motley crew? Was he hiding in plain sight from the authorities? Her father, assuming she had gone to sleep, began to tap his foot again to an irritating tune she could not hear.

A FEW DAYS LATER KATHERINE arrived early in the day, and Sophie lamented that they did not bring her with them when they left the Guildford assembly. She committed her to a walk outdoors in the gardens. Jack had whisked away to his lessons, and Mama disappeared into the library.

"You must forgive Mama," Sophie apologized. "She's become engrossed in that Defoe adventure."

"I understand," said Katherine, though she did not read books at all. "How do your roses fare this year? Are they budding?"

"They look very well," Sophie replied. "I'm pleased you asked. I know they are Mama's flowers, but she does not like to get dirty in the garden, and the insects startle her more than she can bear."

"She seemed content at the dance. She spent a great deal of time with Mrs. Porter."

"Yes," said Sophie. "I was happy she came. What do you think of Mr. Porter's nephew?"

"He is most handsome, and I don't believe I've seen a man dance better."

This pleased Sophie, but she said in all seriousness, "Papa is sure he is fit to pursue me, though of course, he is not a Billingham." She looked sideways at Katherine and grimaced.

"Do you wish him to pursue you?" said Katherine.

"I find him engaging and handsome, and I confess I am ready to settle now and leave the marriage mart behind. I never knew it could be so exhausting."

Katherine frowned. "Did you find him to be the most wonderful of men?"

Sophie thought before raising her shoulders and letting them fall. "No. He was quite likeable though, and I can only think perhaps I would like him even better if I had the opportunity to meet him again."

"What a curious approach."

"Yes," Sophie replied with a dry chuckle, "so Papa can be rid of one more child."

Katherine wrinkled her nose and said, "Hmm," to this, then, "Your new neighbor, Captain Murdock? Is he really some kind of pirate?" Her eyes brightened with curiosity.

"So Papa hints, but I do not know it to be fact."

"We were introduced at the assembly."

"Indeed?"

Katherine nodded. "Yes, while I was with my father and yours, too. Your papa seemed indifferent."

"I imagine the captain was indifferent, too. Papa does not approve of Captain Murdock coming to Pembroke. He's a sea captain, this Murdock, but whether naval or a merchant no one can agree. Either way, they are both beneath him, do you not think so?"

"It's true," Katherine agreed. "He's not like Mr. Devlin. He'll fit right into Higfield, whether he takes up law or moves to the country. Do you not think it's important to know how to work the land?"

"He won't actually work the land," Sophie pointed out.

"Yes," Katherine agreed in a breathless tone, "but he will understand what's being done and why."

"I'm sure Richard would approve," said Sophie, "though if Mr. Devlin is going to be a solicitor of some sort, I do not know why he needs to trouble himself with farming."

"Why, because he will inherit the Porters' old place."

Sophie frowned. "It's a nice home, and very comfortable, but if he is going to take up law he will live in Town. You should concern yourself with his address in London, for I suspect if he does inherit the Porters' place, he will rent it out to some crusty, old naval officer."

"Why would anyone want to live in Town with noises and smells and crowds of urchins and criminals? Everyone knows I like a good supper and monstrous ballroom, but I wouldn't leave Higfield for such stuff."

"Then I hope Mr. Devlin is as attached to parks and woods and pastures as we are."

Katherine smiled in satisfaction. "He hasn't come to call, not officially, but he might come to see Papa about a new colt." She sighed. "I wish you would be there, Sophie. It would be a lovely time."

"Now that Papa has invited him to dine, and with Lady Mary, too, we shall all get down to the truth of his intentions. Besides, I know I can count on you to clean out my rose garden. It's wild and unkempt from winter's cruel hand."

Katherine put her hands over her face. "I was not born to be a gardener, and neither were you."

"I don't mind a little dirt," Sophie pouted, but not for long.

The men of Leatherbury went off to hunt rabbits, and the ladies went indoors. Sophie and Katherine busied themselves with wardrobe preparations for the Season. This entailed new ribbons on old bonnets and a pretty ruffle on a tired dress hem for Katherine. They babbled with enthusiasm about their expectations for the year.

Jack burst into the drawing room with his face white as rice.

"Where's Mama?" he demanded.

"What's wrong?" Sophie jumped from her seat and went to him. "Has someone been hurt?" Her mind began to reel with pictures of twisted ankles, bleeding foreheads, and bullet wounds.

"No," said Jack. He looked at her with surprise. "Papa sent me on," he explained. "Which I scared up a rabbit, and shot three times as many as Old George, and then from out of nowhere came the pirate with four other men on horseback." He took a deep breath.

Sophie felt her eyes widen. "Captain Murdock of Pembroke?"

Jack nodded. "They were fine horses, too."

"What did he do?"

"He said we were on his property."

"Again?"

Sophie looked up in surprise at Katherine's exclamation. Her friend shook her head, both delighted and dismayed. "That's unkind and ungentlemanly, isn't it?" She looked at Sophie. "As ungentleman-ly-like as not asking a girl to dance, isn't it darling?"

Sophie exhaled in frustration, wishing Katherine had not been party to her accusations against Captain Murdock, which she had doled out to her in whispers before leaving the assembly and learning of his handicap.

Dismissing it like a man would do, Jack continued: "He said we were welcome to shoot all his rabbits to our heart's delight, because there were more than he needed this year with a small household and only himself."

"He what?" Sophie was sure Jack was spinning lies for his own entertainment.

"They heard our shots and thought we was poachers."

"*Were* poachers," she corrected without thinking.

Jack frowned and said, "No, we weren't poachers. It was just accidental."

Sophie raised her brows. "I bet you were according to his estimation." She made a grim face. "Whatever did Papa do?"

"He thanked him, of course, and was quick to remind him the boundaries ain't fresh on our minds since no one's lived at the place besides the old hermit all these years."

"What happened to the groundskeeper who kept the place up?"

"Pope," Jack reminded her. "He's dead."

"Maybe they keelhauled him," said Sophie, unable to resist teasing.

"It takes a ship to do that."

"Well, I'm glad no one was hurt. I hope you and Papa can mind the boundaries of Pembroke now."

"Do you want to know what else?"

"Tell us."

"He noticed my rabbits, and said I was quite the shot."

Sophie grinned. "Perhaps he remembered the walnuts."

"He sounds civil," Katherine pointed out. "Perhaps your father will have a changed opinion of him since the rumors have not been proven true."

"Oh, I doubt that," Sophie replied. Papa would not take kindly to anyone reminding him of the boundaries of his ancestral home. Besides, he rarely ever said a kind word about Sir Edward that she could ever remember. She nudged Jack toward the door. "Mama is in the library. Why ever must she know so urgently?"

"Papa invited him to supper, but he refused on account of feeling ill, so Papa told me to tell them in the kitchen to send over the best strawberries that come in. Our imposing on his land gave us no choice." Without another word, he scrambled off in search of his mother.

"You've gone pale," noted Katherine.

Sophie swallowed. "I haven't seen Captain Murdock since the assembly, and truth be told, we have not been properly introduced."

"Well," Katherine said, "no one is certain why he's come and what he's all about. If the rumors are true..."

Sophie put her hand up to her neck. It felt warm. Her hand was cool. She had in fact, seen the captain from the distance, while she walked through the trees growing heavy with young leaves. He often could be spied on horseback, riding the distant hills of Pembroke that rose up behind Leatherbury like swells of guardians over the horizon. A dark, solitary ghost, he wandered about as if looking for some unspoken answer to a riddle only he knew. It did not surprise her in the least he would spurn her father's invitation to supper. It was poorly done, she thought with a shake of her head, and would not sit well with Papa.

CHAPTER THREE

Spring showers swept in with little warning, pushing away the blue skies. With the rain, Katherine took her leave before the roads became too muddy to travel. Days later and feeling alone, Sophie found herself at the drawing room's north window, wishing her cutting garden was not on the other side of the house. There stood only a small grove of elms for a view and then through their thickening greenery the curve of the gravel-strewn road as it turned from the drive and set off to the northwest.

She dragged herself over to the settee and picked up the atlas she had brought from the library. It fascinated her now more than ever, as she contemplated the places Jack so dreamed to discover. She had once daydreamed with him, and planned their own tour of the continent and then a sea voyage to India, but all of it had been useless childhood fancy. For her anyway. She put her finger on a line of latitude and followed it to St. Kitts.

"I'm sure it's a nice place to see, and I'd walk there if I could, but Guildford will have to do, or wherever my attachments take me."

The soft patter of footfalls interrupted her reverie. Jack pushed open the drawing room door. He looked pale and bored. "The rain's dropped off. I'm going to the lake to check the water level."

"You mean you're going to fish or take a swim." Sophie set the atlas down in her lap. She pursed her lips and narrowed her eyes at him. He almost grinned but caught himself.

"You said if I tell you when I'm going, you won't have to come after me."

"I did say that, didn't I? You need me to tell Papa your where-abouts when he asks if I've seen you."

Jack held out his hands in surrender. His jacket hung from his shoulders, messy and crooked. "He won't let me be off if I ask him to go."

"For someone who fancies himself fit for the Navy you struggle with the proper channels of authority," Sophie admonished him.

"I'm going for a turn about the lake. I'll be back."

Sophie looked behind her at the grey and dreary late day through the window. "Wait. I'll go with you. We'll tell Margaret, and then we'll both be in trouble for sneaking out into wet weather."

Jack sighed in exasperation. "Hurry then, before it starts to rain again."

Sophie dropped the atlas on the sofa and hurried for her old boots. She wrapped herself in a dark blue pelisse heavy enough to keep the damp out and snatched a sturdy straw bonnet.

Jack waited for her outdoors by the garden, and when he saw her trussed up against the weather, he laughed. Hatless, his red hair was already molded around his crown like a cap, and the light smattering of sun spots across his face stood out in the gloom of the dreary day.

They walked across the lawn of Leatherbury and into dripping trees that made clumsy, unorchestrated notes. The wet earth smelled coppery and stuck to the bottom of their shoes. The birds were silent. Sophie imagined them huddled down in their little nests to stay warm.

There were no fish to be seen at the edges of the lake either. Jack had a trapping line running up onto an embankment, and he pulled at it and raised one end up into the air. One lone and pitiful tur-tle was snagged, so he set to work unhooking it while Sophie leaned against a dead, limbless tree and watched.

"He'll take your finger off," she teased, and her brother fumbled with the hook and line. He ignored her, freed his captive, and set the turtle free into the water.

Satisfied, Jack scampered back up to the top of the bank. His line was tied off to a makeshift stake he had whittled down from a stick. Sophie strolled over and watched him tie off an intricate knot she found impressive.

He gave it a good tug. "There see, nothing could slip through that knot. You could tie a man to the grating and give him his punishment."

"Jack, that's wicked."

"It's necessary to keep every man to his duty."

"Let's see how right you are." Sophie turned and put her hands behind her back. "Bind me up, and we'll see what kind of captain you will make."

He smiled, but with a flash of hurt in his eyes. "I'll be a great captain, you'll see. You and everyone else will be proud of me."

Sophie backed up against the bare tree. With wrists together, she motioned behind herself. She stood straight and tall like a resolute prisoner ready to walk the plank. Jack darted around her and busied himself with the thin, wet rope. "I'm already proud of you," she said.

"Is you?"

"*Are* you," she corrected. She gave a quick jerk, but her hands did not come undone. "Don't speak like a lower deckhand. Now untie me."

The little imp in Jack's heart surfaced, and he swung his hands behind his back and strode off calling, "You didn't say 'Please, Captain.'"

"Untie me this instant."

Jack laughed. He disappeared into the trees, taunting her.

"James Crestwood, you get back here straight away." His laughter echoed through the quiet trees. Sophie's temper climbed a notch.

She twisted and pulled to free her hands from the loops around her wrists, but they only seemed to tighten. "You wicked boy. I'll thrash you myself." Thunder rolled off in the distance.

"Jack!" she called angrily, but he did not reply. "You're hiding and spying on me, too." Sophie gave the tree a hard kick with the back of her boot which hurt her heel. Dark clouds moved in overhead, and the wind picked up in a burst of speed. It would only be a matter of time before the rain began to fall again. She began to perspire as she twisted her hand this way and that, but the bounds only chafed her skin so that it began to sting.

"Come back!" she cried out one more time. She was too uncomfortable to be angry. She sighed and waited, blinking back her vengeful fantasies. She was too old now to punish him in ways that he did her. Rain began to fall slow and heavy in big, fat drops. "Oh no," she sighed. She squinted to see through the tangle of trees. He wouldn't leave her. Surely, he had not grown that surly and mean during his time away at boarding school. What did boys do to one another when no one watched anyway?

Without warning, lightning struck in the distance, and the ground beneath her shivered. The blast of it left her faint and her heart pounding. Irritation turned to worry, and she began to pull with determination at the rope as the rain began to blast down from the heavens. "Jack!"

The sharp raindrops hurt, almost more than the wet rope scraping across the tender inside flesh of her wrists. Sophie felt ridiculous and angry. The wind sped up, carrying the shower of water along in slashing waves. Against her will, a sob escaped. She could not see what she was doing; could not think of any reason why her brother would leave her out to catch cold. Papa would punish him cruelly now. Jack would never be allowed outside again. If she were to fall ill—oh, the stories Mama would imagine, she thought with misery. Mama would make herself sick with worry.

A loud crash of thunder clapped nearby, so close the earth moved, and Sophie's ears cracked with pain. She screamed, jerking her arms one last desperate time, and the rope slipped over her wet hands taking skin with it. She collapsed to the ground, shivering as her head swam with noise and confusion. The rain felt like needle hooks on her neck.

Her mind ordered her legs to stand and start home as she shielded her eyes from the wild deluge. Tree limbs slapped wildly at her escape and pulled at her hat. She jerked free, loosening the bonnet and continuing through the storm until she stumbled into a thick forest canopy with some protection.

Mud sloshed up her legs and seeped through her petticoat. The torrent was not going to let up; the day had almost gone black. She felt disoriented. Until it cleared, she would never find her way home. Seeking out the largest evergreen she could find, Sophie crawled like a drowned kitten beneath the thick branches and curled up at the trunk. A dull stupor fell over her as she concentrated on shutting out the damp cold and inhaling the piney, comforting scent.

Total blackness soon descended around her, making the dark night feel like it would last forever. Never had she experienced such an eternal bout of discomfort. She ground her teeth to keep her jaw from trembling in the cold and imagined the punishment Jack deserved. Even when the rain receded to a light whisper, it would last only minutes before galloping back to a full and violent barrage.

Once she imagined she heard her name, but it was never quite clear enough to trust leaving the tree's safety. Her trembling would not stop. She shook so hard at times her teeth chattered. Then finally, at long last, she heard the thudding of horses in the distance through a pause in the rain and was grateful for what must have been an early, dark dawn. The wind had not quit shooting punishing blasts across Leatherbury's grounds, she discovered, as she broke free from the soppy shelter. Strangely, she could not stand or make her body do what she wanted it to do. She huddled on the ground, numb with cold and exhaustion, praying anyone or anything would come along and find her. She raised an arm and waved as pounding horse hooves drew closer.

A rider, holding a lantern aloft, pushed into the grove of trees, and she looked up with joy. Water oozed down his oilskin coat and wide-brimmed hat. She thought it was Old George, and sighed with relief. She should have known Papa would send him out to look, but he was almost blind. Where was Papa?

"Miss Crestwood," a strange voice shouted, above the din of the increasing gale. Solid arms scooped her up, and sharp branches flapped up and down around them. She felt warm in an instant against a damp coat that smelled of something odd. Sophie surrendered to the stranger's protection, knowing somehow as she slipped into a swoon, she would be safe and returned home to Leatherbury as fast as the mount could carry them.

HEAT CAME, THEN COLD, and then heat again. Chills rattled Sophie's bones then went away leaving her aching. She opened her eyes at last and knew only that she was awake. Everything around her felt still. There were no sounds but for a steady rain and a distant ticking time keeper.

She gazed with wonder around the room in which she'd revived. It wasn't her home at all. A dark, navy chaise reclined near half-covered windows. Polished mahogany furniture gleamed, and blue silk walls shimmered in the low lamplight. The canopy above the enormous bed was a beautiful golden tapestry. Sophie sniffed through a clogged nose and detected the tang of unpleasant tonics. She gazed down at her covered body. The coverlet on the bed was blue, too, with gold ribbon trim, and beneath it, her legs slid across soft, cool sheets. White pillows. White gown. She weakly lifted an arm and examined her frail fingers. White Sophie.

She had no idea where she was.

Movement beside the bed made her look, and she saw she was not alone. Sitting back with his neckcloth undone and a curious light in his pea-green eyes was the pirate from Pembroke. The surprise of finding him beside her made a surge of heat streak through her from head to toe. "I'm ill," she said aloud, confused as to why he sat at her bedside.

The quiet man resting beside her cocked his head. "You are not ill." His voice was stern; low and husky. "You are perfectly healthy, and your family is waiting at home for your return. They cannot come in this violent weather."

"How long have I been sleeping?"

"Only a few hours, Miss Crestwood. You have not been comatose for a season nor have you tossed and turned with raging fever."

Sophie sniffled and was sure she felt an irritable itch in her throat.

"Where am I?" she demanded. She tried to sit up then changed her mind when she saw she wore only a loose, white shift. Her long hair was down. She smoothed it with her hands and pulled it off to one side behind her shoulder. "I want my mama," she said stubbornly.

"We already sent word to your family, though they have not had any rest themselves since your promenade into the forest." The bottom of the cane struck the floor, and the captain pulled himself up to his feet.

We? Sophie gazed around the antique room once more as understanding settled upon her foggy mind. "You have rescued me. I'm at Pembroke." Her heart tumbled over itself, and she wondered at the prospect.

Captain Murdock bowed but a derisive look on his face hinted he thought she should have long before deduced it. In a hollow tone, he said, "I did not rescue you, Miss Crestwood. Your heroic knight is Mr. Howard—the cook; and by the by, welcome to my home." The dark shadows in the room seemed to close in around her like dancing ghosts and sprites. She shrank back down under the covers.

He lurched across the room and disappeared without another word. Pembroke! How she had always wanted to sneak inside and tiptoe through its halls with Jack. It was once the palace of the county. The entire village used to gather at Pembroke for balls and hunts. Friends met old friends and introductions made new ones. Matches were arranged, and hearts were broken. Sophie gazed up at the golden topper over the bed, following its swag from one post to the next. It looked luxurious even if it was not new.

Before she succumbed to the temptation to climb out and walk around stroking the furniture and opening drawers, an elderly woman burst into the room. Sophie flinched, startled out of her admiration. The stranger was hunched in the back and had leathery cheeks. Her pressed cap glowed, yet it was not as cheerful as her eyes. She stared, waiting for Sophie to acknowledge her.

"Yes?"

"Miss Sophie Crestwood." The woman crooned her name with a smile of warm sincerity. She made a clumsy curtsey that looked foreign on her then set down a wobbling tea tray. "We've sent word to your family you're awake." When Sophie did not respond, the woman added, "I'm Mrs. Brooks, and the captain has told me to watch over you." Her voice had a faint Irish lilt.

She hesitated; waiting it seemed for Sophie's approval.

"I'm sure you'll do," Sophie said with an effort of courtesy. She saw uncertainty sweep across the servant's face and felt pity. "Thank you ever so much," she added, with an encouraging smile at the informal service. "How long have I been here?"

Mrs. Brooks came up alongside the wide bed and clasped her hands over her rotund belly. "Why, just this long day," said she. "You tossed with a bit o' fever for a time, but the doctor your family sent up said you'd recover."

Sophie bit her lip. "My parents must be ill with distress."

"Oh, Captain Murdock put them at ease, he did." Mrs. Brooks smiled. Short, white curls bobbled on either side of her temples when she grinned. She was missing a side tooth. "He explained everything when he delivered your clever lad home. He assured them you'd be tended to throughout the day and into next week if necessary."

Sophie could not help but stare at the space between Mrs. Brooks' teeth. "Uh. Um. Jack was here?"

"Oh, yes, Master Jack come running right up to the door in the driving rain. He was soaked to the skin and frightened, I tell you." The woman looked down like she wanted to sit on the bed beside Sophie to converse, but she caught herself. "He lost you in the woods and was a feared you might wander into the next county."

A smile crept across Sophie's face, because she recalled Jack had left her tied up and alone in the rain to begin with. "I did get lost. However did your men find me?"

Mrs. Brooks grinned. She made a startling portrait of a housemaid, or whatever role she pretended to play for this household. "The captain and some o' the crew saddled up with lanterns and searched along the east side of the property until you was seen. The men brought you to Pembroke."

"I did not know I had wandered so far, and in the dark, too." Sophie looked down, wondering how Captain Murdock felt about having to rescue a silly girl on his own grounds.

Mrs. Brooks waved her hand, sweeping away her concern into the musty air. "Now don't you fret, little lamb. It's brought some excitement here at Pembroke, and we ain't feeling so dull no more."

Sophie smiled her appreciation.

"Here, Miss Crestwood. Take this soup and let it warm your vitals. Mr. Howard made it up special with early vegetables we found growing wild in the garden." The servant placed the tray on Sophie's knees and asked whatever else she could do. Sophie assured her she was well enough to eat and thanked her again for all her kindness. Pleased, Mrs. Brooks tottered out on small, unsteady steps, the bump in her upper back a queer burden she herself did not seem to notice.

Sophie stared at the vegetables floating in the warm, brown broth. She could not forget Mrs. Brooks' comments. It was not so much the explanation of how Sophie had come to Pembroke, but the woman's inadvertent statement about the Captain's *crew* going out to search. Shouldn't a crew be on a ship? Sophie reached for an ornate spoon of heavy silver resting on the tray beside the bowl. She picked it up and examined its fine craftsmanship.

What kind of gentleman staffed his estate with a ship's forecastle? In her mind, Sophie saw Jack's wide-eyed expression at the breakfast table not a fortnight ago. "Pirates," he had said. She was almost afraid to taste the thin, suspicious broth. If Captain Murdock had sailors on his estate pretending to be cooks and groundskeepers, what else could he be hiding?

SOPHIE MOVED HER TRAY to the table beside the bed and fell back on a fluffy pillow. Neither Captain Murdock nor Mrs. Brooks returned to check on her, and she wondered if she'd been forgotten. Warm under the covers and thankful for a small fire flickering in the hearth on the opposite wall, she drifted away, wondering how a room vacant for almost thirty years could be so well polished. Her thoughts faded into quizzical ideas about what her family was doing at Leatherbury and what they must be thinking. The rain continued to spatter the outside walls.

A crackling voice in the distance jerked Sophie's eyes wide open. She lay still, frozen at the sounds she heard. After a long silence, she told herself she must have dreamed it and relaxed back into the warm blankets. Then a low, moaning creak sent tingles dashing down her spine.

She bolted forward, sitting up so quick she gasped. She tried to catch her breath without making too much noise and looked around the room for something to protect herself. Heart pounding, she waited for the noise to come again, but after several minutes when it did not repeat itself, she took a slow, deep draw of heavy air.

"My heavens," she muttered, afraid to lie back down again. Perhaps Jack was right. Pembroke was filled with all kinds of peculiar things. Sophie looked down at her thin shift. She had never seen the inside of Pembroke before, not when it was reputable or when it fell into decline. Her stay might be the only opportunity to inspect it, but that was just the beginning of things. If there was any truth to Jack's suspicions, there might be some sort of intrigue underfoot. She could not have a pirate for a neighbor. The smiling countenance of Mr. Devlin shot to the forefront of her mind. No, a pirate next door would never do.

Without concerning herself about the particulars of her wardrobe and unkempt tresses, Sophie slipped out of the bed, pulling a sheet with her. She wrapped herself up like a caterpillar and after finding no shoes or stockings around the bed, tiptoed to the door and listened. Hearing no sounds, she carefully turned the knob. It screeched with an ugly, pitiful cry, but after waiting to see if anyone heard, she felt convinced the hall outside her room had been abandoned. She slipped between the door and its casing, and quietly pulled it closed behind her without shutting it tight.

Sophie had been assigned the first bedroom at the beginning of a long, dim hallway that ran the length of a narrow wing. Several doors lined the hall on both sides to what she assumed were more bedchambers. Smooth, dark-stained planking underfoot looked pitted and scratched with use, while a narrow carpet dreary with dust and age camouflaged their faded stains. Small tables with ornate, empty vases rested against the walls. They were once painted a rosy salmon, but now they peeled with age. The plaster behind the paint had been wiped clean, but it was still a gloomy shade of grey that accentuated the cobwebs fluttering from the corners and ceiling. Drafts hinted at an open window or holes in the corners.

Sophie chose to sneak around the corner at her left shoulder, glancing at the watchful paintings of Pembroke's previous inhabitants. Her wing was attached as the short end of an L, to another long hallway fragmented with more doors and the occasional flickering candelabra on the wall. A wide stairwell climbed up to the landing upon which she stood and continued to another floor overhead.

She stopped and listened, hearing only her breathing at first, then came the faint moaning cry she'd heard before. It sounded like the distressed cry of a strange creature. She put her hand on the cracked handrail at the top of the stairs and listened harder over the thumping of her heart. The whine pitched up then woefully fluttered down before slowly dying out. She shook her head at her silly ideas. It wasn't a wounded animal, but strings of some sort, and whoever played did so beautifully.

Except for the dripping candles on the walls, the main hall of the great house beyond the staircase where she stood looked as vacant as the wing she'd just abandoned. Sophie gazed upward to where she had heard the melancholy tune and decided to follow the music. She padded up the dark mahogany stairs in her bare feet, hoping she would not be discovered, yet unable for curiosity's sake to turn back to her room. The steps led her up to the next floor, where looking down over the banister, she counted two lower levels. The music began to resonate again, and Sophie followed the sound around the corner to the shorter wing set directly over her room.

This floor appeared even dustier than the previous one, only a few candles were lit, and a layer of grime on the long hallway rug made her feet feel dirty. She sniffed, realizing her nose was beginning to drip. The musk and age in the air smelled thicker up here. Her nose itched and tickled inside, but she didn't dare sniffle so loud again. Long cobwebs dangled like nooses from the ceiling overhead, and she shuddered.

The sad sonata continued its siren's call. It echoed a passionate and haunting melody, just like the dark halls of Pembroke with its soiled paintings of aristocrats from long ago. Sophie examined the chamber doors through the gloom and decided the door to the second room on the left was slightly ajar with a dim light shimmering around it. She moved in silence to the small gap and caught her breath.

Captain Murdock stood in front of a languid fire burning beneath a marble mantel. One bare foot was balanced on a low, milking stool nestled up against a heavy, velvet-covered chair. The other kept time on the floor. With his cane leaning against the fireplace, Murdock stood balanced on his own. In his hands, a violin tucked underneath his chin swayed. It moved in time with his body as he performed a strange dance to the music. His profile in the firelight was sharp and clear. He stood slender and tall. In these private bedchambers, half-dressed in loose buckskin breeches and an untucked shirt open at the neck, he did not seem as rigid and menacing as before. From his dreamy stare, his thoughts were somewhere inside the flickering blue and orange flames. The reflection of the firelight made his pale eyes glow.

Sophie noticed his hair was undone. It hung far past his neck, with slight waves resting on his broad upper back on either side of his shoulders. She put a hand to her mouth realizing it had fallen open, and at the same time, that it was scandalous to spy on her host. She swallowed and stepped away. The music stopped in mid-cry. Her heart jumped in her chest, and for a brief pause, the only sound to be heard was her own loud breathing. She stepped back and pivoted on her heel.

Horrified he might have felt her examination, she strode down the rug-lined hallway as quietly as she could, but each footfall sounded like muffled thunder as she hurried back to the stairs. She reached the banister and slipped down the first step, but her shift snagged on something, and she spun about to free it.

Captain Murdock stood behind her, silent. He held a handful of her shift in his fist. She had not snagged it after all. Rather, he had snagged her. She jerked in surprise, but his hold kept her from falling backward and tumbling down the stairs. His other hand trembled as it balanced precariously on a carved dragon head at the top of his cane.

"What do you think you are doing?"

"I... I heard music and followed it."

His eyes blazed with accusation, and it unnerved her.

"I'm so sorry," she said in a choking voice. Her nose tingled again. She touched it with her fingers to make it stop.

"It's not possible you heard music from all the way down in your room."

Sophie took a nervous breath. He stood there, one step above her like a giant, her bedclothes gripped in his hand so tight it shook. She hadn't heard him shuffle down the hall after her. He moved as silent as a ghost when he wanted—even with a cane. She found the courage to meet his penetrating gaze. "I did hear something from my room. Then I was in the hall."

Captain Murdock waited for a long pause, while the dust they had stirred up in the rugs pirouetted in the air and into Sophie's eyes and nose. "You should not be out of bed," he said.

Sophie swallowed down her frightened apprehension. She tried to beg his pardon, but her lungs failed her, and she coughed in reflex.

She covered her mouth with her fingers. "I'm so sorry," she repeated between them, her cheeks hot with humiliation. She stared at the fistful of her garments he'd snatched, aware his eyes examined her from her straight, waist-length hair down to her naked ankles. With a jerk, he dropped her shift like it burned his hand.

"Go to bed," he said in a quiet voice.

Sophie's nose had not quit tingling and itching. "Yes, sir," she said at once, but not soon enough to keep a sneeze from erupting. It came so fast and without warning, she had no chance to catch it before it doused him with all her rejection.

Horrified, she stumbled down the next step, thankful the old handrail held fast. When she glanced back, he was wiping off his shirt with a look of disgust.

She fled. In the dark blue room, she pinched out the candle and slipped into bed like a naughty child. The bottoms of her heels felt grimy, but she didn't dare get up again to wash them. Over time, her thudding heart slowed to a steady, nervous trot, and she felt warm again. The house was cold, and it was foolish running about undressed in her bare feet.

The room felt gloomy. Mrs. Brooks had not drawn the curtains, so starlight shined in from the tall window beside her bed. Sophie rubbed her eyes. Captain Murdock was entirely in the way of things to order her to bed. The dark, haunting halls and melancholy music had hypnotized her, and she had forgotten herself and her manners. To make it all the more distressing, she had sneezed all over him.

She sniffled to herself and fought back another one. If she were to fall seriously ill, she might not ever be allowed to leave. Perhaps she might die here. Sophie pulled the blanket up over her nose to just under her eyes, so she could watch the mysterious shadows dance in the corners of the room. They shifted with the wind that whistled outside the window through a light rain.

Maybe Pembroke Hall haunted its new lord. Possibly he would find it worse than life in the West Indies; a world with savages and wild animals; a place with boiling sunshine and devilish storms. She shuddered. Closing her damp eyes, she prayed for protection and clarity. The covers around her seemed to tuck themselves in closer.

Tomorrow would be better. Another day would see her improved, and with luck, she would return home. Hope warmed Sophie's heart as she slipped away into her foggy dreams. In the distance, before letting go for good, she thought she heard the grieving cry of a faraway loon.

CHAPTER FOUR

Sophie awoke to sunlight flowing through the window in yellow streamers. Mrs. Brooks had not returned to shut the draperies, but someone had stoked a new fire. The air in the room made Sophie's nose cold, but the rest of her felt cozy under the blankets. The bricks of Pembroke did not retain much heat, but the bright light made the masculine room feel cheerful.

She scurried out of bed to take care of her morning priorities, wincing at the chilled floor beneath her feet. Mrs. Brooks arrived with breakfast just as Sophie brushed through her hair with a brush sent from home with her other things. She climbed back into the bed as Captain Murdock's housekeeper fussed over her health and fluffed the covers up to her waist.

The eggs, cold meat, and sliced bread went down very well with hot coffee. It would have made her drowsy if she had not had so much rest already. Her nose still felt rather puffy, but she did not feel feverish and had not developed a dangerous cough or a sore throat.

After breakfast in bed, Mrs. Brooks led in Doctor Stephens. Having treated the Crestwoods at Leatherbury for some years, he proclaimed Sophie in robust health, only warning her to wear a shawl and stay out of the cool evening air. When the tall, balding man strode out with all the confidence his position granted him, Mrs. Brooks brought Sophie's freshly laundered clothes she'd been wearing the afternoon of the storm. With no lady's maid at Pembroke, the woman helped her dress. She braided Sophie's hair neatly, leaving a few short strands loose at her temples.

"I'm happy to go home," Sophie admitted as she moved to sit back on the bed, "but please don't think I'm anxious to leave on your account. I would have been helpless and lonely without you."

Mrs. Brooks smiled with satisfaction, the little dark gap in her upper teeth seemed hardly noticeable to Sophie now. "Which there are not a lot of females in this place," she said with a grin, "although I'm used to that. There's only the girl in the kitchen from one of the tenant houses, and she helps with the wash."

"Considering the cleaning and repairs to be done, you must be overworked," Sophie observed.

"Oh, no, not so much, ye see," Mrs. Brooks confided. "Captain Murdock brought most the... servants with him from St. Kitts." She lowered her voice. "Not that they know how to run a big house."

"They are lucky to have you." Sophie smiled.

The woman shook her head with some doubt. "I'm new to this kind of living, too," she said. "I sailed with my husband until he passed, God rest his soul. Captain Murdock kept me on in St. Kitts, and I had a little learning, but I ain't ever been a maid, and I sure won't be marrying Sykes."

"Sykes? Who's he?" Sophie said with growing curiosity.

"He's the butler, he is." Mrs. Brooks burst into guttural laughter that flushed her cheeks, then wiped her mouth on the back of her fist. "We got only two footmen, and that's because they done it before they was pressed."

"I'm sure they keep you busy."

"Oh, if Mr. Howard don't. He's only the cook, but he thinks he has just as much say when we was aboard *Constance*."

The *Constance*? Was that Captain Murdock's ship?"

Mrs. Brooks' face drooped, and her eyes misted over. She stepped back and clasped her hands together. "You look very fine, Miss Crestwood."

Sophie rose and thanked her. "What should I do now? Will my parents come?"

The woman curtsied, a late and unsure realization of the new manners required in this new life. "Which Captain Murdock says if you're feeling better I can take you to the drawing room to sit a spell."

"That sounds nice," Sophie said, eager to see more of Pembroke. "I haven't seen much of the house. It's been empty for so long."

"Yes," said Mrs. Brooks in a slow and thoughtful way. "It's all bright and done up downstairs, nothing dreary like it was when we first came."

Sophie let her pass to lead the way. She followed her out of the room and down the hall. They went around the corner to the wide staircase, but this time she went down instead of up.

On the lower landing, an enormous tapestry hung on the wall. Sophie studied it as she held onto the polished rail for balance. The long, red textile had an impressive coat of arms set over a hunting scene from some other age. The lords looked knightly, and the horses angry or deranged. Her nose tickled as she followed Mrs. Brooks down. Her heart recoiled at the memory of sneezing on her host.

When she reached the ground floor of Pembroke Hall, she looked about awestruck. It was not as open as she had expected, but for the impressive, hand-carved staircase. The vestibule did not have beautiful marble tiles, but a layer of polished limestone blanketed with luxurious rugs. They looked soft and rich, and she wondered why she had been cast off to an unrestored wing full of dust and shadows.

Like the staircase, wood panels on the walls were polished to a shine. There were no fingery cobwebs drifting from the corners but an eclectic assortment of candelabras in different finishes. A great round table with a gold leaf top shined and reflected light. It anchored the space with its large urn of Greek figures holding a wild collection of flowers. They looked like they'd been pulled from the meadow rather than a proper cutting garden. It was a pretty attempt, and Sophie smiled to herself. Why not? She knew her mother would find them strange and romantic, but Papa would call them weeds.

Mrs. Brooks tottered ahead and pushed open a door across from the stairs. There were no footmen or other formalities. Sophie hurried across the carpets and entered with enthusiasm. This room glowed with sunshine. Expansive, it had windows running across the front of the house and its southern walls.

She realized Mrs. Brooks waited for some expression of approval. "What a spacious room," said Sophie. The woman looked about, half smiling, half unsure. "You don't have to stay," Sophie excused her. "I'll find something to do."

"As you say," Mrs. Brooks said with a satisfied smile. She motioned toward a little bell resting on a marble-topped pedestal beside a very long settee. "You ring that if you need me, and I, someone but prolly me, we'll be right along."

"Thank you," Sophie said, "for everything."

Mrs. Brooks smiled. She stopped herself from dashing out and gave Sophie a curtsey then toddled off.

Sophie dropped onto the settee. It was very French, covered in a gold-on-black pattern that hinted at a *fleur-de-lis*. Across from her, a pale blue couch rested on the floor with carved long legs that curved up and around like a sleigh. Beyond it, an enormous fireplace commanded the eye. There were tea tables and an assortment of stands and benches with dark wood and gold hinges. Some were painted with queer Eastern designs of pink blossoms and green stalks. A fierce dragon looked carved straight from stone. It rested on an ordinary writing desk between the fireplace and windows. "Quite the paperweight collection you have," Sophie whispered in the quiet. Over it, a frightening savage mask in red and black hung from the plaster.

The drawing room had a high ceiling, too. Sophie thought the space would have served a large household and many friends, but with only her presence, it seemed vast. She glanced at the door and seeing no one, peeked out the windows that faced south toward Portsmouth. She studied the flat meadows that became woods then rolled into distant hills where the sky looked as blue as robin eggs.

Pembroke had once been worked for agricultural means, but its primary history was a longstanding tradition of fine game and popular hunts. She leaned her forehead against the cool, recently washed glass, and studied the overgrown grounds. Ivy framed the outside window from all sides, and she suspected it had just been cut to open the view. A small herd of goats wandered across the grounds, and she chuckled. Surely, they had been as hard at work as the curious servants here. A floorboard creaked, and she swept her chin across her shoulder.

Captain Murdock stood across the room, stiff and gripping his cane. He looked somewhat put out, but whether that was because of her presence or his infirmity, she could not tell. He nodded, and she returned it with a bend of her knees.

"You are feeling well enough to be downstairs."

"Yes," Sophie said. "You have guessed right."

Captain Murdock looked around the room like he had not seen it before. He wore a pair of dark breeches, a soft linen shirt, and a simple grey waistcoat. His unruly hair was combed back over his ears and loose, almost to his shoulders. If he had been a true gentleman, it would have been cropped short with slight waves tamed neatly on his crown, and what a fetching picture he would be; even more handsome than George Devlin. No, Sophie caught herself. A man of no great reputation could not be too handsome.

He finally said, "I will have Mrs. Brooks sit with you and send word you are recovered."

"Oh, no, please." Sophie forced a smile. "She is too busy and advanced in years to play lady's companion."

"Then I'll send word to Leatherbury, and you shall be delivered home before supper. Your mother was anxious to come, but the roads were still poor this morning, so I put them off."

Sophie couldn't help but wonder that he did not wish to dine with her. Since it was he and she alone, with no chaperone or companions, she thought it a great deal sensible to be taken home straightaway. "I think that would be best," she agreed. She waited for him to offer her a book or cup of tea.

Instead, he studied the floorboards at her feet, and she was glad her walking boots had dried out enough to lace them up. "Well," he said, in the agonizing quiet, "it is recommended I show you the grounds since you are so fond of the property."

Sophie pursed her lips at his subtle reprimand but decided to take advantage of his offer wondering who had recommended it. "I would love a walk, and Doctor Stephens said I may go out as long as it's not too cool or damp."

Captain Murdock looked disappointed he would have to exercise and with his handicap, too, but he bowed with a slight bend at the waist. Without another word, he tapped out of the room, and Sophie noticed for the first time he wore a black crepe armband. No one in Higfield had mentioned he was in mourning; not even Papa.

It grew quiet, and she wondered if he had run away as the tap of his cane faded.

She wasn't certain if he meant for her to follow. Perhaps he had decided to lock himself in his bedchambers with his violin on the third floor. She wondered if his reticence had anything to do with the black armband. He did not smile, he had little to say other than the polite requirements of social conversation, and he only appeared to have interest in his neighbors when he was informed one of them had set foot on his property.

Sophie wandered to the drawing room door and seeing no servants about, stepped out intending to let herself outside. She had only seen Pembroke's front façade up close once or twice in her life, and both times the lawn and shrubbery were overgrown, and the walls tangled like mad with vines. She had a certain expectation in her mind, a picture of a long, pitted drive yawning up to a foreboding stone fortress with diminutive gargoyles staring from the eaves, but it fell away when she swung open the doors to a beautiful scene.

Before she could utter a sentiment of surprise, Captain Murdock appeared from out of nowhere, his boots and cane silent on the floor. How he managed to arrive so quietly yet disappear with such a clamor, she did not know. Next to her, he looked tall, and she could smell a spicy flavor that reminded her of cider and Christmas. She glanced up at him through her lashes, surprised at his approach and that she felt it so.

Looking somewhat uncertain, he handed her the rescued bonnet, now dry, and a large shawl folded over in half. She unraveled the long length of light wool and marveled at the rich, indigo color as deep as the sea. "Thank you," she murmured, knowing it must only be borrowed. Taking his arm that he jerked out alongside her, she felt certain he would never part with such a thing unless he had a sweetheart.

They stepped out into the sunshine of a more deliberate spring day than the one that brought her to Pembroke. The treetops were entirely in their green glory, and the earth had a rosy, golden gleam that promised fruit and flowers. Sophie breathed deep, relishing spring's fragrances and realized with sadness that the hot summer days were not far away. After that, the cold would come again.

"I don't like the winter after a time," she confessed, as they stepped out onto a fresh, cleared but wet drive. It was smooth and looked like new. She gazed up in admiration at the long wing attached to the hall's main body.

Murdock followed her gaze. "I have never seen it here. I only know one season."

"You have never seen snow?" Sophie considered it an oddity to have never experienced wintertime, but then Captain Murdock was a curious card after all. "Then you have not been sleigh-riding at Christmas. That is one great advantage of the season. It's great fun and my favorite thing to do."

She glanced at him, and his eyes shifted away as if he'd been studying her. He concentrated on his leaning gait.

"I've seen ice," he replied.

"In the West Indies? How curious." Sophie closed her eyes and tried to picture the atlas from Leatherbury's library again.

"No," Captain Murdock corrected her. "South of Brazil and down around the Cape."

"Oh, but of course. You've been all around the world, haven't you?" This was an interesting tidbit.

He remained silent for a step. Then he said, "Around the horn, Cape Horn, yes, and to the East Indies round about. I never sailed as far as Africa and have never seen England's shores until this year."

"It must be as foreign to you here as the Cape," Sophie wondered.

"How does your geography fare, Miss Crestwood?"

Sophie smiled. "Not so much, but I'm somewhat familiar with the world's arrangement as Jack fancies himself an expert."

"He fancies himself an expert at a great many things." Captain Murdock made a noise in his throat that sounded to Sophie like a soft chuckle, but when she looked at him sideways his face held no expression.

"Most twelve-year-old boys do. I have an elder brother, too, and he was the same way at that age and for a great many years afterward."

The top corner of Captain Murdock's mouth twitched, and it almost distracted Sophie from a great round fountain in the center of the grounds. It was surrounded by an unkempt patch of overgrown roses that were circled about by the drive.

"I cannot say I've never met a young boy that did not fancy he was proficient at some mischief or another," said the captain.

Sophie could not pull her eyes away from the lovely fountain. She nodded to show they shared a common understanding but could not help but direct him toward the two cherubs dancing in a gurgling stream of water. "I never knew this was here," she confessed with a small gasp of pleasure. "It's impressive, though I'm not sure it suits the facade of Pembroke."

"Does it not?" The captain studied the water work. He glanced back over his shoulder toward the house then back at the fountain. "I found it overgrown with weeds and had it cleared. The story, I understand, is that my father's first wife chose it not long after she came to Pembroke, and although he did not like it, he was newly wed and thought it safer to indulge in her wishes then provoke a disagreement."

"A wise man." Sophie watched the water trickle from one pot down into the arms of one of the cherubs. "It's quite pretty. I did not mean to criticize it. It has a lovely sound."

"Yes," the captain agreed, "the water." He stepped around it, the soft pull of his arm inviting her to follow. They walked across the lawn to the drive and strolled along. Beyond the fountain lay more shrubs in disarray. Sophie tried not to stare or show her disapproval, but the captain guessed at it.

"The garden has just been cleared. It still needs some weeding, and all of the roses clamor to be cut back and trained again."

"They're a wild mess, aren't they, especially the roses?" Sophie frowned at the tangled bushes. They were overgrown and choking out one another's light.

"Yes, but it's nature's way. Once we find someone with the right experience we'll have it shipshape, though I like to try my hand at it when I can."

Sophie tried to imagine Captain Murdock helping her in her own cutting garden and almost grinned. "It'll be lovely in a season or two," she said. "I love roses. We have them at Leatherbury, too; a great variety. Red, pink, peach, yellow, white... I'm sorry. You're bored."

"No, I'm only listening." His forehead furrowed, and she flushed that she may have insulted him.

"Then you are planning to stay at Pembroke?"

Whatever small expressions that had shifted on Captain Murdock's face while talking about improvements and roses disappeared, and he became unreadable again. His eyes narrowed like he'd found something in the distance to study beyond the painted black gates at the end of the drive. He was such a mix of English and something wild.

"I'm sorry." Sophie shook her head to clear her thoughts and undo her prying words. "I did not mean to meddle."

The man beside her took a deep breath and exhaled. Sophie could almost hear his sudden burst of temperamental irritation recede. "I understand you are only curious. No one has lived here for a very long time."

"No," Sophie agreed. "Not since your father, I understand."

"We had property in the West Indies. That's where I was born."

"Yes," Sophie said, ashamed for knowing so much about a total stranger. "That much is village rumor."

"Village rumor," he repeated like he was curious and uninterested at the same time.

"I know very little of the details," Sophie admitted. "Perhaps once you are here awhile and people become familiar with your history, the gossip will fade away."

"What gossip?" Captain Murdock inquired. His tone suggested she'd committed another offense.

"Oh, nothing of much interest," Sophie reassured him, trying to think how to talk her way out of upsetting him. She couldn't suggest he might be a pirate. "It's just you've come from the Indies and your father passed away, and that there *was* property."

"I never planned to keep it."

"You do not hope to return?"

"I do not wish it. Not now."

Again, Sophie realized she'd overstepped her bounds when the captain clamped his lips together. Of course, he did not wish it. Why would he if he had secrets to keep? A little tremor ran through her when she considered the possibilities of his past.

He frowned, and she guessed he'd revealed too much. They'd reached the gate, so she turned to view Pembroke as it was meant to be seen, not from Leatherbury peeping through the trees or sitting on the old rock wall gazing up at the hall's stone chimneys. She forgot about buccaneers and let out a small gasp.

"Why, it's a beautiful place, it really is," she said with delight. "The sun hits it just right, and with the bricks clean and the window trim painted, it looks very soon to be recovered. Once your gardens are tended, Pembroke Hall will be a handsome estate indeed."

She glanced at Captain Murdock to see if her compliments pleased him because she meant them, but a peculiar look of suspicion clouded his features.

"I'm happy you think so, Miss Crestwood." He didn't sound happy, and Sophie felt a pang of disappointment that his amiable feelings toward her seemed to have dissipated. They walked back toward the towering hall in silence. She tried to make it as pleasant a silence between them as she could, but his withdrawn spirit dampened her own. She took the opportunity to study the windows on the top floors that still needed washing and noted the roof was in dire need of patching.

"How the rain must get in," she said to herself, and he glanced at her. She motioned with her chin toward the pitted rooftop over the east wing and he said with a calm tone, "There is still a great amount of work yet to do at Pembroke. I can't see to it all at once."

"No, of course not." Sophie smiled at him but feared it came out more a grimace. He led her back inside out of the sun, and when no butler or footman came to see to them, offered her tea in the drawing room. Before she accepted, she unwrapped herself from the beautiful shawl and handed it back to him. He accepted it with a curt bow and limped toward the stairs. To where he vanished she could only wonder as she let herself back into the strange drawing room. She had probably tired him out, and he needed rest. Curious soul.

The little brass bell still stood on the marble pedestal. After waiting so long she was sure he had forgotten her, she picked it up with some timidity and rang it. A few moments later she shook it again, and Mrs. Brooks burst into the room with a happy smile. "Which did you enjoy your turn about the old place?"

"Oh, yes," Sophie said with a grin. She tried to imagine the roses in bloom and the grounds trimmed. "I can hardly wait until summer to see it," she confessed, "but I'm afraid I asked too much of the captain."

The servant clapped her hands to her bosom. "Oh no, he needs to get out and about. I'm sure it done him good. Now, what can I do for you? We have word from Leatherbury and will carry you home within the hour.

"Oh," said Sophie, uncertain if she should trouble the servants at all. I was only wondering about tea because the captain had mentioned it."

"Oh, tea! Yes!" cried Mrs. Brooks. "I'll see right to it, Miss Crestwood." She turned on her heel and chuckled on her way out, "Tea time, is the order of the day. No grog here at Pembroke, ha-ha!"

AFTER TAKING TEA AND waiting for Pembroke's rather new carriage to ferry her home, Sophie found herself bouncing along home at last. The small vehicle swayed back and forth along the lane, and Sophie's stomach rolled with it, too. She felt warm enough, bundled up in her pelisse and worn bonnet. She watched the wild grounds of Pembroke sweep by like an oil painting. It made a pretty blur.

A stern Captain Murdock had warned the driver to see Sophie came to no harm as he helped her into her seat. Once his cane slipped, and he pitched forward catching himself against the carriage door. She did not expect him to keep her hand, but he did and with a strong grip, as she tried to take her seat without looking clumsy. She pretended it did not happen at all and that his cheeks did not grow ruddy.

Mrs. Brooks came, too, settling in beside her patient as if they were going to undertake a dangerous adventure. Leatherbury, Sophie knew, could not be more than a mile from one drive to the next. Low branches arched over the carriage, as trees shook hands from either side of the road. Leaves fluttered in a light breeze, and birds twittered. She tucked her hands into the folds of her pelisse but not before Mrs. Brooks patted them.

"I'm sorry for your distress, Miss Crestwood; for the situation that brought you to Pembroke, but we're ever so happy you did. Not that I mean we're happy you was frightened and nearly ill, but that we made your acquaintance. I mean," she corrected herself as she prattled on, "that you made the acquaintance of Captain Murdock."

Sophie did not have enough time than to reply with raised brows and a pleased smile.

"My real meaning," Mrs. Brooks continued, finding her tongue again, "was that I am pleased you came to Pembroke. Captain Murdock is a bit lost with no ship under his command."

Sensing the woman's pity, Sophie wanted to hear more. "The sun sets on the horizon in Higfield, too, Mrs. Brooks. Why would he be lost here? It's his family home after all."

"He ain't never been to England before and everything is different."

"I hear it's very much the same."

"Oh, my no, well, maybe the gov'ment and all those types, but no, the air is different and the trees and the birds... even the food ain't quite what we been used to eating." Mrs. Brooks put a finger to her chin. "Some of it is a great deal better, I say, but there ain't no breadfruit to be found."

"Yes, we probably eat a great deal more variety here," Sophie agreed.

Mrs. Brooks warmed up to the conversation. "The ladies, they're different, too. All the people in the village act like the captain is either royalty or criminal. I don't think they can much make up their minds."

"No, he's quite the paradox."

"Yes, and a riddle, too, I'd wager. He's lonely since Cottle..."

"Cottle?"

Mrs. Brooks swallowed, looking guilty and then sorrowful. "He's just lonely, Miss Crestwood, and since the ladies in St. Kitts found his fortune so comely until it was gone, he's prone to suspicion when it comes to females." She giggled. "Not like me, no, or you, I dare say." She smiled at her with approval.

"Me?" Sophie turned her face straight ahead, so Mrs. Brooks could not see her expression. A warming in her cheeks exasperated her.

"I just mean you're a kind young lady, Miss Crestwood, and don't seem to mind Pembroke in its pitiable state."

"To be fair, I must say that neither does Captain Murdock, and you have made a good job of it, Mrs. Brooks. It's coming together quite well."

The woman pressed her hands together, thinking as she steepled her fingers over a worn grey cloak. "His father had distractions to be sure, and the captain did not have much attention as a lad, but he's done a great deal of good and has a heart of gold."

"Gold?" Sophie smiled to herself.

"Yes," Mrs. Brooks insisted, but she sounded more careful now. "He ain't had much to be gay about even with his situation, but he's a good sort underneath all the scowling."

Sophie tried to picture him without a scowl. She could only see him staring into the fireplace in his chamber and the grip of his fingers on the violin bow. Granted, he had lost his frowns and detached tone while walking with her on the grounds of Pembroke; at least for a bit.

"Perhaps someday he will come to love his home as much as he did the sea."

"Yes," Mrs. Brooks said in a hopeful voice. "Find something to love. That is all we can wish for him now, I suppose, since he won't ever go back."

Leatherbury came into view. Sophie sat up tall and stretched to look. "Why can't he go back?"

"There's nothing to go back to now," Mrs. Brooks said in a quiet, sad voice, "and he's got his 'heritance at Pembroke. He's a big, important man here."

Sophie decided not to press Mrs. Brooks further. "Here's Leatherbury now, Mrs. Brooks." The enormous old elms scattered about the large yard waved in the afternoon sunshine.

The woman beside Sophie clapped her hands as if she heard music playing in the wind. "It's a handsome place indeed, Miss Crestwood. What lovely roses."

IN THE MORNING, MARGARET helped her pin up her hair. Sophie felt ready to work in the garden and investigate the new blooms on her roses, despite anyone's opinions of her health.

"Oh, Sophie, I was going to have your breakfast sent up," Mama scolded when Sophie took her regular seat at breakfast.

"I cannot miss the news," Sophie insisted, looking at her father. Papa piled sausages onto his plate, crisscrossing them in a pattern that reminded her of embroidery.

"You look well enough," he agreed. "I'm happy you are come back, for it's all over the village now." His brows crinkled over his eyes.

"I am well, and what could the village possibly talk about regarding me?"

"One never knows to be sure," Papa answered. His mouth turned down as he plunged his fingers into his sausage pile and plucked out the fattest one.

"It was an accident," Sophie insisted, "and nothing more."

Mama said in a quiet voice, "You do know he practically refused to let me come, and you my own daughter. Was there anything... untoward?"

"No, Mama." Sophie shook her head in a firm motion. "Pembroke was tidy, Mrs. Brooks attentive, and when I saw Captain Murdock, he behaved politely. I was hardly there a full two days, and the roads *were* terrible." Sophie decided to neglect the fact Murdock had taken her on a tour of the grounds should Mama send her to bed again and stack more blankets over her.

"You could have been killed or worse. What if you'd died?" Mama's eyes watered, and she dabbed at the corners of them.

"Oh, Mama, we must be grateful it did not come to that. You can see I'm as well as can be expected." With that, Sophie scowled at Jack, who sat staring into a small bowl of porridge. "Lucky for you, I am anyway."

Papa raised his head. "Jack did the only thing he could do when you wandered off, although Leatherbury was not further away." He pressed his lips together to show his displeasure that Jack had called on Pembroke for help.

"Yes, I should not have wandered off," Sophie said, relenting to Jack's sudden, pleading stare. It was clear he had not provided all the details.

"Which Pembroke was closer," Jack muttered, and Papa harrumphed.

"Well, I am thankful for Captain Murdock and his kindness, nonetheless," Sophie admitted. She happily took two eggs, contemplating how many days had passed since she'd eaten a real meal.

Papa swallowed a bite of sausage then said, "There's no excuse for you wandering out alone in a storm and away towards Pembroke. It's been abandoned since you were a baby, and it's in no better state with a... with that captain taking up there."

"Upon my word, he was genteel," Sophie said.

"It will not do," her father insisted, "to have everyone knowing you stayed at Pembroke with no chaperone; with not even your Mama or Margaret there."

"I had Mrs. Brooks," Sophie replied, though she did not know why she rushed to the captain's defense.

"We know nothing about Murdock. No one seems to be able to recommend him or to account for his reasons for coming to Pembroke, and now the entire village knows you've been under his roof."

"Nobody ain't ever minded an officer before. If Murdock's an heir and has an inheritance, what does it matter?" Jack interrupted the conversation, unconcerned about his place.

"Because," snapped Papa, now red on his cheeks and squeezing his fork, "he has made no effort to be neighborly, does not play cards, and has little interest in hunting on his own land." He shook his fist in the air, and Sophie guessed it was because her father could no longer hunt on the land either.

Mama patted his hand, trying to reign in his temper. It was too late now, for his worries spilled out like crumbs as he pushed his plate away. "The village says he is hiding out, and from what, we do not know. It is unwise to wander about his property or to lie ill at Pembroke. He could be mad." Papa took a long sip and wiped his chin with his hand. Sophie cringed.

"We must consider that Jack may be right," Mama murmured, trying to restore calm. "He certainly does not behave like an officer, not that anyone minds a captain in Higfield, and he does refuse to divulge any details about himself. He could be a murderer for all we know, though knowing his father, it is unlikely."

Papa frowned, and Sophie blinked in surprise at the glare he gave Mama. It was so accusing she looked down at the table.

"A pirate," Jack agreed. The rest of the family stared like it was the first time he'd suggested it. "I told you so. He's come here to escape being hanged, and when he's found out, they'll take him to Execution Dock."

Sophie shuddered. "Don't say such things, Jack." The thought that their neighbors might very well be criminals in disguise made her ill. "It was told to me by a servant that he had a ship and was reputable." Well, that was not entirely true, but he did have his own ship.

"Someone should say it," Papa said. "We live too close and may fall under his cloud." He chewed for a moment, thinking. "It would be well to find out the truth of things before anyone else. Until then," he stared at Sophie as if the accident was her fault, "no one should leave the grounds of Leatherbury, and there will be no other encouragement."

Sophie reared back her head as if she'd been cuffed. Jack said, "Does that mean no more hunting?"

Papa glowered at his son. "That's exactly what it means."

"Come now, Sophie," said Mama in the dazed silence, "let's talk about our supper party. It's only days away, and Lady Mary has promised to come as she has business south. Last she wrote, she inquired about your health and promised us a surprise announcement."

Sophie's thoughts spun in a new direction. "I suspect she is to bring her nephew. She has spoken of little else since Christmas." Her cheeks felt hot despite her attempt not to pay any mind to all the gazes upon her.

"He is not due until summer." Mama smiled to pretend some sort of innocence, but Sophie did not miss the sparkle in her eyes.

"It's kind of her to accept whether she brings him or not." Sophie would not give them more than that. She glared at Jack who smirked with satisfaction at her discomfort.

Mama added, "I suspect her surprise is something more than gracing us with her company. She's fond of you."

"So is Mr. Devlin I hear," Jack interjected. "Papa invited him, too."

Sophie blushed. Before she could complain, Papa said, "Now, now." He shook his head at Jack, and he went back to shoveling food from bowl to mouth.

"Mr. Devlin is entertaining," Sophie said with generosity, "but I hardly know him. Why he would care to come here I'm sure I don't know."

Both of Sophie's parents grinned like she'd told a joke. She looked down at her eggs and decided they were cold. She picked at her toast instead. The popular Mr. Devlin was coming to Leatherbury. What good news. Sophie could put the adventure at Pembroke away in the back of her mind.

CHAPTER FIVE

Sophie recovered from her night in the storm with no lingering consequences, which pleased her father but puzzled her mama. Although he would not admit it, Jack felt relieved. The catastrophe she'd avoided was almost forgotten by the time the drawing room filled with guests for Mama's supper party.

It was a great honor to have Lady Mary of Billingham with them. She had command of the room. Mr. Devlin and his aunt and uncle sat rapt with attention on Sophie's favorite settee. She took a ladder-back chair, quite uncomfortable, and tugged on a gown that had grown tight in the sleeves. It was a pale blue-green that Mama insisted would make her glow in the lamplight.

Lady Mary sensed her unease. "You look lovely this evening," she observed, as Sophie tried to lessen an ache between her upper shoulders.

"That's very kind of you." Sophie did not feel lovely in colors that contradicted her dark eyes. She wished Mrs. Blackburn had allowed Katherine to come. The gown would have suited her far better. "It's Mama's favorite, and she was happy I should wear it."

Across the room, Devlin diverted his attention from Mr. Crestwood and said with great emotion, "There's no need to be humble, Miss Crestwood. Your complexion is perfect for any shade of blue. How it makes your cheeks glow."

He motioned for everyone to agree. Studying Sophie, Lady Mary remarked, "He is right, not that I often credit a gentleman for knowing what a woman should wear. My nephew, Henry Billingham, is one exception."

Devlin glanced at Sophie and then looked around with a smile at the compliment.

"Henry has good taste when it comes to redecorating, too," continued the lady.

"It would be convenient to have a reliable opinion when changing over a room," Sophie agreed. She watched her father's eyes sweep around the drawing room and inwardly chuckled at his concern about Leatherbury's aging interior.

"My nephew," Lady Mary continued, "has extraordinary taste. He is also a great connoisseur of wine, and I've asked him more than once for his advice."

"How fortunate for your nephew," Devlin said, "that you should trust him so. What I know I learned on tour, and if it weren't for the generosity of my uncle, I would be no better suited to tell water from tea."

Lady Mary smiled, pleased at Devlin's modesty. "My nephew did not require much when he went to the continent, but he did take my advice of what to see and to whom he should call. It is a pity you are not yet acquainted. I blame your uncle for keeping you all to himself."

Devlin nodded with a solemn attitude while his uncle, Mr. Porter, looked mortified.

Papa pardoned himself to see to some arrangement, but supper was called in that instant, and Sophie watched his shoulders drop with relief. Perhaps it was Lady Mary who upset the balance of his disposition.

The party moved into the small dining room with Jack trailing behind. He had turned thirteen one week ago and received a rifle for his birthday. Sophie thought him too young for dinner parties, not to mention a large gun, but it pleased him all the same as if it had been a sword or compass. His naval dreams were now a thing of great anxiety with admittance to Harrow looming, and after the first course when Lady Mary saw fit to include him in her inquisition, Sophie was horrified at his reply.

"I don't want to be a clergyman," he answered with a stubborn air.

"Why not?" asked the lady, her white brows raised. "You won't inherit Leatherbury, and the parsonage may pass to you as I've arranged with your parents."

Jack had the decency to look down at his plate and frown rather than scowl at their esteemed benefactress. "Just because some cousin done it until he died don't mean I want to do it, too."

"That's foolhardy," Lady Mary said in a stern tone. Sophie watched the lines in her cheeks sink deeper into her face. "There's nothing more admirable than the Church unless you purchase a commission, I suppose." She did not put down her fork as she glanced at Papa. "I've never heard of such a thing, turning down a respectable living; and at Oak Grove, too."

"I ain't gonna get myself killed in the infantry either," Jack muttered, and Sophie tensed. Papa's face flushed a dark, bloody red, and Mama looked sideways at Jack like he had shamed them all.

Devlin leaned across the table. "What do you aim to do then? Go on tour forever? Study at Oxford until your brain is full?" He laughed, and the top of his coiffed golden hair bobbled with his gaiety.

"No," said Jack, his face drawn. "I'm going to sail under a captain like Nelson and someday command the fleet."

There was a pause in the room then the guests around the table broke into titters. Even Mr. and Mrs. Porter laughed, although with more affection than amusement.

"Children should be seen and not heard," said Papa in a hard voice.

Mr. Porter cleared his throat. Mama set her lips together in a narrow line. "A commission would not be out of sorts, I daresay, but a life in the Church is a far more sensible occupation than living in dangerous and squalid conditions while trapped at sea."

"Squalid characters, too," Devlin added. Studying Jack, with a tilt of his head he said, "Have you ever seen the fo'c'sle, young Jack, or spent time on the docks?"

"Not exactly," replied Jack in a cold tone.

"They're a nasty, savage lot, with no manners or etiquette to recommend them. Their speech is rough and uncommon, and they have no understanding of what is proper and seemly in society."

"I won't be in the fo'c'sle," Jack replied. "I'll manage them well enough from the wardroom."

Devlin grinned. "You'll be forced to occupy the same space, even on a ship of the line. It's risky, dirty, uncomfortable work with little thanks from your superiors."

"How would you know?" Jack's olive eyes flashed under his ginger locks, and Sophie cut him off before he could say more.

"My brother loves the sea, Mr. Devlin, and everything in it. It's only natural he would set his hopes on a career that holds his interests."

The gentleman acquiesced, and with an air of patience said, "There's nothing wrong with a fancy, Miss Crestwood." He chuckled. "I admit I've had my share or two." He gazed at her a bit long until it made her uncomfortable, and she looked away. At the same time, she fully expected Jack to bolt up from his chair and shout, "It ain't no fancy!" but he said nothing at all. Instead, he gripped his spoon tighter; so much so his knuckles paled.

"Oh, the strawberries," said Mama as another course was served. "Lady Mary, you were so right to tell us to thin them out. We've more this year than any other time I can remember."

Everyone gave a great deal of compliments to the berries, and just like that, Jack's poor behavior was forgotten, except by Devlin. He stared at Sophie. His eyes shifted to Jack and back, then he shook his head and widened his eyes. She bit her lip to keep from grinning but let a tiny smile slip out instead. Devlin did not mention it again, and when the ladies rose to retire from the room, he stood up and helped Sophie from her chair.

Sophie thanked him and ignored the pleased look on Papa's face.

LADY MARY REIGNED OVER the drawing room again by taking the seat closest to the fire. Mrs. Crestwood and Mrs. Porter shared the settee, and Sophie found herself settled in the unpadded chair once more. Lamps and their best candles lit up the room though dusk had fallen over the day later than usual.

"Well, Miss Crestwood," said Lady Mary, as soon as she finished complimenting Mama on her strawberries, as well as her home and garden and the lovely necklace she'd worn to supper, "I have exciting news to pass on to you."

Her mother smiled at this and so, Sophie noticed, did the other two ladies. She clasped her hands in her lap. "Your ladyship has always been kind to me, and if you have news, I am happy to hear it."

Sophie thought her response sounded well and polite, but she was surprised by the sensation she felt of falling from a great height. It started in her bosom and plunged down into her stomach, and then it trickled to her toes.

"With the heat soon to come upon us and trap us all indoors in the afternoons, I've decided to have a house party when my nephew arrives. He is much used to the variety of activity in Town."

"How generous," Sophie answered. Truth be told, a house party at Oak Grove held more interest than sitting in the drawing room of Leatherbury all summer.

"I intend to host a house full of young people for a fortnight or more, and all of it at his pleasure. Would you not find that stimulating?"

Mama smiled ear to ear as if it were indeed the most amazing of proposals. Sophie concurred to please them both. "I think it is a wonderful idea, your ladyship, and very generous, too."

"Well," continued Lady Mary, rapping a closed fan on her palm, "I'm happy you think so, my dear girl. I've already discussed it with your papa, and I intend to be your chaperone. You will be our special guest." She stopped, beamed, and watched Sophie for the expected expressions of gratitude.

Sophie squeezed her fingers and tried to look appreciative and demure. "I can't thank you enough. How kind of you to think of me, and how charitable, too."

Mrs. Porter sighed loud with pleasure. "It's an excellent idea, your Ladyship, and so generous." Turning to Sophie she reminded her, "You must remember her ladyship introduced me to Mr. Porter in much the same way." She smiled to herself at what seemed to be a happy memory.

"I remember, Mrs. Porter. We speak of it often."

"Oh," said Mama, "and I was fortunate to have the same opportunity." Her eyes clouded with memories, but she blinked them away.

"Hmm," mused Lady Mary. "Mr. Crestwood had a mind of his own, but he did ask for my advisement. You have a good home and family, Mrs. Crestwood, even though you brought no money into the marriage."

Sophie glanced sideways at her mama, who colored and looked toward the low fire. Mrs. Porter smiled at her friend's good fortune. Sophie tried as much, but it felt a bit strange to be more grateful for an income than for a happy heart.

"Papa can never refuse Mama anything," Sophie said, and the women chuckled.

Lady Mary caught Sophie's eye with a firm stare. "You would do well to be half so content."

"I will, your ladyship," Sophie promised. In her heart, she wondered what Lady Mary expected of her.

"There will be several other young ladies invited, of course you know."

Sophie swallowed. The women around her were quite serious. Oak Grove was so... large. Pembroke popped into her mind like an unexpected mouse. Why, Oak Grove made Pembroke look shabby indeed, and compared to her own humble abode—

"You are nigh on twenty now, so one would expect you to be sober and well behaved."

Sophie glanced at her mother with consternation, a flush rising on her cheeks. No one mentioned her not having made a match in two seasons, not to mention the following year. She cleared her throat and whispered, "I assure you I will be in earnest, your ladyship."

The idea of a house party now filled her with prudish uncertainty. She had first thought it a wonderful idea that would provide opportunities for fun with young people her own age, but Lady Mary made it clear this party would be business: matchmaking, just like the social season in London.

"Now, Sophie's dowry, Mrs. Crestwood," the lady said. She went on to lead another discussion on inheritances and some victorious matches made in London among the Ton in the season past. It was as if the upcoming party was for Sophie's own good rather than Mr. Henry Billingham. She felt like an advertisement.

She understood Jack, put upon by the expectations of others. Perhaps she dawdled over Leatherbury's grounds too often like her brother. Maybe she was not quite ready to grow up either. Despite the occasional irritation, she felt fond of her dreamy Mama and expressive Papa. They were their very own little society, happily wiling the days away at a fine country house with roses and a vegetable garden, and a fine pond with fish that were easy to catch—for a boy at least.

The idea that Lady Mary might have schemes filled Sophie with some trepidation. It was true she did not have a dowry of royal enormity. Though it was notable when compared to others in the county, alone it would be no temptation for a titled gentleman.

Sophie reached up and brushed her hair back towards its pins, wondering if she was not quite as handsome as she'd decided. She had grown up thinking she would marry young like her mother and be happy with a dashing gentleman who found her as irresistible as Venus. It now appeared it had been too romantic a notion. Papa had married for love. Mama had, too.

Hadn't she?

Sophie glanced at the circle of women making plans for her while she sat in the same room unseen. It did not feel well, almost as unpleasant as her first ball. She'd loved the gowns and dancing and fun, but in her heart had echoed the funny, unsteady tapping of some disgruntled march. She had not tried to think, when passing gentlemen caught her eye, that they were calculating her income and measuring her beauty against the next girl in line, and the next, and the next after that.

"Much like a window dressing," Sophie muttered.

"What's that?" Mrs. Porter leaned her direction, and Sophie shook her head. "It's nothing," she smiled, forcing it to be true.

The door swept open, and Papa saved her. For a man who cared very much what Lady Mary thought of Leatherbury, he smelled of spirits. She wondered what Devlin had gotten him up to with all his happy encouragements. She would have frowned, but Devlin's beautiful features brightened the room as he strode in with a determined look. He spied her on the little chair and made a beeline to join her. His cheeks were flushed, and his eyes bright with satisfaction.

"Your father is a gurgling spring of information," he declared.

"He's lived here all his life and knows everyone in the county." Sophie looked up and found Devlin inspecting her.

He put a hand on his hip and tossed his head back to laugh like she'd told the funniest joke he'd ever heard. "Miss Crestwood, you must take me at my word. I think it clever and intelligent to keep abreast of news in the neighborhood. It's just as important as reading the naval news, or the on dits if you like."

Sophie smiled. "I'm not certain I find reading common gossip that important unless one wants to know where to be seen."

Mr. Devlin bowed to express his agreement. "Exactly. On a fine estate such as Leatherbury, one would want to know what the tenants are up to, who the neighbors are, and what of their plans."

Sophie did think it important to know the conditions of certain livings, but she wasn't sure she needed to know her neighbors' plans. She thought of Pembroke Hall and couldn't resist saying, "If you are speaking of Pembroke, I have it from the highest authority it is to be restored for what it was intended."

"You mean the hunting, I presume." Devlin leaned down so Sophie could see into his golden eyes. "Yes, I've noticed it on rides through the county, and I must say it has a great deal of forests and hollows."

"There are many trees," Sophie agreed, only because she had staggered beneath one.

"It would be an inconvenience to live next door to such a great estate and never get an invite." His eyes sparkled, tempting her to come near.

"Oh yes, but," said Sophie, lowering her voice so he had to move closer, "there is quite a bit of inconvenience yet at Pembroke."

Devlin's brows furrowed. "Do say."

Without thinking, she shook her head to emphasize her words. "There are only a few servants, and the air is musty and dank. The gardens are so grown over, only a few late vegetables are ever found, and Captain Murdock does not like company, not at all."

"That's a shame," exclaimed her confidant. "I would think to restore it to its original glory one would throw fine hunts and parties."

Sophie pressed her lips together and shook her head with a sigh. "It's been cleaned up a bit, but there's still more work to do."

"With a neighbor such as you, Miss Crestwood, I'm surprised the captain does not feel to 'waste not a minute' as those types say."

Flattered, Sophie grinned. "He is the type indeed, but I find he's taken to solemn contemplations far more than are suitable for society."

Devlin straightened and made a face of pity. "You never quite know, do you? A shame you had to recover there after your accident. I'm sorry for it."

"Oh, I was treated well," Sophie said, hurrying to excuse the unfortunate affair, at least on behalf of Mrs. Brooks. "He keeps a kind housekeeper there who saw to my every need."

"Does he now?" Devlin narrowed his eyes and gazed across the room to where the evening fire flickered. "She must be an attractive sort or quite used to his kind." He grinned with a wryness that showed his teeth in the firelight.

"No, she's not that exactly—what I mean is—she was kind and helpful. Though I must admit I exaggerated, Mr. Devlin. She was no more a housekeeper than I am a cook." Sophie winced at the thought, but it was true.

The gentleman laughed. "You do not belong in the kitchen, Miss Crestwood. You are far too elegant to be washing pots."

Sophie's heart tingled at his compliment. No wonder Katherine found him so captivating. "You are too kind, Mr. Devlin. I'm sure I am not as elegant by half compared to your acquaintances in Town."

Devlin raised his brows, thinking. "Not all elegant females choose to stay in Town, and a great many I find to my personal and selfish delight, keep to the country and their fine homes. She smiled in satisfaction at his generous words. Before she could thank him again, he told her, "They are having a house party at Oak Grove, and I have been invited. I do hope you will consider it since your father has told me you are welcome there, too."

She shook her head in agreement. "Her ladyship has invited me, and I cannot wait to see the grand rooms of Oak Grove once more."

"Then we must make it sure," Devlin said with cheerful promise. "We will play and dance and sing until you miss your family and beg to go home."

"If I am having so much of a grand time," Sophie warned, "I'm sure I will not wish to come home again at all."

A WEEK AFTER THEIR guests' visit, a letter arrived from Katherine with news Sophie found both exhilarating and relieving: "*I have received a letter from the Lady herself and can you believe, I have been invited to the house party, too. Mama insisted I have two new gowns. I have not slept at all since the post arrived...*"

Sophie felt satisfied. Katherine's companionship at Oak Grove would make everything more comfortable and jolly. She had just sat down with an ink bottle to reply when the low creaking groan of her bedroom door told her someone had sneaked in for visit.

She looked over her shoulder expecting to see Jack. He did not apologize for not knocking first. He shut the door with care, so no one would know he was out of bed and walked across the floor with bare feet. Sophie frowned and pointed this out.

He shrugged and made a corresponding expression of carelessness with a drooped chin and bugged eyes. She caught a laugh before it sounded too loud and permissive.

"What are you doing out of bed?" Comfortable with him in her room, which had been a common thing since the day he could walk, she began writing again, mindful of her neat, flourished script.

"I can't sleep," he said. After a pause in which Sophie offered no advice, he went on. "They want to send me away, Sophie."

She turned about to face him, old quill pen hanging in the air like a question.

"I heard them talking." Jack backed up to her bed until he bumped into it, then he sat down without permission.

"They was in the drawing room—"

"Were."

"They want to send me to Harrow, and then on to Oxford. They want me to learn *scripture*." He wrinkled his nose as if saying the word was shameful.

Sophie opened her mouth to respond, but nothing came out. There were no words in her head, no words in her mouth; only a heavy feeling in her stomach much like rocks.

"Perhaps you misunderstood," she said at last.

Jack stared at the floor. His shoulders slumped. "I'm old enough now," he said in a desperate tone. "If they would just find someone to recommend me, I could start at midshipman. I would even be a ship's boy." He exhaled, his frustration evident. "I'm not afraid to work. You know I ain't."

Sophie's mind churned. So often she had answers to her brother's questions, logical and appropriate resolutions, but she could not advise him to go against her parents' wishes. "Maybe you could talk to Papa, alone, when he takes you shooting next time."

Jack shook his head. "Don't you think I've tried?"

"What does he say?"

"Not too much. He just changes course. I do not think he would mind it so much, to have an officer in the family, but everyone is set on me taking the living at Oak Grove."

"You mustn't fault, Mama. She just finds the cottage and career a bit romantic, and besides, it's in part to her connections you have the opportunity at all. I suppose you should be thankful for it."

Jack looked up, and his green eyes glinted with determination. "I ain't thankful for that cold, dusty place at all. I don't even like church."

Sophie crooked her head in admonishment.

"I don't," he insisted. "Why should I pretend I do?"

She covered her mouth to muffle her shocked giggle. People pretended all the time. That's what one had to do, wasn't it? "Why, I like church, Jack. I like it to be sure. It can be a bit long, but I do feel happy and peaceful-like when I'm learning about God and His ways."

"His ways include the sea, too," Jack spat. "He created the oceans. Not just the land."

"Is this really what you want to do?" Sophie said, but it did not matter whether she asked it or not, for she already knew the answer.

"I do," he said. "I wouldn't be so stubborn if I didn't know it was for me." He pressed his crimson lips together in an even line.

"I think you are stubborn about everything for the joy of it," Sophie said with a sigh, "but if you are so sure..."

"I am."

"I will talk to Mama. Maybe I will help her to see reason; that this is what you truly desire. Though I must say, Jack, I'm well older than you, and even I'm not sure what I want to do."

Jack's chin dropped, and he scowled. "Yes, you are, Soph. You want to be married and all in love. You just don't know who to like."

She laughed at his assessment. "You make me sound romantic and silly. I do want to be married, but I... Well, truth be told little brother, I'd rather just prune flowers in the garden, but don't tell Mama. She says I spend too much time in the dirt already."

"Walking, too," Jack added. "You wander off as much as me, but no one ever gets put out about it."

"Because I do not go far, and I always come back," Sophie answered in a wry tone. "I do not have lessons to continue like you do. Poor Mr. Lyman."

Jack folded his arms and crossed his ankles. He looked like a churlish leprechaun.

"Off to bed, brother dear. We'll figure this out another day, and don't you forget that you promised to walk with me to the village tomorrow."

"I will. Do *you* promise?" he said.

"You have my word I will speak to Mama, but you must give me time to find the right moment. Don't blurt it out at breakfast like you are prone to do. Keep your battle quiet for now."

"It's hard not to speak my mind," the boy muttered.

"I know," Sophie said with a gentle smile, "but you must rein it in until we come up with a perfect and convincing argument."

He nodded and slid down off the bed, dodging her before she could hug him like a little boy. He strode off to his room with a solemn face.

Sophie watched him go, her heart dangling in her chest. Was it wrong to give him hope?

SOPHIE DID NOT HAVE the opportunity to talk to her mother about Jack the next morning. The usual rain expected for Higfield held off, and with Papa's permission and the cutting garden pruned back as much as she dared, Sophie put on a walking dress and her nicer boots and chose a light shawl for the exercise that would warm her aplenty.

Once downstairs, Jack was nowhere to be found, and she paced the front drive impatiently, glancing off toward the trees where she refused to fetch him. At length, with no other alternative, she begged Margaret to walk with her into the village to purchase a length of ribbon to trim a dinner gown for the house party at Oak Grove. They set off toward the little village, walking south along the rutted country road, bypassing the fork that bent its way toward Pembroke.

"Look there," Sophie pointed, when they passed Pembroke's south end, and Margaret stood on tiptoe to see as much of the behemoth in the distance that she could. The grey façade seemed to shimmer a bit in the sunlight, at least to Sophie, but Margaret exclaimed, "It's as threatening as the Tower!" as she dangled a basket from one arm.

Higfield did not have cobbled streets much as Sophie would have liked. They would have kept the mud off her hem and besides, pattens made her feel clumsy and too tall. A bit dusty and damp, they arrived in the village while the day was still sweet and pleasant. They walked past the cobbler's shop without interest. The milliner was across the street, and when there was no traffic, they hurried across to the other side to see the window display, dipping and smiling and saying hello to the familiar faces of those who thought the Crestwoods esteemed and good company.

Sophie prided herself on being kind to everyone she met and not putting on airs because she was a daughter of Leatherbury. She greeted Mrs. Kane outside the shop with a broad smile and asked after her granddaughter who would soon be old enough to come out.

Mrs. Kane, a neighbor of the Porters, asked after her mother and then said in a low tone, "You may want to avoid passing by that shop this day." She gave Sophie a meaningful look with eyes that shifted down the street, and of course, Sophie could not help but look over her shoulder just as Margaret did. The servant gave a little gasp, and Sophie was sorry she had asked her to come along.

Sophie gazed heavenward in exasperation. "Why, Mrs. Kane. I'm sure no harm will come to me should I walk past the tailor's shop, even with menfolk milling about. This is Higfield after all."

"Yes," said Mrs. Kane with a sniff, "but some menfolk are more questionable than others."

Sophie looked again, narrowing her eyes to see through the throng, when out of the door of the tailor's shop strode Captain Murdock, as much as he was able to stride with sharp, determined steps.

He moved quickly for a man with a cane, in a sort of stride-skip-jump. He'd quite mastered the hang of his aide, she decided. His jaw was set hard, making his face look as stony as Pembroke. He did not want to dawdle, that was to be sure, but perhaps it was the men outside he did not want idling.

Sophie realized they were not farmers or servants, nor any of the country gentry, but rough looking men with hard, red faces. Some had scars, and others queer clothes, more like what she had seen in Portsmouth than what Higfield had on its streets. Two of them looked familiar. She had seen them before on the grounds of Pembroke.

"Sailors," she murmured, and Mrs. Kane's face twisted with disgust. "Indeed. Loud, uncouth, and laughing like drunkards. I wouldn't be surprised if they were drunkards, and some of them..." She stopped, and just when Sophie thought she'd found a morsel of self-control she proved it wrong by uttering in a harsh whisper, "Pirates. That's what I've heard. Look at them! Brown and dirty and too jolly by far, staining the halls and dignity of our Pembroke."

Margaret gasped again, this time covering her mouth with her hand. She looked back at Sophie wide-eyed, and when Sophie said nothing, not letting her face reveal one hint of what she was thinking, a smile curled up on Margaret's face behind her fingers, whether with excitement or pleasure Sophie could not tell.

The women watched as Captain Murdock had words with one, and the spirited banter outside the shop ceased. He was clothed in dark trousers, with a loose shirt and plain waistcoat. His long, sweeping jacket was the black one, and though he had a properly tied cravat, he was as natural and mussed as Sophie had ever seen him—with the exception of the private recital where she had spied him playing the violin in his room. It would not do to be dressed less than impeccable, she decided, under the critical eyes of the village.

A horse, the tall fine bay Sophie had seen before, stamped its feet as its master tapped his cane over to it. Another man took the walking stick and helped him up, and Captain Murdock became towering and foreboding once more. The sea of bodies parted and began to straggle away from the shop to the other end of the village, and the Captain cantered his ride down the center of the street either unperturbed or unaware of the stares from windows and open doors.

A strange, warm feeling melted across Sophie's chest, and she thought as she watched the gentleman settle in his saddle that this was no villain at all. He did, however, carry himself with a determined streak of pride, and should Mrs. Kane point out and accuse him of piracy for all of Higfield to hear, she felt certain it would not ruffle him one bit.

He was, after all, quite a mysterious fellow. True, he was somewhat melancholy, but that did not make him what the whispered accusations said. Such hints that he may have been involved in something as filthy and cruel as piracy she knew to be silly, and she laughed inwardly at them all despite his suspicious fortune and odd ways.

She must have smiled, just a little, for he glanced her direction as he approached the milliner's shop to pass it by, like he felt her watching him. When their eyes met she caught herself and tried to turn down the corners of her mouth, but it was too late.

He reigned in his horse and brought it to an abrupt and prancing halt. "Miss Crestwood," he said in a low tone, not at all rude but polite. He doffed his hat, the black bicorn, and she curtsied politely. Beside her, Margaret did the same. Mrs. Kane huffed and looked askance, but from her lowered glance Sophie saw her dip at the knee although it looked rather stiff.

"How are you faring this good May morning?" Sophie asked in a burst of gaiety. She could hardly be boorish. He was her neighbor after all.

Mrs. Kane said in a rush, "I must be off. Mr. Kane expects me, my dear." She hurried away as if something smelled very foul, so foul she would be sick if she lingered.

Captain Murdock hesitated like it took a great deal of thought for him to converse. "I'm certain it is well past morning, Miss Crestwood, for I spent it in my orchard with your brother, I'm sure you know."

Sophie frowned. "I'm sure I did not know. He promised to walk me here today, but was nowhere to be found."

Captain Murdock glanced over her head, and she almost turned to see what he was studying, but then his gaze caught hers up again. "I apologize if I kept him longer than needful. He offered to bring me a day's catch of his fish, and we had further conversation."

Sophie was certain there were fish in the streams at Pembroke, for it was a good-sized property. "You are kind to give him excuses to be out of doors."

"He's just a boy. That's where they belong."

"Did you dodge your lessons and play out of doors when you were a lad?"

Captain Murdock smiled, and the brilliance of it made Sophie stare. It was a smooth, snaking grin that lifted the corners of his mouth into the apples of his cheeks, and his eyes crinkled around the edges making him look clever and amused and mischievous all at the same time. "I'm afraid I am guilty of that as well, Miss Crestwood."

A small step sounded behind her, and Margaret made a noise like someone had poked her in the backside with a stick. Sophie had forgotten she was there.

"I'm sure that is not at all what you are guilty of, Captain," she said, meaning boyhood pranks, but it sounded all wrong after Mrs. Kane's accusations of piracy only moments earlier. She saw the impact of the mistaken meaning pass over his face in a cloud. It was evident he had heard the gossip. His expression became its usual blank self once again, and he put his hat back on his head with a curt pat.

"Good day," he said, and Sophie dipped at the knee again, calling as he rode away, "Good day, Captain Murdock." She felt sorry he had taken her words the wrong way and wanted to salvage some sort of innocent dignity.

A few of the captain's men made their way after the departing horse and examined Margaret and Sophie in a rather vulgar way as they passed by. Sophie grabbed Margaret by the elbow to drag her into the shop before any more offensive pleasantries were expressed. The door was not quite shut when Margaret exclaimed all too loud and out of turn, "Good show, Miss Crestwood! Guilty, indeed!" and then broke into giggles that turned into a gasp when Sophie elbowed her sharply in the hip.

"YOU PROMISED!" SOPHIE hissed like a cat once she and Jack were alone in the drawing room before Mama came in to sit after supper.

"I forgot," Jack insisted. The tips of his ears grew red, and Sophie suspected he was telling a lie to save himself. Of course, the last place any boy wanted to linger was in village shops with his sister, but he shouldn't have said he would do it if he had other plans.

"I had to take Margaret with me to Higfield today because I could not go alone. You know Papa will not approve of you crossing the boundaries to Pembroke, and with our fish, too."

Jack paled.

"Don't look so surprised," said Sophie. "I have no doubt where you ran off to, but I would like to hear it from you."

Jack licked his lips. "I needed something to trade, don't you see?"

"No, I do not."

"I can't use my own money, and the fish are part mine after all, ain't they?"

Sophie tossed down the knitting she had picked up. "Must you always speak like a deckhand? Papa detests that ignorant talk."

"Since when did you put so much stock in what Papa thinks? Half the time you act puffed up and like you think he's daft—like we're all just silly people living with you here at Leatherbury."

Sophie cringed at the mild sting but put it away in her mind to think about another time. Her brother needed something to trade for some mysterious reason, and that did not bode well in any way. "What did you need the fish for exactly?"

Jack, standing only steps away, backed further away from her like he feared she might grab him by the ear, one of her former unkind habits when he was little.

She almost stood and put her hands on her hips, but squeezed her knees together instead. Waning sunlight changed the drawing room into a reflecting pool of salmon and lavender puddles that shimmered up one wall, trickled off a portrait, and rippled back down onto the floor. Someone had left a window cracked, and a dangerous but pleasant cool breeze that smelled of sweet grass crept in. It would make them all ill if she did not get up to lock it. "Tell me at once, or I'll tell Papa."

Jack's face flushed as scarlet as a marine's coat. He slammed his closed fists against his thighs in frustration. "I asked the Captain for lessons, is all. We made a trade, nosey sister, and it's none of your business."

"You are still a boy," Sophie replied, although she knew he hated to hear it. "It's for your safety and reputation that I'm asking. We still do not know that much about Captain Murdock.

"Heaven and earth, Sophie! He's just a man who's come to live in his family home. I don't even think he wants to be here. There's no harm done."

"You're the one who said he was a pirate. Tell me more." Sophie pressed her lips tight and tried to look severe and determined at the same time. Inside, she reeled with curiosity. What could Captain Murdock have to trade for fish? Jewels? Exotic pets? Shrunken heads?

Jack sighed in surrender. "I thought maybe his lake had been poached over the years and there weren't no fish left. Least I hoped so."

Sophie waited, trying to be patient as she listened for Mama's footfalls outside the drawing room door. She dropped her head to one side and gave Jack a demanding stare.

"I asked him to give me lessons on naval etiquette."

Sophie felt her eyes widen in surprise. "How do you even know how much he knows?" From somewhere in the house, Mama called to Margaret to fetch her book if she had seen it last.

Jack jerked his head toward the voices. In a low tone, he added, "I asked him. He was in the Navy a little while then he got his ship. I go over there all the time now when I'm getting my exercise. They don't pay me no mind on the grounds anymore. Sometimes I even take the dogs with me."

"Jack!"

He stiffened and crossed his arms, pursing his mouth as if he might blow some imaginary girl a kiss, but his eyes blazed with emerald stubbornness. "He's smart, and he talks to me like a grownup; not like I'm still in strings."

"You can't take instruction from Captain Murdock without first asking Papa."

The swishing sound of Mama's approaching slippers could be heard. For three ticks of a heartbeat, neither of them said another word. Then as the knob turned Jack whispered, "He didn't ask me if I had Papa's permission, and I didn't say."

Mama entered the room, and Jack spun with a flourish like she'd caught him dancing. She laughed at him and opened her arms for a hug. He swept past her close enough for her to give him a gentle squeeze then scurried off like the bilge rat he was sure to become.

Captain Murdock, Sophie thought, as she pretended to be engrossed in untangling a ball of yarn, was either a pot-stirring trouble-maker or a patient and kind man. The confusion she felt about his character vexed her the rest of the day.

CHAPTER SIX

Sophie determined she could not let anyone know the pirate at Pembroke was schooling Jack on life at sea. Mama had begged her to start packing for Oak Grove, but she would not think of it until she spoke with Captain Murdock. Should Papa find out Jack was disobeying him, he might very well send her brother straight to Oak Grove's parsonage.

Margaret tiptoed into the drawing room and reminded her Mama needed her upstairs. Sophie exhaled. There were other conversations to have, ones she had promised. She must find out if her parents really meant to send Jack away, and do everything in her power to keep him free at Leatherbury for a little more time.

She found her room in disarray with Mama standing in the middle of it. "Oh, Sophie, dear, look at this!" She held up a lavender shawl that Richard had given Sophie for her birthday the year before. "You must wear it in the evenings at Oak Grove. It makes your cheeks pink as rosebuds."

Sophie tried to smile. She tiptoed through the mounds of clothing thrown across pillows and trunks to protect them from the dusty floor. Sitting with a heavy *poof* on the edge of her mussed bed, she clasped her hands in her lap and tried to look agreeable. "With all the excitement of me leaving, we shall all forget that Jack is here."

Mama looked up from folding the shawl into neat little squares. "I'm sure we cannot forget about Jack. The moment he's out the door the whole house falls silent as the grave."

Sophie forced the corners of her mouth to turn up at the candid observation. "I think so, too. Papa starts writing letters, you start reading, and I—I pick up mending or wander around like a ghost."

"Mmm... yes," agreed Mama. She reached up and tucked a loose lock of pale yellow back up under her cap. She reminded Sophie of an elegant but fading flower. "Now Sophie, you must not wander around Oak Grove like a lost lamb. You need to get used to having Jack out of the way. He can't be around forever to entertain you."

Sophie laughed outright. "I'm sure I will find plenty to do. I'm not that dependent on him."

Mama looked up from Sophie's traveling trunk, where she had placed the shawl with great care. "My dear, you do not spend any more time studying than your brother, and since you aren't fond of reading or letters, I fear you may be very dull at Oak Grove unless they have a tambour frame or box of ribbons."

"Mama!" said Sophie. "I only like to keep my own mending up, and I like ribbons. They're like kite strings. I love to wear them long just to watch them snap in the breeze. Sometimes I imagine the wind may pick me up and carry me away."

"Aren't you a fanciful thing." Mama chuckled.

Sophie hesitated, thinking about how to bring Jack up again. "I'm sure I am not fanciful," she said with stubbornness. "I pride myself on being practical and reasonable."

"Yes, I know," Mama agreed, but with a queer smile that made Sophie feel young and foolish."

"About Jack," she blurted, determined not to let her mother tease her today. "I'm worried, Mama. He's so happy here at Leatherbury, except when we speak of Harrow or Oak Grove. I'm afraid he is determined to go to sea. Is there nothing we can do?"

Mama bent over the trunk to put a pair of pattens in should it rain. The half-smile on her face melted away, and she gazed deep into the bottom of the chest like she saw something there she did not like.

"I only mean I think we should not tell him what he must do if it makes him so unhappy."

Mama stood, arms hanging at her sides. "He's just a boy. Don't you understand, Sophie, he will have no worries about a career, but a good position and a comfortable home, too. It would be foolish to throw it away on a whimsy."

"I don't understand why you feel so fervent about it."

Mama picked up another shawl as if June in the country would not be hot.

"I must tell you," Sophie whispered, "his heart is set on a naval career. I do not see why it should matter one way or the other if he's willing to risk it." Her heart thudded in her chest, getting louder with each line of reasoning.

"Clergymen do not drown or get blown up," Mama muttered. "They do not go away and not come back. They do not run off and fall in love with other women."

Sophie felt her forehead wrinkle, puzzled at her mama's concerns. "Jack's troubled, Mama. He's afraid he's going to be sent back to boarding school when he loves it here at Leatherbury so much more. What a waste it would be, too, if he dreams of being an officer."

"Sophie," Mama said in a cross tone, "we don't always get what we want in life. It is like you said, practical and reasonable."

"I would think you would find it romantic."

"There is nothing romantic about going away forever. I don't want to hear another word about it." Mama dropped the lid down on the trunk, although it was not yet full. She took a step toward the bed to rescue the gowns Sophie had wrinkled with her bottom, but their gazes met, and Sophie saw tears pooling in her eyes. She jumped to her feet with worry as Mama spun about toward the door.

"I did not mean to distress you," she said, feeling sorrowful and confused. She hoped Mama heard the remorse in her voice because she left Sophie alone in the room after closing the door with an abrupt click.

JACK DISAPPEARED DURING tea time on a day of sunshine and light breezes; a welcome relief after so much rain. Turning from the library window, Sophie picked up a lightweight spencer, so brown it reminded her of cinnamon sticks, and dressed for a long walk. She chose her old straw bonnet with new ribbons, and remembered her words about kite strings and flying away with a whimsical smile.

He was nowhere to be seen when she knocked on the door to his room. After waiting for a long moment, she turned the knob and peered inside. It lay empty. She rushed downstairs, peeked in the library once more, and then bid her startled mama goodbye. Hurrying out the door with her clumsy pattens, she strode past the garden scanning the distant fields of Leatherbury. Irritation rose in her chest as she concentrated on finding her way to the pond alone. She assumed Jack would be fishing, but no one was there.

From the murky water's swollen edge, Sophie stood on tiptoe and tried to gauge the distance to Pembroke. It must be that he had sneaked off for his "lessons", she surmised. She could see the manor's roofline, steady as ever above the trees, and a glimpse of the stone wall dividing the properties. It was time she had another word with Captain Murdock.

Using the ancient stone wall as her guide, she made a conscious beeline for the estate and managed not to get lost. Azure skies chased away low, mist-colored clouds. The wet, long grasses squished, and the wispy wind made the warming sun feel just right. Blooming shrubbery made a pretty pink and white parade until the forest swallowed them back up again.

She came to the long, stone wall and studied it. Some of the crumbling rocks had been replaced or set back into position. It looked well patched up. Ignoring the stile, she hitched herself over the rocks, scraping her leg through her stockings as she went.

Sophie retied her bonnet, resolute. It would not be pleasant or easy, but it had to be done. She lifted her hem off the damp ground and continued up the slanted pasture toward the grounds of Pembroke, expecting at any moment to be stopped by riders on horseback.

The sun overhead grew hot, and she wished she could shed her spencer and trudge bare-armed in the sunshine. The caked and muddy pattens she'd left at the pond. Her boots accumulated their own layer of mud and felt heavier with each crest of the hill. The exertion caused her to perspire, something she did not let trouble her too often since it came with playing in the garden, but this was a stickier and more formidable wet that reminded her the earth was still full of damp. She prayed she did not catch a cold.

At last, she reached the grounds, a bit out of breath and wondering where all of Pembroke's pirates were this day. She chose to explore the back of the house after hearing the lowing of animals in the near distance. When she came around the rigid back corner of Pembroke, she stopped in surprise. Behind the crumbling rockwork was a pleasant view of a stable and a large vegetable garden that looked like someone had been hard at work. Mrs. Brooks she imagined, or maybe Mr. Howard, the man whom she called "Cook" with some amusement.

Rows of tidy green sprouts poked up like fingerlings of hope through the tilled ground. Sophie admired the effort. She peered over a gate that allowed entrance to the back courtyard between a tall, stone wall. Beyond it, she could see an old door and a worn footpath that emerged from out of a row of hanging clothes. The kitchen wall was very good to keep the chickens in and the laundry from prying eyes. She smiled to herself wondering what kind of underthings would be hanging on Pembroke's lines.

The stamping of hooves forwarded her attention to the large stable. She ambled toward it like she belonged there, should someone see her wandering about the grounds. Perhaps they had become so used to the inhabitants of Leatherbury running wild over Pembroke's pastures they had given up chasing them back home.

Curious as to what new livestock lived under the hastily-patched building, she quickened her pace. A clash of metal and high-pitched shouts made her stumble, and she froze. Accusatory voices rang out from inside the stable, amid the prancing and pounding of horse hoofs.

"Villain!" Her brother's voice echoed across the yard.

"Jack," she nearly shouted, but caught herself and called him only loud enough for the laundry to hear. "Oh, Jack," she whispered, shaking her head in worry and frustration as she set off at a near run. She rushed through the wide, open doors, sucking in the heavy odor of hay and manure all at once. Clouds of dust filled the air.

She heard the scramble of boots over stone just as the tall silhouette of Captain Murdock tripped backward toward her. A line of sweat ran down the back of his shirt. Over his shoulder, she saw he was waving a gleaming rapier, and then she spied Jack.

Jack was on the attack. He had a sword, too, a real and dangerous blade in one hand while his other flapped up and down to keep his balance. He slid across swept pavers on the stable floor. His copper hair lay plastered to his head and glowed liked dark rubies. Small bits of hay fluttered around him in the air.

Sophie could not move. She was frozen by Jack's wild cries and his aggressive attack on the crippled, floundering man in front of her. Murdock scrambled back again in a rush. He would not see her if he did not turn about. Sophie noted he hardly used his cane now, as he tossed it back to steady himself, almost landing it on her foot.

"Oh dear," she said, not sure in the madness of the crashing swords if she should cry out for the captain or her brother.

Jack saw her and drew back from Captain Murdock with slow steps, lowering his sword and nodding toward Sophie. The captain pivoted around with such speed she thought he expected another attack from behind.

She jumped backward when his sword cut through the air like a guillotine, then tripped over the soggy back hem of her gown and fell with an unladylike, *umph!* on her backside. Had she not, the sweeping sword might have taken off her head. She gasped in pain.

Captain Murdock lowered his weapon. He was out of breath and huffing fast and deep. His usual scowl was replaced with a healthy glow. He did not look angry or overcome with aggression. Instead, he beamed like polished coppers. "Miss Crestwood," he said in a tone full of surprise.

She glowered back up at him from the ground as mortification set in.

If he had dressed properly this morning, she could not tell. There was no waistcoat or jacket lying about. Her eyes traveled down the length of him, noticing his dusty breeches and dirty boots. When she looked back, he met her eyes unabashed, once more in complete control of himself and the situation. He shrugged his shoulders to right his bleached muslin shirt.

"I thought you were fighting." Her cheeks burned.

Murdock handed his sword back to Jack and reached out a black-gloved hand toward Sophie. It hung in the air above her head, dark and strong. She pursed her lips in disapproval to distract him from her ungraceful plop onto the pavers but reached up a hand so he could pull her to her feet. He did so in one strong tug, and she noted he did not use his cane at all. It was a mere accessory now, one that he depended upon for occasional balance, she suspected. Nothing like the heavy dependence he had on it when they first met.

She dropped his palm and looked down at her rumpled layers. "Well," she said, realizing she may have the upper hand at last, "whatever are you doing with my brother?" She tried to sound cross. She felt impressed, almost moved, but she had to be angry. It was the proper thing to do.

Jack appeared beside Murdock like a page. She had forgotten he was there. Her nose itched. The awful dust was settling, and right up her nose, too.

"I told you he was giving me instruction."

Captain Murdock gave a quick nod. She watched him lick his top lip and realized he was thinking of a response as crafty as Jack's since they were both caught.

She eyed Jack like Mama would when she caught him in a half-truth. "You told me he was educating you on naval etiquette."

Captain Murdock looked down sideways at the red devil.

Jack threw up his hands as if she was the stupidest thing he'd come across in his short lifetime. "This *is* naval etiquette!"

Sophie clenched her jaw and raised a brow. She shifted her stare from Jack to the captain and gave him her hardest look. He would not get out of answering questions today.

Instead of looking ashamed, the corner of Murdock's mouth quivered. He had a small mouth, she noticed, with thin flushed lips that looked like they were trying not to smile. His gaze roved over the beams above her head as if an explanation hung in the rafters. When he met her stare, she noticed the haunted weight in his eyes had disappeared. They glowed with warmth and to her surprise, pleasure.

Feeling her nose all watery, Sophie sniffed. "You're amused? My parents know nothing of this naval etiquette. She crossed her arms over herself, alarmed at the man's change of attitude when caught doing something questionable. "You are trespassing on my family," she choked out. She inhaled sharply and took more dust in with it.

"He did no such thing," Jack answered in a loud, angry tone.

Sophie's nose burned, and she touched it to keep from sneezing all over the man.

"I apologize, Miss Crestwood," Murdock said in a repentant tone. The animals around them quieted, too. "I was under the impression the boy's lessons were approved."

Jack's flushed cheeks turned redder at the captain's words. Although Murdock did not look at him directly, he made his meaning felt.

"I told her," Jack said. He glared at Sophie. "Why are you here? You said you wouldn't say a word if I did my studies."

"I didn't say I wouldn't come with you." Sophie tossed her head, and her bonnet slid back onto her shoulders.

"You didn't say you would." Jack did not stomp his foot, but he spat out the accusation in angry staccato. He took a step forward, daring Sophie to meet him at some unseen line.

"I don't have to say what I will or will not do, not to a thirteen-year-old boy."

"But—"

"Children, please." Captain Murdock held out his hands, signaling he would push them back into separate corners if they did not reign in their tempers. He had control now. Tall, with his shirt retucked and his blowsy locks smoothed back down, Sophie was sure he was trying not to grin. An arrow of offense shot right through to her center. Her nose tingled. Lud, she had to sneeze.

She rubbed her nose and declared, "I am not a child," in a haughty voice. Something inside her nose began to drip, and she sniffled again. "You have no right to give my brother fencing lessons without first discussing it with my parents."

Her voice high, Sophie realized she sounded like a grumpy, old shrew. Huffing, she tried to right her bonnet and retie it. Murdock reached out a gloved hand to help, his gaze locked on hers. Looking into his deep eyes felt like staring down a wishing well. His thumb brushed her cheek. Sophie jerked back. A bubble of air trickled down her throat and went the wrong way. It was no good. Twisting away, she sneezed into the air so hard it jerked her spine in the wrong direction. She winced.

Jack laughed, and she felt her face go warm.

"You sneeze like a storm, Sophie."

"Shut your wicked mouth," she snapped, her eyes wet and nose tickling. She sneezed again, but this time managed to catch it with the back of her hand.

Horrified, she glanced at Captain Murdock. He was smiling very broad now. How odd. He had a fetching dimple in one cheek. She tried to glare. Why did Pembroke always make her sneeze?

"I'm sorry," he said. "I do not have a clean handkerchief with me. Had I known we would be interrupted—"

"Interrupted?" Sophie sniffed again. It was a mistake, the sniffling. "Oh, blast!" she cried and fled the stable into the fresh air. Jack was right on her heels.

"Please do not tell, Soph," he pleaded in a low tone. "I asked him to do it. I need all the training I can get and from a reliable source." His olive eyes bored into her and softened her irritation.

Sophie wiped her nose in as ladylike a manner as she could, glancing toward the stable to watch for Murdock to come out. "Go home at once."

"I never promised Papa I would stay away. I never said it. Say you won't tell. Swear it."

Sophie swallowed. She could not be angry with such pleading words that echoed the dream in his heart.

"I won't tell for now, but we have disobeyed Papa in truth, and he will be furious. A lecture is one thing. Sword fighting is another. You must go home at once while I talk it through with the captain." She waved to the rolling hills and Leatherbury. She could see it better from this vantage point than one could see Pembroke from the other. "Go check your trout lines, and I will be along soon."

"You swear it?"

Captain Murdock stepped out from the stable door. He used his cane to glide across the space between them like he and the attachment had come to some sort of agreement to work together. He also carried the blank, determined expression on his countenance that was more familiar. Sophie knew he had collected himself and would be ready.

"Run along," she muttered. Murdock had not donned his black bicorn either. Apparently, he felt comfortable dashing about Pembroke on three legs and in only a loose shift.

Jack gave her one last pleading look then approached the captain. They had a conversation, low and whispered, then Jack trotted like a well-trained colt for the open pastures.

With her sneezes under control and gown smoothed down, Sophie braced herself for more discussion. Captain Murdock gave her a half-hearted little bow. "I would invite you in, but I'm not certain it would be proper since you are not ill, and we are not popular enough for tours, and by the by, you seem to be allergic to Pembroke, Miss Crestwood." Despite his teasing, he seemed in a more amiable mood than he had ever been before.

"Perhaps I am allergic to you, Captain," Sophie retorted. She surprised herself with the reply, but it did not seem to offend him. She had to look up to meet his gaze. He smiled at her. "*Touché.*"

When he smiled, it changed his entire appearance. His brooding brows raised, his pale eyes shined, and a hint of color tinted his cheeks. It made him affable and attractive; a much better look than the stalking, shifty scarecrow.

She blurted, "You are in good spirits and looking much better than when you first came to Pembroke."

"We are recovering, the house and I." He nodded back toward the stone monstrosity behind her.

"I am glad to hear it, though I cannot be diverted from the reason I came for my brother today."

Murdock's free hand hung at his side. Through his gloves, he tapped a thumb against a finger to an unheard song. An abrupt breeze rippled his hair, and she watched it dance about. He caught her off guard when he offered his arm. "Shall we walk?"

Surprised, Sophie took his arm. His cane moved over the damp dirt and clumps of weedy grass with deft skill, and she matched her pace to his slight skipping rhythm. The wall protecting the poultry and laundry was formed of the same stacked stones that lined the boundary between their two estates.

"I wonder that Pembroke was never red brick," she mused aloud.

"It is far too old for that," said the captain. "I know very little of its ancient history, although there are dusty books in the library I assume would give a fair account."

"I have not seen your library. Is it very large?"

"For a library, I suspect. My home in St. Kitts was long, low, and level. We did have a library suitable for our small island, but I've never seen such a collection as this."

"The library at Billingham is enormous," Sophie said. "It's larger than our drawing room and library put together. There are two."

"That sounds impressive if one likes books."

"Oh, I'm not especially fond of them," Sophie confessed, enjoying the sunshine and a cooling breeze as they reached the far end of the house. "I mean, I like books about things. Information. Sketches. I'm just not fond of... novels. Papa does not find it healthy anyway."

Sophie saw the captain glance at her with a curious expression. "Information. Things. I would have supposed you had no interest in such."

"Why is that?" Sophie met his gaze, but he looked away.

After a pause, he said, "My first outing was the assembly in Guildford."

"Oh." Sophie considered this statement with a quizzical brow. Her eyes widened in alarm. "Was I that silly?" She remembered the excitement of George Devlin's arrival, and her cheeks warmed. Murdock chuckled under his breath, but she could not look at him. "If you mean Mr. Devlin, I assure you I was only welcoming him to the county."

"Indeed; as did your father and the rest of your friends."

Sophie frowned in annoyance. "I don't know what you mean."

"I mean nothing." He cleared his throat. "I suppose enthusiastic conversation and dancing is not the best time to form an opinion of one's neighbors."

Sophie thought of the happy Mr. Devlin then Captain Murdock sulking in the corner. "I think it may be a very good place indeed, but one must not form every opinion from just one meeting."

The captain nodded. "We agree, then, somewhat. However, we do not agree on your brother's activities beyond his studies."

Sophie realized she had forgotten her reason for coming to Pembroke. She glanced up at the sun and wished she had brought a parasol. Taking her hint, Captain Murdock steered her through the tall grasses outside the drawing room window to a grove of old, towering trees.

"He's quite the fisherman, young Jack, and a quick study, too."

"How long have you been teaching him to fence like a Moor?"

Murdock laughed; a soft chuckle that came out in one swoop of breath. "Only a fortnight, but it helps he's had some previous instruction."

"Yes, he insisted, and Papa did not see any harm in it at the time since he would need to become proficient sooner or later." The captain glanced at her as they walked beneath green bows and among sprigs of violets here and there beneath the trees. A little stream ran alongside them, and the flowers made a thick purple carpet on the muddy banks.

"How beautiful. Your wildflowers are almost as pretty as my roses."

She felt him studying her and tried to ignore the skip in her heart from his furtive appraisal. They stopped, and she examined the bank, seeing animal tracks much larger than chickens but smaller than horses.

"My goats," said the captain with a chuckle. "They are clearing the property for me. Those over there are from a deer; a large eight-point according to my groundskeeper. The beast is not used to residents at Pembroke and has lost some of the proper precautions one must take among people."

She thought he would say "us", but it seemed too difficult for him. "My brother," she said in a halting voice, feeling overwhelmed with contradictions, "he's taken a shine to you, sir." She paused, and he dipped his chin. He already knew it.

"It's very kind of you to tutor him, but our family connections assure him a living in a parsonage at a larger estate up north. Oak Grove."

"He's mentioned it."

She waited and when he said nothing more, Sophie explained. "Mama feels convinced he must not go to sea, and she is not fond of a commission in the army either. She thinks it far more reasonable to spend one's time serving God in the countryside than wallowing in filthy conditions aboard a man-o'-war."

Murdock stiffened, and Sophie realized she'd insulted his occupation. In a chiding tone he said, "Contrary to some opinions, a man-o'-war can be as clean as a kitchen."

"Yes, but the danger." Sophie winced. He could not argue that seamen lived far safer lives than clergymen.

"Yes, I am well aware of the dangers, Miss Crestwood." He tapped the knee of his bad leg with his cane. At some length, he added, "While I do not feel it right to determine a man's destiny, even the dreams of a boy, I understand your parents' concern for your brother's safety. Perhaps you are right. He is not aware of the sacrifice one makes choosing a life at sea."

Taking a deep breath, Sophie dared to inquire about his injury. "You mean the sacrifice of life and limb?"

He did not take the hint, but said, "Of bloodshed and battle, specifically, but yes. People... die." He sighed, and his pace became uneven and heavy. An invisible dark cloud seemed to descend over him.

"I should go," Sophie said with as much cheer as she could muster. They were around the front corner of Pembroke now, with the drive and fountain in view. They had almost circumvented the entire house.

"Your roses," she cried. Her legs wanted to pull away and hurry, but she restrained herself. The captain remained quiet. The grass under their feet turned to gravel and narrow trenches of mud from heavy carriage wheels.

The roses surrounded the clean and trickling fountain like a rainbow crown. They were blooming, somewhat haphazardly, but flowering in shades of peach, yellow, pink, and red. It took her breath away. There were even buds of snow white, just like her flowers at Leatherbury.

"Remarkable. We have white roses just like that at Leatherbury. Why, they look exactly alike."

She looked at Murdock to see if he was impressed. His mouth twitched in contemplation. "I suppose," he murmured, "they might very well be one and the same."

"I'll have to ask Mama. We thought we were the only house in Higfield to have Bengal roses from India. I confess I adore them."

"Yes, you shared that with me the last time you were at Pembroke." The captain gave her a tight smile. She could not see his dimple this time.

"Well," she said, looking up and feeling a bit chagrined she had imposed herself on his day, "I should go before Jack comes back looking for me instead."

"I'll walk you to the wall."

Sophie shook her head. "Oh, no, I've tired you out. It's not your duty to chase me back home when I came uninvited."

"You need no invitation to come here," Murdock said in a mindless manner.

She was sure he was finished entertaining her. It was entirely out of the way of things for her to call on Pembroke after all, and alone, too. It looked improper, indeed, and Papa had insisted everyone avoid the place.

Sophie swallowed. In a voice she forced to sound both determined and lighthearted, she said, "I found myself here. I'll find myself back."

The captain turned the dragon head on the top of his cane in his hand and squared his shoulders. "You have a poor record of not finding your way home, Miss Crestwood. I insist I help you back."

"Your leg—"

"It is my knee essentially, and it is no worse off walking the grounds than sitting in a chair all the dull day long."

He gave her a gentle nudge, and they continued on their way. Sophie felt tired herself. It seemed like she'd walked miles already.

"If you insist," she whispered.

In a stronger and more confident tone, the captain said, "I do."

It all became very formal then, the captain walking Miss Crestwood back to the boundaries of Leatherbury after sending her brother home. They said very little as they worked their way down the uneven ground of the pasture to the stile. It was pleasant though, and

Sophie believed she'd had a satisfactory afternoon even though it'd involved unpleasant business.

"I will not tell my parents just yet," she told him when they came to stop beside the wall. "I will leave that up to Jack, but I must insist you or he speak with them if the lessons are to continue."

Captain Murdock had made up his mind on the long walk down. He did not seem happy to say it, but he promised, "I will speak with the boy myself. The lessons are a poor idea if he is going to take up the cloth."

Sophie knew Jack would be furious with her. In her heart, she hadn't meant to end them. "I don't mean to ruin your fun," she said. "It is only my father would be angry. My parents do not understand his persistence."

Gazing toward Leatherbury as if it were a faraway world, Captain Murdock replied with a heavy breath, "No, you are entirely right. A church calling is far safer than the sirens of the sea. I could not bear to lose another—"

He stopped, raised his gloved hand, and helped Sophie up the wooden stairs that crossed over the wall. She took them with practiced skill, not coming close to a scraped ankle. She turned back to wave at him, but he merely pointed with a grimace and said, "It's that way now, Miss Crestwood. Keep the sun to starboard, and go straight through the trees until they clear out."

"Yes, right," she promised and waved good-bye.

He nodded back, unruffled by the sun on his head, but turning the cane before him over and over in his hands in a queer manner.

"Lose another what?" Sophie wondered as she made for the trees.

SHE FOUND HER WAY BACK home without becoming lost. It had not been such a terrible visit to Pembroke after all. Sophie assumed Jack would be loitering at the pond, but he was not there.

Once home, she spied him through the library door sitting at the writing desk. The scowl on his face either meant he did not enjoy his labors, or he was cross with her for coming home long after he did. She wondered if he had divulged to anyone where she had gone off to, but realized that to inform Mama would mean answering questions about his own activities.

She bypassed him and went up to her room to change. Margaret was busy downstairs, so she did the best she could with an old but clean muslin gown. The looking glass reflected a rather pink Sophie which ruined her chances of omitting her afternoon schedule at supper. A bell chimed, and she hurried downstairs hoping Jack felt better. Their father must have trapped him in the library as soon as he'd returned and ordered him back to his studies. She grimaced as she closed the door behind her to go downstairs. Jack would not be in good spirits.

The dining room shined bright with late afternoon sun. Margaret had not shut the curtains, so Sophie saw to them herself before Papa realized it and complained. The fragrance of roasting vegetables drifted in from the kitchen, and her stomach rumbled. She smiled at Mama who waited at one end of the table, lost in thought.

"My, you're flushed," Mama said, as she shook off her faraway stare. Sophie slid down into her chair and scooted up to the table. "I had a nice walk today, but it went on too long."

"Did you take your parasol? It's in the corner of the drawing room where you left it last."

"I didn't think of anything more than a bonnet, and it warmed up so much I felt hot most of the day."

"Better to be hot than spotted," Mama observed. She glanced toward the window, but Sophie had closed the curtains. Sighing, she pulled herself out of whatever thoughts were drawing her inward. "What did you find so interesting today you stayed out in the sunshine too long?"

Sophie tried to appear nonchalant. She gave a little pitch of one shoulder as her mind spun with possible replies.

"Yes, my dear, what did you find so diverting that you had to walk the grounds of Leatherbury until supper?"

Papa strode into the dining room, his tardiness unusual, with Jack right behind him. Papa's face looked flushed and his jaw tight. Sophie's stomach sank. It seemed certain her brother had found some sort of trouble.

Sensing tension in the air, Mama pressed her hands together then held them under her chin. Papa sat down with a thump, and they waited for the courses.

"I understand you walked to Pembroke with your brother today." Papa looked up from his soup bowl to Mama and then his gaze riveted to Sophie and pinned her to her chair.

Sophie looked down while her dish was filled. "Oh, Papa, I um, well, yes, we did wander beyond the wall today."

With ruddy cheeks, Papa countered in a low voice, "You did not think to mention it?"

Sophie hesitated. She did not want to tell a lie. "I did not think it was that important," she stalled, thinking as fast as she was able. "We found Captain Murdock very cordial and only spoke briefly. I did not want to trouble you with such a minor thing."

"A minor thing?"

Mama picked up her spoon and began sipping her soup, glancing back and forth between Papa and Sophie like one of them might raise their voice and ruin her evening.

Avoiding Jack's watchful stare, Sophie felt all eyes upon her. After a painful silence with her father's penetrating gaze, Sophie glanced at him and whispered, "I'm sorry, Papa. I did not want to upset you since you do not find him amiable."

"Surely you do not."

His voice was cold and stern, a Papa she rarely heard. It made her heart *thunk* with discomfort.

She swallowed. Her supper sat before her growing cold.

"I said, Sophie, surely you do not. He has done nothing to earn our esteem."

Sophie replied, "Perhaps Pembroke is not ready to have suppers, and he did take me in during the storm after inviting you to hunt on his land."

This was a mistake, she realized, as Papa's ears turned scarlet, and his jaw tightened so much she was afraid he might snap his teeth.

"I only meant after being rescued from the storm and treated so well, I do not find much frightful about Pembroke or Captain Murdock."

"I find him frightful. It is no matter he has inherited Pembroke. His father was mad, the house fell to ruins, and whatever the family's business in the Indies should stay there, and he with it."

Papa picked up his spoon and splashed it into his soup, making Sophie give a little start. Looking around the table again, he said in a rare and thunderous voice, "I do not want to hear another word of Pembroke in this house, and no one in this family is to entertain its heir there, here, or anywhere else for that matter." A last stabbing stare he sent to Jack, who cowered over his bowl with a face so pale his sun spots looked dark brown.

Staring into her soup, Sophie felt connected to Jack and very sorry, too. There was no way he would be able to continue his fencing lessons with the captain even if the man could be convinced to take them up again.

Everything felt unnatural in the drawing room after they'd eaten in silence. She quickly hurried to her room to try to study in private, but the dull book did little to hold her concentration. In frustration, Sophie tossed it aside, changed into her nightdress, and found herself at the window, staring out across the dark lawn. Shadows through the trees danced in an eerie waltz. The entire household seemed to be waiting with baited breath. Uneasily, she took her lamp and tiptoed down to the library. A dim light glowed from beneath the bottom of the door.

Mama sat with her back to the door, the gentle curve of her neck creamy and white. Her hair was still up, Sophie noted. She had not undressed. Sophie tiptoed in and closed the door behind her quietly. Sensing her, Mama turned about. Her face still carried the look of discontent it held at supper.

"You startled me," Mama whispered, closing a novel in her lap. Sophie padded across the room and joined her.

"I'm sorry. I couldn't sleep." Sophie sat down with a little bounce beside her on the settle.

"I'm sorry you were treated so harshly tonight."

Sophie shrugged, though her shoulders felt tight. "I did not mean to make Papa angry. It came on so quick, too. I don't understand it."

Mama looked across the room at the lamp burning low on the mantle. "I'm afraid we had a disagreement before supper. Your interlude with Captain Murdock did not help matters at all. In fact, it was very poor timing."

"I'm sorry," Sophie said again. "If I had known he was so violently opposed to Captain Murdock or his company I would have avoided him."

"There's no need for us to be rude," Mama said in a quiet tone. "It's not Captain Murdock's fault he is Sir Edward's heir, nor is he obligated to explain his business to this neighborhood, not if he truly does not wish to do so."

"I suppose everyone is unused to someone living at Pembroke."

"Yes," Mama agreed, "someone who is not a ghost."

"It's a pity," said Sophie, "that Sir Edward was so well liked only to become so unpopular."

Mama sniffed in disdain. "Some people like others well enough only when they are rich and throw parties and hunts."

Sophie studied her mother in the low light. "You liked to go to parties when you were young, did you not?"

"Yes. Most of us are drawn to fun and society when we are young. It's how the best matches are made. I was fortunate to be under Lady Mary's favor since my mother was a best friend to her younger sister."

"Yes, I remember, and she does always treat us so well."

"She did then, too," Mama agreed. "Of course, others did not approve of me."

"Why ever not?" said Sophie, although she knew the answer.

"I was too common. Your Papa could have married two other girls with better connections and more income, but he set his heart on me despite my lack of it."

"It's no matter, Mama. You married as well as we all should if we can. Papa had the luxury of choice, and he chose you because he wanted you. How wonderful that must have been."

"Yes," said Mama. "I was lucky."

"Did Papa not enjoy the parties at Pembroke?"

Sophie smiled to herself, imagining her parents facing one another with outstretched hands properly sheathed in kid gloves. Did the ballroom floor gleam like sunset in the glow of a hundred candles? She had yet to see the ballroom at Pembroke. Sophie glanced at her mother who stared at nothing. The silence began to feel uncomfortable, then Mama said, "No, Sophie, I did not dance with your Papa at Pembroke. We had not been introduced."

Sophie felt her eyes widen in surprise. Why, she had just assumed. "Then who?"

Mama stood up in one abrupt motion. The novel in her lap fell to the floor with a thump. "Come, dear girl, we must get off to bed. Tomorrow is the last day to prepare for your triumph at Oak Grove.

CHAPTER SEVEN

As the modest carriage pulled away from the comforting sight of home, Sophie fell back against the stiff seat trying to soften the ache in her throat. She did not know why she felt like crying. Perhaps it was because she was tired. She had slept poorly. Her conversation with Mama had left her dazed and confused.

Papa and Mama had been acting differently of late. Not that Mama spent any more time in the library than she already did, but she said things she had not said before and expressed her opinions more often and in different ways than Sophie had ever heard her speak.

She chewed her lip and winced, as the carriage wheels shuddered over a crevice in the road too wide and deep for comfort. She'd expected Mama to accompany her, but because it was only a half day's journey to the next county, and Mama complained of a great anxiety over Sophie's departure, Sophie was packed up into the carriage and sent on her way with the drivers Papa trusted most.

The early morning sunshine was a welcome sight, even though Papa had been upset with her for ruining her complexion right before the house party. Margaret had tried every trick she knew to soften and fade Sophie's cheeks, but it was no good. She could not produce a creamy white complexion for her if Sophie spent too much time tromping around outdoors.

Sophie glanced up at the faint voices of the driver and his companion. They seemed excited about the adventure to Oak Grove. This was Sophie's third visit, but her first official stay beyond the formal invitations to her parents over the years. Truth be told, she sometimes tired hearing about it, and so often, especially when Papa returned from the yearly event when he dined with its mistress.

Sophie leaned her head against the door and closed her eyes. Lady Mary, it was rumored, kept a rigid, organized calendar that included every one of her acquaintances, their standing in society, and how often and when they would be invited to Oak Grove.

She did very well, Sophie admitted, as a lady of a great house. A wise young lady would study her example in both social etiquette and management. Not that Sophie would ever hold such a position. She smiled to herself, amused at her parents' ambitions that she saw more clearly now with the perspective of a few seasons behind her. The illustrious nephew would be at Oak Grove, and he was marriageable.

Sophie sighed. Some people behaved like a titled match was possible for any girl, but to ignore the low probability of such fairy tales only led to disappointment in the end. Not that she was disillusioned, she thought. She had wanted to be married since she was little and smartly matched, but with her budding maturity had come the acceptance that wishes did not always come true, and it was better to plan for an amiable marriage that suited both partners.

She forced her eyes open, blinking in a slanted beam of sunlight and chuckled at her practical ideas. She was still twelve in her heart. She still wanted to fall in love and be loved back deeply. It did not matter so much to her anymore that her future husband had a superior standing or astounding income. Generous would do.

She snorted to herself. What a sad thing she was at only twenty; already growing tart. She thought of Papa loving Mama so much he pursued her despite her lack of money. It was still romantic no matter how Papa's ideas of marriage had changed these days. As for Mama, well, she was the biggest romantic of them all, so marrying Papa must have been a *coup de grace*, unless the decision had been pragmatic. Sophie sucked her bottom lip at this surprising thought.

She considered the balance between romance and reality. If she fell hopelessly in love with a poor gentleman, she had enough to live on with what she would inherit. Not much, she admitted, but it would do if love was the order of the day. She pressed her dry lips together as fields with budding crops trotted by her view. No, she was being silly again. Maybe Captain Murdock was correct in hinting she could be silly at times. Papa would never agree for her to marry someone beneath her, no matter how madly in love she thought herself. His guidance and direction since the years of her coming out were plain to see. Sophie Crestwood would marry well and there would be no regrets.

A horrifying idea lit on her mind. Did Papa regret his choice? She felt her face wrinkle in distaste at the idea. He certainly was not a romantic now, but he was only looking out for his children. Wasn't he?

As the carriage bounced north toward Oak Grove, querulous thoughts tumbled through Sophie's mind until at last, she managed to shut them out and fade away into an uncomfortable, rattling nap. When she opened her eyes again, the carriage was humming along in a peaceful way. She realized they must have reached a smooth road and tall trees to feel so rested and cool in such a short amount of time.

She rubbed her eyes, pulled up the shade over the carriage window, and drew in a sharp breath. The vast lawn of Oak Grove stretched out for as far as she could see. It seemed to go for miles before the distant low hills and trees signaled the boundary of a wooded park. Between the woods and she stretched a large lake four times the size of Leatherbury's pond. It was surrounded by bushy pink azaleas and other shrubbery trimmed into neat broccoli heads. The lawn looked trim and green.

The carriage rolled to a stop. Sophie wanted to leap out and kick off her heeled shoes, but she knew instinctively what would be waiting on the other side. On cue, the door across from her opened with a jerk, and she sat upright. A liveried footman was waiting, along with the impatient driver who must have tossed her things to the ground to finish unloading so soon. He hadn't even bothered to help her out. Ducking low, Sophie extended a hand and stepped down.

The sweeping façade of Oak Grove towered over her. The house shimmered in the sunshine. Pristine brick gleamed under a coat of oyster-tinted paint, and gold trim laced itself around each long window. Four stories tall, it stretched from north to south; with each wing turning a corner and running straight west in another long hall of several stories. The rooftop shined in the early summer sun, beckoning all visitors to explore its halls and the vast property surrounding it.

She had never been to a finer place short of her one appearance at court where she had been so nervous her knees quivered back and forth in sharp, jumpy jerks. Nestled in the southern countryside of Berkshire, Oak Grove was far more beautiful, and although it made her stomach curl over with apprehension, she was not afraid.

Before she could examine every detail of the awe-inspiring front hall, a servant led her from the black and white marble floors upstairs to a wing painted in a pleasing shade of blue. Flowers and paintings hugged the walls, and she examined them until a door opened, and she was encouraged to enter.

The bedchamber was generous for a gentlewoman of Leatherbury. The walls were bright cream and dappled with yellow posies. A maid stood waiting, dipped at the knee, and said her name was Betsy. She had a small room adjacent to Sophie, more like a pantry from what Sophie could see. She almost regretted that Margaret did not come.

Sophie collapsed into a chair and stretched out her cramped legs, but her respite fell short when a knock on the door was a request from Lady Mary to join her in the drawing room. "So soon," Sophie sighed, her stomach tightening with currents of anticipation and anxiety.

To be under Lady Mary's charge was an honor, and she felt certain there would be others at the house party who felt it too generous an honor, but she determined to make the best of it. Leatherbury, her lovely home, was no match for the great Oak Grove. It could never outdo the stables and chapel she had seen from the carriage. It was like a village in and of itself, with a monstrous town hall.

When she was introduced into the drawing room after changing her shoes and donning a light shawl, she found it a vague and familiar place. The walls were fresh green, and the silk trimmings matched in shades of vermeil. Large portraits with gilded frames hung like heavy loads on the walls; a mishmash of country gardens, a Greek goddess in repose, and distant ancestors of the aristocrats who had walked these halls.

Lady Mary sat straight in her tufted chair, her stiff cap nestled on white locks so stubborn they probably would not take a curl even under the duress of a hot iron.

"There you are," said the lady, nodding her head in unspoken approval. "I expected you on the hour, but you are only a few minutes late."

Sophie curtsied. "It is so kind of you, again, I must express my gratitude," she said, hoping it did not come out all in a gush. She was mortified to arrive later than her hostess's expectations. A few minutes would be a great deal of time at Oak Grove; more than it would be at Leatherbury.

Lady Mary wiggled her fingers in a wave that fluttered away Sophie's words like puffs of smoke. "Young Miss Middleton and Miss Banks have arrived. You may sit," she said, nodding toward a violet settle that contrasted in a sharp way against the emerald drawing room walls. Sophie noted she would not be able to appreciate the view out of the windows as did her hostess, but at least the high back would protect her from any drafts or wayward beams of sunlight.

She walked with as much primness as was possible under the lady's watchful eye. With practiced grace, she dropped with a light motion onto the firm furniture, pulled back her shoulders in a small stretch, and prepared herself for a long, upright afternoon. It began with Lady Mary's guest list.

"As you know," she reminded Sophie with a kind smile, "you are my especial guest despite Lady Milton's niece and of course, Miss India Banks. I understand you are not acquainted."

Sophie shook her head.

"Miss Banks is Admiral Banks' daughter. He is yet in the Channel wreaking his havoc like those men do, but I have promised his wife that Miss Banks is welcome here. Mrs. Banks is an old, dear friend of mine, much like your mother. Her daughter is in great need of refined company."

Sophie supposed her mama must have been a much dearer friend for Lady Mary to offer herself as Sophie's chaperone. She felt humbled.

"My nephew arrived on Thursday last. He is delighted to be in the country, and of course, I have told him all about you and my young friends. I do hope you'll find him pleasant."

Sophie felt her cheeks warm, but nodded, keeping her focus on her clasped hands. She tried to look up with politeness at proper intervals, but she could not do so when Lady Mary mentioned her nephew's arrival. Sophie's stomach surprised her by twisting in agonizing pain. She realized she had pushed all her worries about Oak Grove and matchmaking far from the forefront of her mind, what with Jack and his lessons with Captain Murdock.

"I invited your friend, Miss Blackburn, I'm sure you have heard," continued the elderly woman. "She is not quite your equal, and I have warned your Mama of how it may look, but I suppose there is more latitude offered to one's bosom friends at your age, although you should think of her as more a responsibility than a friend. She will benefit from your acquaintanceship, as she has already by her invitation to Oak Grove."

Lady Mary flicked a wrist again in a queer motion that looked young and careless. Sophie thought of George Devlin, imagined him doing so, and caught herself before she nodded again.

"You understand?" the lady asked, "I do not mean to be harsh."

"Oh yes, your ladyship. Indeed."

Sophie wasn't quite sure if they were still discussing Katherine, which Sophie found a bit cruel and unfair, but she would not admit she had not been concentrating on the woman's every word.

"Four girls under one roof should be more than enough to keep a summer party proper and simple, but entertaining, too. Henry did not want a large crowd."

"Yes, Lady Mary, four is a good number," Sophie agreed. Of course, she found a party of four young ladies tragic and small for Oak Grove. She imagined all of Guilford could easily fit onto the grounds at one time, and everyone could have an opportunity for a turn around the house.

"My nephew has brought a special friend with him, I must warn you. A lieutenant." Lady Mary lifted a slight bit out of her chair then resettled her layers of dark silk which floated around her in eddies. It was a much older fashion which Sophie found impractical and uncomfortable, but it suited the austere face and commanding presence, much like a faded copy of Marie Antoinette.

"His name is Perlmutter. He's on shore leave while his ship is in the dockyard. Those naval men, always waiting for orders, but Henry needed him, and he has come. Dragged him away reluctantly from Whitehall, I presume."

"Yes, your ladyship." Sophie did not feel it appropriate to suggest that if Whitehall or Perlmutter's captain demanded the presence of the lieutenant, even Oak Grove could not force him to stay.

"He's of good family, I know," continued the lady. "They were in school together when they were boys and somehow remained fast friends, although there was no way on my life Henry would have been let to sea. Harold Perlmutter is a gentleman, however, and a respectable second son. I think he would do well to be introduced to your Miss Blackburn, although he does not command a great income yet." She sighed. "Those things can change in an instant for that sort."

Lady Mary's studious eyes penetrated Sophie. She felt them and raised her gaze to look agreeable. Never until this moment had she realized how much of a matchmaking affair the house party would be. Lady Mary took her unofficial calling with great seriousness, but Sophie did not feel half as enthusiastic as Mama and Papa. Expectations of afternoons of whist and croquet were replaced with forced conversation and reading in the drawing room. Sophie breathed a sigh. She had the startling desire to go fishing. The beautiful lake before the great house probably teemed with fish.

Her mind took several steps back to Perlmutter and then the Navy, and then out of nowhere, it settled on Captain Murdock. Was he fencing with Jack this very moment, and in secret defiance of his promise?

"Miss Crestwood?"

"Yes?"

"Where are you?"

"I'm sorry," Sophie apologized. She stumbled over her words. "I was trying to recall if I had met Lieutenant Perlmutter, but we are not acquainted."

"No," said Lady Mary in her calm tone. She kept her gaze on Sophie, watching her to make sure she had her attention. Her small eyes held a sort of amused patience. Lady Mary was still handsome. She would have been a great beauty in her time. Even the lines seeping into her regal countenance could not hide that.

"Lieutenant Perlmutter has been to sea a great many years and only comes home on occasion. Despite the distance and time, he still retains my nephew's favor, and as I said, one cannot deny a great many friendships for they do give us something to lean on. Besides, we have a mutual friend, Perlmutter and I."

"Yes," Sophie agreed. "I do treasure my friends in Higfield, especially Miss Blackburn."

"I'm glad to hear it, but I recommend you reach out to the other ladies you do not know. I have friends all over England, so I feel the weight of responsibility for bringing our children together whenever possible."

"Yes, we know."

The corner of Lady Mary's mouth pulled up toward her creased eyes. "It is more out of duty and due to a great many requests, I assure you." Then she smiled very wide as if sharing a humorous secret. "Do not be too troubled, Miss Crestwood. I do not put half as much stock in matchmaking as I did when I was your age. I only try."

Sophie smiled back. Matchmaking. What else was there when a girl came out?

"Your mother was a beauty, much like you. In some ways, she reminded me of myself." A fine Italian fan popped up out of nowhere, and Lady Mary began to cool herself. In the great rooms of Oak Grove, with ceilings too high to touch even standing on a cupboard, the air already felt cool to Sophie.

"My mother speaks with fondness of your interest in her affairs. She's very grateful to you." This was true, and Sophie tried once again to feel quite grateful, too.

Lady Mary's smile faded. "It was the least I could do. She is the daughter of my sister's very best friend."

"Yes, of course. I met your sister once."

"Out of respect for your grandmother, I had to do what I could for your mama. She was a lovely thing and very practical. I admired her."

Practical? Mama? It was a hard thing for Sophie to imagine.

Lady Mary continued: "She was sensible and headstrong and knew it would not do to run off with the first beau who turned her head." She hesitated. A faraway look in her eye made Sophie wonder at what stories she did not tell. "That's why I knew she would be good for your Papa. He had Leatherbury, and I must tell you," she added, lowering her voice, "he had quite an eye for the ladies." Lady Mary rested her head on the back of the chair and gazed at the ceiling.

Sophie felt alarmed. She'd heard enough. The woman made it sound like Papa was nothing more than a flirt once upon a time. This history of her parents' arrangement from a half-stranger was uncomfortable.

The woman chuckled. Her gaze returned to Sophie. "One look at your serious, lovely Mama, and his heart was won." She blinked, although a small smile creased her lips again. "Your mama took up in your respectable country home, and your papa had a beauty on his arm that was the envy of everyone in the county."

A shadow streaked across Lady Mary's face, and she frowned. When she saw Sophie still watched her, it disappeared. "Yes," she muttered, "everyone was quite taken with your mama. Almost everyone." She cleared her throat.

Sophie pressed her lips together and kept her expression vacant. She had nothing to say to that. Her mind twirled like a weather vane.

The door to the drawing room swung open, and Sophie managed not to cheer in relief. Instead, she took a deep breath and held it. The footman, who had escorted her into the drawing room, announced Katherine's name and in she swept like a queen. Her cheeks blazed with a red luster, and her jaw looked set as if she was determined to keep herself from babbling. Sophie tucked it away with some amusement to tease her with later.

AFTER SHE WAS DISMISSED, and before she could speak in private with Katherine, Sophie returned to her room to find her things laid out for supper. Realizing she was expected in the salon before supper where all the gentlemen would be waiting, she almost climbed up onto the bed and curled into a tight ball like a kitten. She wanted to sleep and pretend it was tomorrow, or even better yet, yesterday.

She was far less prepared to be at Oak Grove than she realized. The vast size of it seemed to swallow her calm and confident demeanor. The infamous Lady Middleton's niece was there and of course, Miss India Banks. Sophie felt insignificant.

Admiral Banks was quite rich. Everyone knew it. The war had made him as rich as a prince. Miss Banks would be a far better catch for Henry Billingham. Her heart shrank in her bosom. She was probably a great beauty, too. Mr. and Mrs. Crestwood had built up their hopes too high. Sophie was a family friend and honored guest and nothing more. She had no title to inherit, and her income looked quite common when compared to what Miss Banks would have in her bank. Why, only Katherine had less, and she was almost no higher up than a lady's companion. Shame washed over her, and Sophie sighed. How dreadful of a friend she must be to find relief in Katherine's situation.

Betsy cleared her throat, and Sophie sat up and smiled an apology. What the servants must think, she wondered, that Lady Mary's charge would lie in bed with such melancholy and take no interest in dressing for supper. She pulled herself up and slipped on new slippers, even if they would be stomped and clomped on by heavy boots.

Turning her back, the buttons of her traveling gown were undone, and the entire dance of the *toilette* began all over again.

Afterward, she strolled toward the salon with slow footsteps. Watching her covered toes slide out from beneath her gown with each stride, Sophie decided they were very narrow, though it mattered little because the hem of her gown was light, and it fluffed itself up in a small cloud with each step, one that made her want to stop and twirl around, but that would not do.

Two footmen on either side of the salon doors bowed then pushed them aside, and she was let in. Her name was announced and to her surprise, she found Lady Mary there already, speaking with great energy to a pair of older, well-groomed ladies whom she could only guess were chaperones for the young people at the party. Her skin prickled, and she glanced across the room. There stood a trio of rather amused looking gentlemen, two in fine coats and a third in naval blues.

Perlmutter. The long sideburns did not hide his weathered face. Her gaze snapped to Devlin, who grinned at her in the middle of a sentence like a satisfied cat. The third man was tallest, quite a good height, even taller than Captain Murdock. He beamed as he gave a little bow her direction, and light brown hair flopped over his head which he swiped back much like Jack would do. Sophie found her attention captivated by the fine rug on the floor. She avoided their stares, hoping her sapphire gown looked fetching enough.

"Miss Crestwood," said Lady Mary, who had changed into yards of gleaming silver. The room fell silent. Sophie's stomach fell a bit, too, into the bottom of her feet. All eyes seemed to rest on her until someone coughed. "Come," she said, and Sophie crossed the room to join her. In the dark red salon, she felt like she'd entered a painting with the other women in varying shades of lavender, green, and blue.

Lady Mary motioned to the gentlemen as well. They moved closer to the furniture, reluctant to be taken from their corner where they could observe the other guests. Sophie noted two girls standing at a long window watching introductions.

"Henry," said Lady Mary in a formal tone, "this is Miss Sophie Crestwood of Leatherbury." From her deep curtsey, Sophie dared look up only a moment, as the nephew bent deep at the waist. His smile lit up his boyish face and made his fair eyes look bright and lively. A satisfied breath escaped her body. Sophie could not keep from returning his kind smile. He was not ugly and did not have a leaky nose.

"Miss Crestwood," repeated Mr. Billingham. "I am so happy to meet you at last." His compliment slid easily into the conversation around the room. He was authentic; it could not be denied.

With relief, Sophie returned, "I do believe we met as children, sir, but I'm happy to renew our acquaintance."

"I'm afraid I don't recall, but you must know, I was never still for long while running amuck at Oak Grove."

Lady Mary chuckled. "You still do not sit for long, Henry. Now Mr. Devlin, I know, is already acquainted with our Miss Crestwood."

"A small bit," said Devlin, and he offered Sophie a cheeky grin. She grimaced. Devlin's smile lit up his face.

"Mr. Devlin," Sophie said with some exasperation, "we are quite known to each other. You have dined with us already at Leatherbury." The trio of men laughed, and Sophie felt her face warm. Devlin, it seemed, had already spoken of their friendship. Sophie turned to the officer, who watched her with arms pressed to his sides.

"Here is my dear friend," said Billingham, and he reached an arm around the man's shoulders in a brotherly embrace. "May I introduce to you, Lieutenant Perlmutter."

Sophie and the officer made the proper gestures. "Miss Crestwood," he replied, "I understand you live in Higfield."

"I do." Sophie stepped closer, aware of a giggle across the room and a low whisper before voices returned to normal. She glanced over her shoulder and spied Katherine standing beside the other two girls, a coppery redhead and one with plain russet hair. All eyes were on the gentlemen, she realized. Even the chaperones sitting around Lady Mary cast sly glances their way.

A pause in the conversation drew her attention back to the men to find them all staring. "Pardon me," she said with a light chuckle. The moment felt ridiculous, like a ball, a very small ball, except there was no dancing, no music, or tapping boots. She strained her mind to think of something more to say, their smiles expectant but growing stale.

"Higfield," Devlin hinted, and Sophie said laughing at herself, "Oh yes, Higfield. I am from Leatherbury, the country house outside of the village and south of the parish church."

"I'm not familiar with Higfield," Perlmutter admitted. "I only inquire because I know a man from the Indies there."

Sophie felt her brows rise. Surely, he did not mean—

"Murdock?" said Devlin. He rocked back on his heels and cast a look of disbelief at Mr. Billingham's questioning stare.

"Yes, Murdock," said Perlmutter, and he looked at Devlin as if did not understand his amusement. "Edward Francis Murdock of Pembroke Hall. I sailed with him years ago, before I reached the wardroom myself. Good officer."

Sophie narrowed her eyes at Devlin to shame him for his behavior. He, in response, snorted. Mr. Billingham followed the conversation with thoughtful eyes, first watching Perlmutter then her. Sophie met his gaze. They were eager and full of interest, no... intelligence. He turned to Perlmutter. "You don't mean the captain?"

"Yes, that would be him. The man we met in Town." He glanced at Devlin. "A fine sailor. We've been in contact since I've been on shore leave, but I haven't made my way to the estate."

"Pembroke," Sophie told him.

Perlmutter dipped his chin. "Yes, his father was titled in one way or another. A knight, was it?"

Devlin laughed. "I'm sure he'd like to think so. It was his father after all."

Sophie chose to ignore this. Devlin could not know how kind and humble Captain Murdock could be after all. "Yes. His father was a gentleman, a knight, Sir Edward of Pembroke. Captain Murdock has inherited and come home."

"That is as I understand it," Perlmutter said in a kind tone. He bowed his head again in assent, and Sophie smiled at him. The long sideburns did not disguise that his thin hair sat too far back on his head, but he did have friendly eyes.

"So," said Mr. Billingham, interested in this caricature, "and are you acquainted with Captain Murdock, Miss Crestwood?"

"Somewhat," Sophie replied. "Our home borders his estate, a vast park and stone hall situated on the hillsides overlooking Higfield."

"It sounds very fine indeed," said Billingham. "We've been introduced as Perlmutter said. He is a serious and thoughtful fellow."

Sophie found herself leaning closer to the officer. Here was a source of information she could rely on. If only Papa were here, he'd have every detail out of the man.

As if sensing her interest, Perlmutter shifted away in a slight movement, and Sophie followed his gaze to Katherine and her chaperone, Mrs. Burke, standing behind her. The widow was an aristocrat and a fine friend to all in Higfield.

"Why, more introductions," said Mr. Billingham with enthusiasm, and he stepped forward, delighted to meet all the guests invited to his party at Oak Grove. Sophie waited, wanting to question Perlmutter again, but he seemed relieved to be interrupted and looked away whenever she tried to get his attention.

SOPHIE MET EVERY PERSON in the room and formed a quick opinion of them. The copper-haired Miss India Banks spoke with great authority. She told Sophie, "I have not heard of Leatherbury, but I do not have time to waste in the country. We have a house near Grosvenor Square, which is my preference since Papa is not home because of that horrible Boney. Mama does her best to keep me entertained, but it is not as relaxing as Oak Grove."

She turned to Lady Mary. "I must compliment you, Lady Mary, to be so kind to—" and on it went with no time for Miss Banks to draw a breath. In fact, it seemed she had an inexhaustible supply of energy and did not need to breathe at all.

Miss Anne Middleton stayed behind her chaperone, a bird-like woman named Lady Fairfield, as if she was the lady's shadow. Sophie could not engage Miss Middleton in any conversation other than to get her opinion of Town which she saw little, and her home, that Sophie was not familiar with. It lay far north and sounded much to Sophie like it was too near the moors for her liking.

Miss Middleton could not have been any more different than Miss Banks, and Sophie wondered how she and Katherine would measure up between the two other girls. Of course, Katherine would always have witty conversation and clever ideas, but even she would not be able to speak over the admiral's daughter, and Sophie had no interest in doing so though she could not afford to be as shy as Miss Middleton.

Sophie was disappointed at supper to find she was not seated next to Perlmutter. Lady Mary sat at the head of the table by Henry with Sophie close by. Between them, Sophie learned Lady Mary's nephew was of a true and enthusiastic intent, and quite interested in everyone else's opinions. Across the table and further down, Miss Banks could speak and eat at the same time without looking improper or rude.

After supper when she retired to the salon with the ladies, Sophie found an opportunity to converse almost in private with Katherine, thanks in part to Miss Banks' volume from the sofa.

"My room," said Katherine with a chuckle, "is quite small. I can hardly fit in the bed, and Mrs. Burke is a-joined in a much bigger room I must pass through to even escape."

Sophie put fingers to her lips to hide her grin. "Why, your papa is only keeping you properly attended."

"In a closet? I'm sure my ankles will hang over the rails."

"Come to my room," whispered Sophie when the other ladies were distracted.

"Mrs. Burke won't have it," Katherine pouted. "I'll have to wait until she's sound asleep. Her bed is far bigger than mine, so it shouldn't take her that long."

"Then do. It can't be wrong to visit your friend after hours."

"Lady Mary looked me in the eye when she said we must be in our rooms by eleven o'clock and not out in the halls."

"Shocking," Sophie replied in a soft voice. She leaned closer to Katherine so that only she could hear her. "She said no such thing to me, so I must be free to roam at all hours."

Their giggles were interrupted by a loud cry. "What's that you say, Miss Crestwood?"

Anne Middleton's chaperone, Lady Fairfield, must have tired of Miss Banks' explanation of how the admiral's stratagem had increased her income and the number of gowns in her armoire. Instead, she decided to listen in on Katherine and Sophie's conversation. Sophie looked up and saw that silent Anne was watching, too. She seemed remote, even seated beside her chaperone and across from Lady Mary.

"I was just telling Miss Blackburn," said Sophie in a halting voice, "that we should all be happy to be in our beds by eleven o'clock. It's been a very long day." *Or something very close to it, cross my heart.*

"Oh, yes," said Lady Mary in a firm voice, "ladies should retire well before the midnight hour at Oak Grove. I am far too old to be chasing scandals into the night." She looked around the room from young lady to lady, her eyes coming to rest on Sophie. "Miss Crestwood, since you are my special guest, won't you play for us?"

She motioned to a polished mahogany pianoforte with legs as thick around as the supper table legs at Leatherbury. It seemed an intimidating beast, but Sophie realized she was fortunate to be invited to play so early in the evening, for the men had not yet joined them.

"I will not wait any longer," Lady Mary declared. "Henry has lured them all to the billiard room, the rascal. I will send for him at once."

There was no need. The low strum of male voices reached the doors of the salon just as Sophie stood to walk over to the pianoforte. In came Mr. Billingham, with a caravan of men smelling of drink. She froze as they thundered into the room.

"The fourth addition to our party has arrived," Billingham announced. "Mr. Byers." He swept his hand toward a stout man in white trousers and an impressive cravat. He bowed and though Billingham had not introduced him to his aunt, Byers addressed her: "Your ladyship. I am ever honored to be included."

Sophie saw Lady Mary's mouth twitch to one side. She refrained from smiling, perhaps at Byers ridiculous posturing, but she dipped her head. "I am happy to see you again, Mr. Byers. How is your father?"

"He is well." Byers planted his boots in the center of the room and placed his hands behind his back like he planned to remain there for some time. Even as he did so, his eyes roved around the drawing room, taking inventory of the company as if they were cattle up for auction.

"I have just asked Miss Crestwood to play for us. Gentlemen, do come in."

The gentlemen did as Lady Mary commanded and found positions around the room. Sophie did not withhold a smile of satisfaction when Mr. Billingham crossed over to the side of the sofa where she had been sitting. Katherine smiled up at him from beneath her lashes, but Sophie pushed her flirtatious friend from her mind and began rehearsing the notes her fingers would find once they touched the luxurious keys.

The music took over her mind as she played her favorite piece, *Robin Adair*, with a flickering flame of contentment in her breast. It was a lovely evening in a lovely home, and most of the company, if not all, were pleasant enough after a long, dreary winter and wet spring.

Their applause made her blush, and when she sat down Mr. Billingham did not move. "You play very well, Miss Crestwood."

"She does," Katherine agreed, leaning past Sophie to look up at him. "She practices with great devotion. I would that I had her commitment."

Sophie laughed with pleasure at their compliments. She smiled up at Billingham. "I do practice but not with great dedication, and I am hardly more than proficient."

"You are too humble," exclaimed Miss Banks. Her energetic red hair had worked its way free of some of its pins and stood high on her crown like a rooster comb. Sophie forced herself not to look and gazed into her eyes instead.

"It is uncommon to find such talent in the country. There is not the same quality of instruction as there is in Town." Miss Banks tilted her head and made a small grimace with her lips.

"Yes, you are right," Sophie agreed. "I'm afraid I am only moderately instructed in
most—"

"Why, of course, I am. I've had a great deal more education since I've come out and moved to Town, and I've found improvement in almost every accomplishment. Don't you agree, Mrs. Hood?"

Her aristocratic chaperone did not speak, but a sharp nod was enough. It suited the sharp face with its sharp nose and sharp chin. They looked quite uncommon sitting together, with Miss Banks round and her hair shaded like rust.

"Tell us then," said Mr. Billingham to Miss Banks before she spoke again, "What is your best accomplishment? Music? Watercolors? How is your French?"

"Oh, my music is very well, thank you, Mr. Billingham. I have painted with great talent since I was a young child. Why, only last year I was in Paris with a master, was I not Mrs. Hood?"

Sophie forced herself to listen to more of Miss Banks' accomplishments. George Devlin stood across the room, leaning heavily against the chair of Miss Middleton's chaperone. His arms were crossed as if to keep himself from falling over, but he gazed at Sophie with such intensity she raised a brow in question.

He motioned with a tilt of his head toward Miss Banks then glanced heavenward at the painted ceiling. The keys of Lady Mary's pianoforte interrupted the growing conversations in the room. To Sophie's pleasure, Katherine attempted a piece of Bach despite her lack of practice at home, even though Miss Banks huffed in a loud way because of her rank and that she had not been chosen to perform before a vicar's daughter.

Sophie glanced at the Middleton girl staring down at the tufted rug under her slippers. The poor dear, she decided, was still quite young, and had no interest in house parties or performing at all. Sophie couldn't help but think of Jack, and her mouth pulled into a little smile. Perhaps Anne Middleton just wanted to play out in the woods and be done with such tiresome nonsense. Sophie caught Devlin's gaze. His eyes narrowed as a sly smile crept across his lips, and she felt her cheeks warm at it, not certain what the intense look was all about.

CHAPTER EIGHT

Sophie settled in front of an ornate looking glass as Betsy brushed out her hair. Oak Grove was enormous and would take days to explore. She glanced out the clear window and saw with contentment that sunshine beamed down promises of a happy morning at Oak Grove.

In the glass, her fair hair had taken on the creamy glow of a soft, summer afternoon. Betsy turned it into a nice, round knot on Sophie's crown, and somehow made the straight locks at her temples accept a curl. True the room smelled like burnt flesh, but it was only a lock or two.

When the maid stepped back, Sophie examined as much of herself as she could see. Her sprigged muslin day dress fell neatly to her toes, hemmed to her height. She admired the narrow pink ribbon in her hair that matched the print on the gown, a soft pink, the color of the underside of the lightest rose. She looked well enough she decided, even with her dark eyes. Someone called for Betsy, and after asking if she needed anything else, the girl curtsied and flew off in a rush when Sophie said with a cheerfulness that there was not.

Oddly, breakfast was in the same dining room as dinner the evening before. Its primrose yellow walls looked bright in the morning light, even with the dark wood panels low around the walls and a matching elaborate hand-carved fireplace. It was because of their numbers she supposed, or perhaps because Lady Mary wanted to keep the breakfast parlor to herself. From the chatter and clinking of china and crystal at the early hour, Sophie certainly could not blame her.

The doors opened, and she passed into the warm room's conversation. Devlin and Mr. Byers rose to their feet; both with such haste they brought up the tablecloth with them. Sophie put a hand to her lips to hide her amusement.

"You should both sit down before you drag the silver to the floor." They laughed together, and Sophie took the offered chair. Eggs, fish, cold chicken, and a platter of fruit made her mouth water. "Strawberries," she said to no one in particular, "and an early melon, too." She had no sooner settled into the seat offered her across from Devlin, when Miss Banks came in on Henry Billingham's arm.

"How right you are," she was exclaiming. "I have known what it's like to have only a bit of weevilled biscuit and coffee for breakfast. It is like that on a ship of the line."

Billingham made a response Sophie did not hear. Devlin, with his cheeky grin, leaned over his plate and said, "How did you sleep, Miss Crestwood? Do you find the rooms of Oak Grove as restful as Leatherbury?"

"I do." She pierced a strawberry with her fork and felt a splatter of juice on her hand. "I find the portraits elegant, the furniture grand, and the courses here are as fine as I have ever tasted."

"You are an admirer of fine taste, too. I did not doubt it."

"You did not?"

"No," Devlin teased. His eyes beamed at her from beneath his thick brows. "From the very moment we met at the assembly room, I determined you are a woman of fine taste and opinion."

"Oh," said Sophie. "I do not think I have too many opinions and would like to think I don't consider myself too high."

"Of course, she is not." Mr. Billingham set his plate down with a clink and dropped into the chair beside her.

"Good morning, Miss Crestwood."

"Good morning, Mr. Billingham. I thank you for your defense."

"I did not mean to imply your character is proud," Devlin insisted from across the table. "Only, that you are always of one opinion or another and comfortable enough to share it."

She looked at Mr. Billingham who chewed his bread looking entertained.

"Should a woman be uncomfortable to share her thoughts?" Sophie wondered.

"Oh, no," said Devlin, shaking his head with great solemnity, "hardly ever." He glanced at Billingham, and they broke into grins.

She could not help but join them with a shake of her head. "Abominably rude," she said with a chuckle, but Billingham begged of her not to find offense.

"We are all under one roof for now and must be tolerant of one another. It would please my aunt so, for she has insisted I make acquaintances with my country neighbors."

"You will not be neighbors for some time," pointed out Devlin, "until you claim your place here."

"It is good you have come," argued Sophie. She nodded at Billingham with satisfaction.

"We want to know if the stories are true," Devlin said in a loud whisper. The gentlemen broke into laughter again, and Byers joined them from a few chairs down.

"Miss Banks was just saying we have many stories to exchange, what with her experience at Whitehall and yours at Oxford." Byers looked fascinated by the possibilities.

"Don't forget mine," said Devlin with a wink. "Who can resist a few hours of law?"

Sophie frowned. "I'm sure I could resist it, Mr. Devlin."

He put a hand on his heart. "Could you?"

The doors to the room opened again, and Katherine flitted inside, dressed in a smart walking gown with blue flowers that looked simple, yet was fetching on her. An assortment of merry ribbons held back her hair.

Devlin leapt to his feet and exclaimed, "How festive you look this morning, Miss Blackburn. I dare say you could lead a dance."

Katherine giggled. "This is not the place, Mr. Devlin, but I will hold you to it at a later time."

"So will I," called Miss Banks in her booming voice from Mr. Byer's left. "I have great expectations of a private ball, Mr. Billingham. I am used to Town and its frivolities and cannot grow bored. You must not allow it."

"I will not," Billingham promised, and he turned to Sophie. "You must not allow it either. I will promise you a dance, Miss Crestwood, if you will hold me to it. Especially if what Devlin promises is true and that you dance like a swan."

So near to him and his flashing blue eyes, Sophie could not help but flush. "If you insist," she promised, then darted her gaze to Devlin who watched her with a puckish smile on his lips. "I'm sure he cannot have such a high opinion of me, as he has only danced with me twice." She watched him count their dances in his head. "I mean, once," she amended. She looked at Billingham and gave him a weak smile as her cheeks warmed. "I meant once. You see, it is even less than I thought."

Katherine, who had taken her seat next to Devlin, said, "Why, she has so many partners she cannot remember them all." She burst into giggles at Sophie's reprimanding stare, but it made everyone in the room laugh all the harder.

AFTER A WALK ABOUT the lush, expansive grounds and then games in the drawing room, the ladies excused themselves to nap before supper that evening. Katherine exhausted herself traipsing up and down the property with Devlin, dodging his attempts to pull the ribbons from her hair. She begged Sophie to let her rest in her room, and once breathing heavy, pushed her so far to the side of the ticking Sophie gave up and went to sit beside the window.

The great pool of water before the house reflected the trees that lined either side of the estate. They were a vast row of giant oaks sturdy and tall, and they promised to reach even higher into the sky with the next generation. Like Henry Billingham, they showed promise.

He had a good family and good name. No doubt he had behaved just as a gentleman should during school and his tour abroad. He seemed to have a genuine love for his family and aunt, and to have accepted his future at Oak Grove. It was an enormous estate, and it came with a great fortune. He was a privileged if not indirect heir. Sophie liked the quality of his first impression. There was a self-deprecating air about him, and she suspected that what her aunt saw in the humble young man must be real.

Growing warm at the window seat, she slid off and reached for her lightest shawl. The halls were cool at Oak Grove, and their shadowed coves called out for her to explore them. If Jack were there, he would already have mapped out the floors and found every secret passage.

She tiptoed out of the room into the quiet cerulean-colored hall. Quiet, except for what she was certain was the echo of Miss Banks chattering in a distant room. She strolled from the wing to the center of the house and its grand stairs then floated down them to the next floor with its linear corridors and rooms of treasure and mystery.

Two towering white doors with gold leaf made her guess she had reached the conservatory, but memory failed her. She pushed one open and slid inside. Impressed, she looked around a box-shaped room draped in greens and golds. Rich, olive-shaded couches lined the room around life-sized sculptures of Greek and Roman heroes. Busts rested on tall square pedestals; masks of those who had once ruled Oak Grove throughout its history. She circled the room, spellbound by the mastery of the art form and the pervading peace broken only by quiet breathing and a snort.

Sophie froze. She listened and heard again, the steady rhythmic breathing of something or someone. A chill ran down her arms as her glance swept across the still room. Nothing stirred except the breath of a lurking stranger. She moved across the room with some hesitation, her slippers making no sound across the polished floor. Two of the long couches in the room, set back to admire the art from all angles, could hide a person or something worse.

Holding her own breath, she inched around the first couch and peeked. Flat on his back, with his arm thrown over his forehead, slept Mr. Billingham. His legs were splayed out together, his boots hanging over the edge. Peering over the top of his head, she wished she had a feather to tickle his nose, but they were not that well acquainted, and perhaps he might—

Two round eyes popped open, and Sophie stumbled back in surprise. Billingham let out a hysterical laugh. "Why, Miss Crestwood! You should see yourself."

She was aghast to be caught peering at him while he napped, but his flushed cheeks and loud guffaws, even as he sat up, convinced her that he had not been asleep at all.

Sophie pursed her lips but could not keep from smiling. "You dog. You frightened me half to death."

"Did you think I was dead?"

"How could I think so when you made such an awful noise?"

"Really, I do not snore," he said with little effort at sincerity. His eyes danced with fun.

"I bet you do," she teased back. "Everyone says that." She put her hands on her hips, finding them easily in the folds of her gown. "You should be reading or playing cards, or whatever you gentlemen do when we are retired."

"Sports today," he said. "You are supposed to resting." Pointing at her then remembering himself, he scrambled to his feet. "I came to hide out. I cannot bear to wrestle and run hour after hour. Cutthroat competition is not for me."

"I would think you need a nap anyway after dragging us around the grounds this morning."

"Oh, I did not mind it," Billingham said with cheer, "and you did tell me you loved to spend time out in the gardens. Stroll with me about this great room and let us admire my aunt's collection."

He proffered his arm, and she took it. He led her to the far side of the room and stopped before the statue of a lean and strong browed woman. She was carved from marble, and so lifelike and beautiful Sophie almost forgot Billingham stood beside her.

"Lovely, isn't she? My very own Aphrodite, or so I have wished since I was a boy."

"One day she will be, said Sophie. "It's quite a wonder, isn't it?"

"Oh yes, I do admire the sculptor's hand. I have so little talent."

Sophie smiled up at him. "I don't believe it. You are so lively and of good disposition, I'm sure you have a great many skills."

"Academics, I suppose. Maybe a bit of learnedness, but no one wants to stand about and admire intellect."

"It's a great thing to be educated, Mr. Billingham. You should be proud to have done so well in school. Your aunt has told me all about it."

"Yes," he said with some peevishness, "I'm sure she has."

Sophie scrunched her lips to keep from grinning, but it was no good. They moved to the next god, and she stared at the statue's cold, white ankle. "She is so fond of you. She speaks highly of you and your family a great deal of the time."

"Yes, and I do love her. She has seen to my every opportunity my parents could not, and I have spent many summers here."

"Will you stay now?"

"It is what she hopes. There are things for me to learn; things I must do to prepare to take on this old place."

Sophie blew out a puff of air. "Old place? It's beautiful and grand, and not half as old as most great houses nowadays. Why, Leatherbury is showing her age and Pembroke, it's practically crumbled to the ground, or it was until recently."

"Ah, yes. The pirate at Pembroke."

Sophie caught a laugh before it fully escaped. "It's quite cleaned up. I should say it's coming along."

"I have not seen it, not in so many years. I cannot say I remember it at all, truth be told. Perlmutter knows Murdock though, as he explained to you."

"Yes." Sophie walked over to the bust of a distant earl. He looked old and fierce and bald. "He is to be admired for taking on such a great project I think, and as for the rumors..."

"Rumors?" Billingham chuckled. He touched her elbow, and they moved deeper into the room, stepping into a narrow slant of sunshine slicing its way through the heavy curtains. "I do not believe half of what I hear, Miss Crestwood. I hardly accept most of what I read."

"Yet you are so educated."

"I learn best by studying all sides. There is also truth in observation I find; even then one must make allowances."

"Of course, you're right." Sophie crossed her arms over herself. "How ever did you hear of the curious rumors of piracy?"

"Oh?" Billingham looked at her like she should already know. "I suppose from Mr. Devlin. He has been to Higfield and paid his calls here and there."

Sophie frowned. "So the news travels on; but I must confess the circumstances of his arrival were suspicious, not to mention his servants. Why they are... and he is... Well, nonetheless, I'm sure if there was evidence he would have been arrested by now."

"It has not made the papers, and I'm sure it's all silliness. Aunt says it is nonsense, and she is right. Perlmutter has known him a great many years, and besides, what pirate would sail right up the Thames and plant his boots in Higfield?"

His reasoning made sense to her, Sophie agreed, even if Captain Murdock did not always make sense. "I must say I am somewhat acquainted with Captain Murdock, and he is a gentleman despite the gossip and rumors going around the village."

"Well, he has made a timely arrival, I must say." Billingham glanced sideways at her.

"What do you mean?"

He laughed under his breath and shrugged his shoulder. "Nothing at all. I only meant opportune for the estate."

Sophie suspected he intended to mean something altogether different. She broke shafts of sunlight hitting the floor with her shadow and dropped down onto another sofa covered in the same green velvet. "I should probably make my way back to my room. Katherine will be awake and wonder where I've gone."

Billingham smiled. "I'm sure she will be sorry she missed the tête-à-tête over marble and terracotta."

"I am sorry to interrupt your nap, Mr. Billingham."

"I was not resting at all. I will be lazy on the morrow and sleep past breakfast."

Sophie laughed. "You will not. Your aunt won't allow it, for you must entertain us all as host."

"Then," Billingham relented, "I will be languid and dull."

Sophie shook her head. "I don't believe it, not one bit."

Billingham bowed, and she stood with a small smile. "I'll let you sneak off to another room." Sophie stepped out into the hall and noted the warm room behind her made the hall seem dank, dark, and empty.

She glided down the quiet passage, making every effort to keep her slippers light on the polished floors. Squeaks and creaks drifted around corners, resonated from the ceiling overhead, or echoed down the stairs much like a dream. Her wonder was short-lived as a narrow door swung inward on its hinges into the hall causing her to jerk back in surprise.

Devlin popped out into the hall like a mouse from a hole. Sophie took another step back with a hand on her heart. "Upon my word, Mr. Devlin, you gave me a scare."

He laughed and said with an unapologetic air, "I beg your pardon, Miss Crestwood. I did not expect to find you here."

"I'm sure you did not."

He must have been alone, for the door he burst forth from led down steep, shadowed stairs. They were probably reserved for the servants, she reasoned, since she had not noticed the door until he rushed out of it.

Sophie gave him a teasing stare. "I presume you are not prone to napping away your afternoons, either? No sports? No games?"

He laughed, out of breath, and his cheeks looked ruddy from some exertion. "Oh, no, Miss Crestwood." He winked at her even as he proffered his arm. "I have just finished my exercise."

"Then you must be very fond of it, like my brother, Jack."

"Exercise? Oh, yes. I do like to be out of doors. You do, too, I've noticed."

"I do like my walks, and the grounds here are one discovery after another."

"I suppose," he said with a careless air.

On the next floor, they reached the blue hall, and Sophie slowed her pace. "You should not be here in the ladies' wing."

He laughed too loud, and she looked to see if someone might come out of a room. "Thank you for the escort. I can find my way from here."

"Very well." He slid his arm out of hers. "Have you been through the maze?"

"Not yet."

"Well, that is a good deal of walking if you like exercise."

"I have the intention, but I should rest now, or I will be no fun at cards tonight."

"Cards. Bah." Devlin frowned. "I think we can find much better things to do than play cards. We only have a few weeks to make merry before it grows too hot, and the lady sends us on our way."

"Then you think of something fun," Sophie suggested, "and I will champion your cause."

"As you wish," he said with a bow. "We are partners now."

His enthusiasm made her grin. Once she made her way back to her room, Sophie shut the door with satisfaction. She thought her time well spent roaming Oak Grove rather than sleeping the hours away. To her surprise, Katherine was nowhere to be found.

AFTER THREE DAYS OF walks, games, and good conversation, Sophie thought life at Oak Grove would be satisfactory indeed. She enjoyed her private adventures in the late afternoons when the house fell quiet. More often than not, Billingham would find her, or rather she would find him, napping in peculiar places or sitting at a palatial window, his forehead pressed against the glass and his expression far away.

She did not trouble him about what drew him apart from the party; especially when the gentlemen took to their own peculiar activities—much riding and shooting—but he seemed to feel like he was as much a guest in the house as she, and she pondered it with mild sympathy.

She found him at the end of the week, after rousing evenings of card games and singing, secluded in the second library. It was a smaller space than the vast collection held in a superior room, rather warm and woodsy with dark trim and comfortable furniture upholstered in shades of late autumn. The stone fireplace had a rustic mantel with a charming painting of the hunt. The books were more recent, she found; pleasant publications on a variety of subjects, and even novels which she would not expect such an estate to procure since Mama collected them at Leatherbury, and Mr. Crestwood frowned on it so.

She tiptoed in, noting how the heavy curtains darkened the room, and made her way straight to the volume of Wordsworth whom Mama found fascinating. She took two steps toward the chair she preferred with its cherry side table before realizing Billingham was on the floor across the room lying on his back. His boots touched the hem of a curtain while his arms were folded beneath his head enjoying a scenic view only he could see through the wall.

He glanced her way and grinned before returning to his staring at the covered windows. She winced. "I'm so sorry, Mr. Billingham, I have interrupted your meditation once again." Sophie squeezed the book in her hands, wondering if she should return it to its shelf and leave.

Billingham sat up in a slow, lazy way. "No, you have not." He sat cross-legged on the floor like a boy with his arms outstretched behind him. "I knew you would sneak into this room again. It's your favorite although you claim you don't like to read."

Sophie chuckled. "It depends on the subject. So then, I will take up the best seat in the room and read anyway."

"You must. You do not trouble me at all. I like the quiet you know by now, and only need a little while to rest myself, but I enjoy your company just as much."

Pleased, Sophie slipped into the chair, stopping herself from curling up her legs as if she were alone. "It must be exhausting to play the part of host here at Oak Grove, and for so many days, too."

Billingham smiled. "I do not mind it, really. You must not think me ungrateful for my good fortune. It's only that I have a great deal of responsibility now, but I am happy to see my aunt and talk with her. She knows and understands what my future holds."

"I admire that you are so fond of one another."

"Yes," Billingham nodded. "She comprehends me, quite a bit more than my own father and mother, and so I am comfortable here."

"It shows," Sophie said with an approving smile. She said nothing about his distant stares when he thought no one was watching. "I do not think the others mind you taking some time for yourself. It is your party after all, and you should have some time to do as you like."

"Oh, I do like a party," Billingham laughed, "and making new acquaintances. Do you know, I remember you now from when I was a boy? Your family came to visit. The children were let outside with a governess, but I was a bit older and not allowed. Your brother... Richard. He is about my age."

"Yes. He is married and stays in Town these days. It is only my little brother Jack and me at Leatherbury now."

Billingham shifted forward and folded his arms. "Do you hope to live in Town or stay in the country?"

Sophie thought. "Town does have its appeal, but I love my home. Leatherbury is quite comfortable. There's room enough for everyone to have their own quarters, and we have a small library, drawing room, and a quaint little breakfast parlor, too. It can be quiet sometimes, especially with Richard gone and Jack nearly grown. We have no near neighbors, except Pembroke I mean, but it has been abandoned."

"Until now that is."

Sophie sat up straighter in the chair. She laid the volume of poetry down in her lap. "Do tell me, how do you know Perlmutter? Oh wait, yes, from school. You have been friends for some time then?"

"Yes. He is brave and ambitious, and I admire his accomplishments although they aren't the paths I would choose."

"Did he want to join the Navy? Was it his wish or was it expected of him?"

"What a curious question." Billingham shifted his eyes to the ceiling and reflected. "I think it was his choice to pursue it. He could have bought a commission in the army, but the sea calls to some more than the infantry, does it not?"

Sophie nodded. "It does. My parents took us to Bath on many occasions, and for my brother, it is the sole reason for his existence, or so he's convinced."

Billingham laughed. "As most boys are. Do you have family connections then? Anyone at Whitehall?"

"Oh, no." Sophie shook her head. My mother is a Crooks, a good family from Surrey but with no naval connections, and Papa is a gentleman's son who loves the land. My neighbor, however," she added, thinking of Pembroke again, "is a sea captain, and I'm afraid it has only excited Jack all the more."

"He is a second son," noted Billingham. "It would be a respectful career."

"Your aunt has arranged a perfectly good living for him at the parsonage, and my mother prefers that he tends to flocks over fishes."

Billingham looked sympathetic. "I understand. It's perilous times." He sighed and was quiet for a bit, and Sophie watched him study the floor, then he remarked, "I have lost a great many of my childhood friends and even some cousins abroad. It makes one feel quite undeserving to be tending over great houses while everyone else is serving King and country."

"You must not let that trouble you. Someone must keep up such things. Where would the tenants go, and who would keep up the estate?"

"My aunt?" offered Billingham with a grin.

Sophie smiled. "I had no idea you felt so uncomfortable with your inheritance."

"Oh," he said, "It's not that at all. I suppose it is just that I have little voice in the matter."

"That I can understand."

"Can you?" Billingham said this with a little laugh like the idea amused him.

"It's true," Sophie said with ardor. "Because I am a woman I do not have all the choices in the world. In fact, you must admit I have fewer."

"True, but if you have not been betrothed and are free to settle with whom you choose, then you are still fortunate."

"I suppose." It was Lady Mary who had insisted Sophie be introduced to her nephew. What she had hoped to come of it, the Crestwoods could only presume, but here was poor Billingham wishing he did not have to endure such machinations. The idea of it made Sophie flush.

"You have a happy disposition, Mr. Billingham, and are kind and intelligent. I'm sure you will be able to make your own happiness even when you find yourself secured at Oak Grove."

"Do you think so?"

"You must insist upon it."

Billingham grinned again. "You, Miss, make it sound quite easy. I only wish that it were."

"You worry too much about what is to come. Things almost always turn out in the end."

"What an optimist you are. Tell me," Billingham stretched out his legs until they were spread across the rug on the floor, "how will things turn out for you in the end?"

"Me?" Sophie ducked her head in surprise, mind whirling. "I—I suppose I will marry a gentleman and raise a brood of children while having a mind to care for my brother, Jack. My parents will be older, and he does have a wild air about him at times."

"Does he?"

"He's not a bad boy; just adventurous and curious."

"Oh," said Billingham, "I think curious is good, don't you?"

"For the most part."

"Are you? Curious?"

Sophie thought some then replied, "About some things."

"Like what?"

"I suppose I do like to know what's going on, and I'm always happy to see new places."

"You would travel?"

"Oh, I'm not sure. I don't think I have the wanderlust of Jack, but I do like to think about faraway places."

"Yes," said Billingham with a smile. "I've noticed that, and maps and globes, too. Are you sure you don't want to join the Navy?"

Sophie laughed. She reflected on the experience of living without a breakfast room, garden, new clothes for the season, and even her comfy old bed and the view out her window. "Ah, no, Mr. Billingham, I can't say that I do. Maybe I could travel for a time, but I mean, I've never even thought of it before since it's not possible."

"Hmm," said he. "Anything's possible." He plopped down on his back, and his eyes fluttered shut, and Sophie realized she had been alone with him too long. The library doors were closed tight.

"I should go," she said in a soft tone, and Billingham whispered, "if you like.""Have your nap," she answered, and he smiled back, eyes still closed. Sophie tiptoed out with the hem of her gown billowing like a sail in front of her small steps. She went to her room and slept easily without Katherine for a half of an hour. Where her friend was she did not know.

CHAPTER NINE

After supper, the party drifted to the red salon at the rear of the house. A line of doors opened to a terrace that overlooked steps leading to the lawn. Lanterns blazed, lighting up the night like glow worms. The scent of evening flowers clung to the cool summer air. Sophie found herself at the top of the stone stairs, gazing out across the vast property, trying to determine where its boundaries met the dark sky. Stars glimmered overhead, and the large moon assisted them in reflecting a bluish heavenly light.

She took an appreciative cleansing breath, relishing the floral scent in the air. Across the yard, the entrance to Oak Grove's Gothic maze beckoned the bold and adventurous with prickly, sharp fingers. The maze of shrubbery spread out across the grounds almost as far as the house itself. Billingham had promised them a game out of doors, but before they could form teams, the guests gravitated to the head of the maze. Hesitating, Sophie watched them go, the arch of her foot rubbing back and forth on the top stair. Her slippers were far too new to be stained running through the grass.

Katherine's high-pitched giggle drifted across the lawn, and she smiled. Of course, she would not hesitate. Not like Sophie. She must think it through and consider whether it would be proper and if her ladyship would approve. She glanced over her shoulder. Miss Middleton hung back at one of the doors, leaning into it as if her tiny shoulder could hold up its heavy frame. Billingham stood abreast of her, speaking with a kind smile, but she did not look up at him, only at the ground.

Billingham saw Sophie and gave her a nod. The candlelight be-hind him made his silhouette glow. She could see the chaperones talking with great animation, one with another, not the least bit con-cerned about the single young women traipsing through the garden in the late evening.

She heard Katherine squeal, then Miss Banks' loud voice, and decided to join the frivolities in the near dark after all. The house party was almost halfway over. She looked forward to the small ball Billingham had promised and fireworks, too; something she had on-ly seen a few times.

A warm hand caught hers up in a friendly grip, and she jumped. "Come, let's give it a go in the night, Miss Crestwood." Billingham pulled her down the stairs so fast she almost fell into him. She huffed, discomfited, as he caught her up in his arms and swung her to the ground.

"I have hardly found my way around it in the daylight, and with Katherine, too."

"Oh, she's already gone in. Perhaps we will beat her out this time."

They hurried across the grass to the laughing group of ladies and gentlemen daring each other to enter. "I'll race you then," Miss Banks said with a challenging tone, and Sophie smiled when she saw in the dim light that Lieutenant Perlmutter did not look like he cared to race; in fact, he did not look like he wanted to go into the maze at all.

Billingham stopped beside him and let go of her arm. He clapped the lieutenant on the back. "Go on, now then, Perl. You'll be the only man without a record to break."

"I'm not partial to running through thorns in the dark," Perlmut-ter said in a low voice, although he mustered an attempt to sound cheerful.

"I suppose it isn't a cutter, and there's no current to pull you along, but I bet you find your way as admirable as anyone else," So-phie encouraged him.

"Devlin and Byers, they have a head start already."

Billingham insisted. "They will keep count in their heads, you can bet on it. Let's beat their time."

"Come now, Lieutenant," chided Miss Banks. "I know this labyrinth like the back of my hand. I've found my way through it all week with Miss Middleton. She's such a sweet girl, but I cannot convince her to come out tonight."

"The night air, I presume," said Perlmutter. He glanced back toward the great house. Miss Middleton was no longer leaning against the door, and Sophie guessed she had returned to her perch beside her Mrs. Fairfield.

"Perhaps a wager, then?" Billingham dared him. "I'll take Miss Crestwood. You take Miss Banks, and may the best pair win."

"I happen to know all naval officers are betting men," said Miss Banks. "Don't you think so, Miss Crestwood?"

Taken aback, Sophie mumbled, "Well, I—"

"I'm sure Lieutenant Perlmutter has won his share of stakes, so we should take this bet." She held out her arm for him to hold, and before the reluctant officer could take it, Billingham cried, "Go!"

He shot off through the brush dragging Sophie behind him like a floundering kite tail. "Come on, dear," he said with great excitement and very little huffing, but Sophie was gasping with the first few steps, her chest heaving from the confines of her stays.

She found her rhythm as they sailed along, turning one corner and then the next without error. Billingham's gay laughs were contagious.

"You know it well, you cheat!" she cried, panting for breath as they raced through the darkness. He laughed again. "I have come here all my life, my friend," he reminded her.

In the murky shadows, they ran along as quick as Sophie's feet and tangled skirts would allow. She heard Miss Banks' voice, loud and impatient, and she pitied Perlmutter whom she imagined was being dragged along behind Miss Banks like a dishcloth.

"We're halfway," cried Billingham, when they reached a large intersection that diverted four directions. A pinch cramped up around Sophie's rib, and she wriggled her hand out of Billingham's grip. "You run like a buck, Mr. Billingham."

"You are fast, too. I knew you would be."

Sophie put her hands on her hips and leaned forward to catch her breath.

"This way. We must hurry."

She waved him off. "We're far ahead of them. I'd wager they'll never catch us even if we walk out." In a cloud of voices rising above the hedges, Sophie picked out Katherine's giggle among the low tones of a gentleman. Billingham strode over to an opening in the hedge. She could not tell if he was listening or waiting. Sophie took a deep breath and tried to steady herself. "You go," she encouraged him, "I'll be right behind you."

"I can't leave you." She heard the uncertainty in his voice.

"You must," she insisted. "I'm walking, but I'm right behind you. I simply can't dash in these... trappings."

"Yes, I do know, and I'm horribly sorry to be such a cruel taskmaster."

"You like to win."

"Don't we all?"

"Yes." Sophie grinned in the dark. The moon broke through some scattered clouds and lit up the path behind Billingham. He studied her in the moonbeams. "Go," she persuaded him. "I'll walk quickly. If you hear anyone, make a run for it."

He chuckled and motioned to her in the dark, maybe a wave or a salute, she wasn't sure, but he disappeared before she could return it. Hitching up her gown and taking a deep breath, Sophie threw back her shoulders and followed him into the night.

She only took a few strides before a rush of new footsteps made her halt. A dark figure burst into the clearing. He had come from Billingham's direction, which meant he was lost, going backward. Sophie giggled.

The man turned this way and that to get his bearings then spotted her in the glow of the moon. "Miss Crestwood," cried Devlin, "whatever are you doing out here alone?"

"I'm just trying to find my way out," Sophie replied. "I think I'm making a fine go of it, considering I have not made a wrong turn yet." She did not mention Billingham had been her guide. It was too opportune to make Devlin admire her and discover the joke later.

"Then I must come with you," Devlin declared. He strode across the trampled grass and joined her.

"I can't promise you I will find my way through the rest of it without any complications."

Devlin smiled at her. "That's half the fun of it."

She could make out the whites of his eyes and his teeth. "What? Being lost?"

He took her arm, and she didn't resist. At least he was in no mood to sprint through the shrubbery like a thoroughbred. "There are advantages to being lost."

"Like what?" They reached a corner, and Sophie peered left and then straight ahead, wishing Billingham's footsteps glowed like fairy dust. She tried to listen for footfalls, but Devlin interrupted her concentration.

"Why adventure, and new places and people."

He spoke softly now; like he worried someone might overhear them. Of course, they should not give their position away. She listened again, straining to hear Katherine's crystal tone or the fading gait of Billingham.

Devlin hung back, but she tightened her arm around his and pulled him forward. She did not think weaving back and forth would get them anywhere, so she plowed ahead straight. "I do like new places and people." The moon withdrew again, and the hedges seemed to tower over them. Sophie added, "I'm afraid I would yearn for home though; some version of it. I do like to come home."

Devlin slowed even further, coming almost to a stop. "Sometimes getting lost is the only way to find your way home." His voice sounded deep and throaty.

It made her pause, and she studied his face. "I'm not sure I understand what you mean. I've never heard you so serious." She tried to chuckle, but it knotted up in her throat and stuck there.

They were sheltered between high thorny walls and truly lost, Sophie realized, with no hope of finding their way out if they didn't pay close attention to the surroundings. Devlin stared back at her with such intensity she could not pull her gaze away. She did not know if he had something to say, or if he needed a comforting pat on the shoulder. The feeling he gave her was suspicious and uncomfortable. It made her hot, and she swiped at a layer of perspiration across her forehead. "It's warm," she said, with a nervous laugh.

"Yes," said Devlin. He had somehow moved quite near so that their faces were too close. She could make out the curve of his lip just under his perfect Roman nose. The curl over his forehead he usually kept perfect hung loose and wild. Sophie cleared her throat. "We should go this way," she said. Her mind tried to separate itself from the apprehension Devlin's mood created.

"Miss Crestwood," he said in a quiet voice, "you must know how much I have enjoyed our meetings in Higfield, at the dance, and of course, the supper in your home."

Sophie could not find words. Her ears strained to hear Katherine or even Billingham wandering back toward her; strained to hear Devlin say more pretty things in a smoldering tone any young lady would be pleased to hear.

"We have spent a great deal of time together here at Oak Grove, too," he continued. His hand had not come undone from her elbow, and he reeled her back toward him like a man with a fishing line.

"Yes. We have... Well, we have had great fun playing cards and riddles, and I do enjoy listening to you read Shakespeare to us all." Sophie did not mention they had not spent any time alone.

"Don't forget our walks. There is no more pleasant a companion to walk the grounds of Oak Grove."

"Oh," she said with a shy chuckle, "we all go out walking together. Katherine is far more entertaining than I am in the morning. She has a more cheerful disposition than I could ever hope to possess."

A stab of guilt pierced Sophie through to the heart. Katherine adored Devlin; his clever wit, his enthusiasm, his great beauty, and his flattering attentions which he gave to one and all.

"Katherine is very well," admitted Devlin, "but I must confess you are far more enjoyable to entertain and the most beautiful by far."

"Me?" Katherine had a wild beauty none could equal. Sophie would have put a hand on her heart to profess her disbelief, but she could scarcely move. He drew her to him, almost knee to knee. She could smell tobacco and spirits, grass, and sweat.

"You are far more agreeable, you must know; such a good listener, and fair and kind."

Sophie blushed in the darkness at his compliments.

"You are a pretty country girl with the style and airs of the finest lady in Town."

"I've been to Town," Sophie admonished him. She wiggled her heel and tried to step back. The closeness of him suffocated her. Ripples of hot chills ran up and down her arms. She felt like any moment a lightning bolt might strike. "I do consider myself a lady, Mr. Devlin, even if I do like the country."

"So do I," the man whispered. He dropped his hand from her arm and wrapped it around her waist before she realized what he intended to do. Time froze, and with it, Devlin pulled her against him, lifting her a slight bit as he bowed his head over hers. She no sooner felt the touch of his damp lips on hers than she shrank away and turned her head. Her knees were so surprised at the turn of events she almost lost the ability to stand upright.

"Mr. Devlin," she whispered in a strangled voice. "We should not..."

"We should," he murmured, trailing hot, slimy little pecks along her jaw. She didn't know whether to be flattered or insulted, but the wave of nausea that flipped her stomach upside down made her realize either she did not like kissing or she did not like Mr. Devlin, not quite as much as she thought she did.

Her knees crumpled, and she slipped through his arms, just far enough for him to lose his grip. He pulled her up again, but she jerked her arms free and put both hands on his chest and pushed as hard as she could. He took a step away, and she stumbled backward, falling with a thump on her backside. Her feet bounced up off the ground, but she did not mind them. Rather, she flipped over on her hands and knees like a turtle righting itself and scrambled to get her new slippers under her.

"Miss Crestwood," said Devlin in a hoarse voice full of hurt and concern.

As soon as she felt solid earth beneath her, Sophie shot off into the darkness. She followed a bright star unfettered by clouds, just as Jack had taught her to do. Altering her course when she met a dead end, and not slowing despite the pain in her side, she finally dashed out of the maze into the circle of guests who stood chattering just outside of it in the moonlight.

THE NEXT EVENING, AFTER a day filled with reading and tea with Lady Mary, Sophie looked forward to a night of music in the conservatory to distract her from Devlin's stares. She had pretended all day long that nothing had happened between them, but Devlin seemed determined to constantly hint at it.

The party had only visited the conservatory on one other occasion, due to the fact there was more than one pianoforte at Oak Grove. Sophie wanted to hear Miss Banks pluck the harp because she did indeed have a great talent for it and because the rippling sounds of it relaxed Sophie's nerves far better than the girl's echoing speeches.

The impressive room not only had a beautiful gold harp and monstrous pianoforte, but several exotic looking instruments displayed on its creamy white walls. Lady Mary even had a cello—a fine piece of wood carved and polished to perfection. It was almost a piece of art and a pity there was no one to play it, but the lady explained she once knew a commodore who often played in concertos when she had visited Corsica, and she had come to admire the instrument.

Sophie couldn't help but think of Captain Murdock and his mourning violin. What a haunting figure he once made with such a sad song in his heart. She decided to ask Perlmutter, who hung back from the group looking out a tall, wide window, if he had ever heard the captain play, but when she mustered her courage to speak she could only ask him if he played anything at all. He did not, and he said nothing about Captain Murdock and his talents. Perhaps the captain only played for himself and at Pembroke.

During their discourse, Devlin stood across from Sophie and made twitching smiles in-between long and sometimes bold stares. "You look lovely, dear friend," said Katherine, drawing Sophie's attention away from the gentlemen.

Sophie glanced down at the lavender gown Mama insisted she pack.

"It's flattering."

"Not many people can wear purple, I must say," interrupted Miss Banks, "but you do it well despite your brown eyes, Miss Crestwood. Now, Miss Middleton, I must point out, you wear buttercup very well, too, although it's not a color I would wear for the evening."

The quiet girl blushed, and her chaperone pressed her lips together in a thin, disagreeable line.

"I think she looks beautiful," interjected Sophie. "Tell us, Lady Mary, what was the color of the season when you came to Oak Grove?"

The lady chuckled. "The color I don't recall, but our stays were tighter and skirts much heavier than you lambs get away with these days. Shocking really."

Sophie looked around the room to see who was shocked the lady was discussing underthings in front of the gentlemen, but no one seemed to mind.

"The music? The dances?" Katherine sat up straighter beside Sophie. Fashion always interested Katherine, almost as much as Miss Banks, but for a different reason entirely.

"Music has not changed as much I must say, but—"

"Should I play your ladyship?" said Miss Banks.

Sophie found her so coarse she thought she might scream, but if she had to listen to another night of Miss Banks' lectures on life abroad or the cost of living in Town she might die. Perhaps playing at something would keep her quiet.

"You may," said Lady Mary, and everyone in the room sighed with relief. "We have had games enough this week. I think we should rest and reflect, but not before welcoming another guest." She looked with some intent at Billingham.

"Ah, yes," he said, moving from beside Sophie to the center of the room. He cleared his throat. "We have some competition ahead of us," he declared, raking the other gentlemen of the room with a challenging stare, "and I mean in the billiard room, of course. I thought it would be a great deal of fun to invite another guest, although I am not well acquainted. My aunt knows him well, and he is a good friend of—"

The conservatory doors opened, and Perlmutter, who had disappeared without anyone noticing, slipped in with a lanky shadow in his wake. He stepped aside, and an invisible needle jabbed Sophie's heart. Whether it was surprise or pleasure, she had no time to decide because Billingham said, "Oh, Perlmutter, you're back."

The officer motioned to his new companion, eyes moving with uncertainty between Billingham and his aunt.

"Captain Murdock, welcome." Lady Mary's voice took command of the scene, and the murmurs came to a halt. Sophie could not tear her eyes away from Captain Murdock. There was no hat and no cane. His oiled hair shined in the candlelight, his was jaw clean-shaven, and his complexion glowed with health. His eyes, however, were as guarded as ever.

Facing Lady Mary, he bowed low at his introduction. When Perlmutter motioned toward her nephew, Murdock saw Sophie for the first time. His gaze switched from Billingham to Sophie seated beside him, and except for only a flicker of recognition, it shifted back to their host.

Miss Banks behaved like she was put out at the interruption but was finally allowed to play after everyone met the captain. Sophie could hardly pay heed to the chords of the harp although they echoed through the room like dancing raindrops. Billingham bent near her and whispered his approval of Miss Banks' talent, and it made her cheeks hot. She waited for Murdock to meet her eyes. He stood across the room, one leg pressed against an empty chair, a step away from Miss Middleton.

At last, he glanced her way and nodded with a slight dip of his chin, and she smiled, and then looked away for fear she would not be able to stop smiling. Why, she did not know. What a refreshing change of company, she thought.

Studying some of the others lost in appreciation of the music, she noticed Katherine and Devlin speaking in low tones while the harp's crescendo washed over them. She bit her lip, worrying about her friend's welfare with such a blackguard. He noticed her stare and met it, then looked away. She saw no shame. No regret or sorrow either.

Sophie glanced back at Captain Murdock with a rush of relief. George Devlin, she decided, would not trouble her anymore. She had nothing to worry about with the pirate from Pembroke at Oak Grove. She was certain if she confided in him what Devlin had done, Murdock would have happily run him through.

CHAPTER TEN

Sophie arose early, anxious to be among the first at breakfast because she had a curious desire to observe Murdock in polite society. In sleep, she'd dreamed a scene of springtime splendor with Pembroke in the distance. Yet instead of crumbling chimneys, she saw
white spires glittering in the sun. By the time she shook herself
awake, grey morning light had found its way through the cracks in
the curtains. She felt tired but could not go back to sleep.

One part of her mind was concerned about the arrival of Captain Murdock to Oak Grove, while another argued that he was not
curious at all, only quiet, thoughtful, and a bit unsure of himself in
new situations.

The previous evening in the conservatory she was restrained.
She'd offered nothing more than a hello to the captain when he was
introduced to her by an amused Billingham, who knew they were already acquainted. Later, she left Murdock with only a curtsey when
she departed, electing not to follow Katherine and Miss Banks to the
salon for a late game of cards.

The yellow dining room glowed in the morning sun. Sophie
stood at the doors, casting her gaze about the crystal and sconces
with the strong opinion it made a much better room for supper. She
did not think anymore of it, however, when she noted the unmistak-
able profile of Captain Murdock.

He sat on the right side of the table, looking out a window that
faced the front lawn. If he was impressed she could not tell, for his
face was its impartial self as he chewed slowly, hinting that he en-

joyed his solitude in the mornings, an agreeable quality. Breakfast at Leatherbury was always so boisterous.

She cleared her throat, for he hadn't heard the footman open the door, and his head turned her direction. He lowered his half-raised hand and nodded at her. She glanced at the breakfast fair spread out on the enormous sideboard and walked over to make up a small plate of fruit before joining him.

"I'd sit across from you, Captain, but I don't want to block your view."

His light eyes studied her, and she could not stop herself from patting down her hair. "Did I dress too quickly?"

"You look well enough and are an early riser, I see."

"I'm not always so, but I thought I would begin early this morning for I don't think there will be much time for exploring with Devlin and Miss Banks putting their plans for a play into action."

He made a sniffing sound, and she assumed it was a chuckle; a rather pained one.

"Do you plan to be in the play?"

"No, Miss Crestwood. I do not like to pretend, and it is my great misfortune to feel disconcerted around others I do not know well."

Sophie popped a grape into her mouth. "You are not as ill-humored as you would like others to think, Captain. You must not pretend you are put off. I must say I'm happy to see you here, and without your cane, too. You are doing much better then?"

He stirred his fork in a watery egg then returned to his study of the grounds outside the window. "I can walk a short distance and with only a bit of a limp."

"I do believe you are right," Sophie agreed. "I did notice you leaning last night. I suppose if you do a great deal of leaning when you stand and resting when you can sit, you will manage quite well."

"That is the idea," he agreed.

"I'm glad you are on the mend," she said with cheer. "I'm sure it doesn't have anything to do with more parrying in your stables."

She only meant it as a joke, but a shadow crossed his face. "No, that is not the reason for it. I'm sure only exercise and too much rest are the answer."

"Rest that has done you well," Sophie replied with approval. The overdone appearance of his skin had faded somewhat so that he did not look as red-brown as a farmer.

He took a bite of eggs, glancing at her again which made her stop staring. She looked down at her grapes. "Have you seen my brother? He has not been in your orchard again I hope."

Sliding back his chair, Captain Murdock relaxed his stiff, naval posture. "I have not; not too often, I must say, but he does find his way over to call on occasion."

"He calls?" Sophie said with mild amusement, hiding any concern she had that Papa would find out and explode.

"I suppose that is the way he looks at it. We've had some walks along the wall between our properties, a few fishing expeditions and the like, and the day before I departed for Oak Grove he asked to see the house and how the repairs are coming along."

Sophie sighed. Papa had made it clear they were not to visit Pembroke at all. Clearly, Jack had not learned to listen to his father. "I'm sorry he is so forward." She shook her head in remorse. "He does fancy himself a part of your goings-on at Pembroke. It was empty for so long, and I realize now he spent far more time over there than anyone at Leatherbury was ever aware."

"It's not safe for a young boy his age to be wandering around the county," Murdock agreed. "He is born to it, though, would be my guess. He questions me endlessly about my career."

"Then he knows far more about you than I do," said Sophie with regret.

She flushed, not meaning to hint she wanted to know more about him, then she realized she was as guilty as Jack for being too friendly. Yet, she could not be rude. Murdock was patient and kind, and whatever questionable history he had before coming to England she would sort out for herself. It was all very unfair, she realized, the rumors and gossip about Pembroke's heir.

The captain broke the pleasant silence between them. "Have you enjoyed your time here at Oak Grove?"

"I must say I have a great deal."

His pale green eyes found hers, and they were warm and friendly. Sitting so close, she realized there was a little blue around the edges of his pupils. "It's pleasant to spend time with others my age and to have some form of entertainment besides hounding Jack to do his lessons."

"I suppose you have found a great deal to explore here since the property is vast."

"Oh, I have not given up my exercise, Captain Murdock. We spend almost every morning out of doors—"

"We do, indeed," said a merry voice. Henry Billingham burst into the room, his hair shiny and sleek except for a handsome curl that bounced up and down in the very center of his forehead much like Devlin's style.

"Mr. Billingham," said Sophie, pleased. "You are up early today."

"I am up early, as usual, Miss Crestwood. I do not sleep in, much like my guests have the tendency to do."

"Oh," said Sophie with a guilty flush, "I guess you must include me then."

"I am happy to see you, and Captain Murdock, too. How did you sleep, sir?"

"Very well, thank you." Murdock nodded at his host then turned back to his plate.

"We were just talking about the grounds, Mr. Billingham. I was telling the captain about your trails and paths."

"Oh, there's a great many to be sure," Billingham agreed. He seated himself across from Sophie and Murdock, ignoring the head of the table. Waiting with patience while coffee was poured, he said, "You have only discovered but a fraction of Oak Grove's secrets, Miss Crestwood. True, there are hunting trails and secret paths, but that is neither here nor there until you conquer the maze."

"The maze? What a puzzle," she said with exasperation. "I found my way out once, and it satisfied me enough so that I have no desire to go back into its confusing twists and turns."

"You can hardly blame the others for wanting to better their time."

"I'm sure it's easier in the daylight."

Beside her, Captain Murdock cleared his throat. "You've wandered the maze in the dark?"

"Oh, she has," Billingham said with glee before Sophie could reply. "We all had a game of it just the other night. We made it halfway through and at a fine pace, too, but sadly we were separated in the darkness and in the excitement, did not finish."

"I did finish it," said Sophie, feeling peevish. "I may not have been first or fast, but I found my way through and all on my own, too."

"Impressive," mumbled Murdock.

"Oh, Miss Blackburn is the one to beat," confided Billingham. He leaned over the table like he knew a secret. "She practices every day with whomever can keep up with her."

"She's quite good, too," agreed Sophie. "I'm afraid I've failed to win any of the contests at your house party, Mr. Billingham."

"We are not here for the competition," Billingham replied.

She flushed, for he was staring at her with a great intensity like he so often did, but she knew it was just his friendly nature. Captain

Murdock did not know it, and she could almost hear the questions swirling in his mind.

"You should walk with us this morning, Captain," she said, turning to Murdock. She saw some hesitation in his look and assumed he would appreciate no mention of his handicap, although it had been obvious when he first came to Higfield.

"Of course," he agreed. He shifted back to allow his plate to be removed then reached for his coffee. It wafted rich, thick, and luxurious tendrils of steam.

"Yes, you must," said Billingham, but before he could say more, two more guests strode into the room. One of them was Miss Banks, talking loud and with great animation. Sophie looked at Murdock and smiled, and he turned up the corners of his mouth in quick return then excused himself.

WITH HATS AND PARASOLS, guests were scattered across the grounds in little groups by late morning, enjoying the sunlight as it dried the damp grass and flowers. The lake mirrored a perfect summer sky. On Billingham's arm, Sophie pointed out bubbles in the lake and inquired if it were fish as Jack had told her. "Perhaps," said Billingham without any great curiosity, but even a turtle made such a disturbance he explained.

She nodded and thought hard about what she could say to draw Miss Middleton into the conversation. The girl trailed behind them whispering to her companion. Past the secretive pair, Captain Murdock caught Sophie's attention as he stepped through the towering front door with Perlmutter at his heels. They did not look enthusiastic about joining the visitors, but Sophie gave him a little wave when he looked her way. She stumbled as Billingham pulled her along around the lake, her shoes sinking in the soft mud. The muck made it necessary to examine her sprigged muslin, hoping the light-colored hem did not stain or ruin the cherry-colored posies scattered across the fabric.

"Mi-ster-Bil-ling-ham!" came a shrill and commanding shout. Everyone turned toward the flowering shrubbery across the lawn at the sound of Miss Banks' cry. Billingham put a hand up to his eyes to shield them from sunbeams, but it looked more like a salute.

"My," he mumbled, and though it was all he said a rebellious giggle burst forth out of Sophie. She smothered it with a gloved hand.

Billingham stared in Miss Banks' direction; Devlin and Katherine stood beside her. Devlin had avoided Sophie since the night of music when she had given him the cut. He seemed over his sudden violent feelings of affection, although she felt his gaze when others were dominating the conversation. He liked to stare. Although she knew him to be handsome and acceptable to her family, she could not encourage such familiar behavior. It would ruin her.

She squinted. Miss Banks was pointing, and from what Sophie could see, there was a spider web of enormous size spread between the branches of the shrubbery. Miss Middleton made a small gasping noise. Sophie declared, "Ew," but Billingham laughed. "Imagine the size of the spinner that made that," he said with interest.

"I won't dare," said Sophie. She hesitated, not sure if she wanted to see it or not. Her companion dared, and he dashed off toward the hedges. Before she could decide whether to trail after him, Miss Middleton was dragged around her by Mrs. Fairfield, and they sped up to stay on Billingham's heels.

Sophie twirled the handle of her parasol. She felt sorry for the spider no matter how big or small, for the entire party was crowding up around its splendorous project with loud voices. Approaching footsteps from behind her made her look, and she found they belonged to the captain and his friend.

She pointed with her free hand. "They've found a monster over there, and I daresay one of them, I would gamble on Devlin, will put an end to it."

"Pity," answered Murdock. Perlmutter disagreed. He puffed out a breath of surprise and strode across the lawn, curious to see the novelty. Sophie had seen large spiders before, unfortunately. Both Richard and Jack were always happy to bring home the biggest ones they could find.

"It seems they grow as big as rats in these woods," she said. "I daresay one has lost his way."

"He won't last long if the gardener finds him."

"It's a shame," agreed Sophie, "since they catch nasty bugs and midgies. I don't mind them if they stay out of my room."

Murdock chuckled. His cheeks stretched into a smile that showed his dimple. "How practical of you." He swept his gaze across the lake then looked over his shoulder past the house to the land that rose up behind it. "They have fine stables here."

"They do, and you like to ride," said Sophie. "Does Billingham know? Should we go see? I haven't been inside the stables. I mean," she said in a quick turn, "Mr. Billingham did take me riding once, but they brought the mare out, and she was a small, timid thing."

"Of course she was," said Murdock.

Sophie frowned, and he smiled as if they shared a joke. He offered her his arm, and she took it, happy to get her shoes out of the muck and back onto the dry grass. They ambled up the drive then crossed over to the other side of the lawn to walk in the trimmed grass. Beside the house, there were patches of pink lilies with gaping blossoms big enough to drink up the sun. Sophie looked up at the fine masonry and said, "I daresay this was brick once upon a time."

"It was," agreed Murdock. "See how it does not quite meet at the corners?"

She bent back her head to look up. Despite its age, Oak Grove's facade was impressive and well maintained, almost too perfect, she decided. Across the dusty courtyard, they made their way to the stables, impressive buildings of red brick and dark-stained beams. Inside, it smelled almost pleasant, like leather and clean straw. The snorts and soft neighs of the horses sounded familiar and peaceful.

"Well maintained," said Murdock looking about.

"Yes. Again, almost perfect." They walked over to the mare Sophie had ridden, and she whispered her name as she stroked the horse gently between its eyes once it recognized her scent.

"Her name is Meriwether," she told Murdock. His hands were behind his back, and he seemed to be watching her rather than examining the adorable little horse she had introduced.

"I suppose she's far beneath your level of expertise, but I really did not mind her although I do think I could handle a gelding at least." Sophie chuckled to herself. With it, she swallowed a great big gulp of air and felt little specks of dust stick to the inside of her throat.

"I'm certain you could if you set your mind to it, Miss Crestwood."

Sophie coughed rather abruptly then smiled. "I'm so sorry. Are you teasing me? I can't be sure. You are unusually agreeable this morning."

"I am feeling agreeable," admitted the captain. "I've been at Pembroke too long without company besides the occasional trip to Portsmouth. The port is not pretty country like here at Oak Grove."

"You do not find Pembroke beautiful?" She stroked Meriwether, and the horse nuzzled her hand in search of a sweet.

"Oh, I'm becoming fond of it, but it's more wooded and less manicured than this great place."

"Much less work," replied Sophie, "though I do not mean to dismiss the task you have before you." Her nose tickled, and she rubbed it, aware of the warning.

"It's coming along. You'll be happy to know the stables are clean enough to be considered respectable, and the front gardens are tidy and trimmed."

"Your roses? I do look forward to seeing those again." When she said this, her heart sank a little bit. Papa had decreed she would not be at Pembroke, no less than Jack, and that meant perhaps she would not see the roses again after all.

"You have a deep affection for flowers."

"Oh, I do," she agreed, "especially roses. They're prim and elegant, yet hardy enough to weather drought and the bitter winters here. They're soft, like velvet, and they smell divine for days and days even after they've been cut. I love the idea that beautiful things can be strong, too."

Murdock stared like she'd said the most ridiculous thing he'd ever heard. He lifted his hand, and she moved back a slight bit. She thought he meant to put it to her cheek, but perhaps that was Devlin's doing, making her suspicious and prone to jump to conclusions over every glance from a man. Instead, Captain Murdock held out his hand to the mare, and she nuzzled it and gave a *crunch*.

"Oh," said Sophie, as her nose tingled, and she knew a sneeze would come. "You gave her a treat! Where—Where did you hide it?" She put a gloved hand over her mouth and sneezed hard and loud.

Murdock laughed.

She sniffed. "Oh dear, how barns make me sneeze."

"It's hardly a barn," he said, but he did not seem to mind it.

"I can't be too ashamed," she confessed. "You have seen me sneeze before and never with a handkerchief in time."

"Ruthlessly," he added.

She laughed as her nose tingled again. "You do not mind the clouds of dust. Did you have stables in the Indies?"

The smile on Murdock's face froze, and Sophie wondered if she had upset him. It melted away, and he said with a distant look in his eyes, "My father had a small stable for a time. He had to let it go."

"Oh, I'm sorry to hear it," she said, blushing at the recollection that Papa had said Sir Edward had gambled away all the family fortune.

"No matter," said Murdock in a somber tone. "I had a fine young thoroughbred for a time. He was a great beauty, so chestnut he was almost red." He gave Meriwether one final pat.

"I did not mean to pry," Sophie said in the quiet.

"You do not," Murdock said. "I have forgotten many things from when I was a boy. I've put them away and do not think of them often."

"Well, you have a fine stable of your own now, and you can have all the horses you please. Your bay is a fine piece of horseflesh I believe."

Murdock chuckled like her equine vocabulary amused him. "He is, and I have come to respect and admire him a great deal; when he does not think to throw me."

"Oh, yes," said Sophie with a giggle, remembering the first afternoon they'd met. "He does have a mind of his own, handsome or not."

Murdock smiled in agreement. "It is a great thing to find a beautiful creature with a strong mind."

"Yes," Sophie agreed, "some pretty things are just silly." She meant baubles, but for some shameful reason, Katherine came to her mind. Her nose tickled again. She had not realized her eyes had watered until a sticky tear escaped. "I must go out," she cried, "but do see their stallion, Whitehall, if the trainer will let you near. He is a great runner and jumper, too. Lady Mary, she—" Another sneeze interrupted their conversation. "Oh, do go see," she sputtered.

She darted out the nearest door to Murdock's laugh, a sound more vibrant and with more volume than she had ever heard from him before. She loitered out in the sun sniffling with the parasol twirling in her hand, wondering if she should join the others, go walking alone, or wait for Murdock to come out. She did not want him to think she expected him to endure her company all the time, for he had come to see Perlmutter and perhaps renew his family connections to Oak Grove.

A pleasing thought struck her mind. Should Lady Mary approve of Murdock and make it known, surely Papa would not be so suspicious that their neighbor had not given evidence of his pedigree, situation in the Indies, or even his income which seemed to be in no danger of short supply.

Murdock was a private man, she understood, who did not discuss his money or his injury, much less his talents, for he had said nothing in the conservatory his first evening although Sophie knew he saw the fine violin there and could play for them.

He is shy in this new world, she thought, and a bit sad, like Miss Middleton, only he is a man and not some young girl. She sniffled, found her handkerchief, and discreetly dabbed her nose.

Billingham caught her at it as he came bounding across the courtyard with a Newfoundland at his heels. He laughed, stopped, and picked up a stick and threw it, and the dog dashed off.

"What are you about? Do you want to go see the king of the forest?"

"Your giant old oak? I love that thing."

"Come." Billingham held out his hand.

The temptation to tarry under the great leafy branches of an ancient wonder even a crowd could not wrap their arms around was too great. She took his arm just as Murdock stepped from the stable and joined them.

"We're going to see a giant," said Sophie. "Do come with us."

He raised a brow, and she giggled knowing he was too proud to question such silliness.

"The king of the forest," Billingham explained. "It's the largest tree for miles, probably the biggest in England if not the second."

"I do not think my pace could keep up," said Murdock. He looked from Billingham to Sophie. "I've promised Perlmutter some practice with the revolvers. I'll have to ask you to pardon me." He gave a slight bow and turned on his heel.

At his abruptness, Billingham glanced at Sophie with concern in his blue eyes. She shrugged easily. "He has missed Perlmutter a great deal."

"Yes, I suppose." He offered his elbow, and twirling her parasol, Sophie trotted off with him to find relief from the overbearing sun.

MURDOCK DID PRACTICE for a time with his old friend. Sophie knew it because of the echoes of gunshots that rang out a great deal of the day. She discovered the other ladies had returned to the house to sit with Lady Mary for instruction and to exchange opinions on the papers Oak Grove received from Town.

They were of great interest to the others, especially Miss Banks, who seemed to know everyone who made mention, no matter whether it was scandalous or not. When the females went to their rooms to rest, Sophie heard the men wander into the great house loud, coarse, and probably, she imagined, sweaty. They were shamed by Lady Mary and so quietly went off to their quarters.

Sophie dozed for a time, wondering why Katherine did not join her, for they had not had a great deal of time to talk in the drawing room while Lady Mary read. Too much rested, bored, and anxious to find Billingham and talk of his books or other curiosities, Sophie tiptoed out of her room, wondering whether to explore the statues, the hall of paintings, or the library, for wherever she wandered, she always seemed to come across the estate's new owner.

If not him, Devlin crossed her path, always out of breath and in a hurry. He was polite but made no effort to see her alone, which she thought wise under the circumstances. She behaved somewhat cold toward him, but she respected the man for admiring her from a distance and trying as best he could to act in a proper way.

Yes, it was best they were not alone at all and did not spend much time together.

She drifted down the hall, her mind turning like a heavy wheel. Paintings twice her height hung from the walls, and aristocrats and nobles peered down at her with little interest. She did not find Billingham in the library, and shrugging it away, crept down the other wing to the conservatory.

With no one about, perhaps she could strum on the harp and sort out how to play it, if not enjoy the trills of the heavenly thing. She envied Miss Banks, she had to admit. Miss Banks had a great education and an abundance of musical talent. Although she rubbed on Sophie's nerves, the girl was confident and clever, something Sophie only pretended to be.

She pushed on the conservatory door and slipped inside, averting her eyes from a housemaid across the hall dusting an enormous vase that suited no real purpose. Sophie shook her head to herself, wondering at the immense collection in the house and the utility of it all, if any. The door clicked shut behind her, and she admired the gilded trim on the furniture, the cherry red cushions, and the fresh, bright white walls with their lovely acoustics.

The harp, a giant in its own right, reclined in the corner of the room, and she made a beeline for it, her fingers tingling with excitement to examine the strings and see what chords she could master.

A dark contrast across the room drew her gaze. Against one panel of the long, thick curtains drawn open on either side of the window, Murdock stood with his back to her, staring at the view. She froze, one foot dangling in the air just above the rug. She nearly lost her balance when his rich tone said with some amusement, "You are not disturbing me, Miss Crestwood."

"I'm so sorry. I should not even be about. It's almost tea time."

"Did you want to practice in private?" He turned from the window, and his gaze found hers.

"Yes," she said, then "no." She pointed at the harp. "I wanted to have a go at that."

"I would like to hear you."

"Oh, no," she said with a sigh and plopped down on the nearest sofa. "You would not. I do wish I had the talent for it, like Miss Banks."

"Yes," said Murdock, pressing his shoulder up against the window casing. "She professes a great many talents."

Sunbeams flickered around him, causing his hair to shimmer. Sophie felt she had no choice but to elaborate. "It's true. She is traveled and fashionable, and her French very fine."

"Her music is fine as well," added the captain, "although she is demanding on the instruments." His gaze shifted to the room's corner and the great harp.

"You play the violin," Sophie blurted. She bit her lip. Why did she speak before her mind considered what it would say?

Murdock answered her dangling question. "My parents wanted me to have exposure to art and culture. That meant music and dance instruction. Well, even some drawing, too, but I did not continue them once I—once I left my youth behind."

"You are a great talent, too," said Sophie with some degree of sadness. "How I admire that."

"Talent is a great deal more than an aptitude for art and music." Murdock turned back toward the window.

Sophie's heart felt heavy. He knew, she realized, that she had little to offer beyond the ordinary and was just being kind. She had no great abilities, money, or connections beyond Lady Mary to recommend her. Why had she come to Oak Grove at all?

"I do not have any exceptional proficiencies," she acknowledged with a thudding heart. "I do know I am tolerable on the pianoforte and my watercolors are not laughable. Well, not too much. I embroider lovely pillows with Mama, but hers are better. I don't have a flair for matching colors, and I dare not sing... Jack has told you I'm sure."

"That you sing like a toad? No, he has not."

"What?" Laughter surged out of her, and Sophie cupped both hands over her mouth to muffle the burst of the sound.

Murdock looked around from the window again, smiling so wide the corners of his mouth almost touched the perfect apples of his cheeks. Mischief flickered in his eyes. "He was a bit more detailed in his description, but I will spare you his schoolboy vulgarity."

"I can just imagine it," Sophie said with a sigh. "You see, I am quite humble, Captain Murdock, and Jack keeps me so."

"That he does."

"You are, too," Sophie said, "for you have said nothing to anyone about your musical abilities."

He shook his head. "I find scrutiny unbearable less I am found wanting."

"That is true for us all," protested Sophie.

He raised one shoulder in a sharp jerk. "I find no reason to suffer through an examination of my talents unless there is a purpose."

Sophie pressed her lips together in a grim line to stop from frowning. Clasping her hands together, she said, "I do wish you would consider it here. You play beautifully. It entrances me."

"Yes, as I recall," he answered with a small grin.

Her cheeks warmed. "Everyone would be impressed."

The sound of the conservatory doors sweeping across the polished wood floors stole her attention. Billingham strolled through, saw Murdock first, and then caught sight of Sophie resting comfortably on the long sofa. He stopped, looked from one to the other, and the small curl bounced on his wide forehead as he said, "My apologies, am I interrupting?"

"No," said Sophie with a welcoming smile, "you are not." She glanced at the captain who seemed to agree with her. "Come sit with us, Mr. Billingham, we are talking about music."

"Oh, music. That is not too dull then, Miss Crestwood," he answered. "I am weary of all of this play practice and sporting. I shall be healthy as an ox when I return to Town, and I resent it."

"I did not think you were fond of it," she teased, "music that is."

"Oh, I don't mind it, but it depends on the musician." He grinned. "What do you enjoy, Captain?"

"Strings," Murdock answered, then shifted his attention toward the open doors. "If you would like to keep Miss Crestwood company, I have promised Perlmutter a bout of fencing in the courtyard."

"Capital of you to keep him fresh," Billingham said. "I understand you're quite skilled."

Murdock dipped his chin. "Generous of you to say." He departed, rather fast, like he was relieved to be let out of the music room to more interesting pursuits. Sophie noted only a slight hesitation in his gait, an almost twisting outward of his foot to compensate for some discomfort in his knee, and yet it did not influence the sudden emptiness once he departed. He had a force about him, and when he left a room the air felt strangely wanting.

"Pity his defect," said Billingham in a low tone when the door shut.

She looked up in a sweeping motion, surprised he had noticed it. "Captain Murdock has made quite the recovery since I first saw him."

"Yes. Perlmutter tells me he nearly lost his life."

Sophie angled herself toward him. Billingham excused himself from standing and sank back into a tufted red chair; a familiar and comfortable repose he assumed when they were alone together.

"Perlmutter has told me very little," she admitted. Curiosity came over her with such force she almost moved across the room to sit beside Billingham to extract every detail that he knew. She had not found much time to talk with Perlmutter since his arrival, in fact, he seemed to avoid her, although he was polite and agreeable in her company.

"It was a horrible affair. I did not see it in the papers, but I don't read the naval news with any regularity. The way I hear it, it made only a small mention, seeing it was not a ship of the line." Billingham chewed his lip and reflected.

With prodigious patience, Sophie said, "What was the story then? He had a ship, I know. I don't think he has one now. Did he sell it?"

Billingham shook his head. "It was destroyed and most his crew along with it. He survived."

"I'm relieved he did," Sophie said in rebellion. "He was in trade, I presume? A merchant ship? Did his family own a fleet of them or was it a ship of leisure?"

"Leisure?" Billingham chuckled. "You don't know then, do you? The way Devlin speaks I thought you did, but you ask so many questions."

Sophie stiffened. "Do not say he was a pirate." She clenched her jaw, preparing herself not to believe a word of it. "I have heard enough of those silly stories, and besides, you did say you could not believe it."

Billingham studied her with an air of decided admiration that relaxed the band of constriction around her chest. "You are quite the champion, aren't you? I would that I had such a loyal friend."

"Was he?" she said in a small voice. Her question seemed to echo around the room like the tinkling chime made by a fingertip when rubbed around the mouth of a crystal glass.

"I'm sorry to tell you the rumors are not all without merit. From what I know, and not from Devlin, Murdock is a privateer, quite the rogue if you ask the French, and even the Americans. He comes from noble stock, you already know, but his father squandered away his inheritance, at least in the Caribbean. I guess he chose the sea to recoup his losses, and... well, when one has lost everything, one has nothing to lose."

Billingham's full lips sank down into a dull frown. "Except a ship and many men, in this instance," he amended.

Sophie swallowed. Her heart beat so hard in her chest she could feel it pulsating in her ears. The room became too quiet. She stared down at her thumbs crossed one over the other and rubbed them together. "I do not find him avaricious," was all she could think to say.

After a silence, too long for her liking, Billingham answered, "His pride got the better of him I suppose, to take on a French 54, for that is as Perlmutter tells it."

Sophie felt ashamed and a growing resentment for the officer. "Perlmutter cannot exactly know," she said in Murdock's defense, "he was not there himself."

"Yes, but his cousin was a great beloved friend, William Cottle. He was Murdock's lieutenant and very best friend, until his untimely death that day. The captain lost his best mate, his crew, his ship, and nearly a limb. Now he has come home to nothing more than a run-down estate and a family name shadowed by tragedy."

"How sad," Sophie said in the quiet, almost choking on her words.

Billingham sighed. "Indeed." He looked up and said with some peculiar approval, "At least he does have a great deal of money from his... privateering." He chuckled to himself, and Sophie grimaced.

CHAPTER ELEVEN

Tonight is the play," complained Katherine at supper. "You did not come to practice again." Sophie expected her to lean across the table and chide her until it became intolerable, but she did not. Instead, Katherine turned to Devlin beside her. "Did she not miss the best rehearsal yet?"

Devlin glanced at Sophie then around the table at the others. That she had hurt him pained her. Perhaps she had been prudish. She'd never been kissed, never done anything so shocking, and he hadn't hinted at any feelings before it happened. The fetching young man swallowed then said, "She did," serious for the moment. "We are all as true to character as we can be and know all our lines."

"I know mine, too," Sophie assured them. She looked at Lady Mary, observing the table's conversation from the head seat. Her eyes watched Sophie for a reassurance that she would pull her weight. "I have little to do," Sophie continued, "why, just a line here and there, and then a tragic death scene."

"You die so well," Miss Banks said with too much sincerity. "You are quite convincing. Isn't she, Mr. Byers?"

At the end of the table, speaking in quiet tones with Miss Middleton and her chaperone, Byers said, "What? Oh, yes, Miss Banks," then went back to his monologue.

Katherine giggled, and Sophie smiled back. "You'll see," Katherine warned in a singsong voice, "we have practiced all week, and you will be sorry you idled away your afternoons."

"At least she's well rested," Billingham said with a wink. Sophie bit her bottom lip to keep from smiling. Rested, indeed. Music and talks were better than rehearsals after all.

They did not tarry long in the drawing room after supper. At Lady Mary's request, they took coffee in the second ballroom and discussed the modest and private ball to celebrate the end of their stay at Oak Grove.

The rules were laid out for what Lady Mary expected of them, and she made it clear there would be no contests in the maze or walks in the gardens during the fireworks.

"It's dangerous," she said with a smile. The chaperones in the room sniffed. "It will be too dark and the explosions close and loud. I insist everyone stay together and in view of the house." She smiled at each of them, her gaze bobbing across the room. It rested on Katherine longer than the rest of the ladies until her cheeks became pink. Sophie put a hand on Katherine's arm. "You won't leave my side?"

"Of course I won't, silly," she promised. "I don't want to be shot."

The gentlemen announced themselves by way of a rather loud stampede, moving into the ballroom where a small stage had been erected. Sophie had watched Billingham direct the servants before supper, to make sure chairs for the audience were lined up in neat rows with good views.

The number of spectators would be modest. Only Lady Mary, Miss Middleton, Mr. Byers, Captain Murdock, and the chaperones would see the play in all its entirety. The servants, too, peeking footmen, and giggling housemaids would also watch when they had the opportunity.

Wrapped in her lavender shawl and a makeshift costume, Sophie whirled out onto the stage with great flair, determined to make her friends believe she was a poor orphan. When she was massacred by the villainous Devlin, she stumbled back with such accomplishment, it became a real tumble, and she fell to the stage floor with a loud thump. She gave a little hiccup for effect and then lolled her head to the side.

From the audience, the ladies clapped with great enthusiasm, their *oohs* rising to Sophie's ears, and from behind the curtains, she heard Katherine and Miss Banks laughing so hard behind their hands that someone had to shush them. A curtain dropped, and she rolled up to her knees, smiling in satisfaction.

Devlin brushed by, ready for his next act, his murder of her complete. "You did very well, Mr. Devlin," she said and smiled at him, forgiving him fully for his former indiscretion.

In a quiet voice, he answered, "I hope I was not too violent."

"You were not, and if you were I would completely forgive you."

"I'm glad of it." He smiled back, studying her until the curtain began to rise. He settled an old top hat back on his head as she hurried off the stage.

"No harm done," she said to herself.

They could set aside the awkwardness and be friends again. Gripping the soft velvet curtains behind her, she watched him from the side of the stage and breathed in a deep sigh of relief. Perhaps now he could reflect on whether he really cared for her, and maybe she would give him another chance. He was a happy fellow, and the play and most of the fun at Oak Grove would not have been at all if it weren't for him. Well, and for Billingham, she amended.

She peeked between the open folds of the curtain, careful to pull each side down around her cheeks. Lady Mary was wide-eyed, engrossed in the final violent scenes of their theatrical. One of the chaperones held a handkerchief over her mouth like she might scream. Captain Murdock, expressionless except for a glint of amusement in his eyes, looked back and forth across the stage like they were a cast of idiots.

His gaze came to rest on the long, overhead rod that held the curtains over the makeshift stage. He followed the seam down until it stopped where she was hidden. Their eyes met, and he grinned at her, an unexpected look that made his face light up, but then he went back to studying the gleaming candles overhead. Sophie's heart fluttered. She put a hand on her chest to feel the tremors and drew a long breath. He made her nervous, that was all. He had spied her spying.

After Devlin's final lines and the victorious Miss Banks took him down, the small ballroom broke into applause. Everyone came from behind the curtains and cheered. Sophie giggled at Katherine's little jig of joy, looking to see if it shocked Lady Mary, and she laughed out loud when Devlin began to pump his arms and dance around the stage in little circles.

The servants cheered. It filled her heart with a strange sort of giddy happiness. Sophie clapped her hands until they stung from her enthusiasm. She looked down, expecting them to be scarlet and swollen, but saw instead she had moved too close to the edge of the stage. She stumbled back, tripped into the curtains, and reached for them with frantic fingers to keep from falling on her backside.

The curtain in her grip went limp, and she continued to fall backward in slow motion. At the same time, she saw Captain Murdock in mid-air, leaping over chairs to help her. How kind, she thought, as she watched the ornate ceiling pass by, aware she would land flat on her back and that something was coming at her in a fast, broad slash.

A scream and a great many gasps echoed in her ears, even as her head slammed into the hard planks of the stage. It came from both sides, pain in her shoulders and the back of her head, and then a crushing weight across her chest like a heavy oak had fallen on top of her.

When the confusion cleared, her eyes streamed with unwelcome tears and a circle of voyeurs stood around her, their mouths agape. Katherine had a hand over her mouth. Sophie looked down and realized it was not a tree or even the curtains on top of her, but Captain Murdock. He raised his head and pushed himself up.

"Are you hurt?" His voice sounded heavy with concern but mild with tenderness. She tried to shake her head, but couldn't. He stumbled to his feet and so clumsily he almost fell again, but Billingham reached out an arm and helped him up.

"Good show," he said in a heartfelt compliment, "she would have been knocked senseless had it hit her head."

Ignoring him, Captain Murdock called out, "Miss Crestwood is hurt. She needs a doctor. Lady Mary?"

"Sophie!" Katherine cried, coming alive as she dropped to her knees.

"Give her room," Murdock ordered. He dropped back to the floor and put a warm hand under Sophie's neck. "Does that pain you?"

"I don't think so," Sophie said with courage. She stared into his dazzling green eyes, the color of a lake's shallows.

"Poor Miss Crestwood," Miss Banks bellowed.

Sophie tried to move her head again, and it obeyed although it wasn't comfortable. "I think I'm not hurt," she said with as much pluck as she could muster. Captain Murdock's tight jaw and clenched teeth gave him a look of pain that disappeared like a puff of smoke once she had his attention. He must have felt horrible she'd nearly been hit. His face looked pale.

"Miss Crestwood, that iron curtain rod nearly came down on your head." Miss Banks sounded impressed. "You pulled too hard on the curtains."

Sophie realized that if Captain Murdock had not noticed it falling, it might have killed her. Billingham patted him on the back, put an arm around him, and tried to lead him away. Sophie forced herself to rise.

"Do not get up," ordered Miss Banks.

Katherine put an arm around Sophie's shoulders and eased her into a sitting position. A small pucker in the shoulder seam of her dress had come undone, and she stared through the little hole noticing with regret the petticoat underneath.

"I am not hurt," she said out loud. "I only fell and had a fright when the Captain shielded me from that monstrous thing." She looked beyond Katherine at the heavy rod laying half on and half off the stage. It would have crushed in her brains for sure.

The young ladies helped her to her feet.

"Miss Crestwood," said Lady Mary from the foot at the stage, "allow Mr. Devlin to walk you to your room, and Miss Blackburn, too." She nodded at Katherine to accentuate her order. "I will call for my physician, and we will have a look."

"Oh, no, your ladyship," pleaded Sophie, "I am quite well." She moved Katherine's hand off her shoulder. "My pride is all that's wounded."

She smiled to make sure her hostess understood she meant it, but the lady replied, "You must lie down anyway, it would please me. I will call for the doctor just to be sure." She glanced out through the ballroom doors then back at Sophie. "Send for me if you need anything at all." With that, she left in an abrupt swish of silks.

The party moved down into the audience's chairs that were rearranged into a small circle. Servants brought in punch and biscuits and after a few minutes to Sophie's relief, it was as if nothing had happened at all. They chuckled over Sophie's performance and applauded Devlin once more.

He gave a little bow. "I could not have done it without my comrades in arms, especially our merciless Perlmutter." They all had a laugh at the lieutenant's expense. He flushed. "I am not a great actor," he admitted, "but I gave my best."

"You did indeed," Katherine said, and Sophie nodded in agreement. He excused himself, claiming he must find Captain Murdock and Billingham, but the rest of the party remained in the soft covered chairs, chatting in the waning candlelight. Even Miss Middleton was full of compliments for each cast member.

"You should have joined us," Miss Banks chided the girl, then took a small nip out of her biscuit that made Sophie think of a pecking bird.

Miss Middleton gave a little shake of her head. "My voice does not carry, but I will say," she smiled, "I am feeling less shy."

This was a cheerful thought, decided Sophie. "I wish Captain Murdock would have tried a role," she remarked to no one in particular. Everyone hesitated, but no one agreed. "Well," she said, looking around the room with obstinacy, "he may not have a loud voice, but it can be commanding."

"To be sure," Miss Banks said, "at least he made it so when he saw you were hurt. He quite took things over." She glanced over her shoulder like she wanted to make sure he was not in the room. Then her features became proper and stiff as they did when she presided over the conversation. "Honestly, he is better suited for a deck than a stage," she sniffed, "certainly not for a gathering such as this."

Sophie nearly choked on a swell of offense. It came out half a gasp and half a cough. "Perlmutter is a lieutenant, and he is good company, on the stage and for a party." She tamped down a flicker of ire that stirred in her belly. Miss Middleton's chaperone rose and held out an arm so that her charge would follow her out.

Devlin said, "I must agree with Miss Banks. He is a hard and seasoned man, and you know..."

"Know what?" demanded Sophie.

Beside Devlin, Katherine sat up straight in her chair and pressed her knees together. Sophie thought she might put her hand on his knee to quiet him.

"Well," said Devlin, for Katherine did nothing to stop him, "it is widely known the family lost everything in St. Kitts. His father was a drunkard, and some say mad."

Sophie stared, aghast he would say such things before others. He gazed at her and continued in an almost apologetic tone: "The captain was in trade or shipping; some kind of activity and lost that, too. Pembroke is in disrepair, and yet somehow despite his luck, he has brought with him an inexplicable great deal of income."

The ladies in the circle said nothing. Some nodded their heads as if they already knew these things. Sophie rose to her feet. "He is not hard or seasoned. He was a good captain and had some misfortunes. Captain Murdock is a gentleman and has been very kind to my family."

"Misfortunes in shipping," Miss Banks snorted. "Really, Mr. Devlin, my family is in shipping. Misfortune does not make you rich. Do you not think we would know of him? He has nothing to do with either of the India trading companies. His kind of shipping and his kind of rank are most likely not even—" she looked around the room and said in a hushed tone, "legal."

Katherine put a hand over her mouth. The other ladies in the room gasped. Sophie glared at Miss Banks, then at Devlin. "He's as legitimate as Perlmutter," she rallied.

"He is not," argued Devlin. "He's an acquaintance of the lieutenant, an old friend, but I'm sorry, Miss Crestwood, Miss Banks is right. He is not in good standing with anyone in Cheapside or even Guildford. He did not come by his fortune in trade or through inheritance. We know what that means." He gave a small laugh that tried to sound sympathetic, but it was cruel and mean. "He is not the best neighbor to have adjoined to Leatherbury. I must say so and with deep regret, too."

Sophie thought she might box his ears. "Captain Murdock is a gentleman's son, a good man, and a..."

Everyone stared. "A what?" asked Miss Banks, in a sly voice that hinted she already had an answer. She gazed at Sophie, her lips pouting like she wanted a kiss. Sophie wanted to slap them.

"How dare you all." Sophie looked to Katherine for support, but her friend said nothing. Instead, she looked away with a red face and would not meet her stare.

Sophie's hands clenched again. She could not say he was a privateer, even though she trusted Billingham's account. "Of all the heartless insinuations, you know nothing of what you speak. Is this what they say in Town, and you help spread it from county to county before you even know if it's true?"

Those in the circle either stared at the floor or over Sophie's shoulder beyond the ballroom doors. Not one of them would meet her eye.

"I won't listen to another word of it," she scolded and spun on her heel and stomped out.

SHE COULD NOT BEAR the idea of going to breakfast the next morning and requested it brought to her room. Before it arrived, Katherine let herself in. She looked rather shamefaced; like a puppy caught with a slipper in its mouth. She sat on the edge of Sophie's bed.

"I thought I would check on you before I went down." She pulled at a thread on the seam of her gown. "Are you coming? You will be agreeable today, won't you?"

"Agreeable?" Sophie pulled the thin blanket up to her chin. "Do you mean that I should not defend Captain Murdock?"

"Well, yes." Katherine raised her brows with a shake of her head. "It was all very contrary last night, and everyone felt uncomfortable. I know you speak your mind when you are confident in your opinions, Sophie, but we should not make a scene, not here at Oak Grove."

"You're offended?" Sophie could not force herself to sound less disdained. "They were speaking nonsense about Captain Murdock."

"It's not nonsense if everyone knows it."

Sophie dropped her fisted sheets in her lap. "It is nonsense. If it's not true, it's not true, and why spread it about?"

Katherine looked at her with clouded eyes. "I think it may be true."

"Don't say that."

"I think you're confused. You're too kind and you... hit your head. He did save you, and it was very gallant, but you can't spend every moment with Captain Murdock while we are here."

"I divide my time equally with everyone. I even sat by Mr. Byers at cards yesterday, and I joined Devlin later."

"Yes, you do all that very well," agreed Katherine, "but when we are free to spend time as we choose, you are always in Murdock's company since he has come; not like before when you spent time with the rest of us."

Sophie thought hard and could not agree with her. "I don't see it that way. He is my neighbor and friend, and he is..." she thought of him leaping over the chairs toward her as she fell and then his smile at the window in the conservatory. "He's no pirate," she finished in a stubborn tone, aware her cheeks had warmed to a blush. She glanced up at Katherine through her lashes.

Her friend stared in disbelief. "Your father will not like it, and Lady Mary hopes you are as fond of her nephew as he is you." Katherine stood. "Don't be a fool, Sophie."

Sophie jerked her gaze up in surprise.

Katherine stared back. "I won't be, for I cannot. I'm just a vicar's daughter. Please, do not ruin this for me." She moved toward the door in slow but determined steps. Before walking out, she looked back. "I beg of you, speak nothing more in defense of Captain Murdock. Just say nothing at all, and enjoy your time with Mr. Billingham. We leave in only two days. "

And then what? wondered Sophie bitterly once the door shut.

SOPHIE FORCED HERSELF to join the ladies in the drawing room. They were making bets on the sporting events the gentlemen had been practicing in preparation for a final contest. With the windows wide open and a small breeze whooshing in and out, the mood was friendly and filled with anticipation. Outdoors, the men called back and forth, teasing and challenging one another. Their voices carried on the wind.

"Oh," exclaimed a chaperone. "They have been at it all week. If not dallying in the ballroom for the play, it's been walking or running or throwing things, and shooting, too."

Sophie did not notice Captain Murdock, and no one mentioned his name.

"Miss Crestwood?" Lady Mary stood and addressed Sophie. "I am going to walk in my rose garden for a moment's peace. I have seen you admire it, and the arbor, too. Do come along and keep me company."

Sophie rose and curtsied. The other young ladies in the room had ignored her all morning. She watched her ladyship's back turn and followed her out, not looking to the left or to the right; not glancing to see if Miss Banks was jealous she'd been singled out by the mistress of Oak Grove, and not caring if Katherine Blackburn fell right out of the window from where she leaned over and flirted.

There came a flurry of activity as bonnets and parasols were brought downstairs to the glass doors just off of Lady Mary's private breakfast parlor. Once they were adequately protected from the sun, her ladyship took Sophie by the arm and led her out of doors.

The rose gardens at Oak Grove were extraordinary. Varieties of roses in different sizes bordered pathways leading past thriving bushes of pink and salmon; then it turned past corners into walkways of white and yellow blooms. There were even plum, lavender, and vibrant orange roses. It was breathtaking, and the air smelled heady and thick with perfume.

Sophie sighed with contentment, enjoying the silence between Lady Mary and herself. She admired a long, overhead arbor with thick climbing vines that held small, wild looking blood-colored roses. They formed a shaded tunnel of elegance and privacy.

"Oh," she said at last, unable to hold her tongue, "I do admire your arbor. The time and skill it must take to grow something so fine."

"It is a great many years old," said Lady Mary. "Generations." Her reedy form and unruly petite curls seemed to float down the path. "I cannot take credit for it. I only see it is tended, and I take every opportunity to enjoy and share it, too. It's a sad sight in the winter, though; a brown, withered spectacle that troubles me so much I can't bear to look upon it with any degree of pleasure."

Sophie tried to imagine it in January.

"I do not like growing old," the woman beside her said.

Sophie looked up in surprise. She would have laughed if it had not been Lady Mary.

"You're so..."

"Good at it?" The lady's eyes twinkled.

"No," said Sophie with a flush. "I only meant you are wise and gracious, and very elegant, too, like your roses." She finished with a stammer, and Lady Mary laughed.

"Oh, to be young and so full of enthusiasm, my girl." She sighed and said, "Come," leading her from underneath the rose tunnel down a path with pastel blooms. "There is something I want to show you."

They walked side by side between the rows. Sophie tingled with curiosity. Lady Mary stopped before an enormous, manicured patch of white roses. They were delicate and soft, with a touch of soft yellow in the centers. The plants were so established and in good health that the blooms were the size of dessert plates.

"The Bengal roses?" said Sophie. "It looks like a cloud, and these look just like Mama's roses." She leaned over to smell one and said in surprise, "They smell just alike, too."

"Yes," said Lady Mary with a smile, "they are related."

"Our roses and yours? I had no idea. Did you give a cutting to Mama?"

Lady Mary pressed her lips together and stared at Sophie with a level brow. The meaningful look made her uneasy.

"I am not shocked you do not know, although I thought you might." Lady Mary reached out her gloved fingers and plucked a fading petal from its parent.

"I know they live almost forever," said Sophie. "I do love them. How *did* your roses get to Leatherbury?"

"These roses belonged to my sister. You may not remember her."

Sophie shook her head. "I saw her once when I was a child."

"She asked me to plant these here."

"Did she get them from my mother?"

"No," Lady Mary replied. "Both my sister's roses and your mother's are from Pembroke."

Sophie's head snapped back in surprise. "How... I mean... Yes, I have seen the white roses at Pembroke. Captain Murdock cleaned up the front gardens all around his fountain. It's a great fountain, and the roses are pruned back and look very well. But how did—"

She stopped, aware she had run away with her thoughts and out loud, too. Grimacing, she waited for Lady Mary to speak.

Lady Mary gave her a patient smile. She took Sophie's arm and with one last glance at the flourishing bushes, led her away. "Has your mother ever spoken about Captain Murdock's father, Sir Edward?"

"A little, I suppose."

"I mean about their flirtation."

Sophie stopped with a jerk. "Flirtation," she gasped, "my mama?"

Lady Mary laughed. She looked over her shoulder to see if she had been heard then urged Sophie to follow her on. "My dear, the young think they are the only ones who ever make romance."

"Mama." Sophie stared at the lady next to her, waiting for a signal their conversation was a joke.

"Oh, Sir Edward, that charming devil," said her ladyship instead. She looked into the distance to gather some memory there. "He was a happy, cheerful sort, much like my Henry. Everyone wanted to be his friend, and every lady wanted to be his wife."

She chuckled in a soft way. "He did not mean to be a flirt. I sincerely don't believe he did, but he saw the good in everyone, much like you, Sophie, and with no manipulation on his part he made everyone fall in love with him."

"My mother?" Sophie's mind reeled over the idea that Mama had loved anyone other than Papa. "I knew she found him handsome, and that she went to balls, but..."

"Your mama met Sir Edward in Town and fell head over heels for him. She soon realized he did not return her affection to the same degree, and so we found her someone else just as suitable."

"Papa?"

"Yes, he was quite taken with her good looks. That she did not have a title or any money did not trouble him at all."

"He had Leatherbury," murmured Sophie.

"Yes," said her ladyship, "and it made very good sense to her. She became pragmatic after losing her heart to someone above her that would not have her. Your Papa was a sensible choice."

"I can hardly imagine Papa taken with anyone."

"Oh," said Lady Mary with a chuckle, "he was quite the romantic in his day. Most young men are, especially those with some living promised to them. True, he did not marry up to expand his holdings, but he married for love and that is not always a given to everyone, my dear."

"People must have thought he was foolish," said Sophie, as small parts of the curious relationship between her parents made more sense to her. It was almost clear enough for her to see, but not quite.

"Can you blame him?" Lady Mary tapped Sophie on the shoulder with the tip of her parasol. "Your mama moved into Leatherbury and brought roses from her family home that had been given to her by another man."

"How did your sister come to have them?"

"Oh," said Lady Mary, "Edward was not the first Murdock to give roses to his sweethearts. His father was so proud of his cuttings from India—the Murdocks do love to travel—that when he could share them with others he did so to any that admired them.

"I see," said Sophie, "so there must be Bengal roses throughout the county and maybe even more." The idea of it made her giggle. She quieted herself with a glove to her lips. Once composed, she inquired, "You do not mind that your sister... that she..."

"Was jilted by a Murdock, too?" Lady Mary laughed. "Oh no, I cannot do that. I have known three generations of Murdocks. I knew Sir Edward well. He had a good heart. It's a shame he lost almost everything in his grief, but it's admirable in a way. Once he loved, it was etched into his heart like the stones of Pembroke. When his first wife died it became a dark and disagreeable time for the family. She was a lovely little bloom herself from Hereford. Those were dark times for Pembroke then. They lost a child, and she went, too, and before long he packed up and sailed to the Indies to oversee the plantations there."

"Sugar," Sophie assumed.

"Oh yes, that's how most of these old houses stand today. I do not claim to understand it all and feel relief that my income is not dependent on such things. Sir Edward left a dark scene here, but then he found himself in a strange land where he saw firsthand how his living was brought in on the backs and lives of human chattel."

Sophie's nose wrinkled. "It's a shame he did not understand it beforehand, and to lose a second wife again. Poor Captain Murdock grew up without a mother after a time." She swallowed and confessed, "I really do not think of him as poor Captain Murdock, although I say it often. He's rather a strong sort."

"He is. You may not know that he injured his knee last night when he bolted over the chairs to reach you. I called the physician for him, and used you for the excuse."

Sophie felt her eyes widen in concern. "Oh no, and he had been doing so well. I hope it's not too serious." She glanced at Lady Mary and asked with some reluctance, "Have you heard what they say about him?"

"Murdock? Oh, yes, of course. Utter flimflam," the woman decreed. "We all must take up some occupation or another to survive. His father may have been titled, but he was terrible with money. Captain Murdock had to make a living some way once the income was gone. There isn't much choice on the far side of the world."

"If left with no choice I suppose... trade will do," said Sophie. She cleared her throat and peeked at Lady Mary from the corner of her eye.

"You mean shipping? Oh, no my dear, he had a letter of marque."

"You know about it," said Sophie in surprise.

"I do. His father and I were good friends. I wrote him often to offer my advice and warn him of his foolish, destructive habits, and he did use my connections for Captain Murdock when he first chose the Royal Navy."

Sophie's mouth made a small 'o'. Her mind could hardly keep up with her companion's revelations. "That's why you welcomed him here."

Lady Mary snorted. "Who do you think Murdock wrote for advisement when he considered returning to England? I practically invited him to this house party myself. Perlmutter made no effort, and since my Henry hardly knew of him, he did not. At first, I did not think of it, for it made the numbers uneven, but then I changed my mind and insisted that he come. No good can come of hiding away in that crumbling old place like his father did."

Sophie lifted her chin. "I'm glad you did, and it was very good of your nephew to accept him."

"I'm glad you approve, and I must compliment you on your defense of him last evening. Oh, do not be surprised. Of course, I would hear of it. People are strange, Sophie dear. They hear what they want to hear, see what they want to see, and believe whatever sounds the most exciting at the time."

"I'm glad you know the truth. I never knew gossip could be so cruel."

"Did you not?" Lady Mary tilted her head. "Well, now you do, and it's something to be aware of my dear, to separate yourself from. It's a terrible habit and does not reflect well on anyone who takes pleasure in such a thing."

A flitting picture of Papa passed through her mind, but Sophie pushed it away. "Yes, your ladyship, I am ever mindful of it now. It is no mere game or way to pass the time."

"Good." Lady Mary patted her hand. "Now let me tell you something that is not gossip at all."

"What is that?" Sophie grinned in anticipation.

"Your friend, Miss Blackburn, has set her cap for that silly Mr. Devlin, and I fear she will face a great disappointment."

Sophie's smile slipped from her face, her initial amusement dampened by a splash of cold truths she had ignored for too long.

CHAPTER TWELVE

Cheers for the long-distance race could be heard when they returned to the house. Sophie ducked into the cool shadows of the hall outside of Lady Mary's breakfast parlor, fanning herself with the gloves she had removed. Overheated, she was not sure she wanted to join the others even though she'd wagered a little money. In her room, she wiped herself off with a cool towel and re-pinned a few limp curls before making her way down to the drawing room.

On the front lawn, Billingham appeared to be lining the men up for a final sprint. Sophie squinted down the long drive. It would be a quarter mile at the least, past the lake to the front of the drive that turned onto the grounds of Oak Grove. She did not spy Captain Murdock. He had obeyed his hostess's orders and kept to his room, probably with great frustration as there was no one for him to order about, nothing for him to see to repair, and not even a Jack Crestwood to pester him to fish or fence. She realized it was not his leg but his knee that once caused him to limp so, and that his attempts to save her onstage had injured it again.

A shot rang out, and off flew the runners. Beneath an awning on the lawn, Miss Middleton waved a stick festooned with ribbons, one of them bright silk like the ribbon around Billingham's waist. Katherine, Sophie noted, had a wand covered only in green ribbons like Devlin wore, and she bounced up and down like an excited puppy much to the irritation of the chaperones who could not see around her.

Sophie chuckled as the young ladies squealed. Perlmutter lost the advantage; his legs were too short, and it was Billingham and Devlin dashing down the drive for the finish. Sophie thought Katherine might throw herself at them as they crossed the line, and she cringed. Her old friend had been so adamant Sophie not come down to breakfast in a cross mood, yet she completely forgot herself when she became excited.

Devlin edged ahead, and Katherine whooped like a boy. He certainly thrilled her. Sophie frowned. It was good, she realized, she had not confided in her friend about his indiscretion in the maze. Katherine would have been disappointed and hurt, and maybe even angry with Sophie, not that she could have helped it.

Her line of thinking was a distraction from the clapping and encouragements. She watched Devlin cross the finish mark just a blink before his host, raise his hands in victory, and stumble to a slow walk shaking his fists in the air. Billingham staggered to a walk, too, gasping for breath. The other gentlemen slowed to a walk to the finish mark. Sophie gave one last shout for Byers who was folded over in half at the waist, his face red as beets. He looked like he might faint.

"There you are."

A voice below the window made her look. Sophie peered down and saw Billingham with his hand against the stonework, bracing up his frame. His face was flushed, but the relentless smile he kept beamed up at her. "I had no supporters," he complained. "Not a one!"

Sophie laughed. "That's not true."

"Oh," he shrugged, looking around, "maybe Miss Middleton, but Devlin has the crowd today. All of it."

"You jealous thing, you should have run faster."

"Yes, and walked and hopped and shot," he returned.

"I spent the morning with your aunt. I lost track of time in the gardens."

Billingham grinned. "What are sweating, sporting men to shrubs and flowers?"

"Not a great deal, I'm afraid," Sophie admitted with a laugh. "I did bet on you, Mr. Billingham, but I fear I have lost it all."

"I'll make it up to you." Billingham pushed away from the wall. "Come down," he said. "Come sit with us and have some punch."

She nodded in agreement. The book she had no intention of reading but had brought along should she need to look preoccupied, she left on a side table. Hurrying down the hall toward the staircase, she realized she did feel thirsty. It would be entertaining to hear Miss Banks' opinions of the day's events, and whom she had predicted would win. Did every girl and chaperone have her heart set on George Devlin?

Sophie shook her head. To think the host himself and heir to this great estate was no match for Devlin's looks and charms. She sighed, feeling somewhat flattered it was she who had turned Devlin's head after all, although he hid it well in public.

A presence across the hall caught her attention before she reached the top of the stairs. It was not a servant, but Captain Murdock, leaning hard on his cane outside the door to the small library. She stopped in surprise. "You should be in bed," she said, without considering where they stood.

He put a hand on the door like he meant to go in. "I have rested all the day long."

"They have finished their games at last," Sophie informed him. "I'm going out for punch." She motioned down the stairs, but he shook his head.

"It's too hot to sit outside like an invalid. I'll find a book to read; something quiet."

She nodded, her shoulders dropping in disappointment. He was not dressed for outside or company she supposed, in a loosely fastened waistcoat and shirt undone at the neck.

"I understand." Forgetting her intentions, she let go of the banister and walked around the staircase to meet him at the door. He paused, though he pushed the door open like he could not wait to sit some more. She stopped just close enough to reach out and touch his shoulder. His hand rested on the pommel of his guardian dragon.

"You have injured yourself, and it is all my fault."

The corners of Murdock's mouth turned up a bit, but the look was wry. "You are not at fault, Miss Crestwood. I simply saw the rod coming loose over your head and moved faster than my leg would go."

She chuckled. "Don't play valiant with me. You hurt your knee again. I see it is the same leg. Now you are back on your walking stick, and I don't like it. I feel horrible."

"You must not," he said. "It's only a small sprain."

His eyes were soft, holding her gaze with such a natural expression of familiarity she wanted to touch his hand. "Well then you are bruised for my sake and for my brains, so I thank you for it."

"I thought you might need them."

"Oh, did you?" Sophie laughed.

He smiled. "You are welcome to come in and read with me a spell. This library is better stocked than Pembroke."

She inclined her head just so and opened her mouth to accept, but Billingham's loud baying, much like a dog on the scent, echoed up the stairs. "Miss Crestwood," he called from somewhere below, "we are waiting for you."

"Oh, punch," Sophie said, feeling somewhat reluctant to return to Billingham and the others. "I did promise him I would take punch and hear all about the wins and losses."

"You did not attend the games?" Murdock glanced over his shoulder like he expected someone to come bolting up the stairs.

She shook her head. "No. Lady Mary asked me to join her in the gardens, and in truth, I did not mind." She thought of the Bengal roses and smiled to herself. "Your roses," she announced, "the white ones in your garden, they are... they are here, too."

Murdock's brow crinkled. "Are they?" She surmised he did not know why.

"Some just like them," she said in a casual tone. "I suppose they are a popular import. No matter. Are you sure you won't come out?"

He looked at the stairs, and it was obvious he was calculating their number. "I'm sure her ladyship will not like it, and I have no intention of offending her sensibilities."

Sophie pursed her lips but shook her head in agreement. "Nor should I—"

"Miss Crestwood!"

"—which means I should go down before Billingham hurts himself."

Murdock gave a soft, dry chuckle and swung the library door open all the way. "I will see you at supper then."

"You will," Sophie replied as she curtsied. The faint smile on her lips lingered long after the door shut behind her. She could not help it.

SOPHIE DID NOT WAKE to sunlight streaming through her window. Rather, a loud rumble jerked her up with a start. She groaned inwardly, for although the rain was needed, it would ruin Billingham's plans.

She almost crawled to her knees to pray, but instead, she stretched out with a groan beneath her blanket and muttered a request to heaven that the weather be agreeable by the ball. She then sat up with her mind whirling. Supper the night before had been chaotic. Devlin had flirted with her with no shame when no one was looking, and Captain Murdock sat across the table from her staring at his plate. He did not seem content with the seating arrangements, and there were moments it felt like he knew exactly what Devlin was playing at beside her.

Sophie shook off her dull mood. There was much to do, and the day would be fine if she made it so. She missed home, but she wanted to enjoy her last day at Oak Grove. It would be some time before she saw these acquaintances again. Of course, she must count Billingham as a new and good friend, and she did not mind Miss Banks or even Devlin so much if they would keep their opinions about Murdock to themselves. Her sharp retreat after the play had been forgotten. She hoped they had put their gossip behind them, too.

She washed and dressed, not concerned with taking too much care, for the wardrobe change in the afternoon would be more demanding with the dancing and celebrations to come. Her best morning dress with the red posies would do well enough. Before she left her room, the rain began to spatter on the window panes, and with a sigh, she went down for breakfast. It was already a lively affair, with Devlin laughing at Miss Banks' stories, and Katherine giggling at the pair of them.

Sophie smiled when Captain Murdock caught her eye. He seemed to enjoy listening to people converse and comfortable enough to say little unless he was asked a question. She knew he was a man of solid opinion if one took the time to talk with him. As proof of it, Perlmutter sat across from him speaking in a quiet tone.

Sophie took a seat beside Miss Banks, two chairs away from Murdock, her back to the window and the wet, dismal view.

"You look well rested," said Devlin in a teasing voice.

"I thought you would sleep the whole day through," added Katherine.

"When have you ever known me to sleep an entire day?" Sophie chided her. Aware of the captain so close; feeling him she realized, as much as seeing him, she tried to think of something to say whenever

Perlmutter took his next breath. Miss Banks riveted her gaze around to Sophie and cut in.

"Well, have you heard? The picnic is cancelled." She sounded irritated that Oak Grove did not control the weather.

Sophie looked about. "Where is Mr. Billingham? Has he gone anyway?" She grinned at her own joke, and Devlin laughed. He motioned toward the window. "I wouldn't put it past him, but no, he has other things to see to for tonight. Her ladyship will keep him preoccupied most of the morning."

"Then you must entertain us," said Katherine, and Miss Banks insisted, "Oh yes, Mr. Devlin, you must keep us from growing bored. We should have another play—" she glanced at Sophie "—one without any real tragedy of course."

"Or read," Katherine interrupted. She put a hand on Devlin's arm. "We do love to hear you read poetry." She beamed up at him, and he smiled at the compliment.

Sophie watched, amazed at Lady Mary's acuity. Katherine was quite a bold flirt in her own right, but perhaps Sophie had grown so used to it she did not see when it mattered. She almost flinched at what the others must think of her friend. Katherine had been invited by Lady Mary on Sophie's behalf and set her cap for the lively and soon to be very well-off George Devlin. Sophie glanced down to the other end of the table.

"Gibraltar," Perlmutter was saying, and Murdock lifted his chin in silent agreement. He cleared his throat, put down his fork, and said in a low tone, "If the admiral has his way we will all be in the channel, with or without illnesses and injuries."

Sophie's ears pricked up. "It would be well for me," murmured Perlmutter, "for no prey means no pay." He gave a dry laugh, then cutting it off, looked away.

Murdock said nothing. In fact, he looked uneasy. Glancing around the room he noticed Sophie listening and said to her, "You are disappointed the rain is here."

"Oh, no," she said, not completely honest but making every effort to be cheerful. "We must eat. If there's no rain, there's no breakfast." She motioned toward her toast. "No prey, no pay? Does that mean what I think it does?"

Perlmutter rose with a jerk, his plate clear.

"Oh, I'm sorry, I didn't mean to listen in."

"No bother, Miss Crestwood," he said with a placid smile. "I am only finished and off to see to my packing. Would you excuse me?"

She nodded, and he bowed and drifted away. The rest of the table's occupants, she realized, were listening, too. They looked curious about her question, or perhaps it was the answer.

Murdock scraped his plate like he was finished, but he was not. His cup steamed beside his half-eaten food.

"Did you know, Mr. Devlin, there is a great collection of sculptures upstairs?" Miss Banks moved the conversation off in another direction over the aroma of ham, toast, and roasted coffee beans. When the attention swung back to the other side of the table, Sophie stood up, moved her dishes down beside the captain, and sat beside him. No one seemed to notice except a footman who scrambled to help her before she made a mess of the place settings.

Murdock glanced at her but did not seem offended or annoyed he would not be left to the remainder of his meal alone.

"I apologize, I did not mean to pry. Was I out of turn?"

He half-smiled at her, but his eyes were distant. "You did not."

"I only was curious, what with Jack's interest in such affairs."

Murdock leaned his head close to hers. "I am going to have a stretch in the conservatory," he said, "and maybe listen to Miss Middleton if she is practicing early this morning. You are welcome to join me."

"She does play the pianoforte well," Sophie agreed. She looked down at her plate. "I'm not so hungry after all. Let's go find her."

They excused themselves from the dining room. Despite all the pleasure she had shared with these guests over the past few weeks, the sudden quiet that dropped over the room when Sophie rose to leave with Captain Murdock felt awkward. It seemed like minds were whirling away, forming opinions or perhaps, restraining themselves from commenting on their withdrawal from the room together.

She shrugged her shoulders as she went out the opened door. Ahead of her, Captain Murdock hesitated then looked back, and she hurried a few steps ahead, so they could walk up the staircase together.

On their way up, she told the captain, "You seem less enthusiastic about Oak Grove than you did upon your arrival. I am still sorry I put you in a position to hurt yourself after the play."

"You must not burden yourself with guilt, Miss Crestwood. It was instinct, and I would have done it for anyone."

"Oh," she said in a small voice. Her mind sifted for meaning in his words.

Gripping the handrail to wrench himself up each step, Murdock held out his other elbow for Sophie to hold. She took it, smiled at him, and in a subtle manner, gave him a little lift with each hop he took up the stairs.

"Was it a vulgar thing?" she asked when sure no one would hear, "to ask about the expression?"

"No prey, no pay?" Murdock chuckled. "It's a common expression, my—Miss Crestwood."

"I don't suppose there's anything wrong with praying for income. We all have to manage it one way or the other I suppose."

He glanced at her with a wide smile like she was amusing. They reached the top of the stairs, and he breathed a heavy sigh of relief.

"Just a few more steps." She pointed toward the conservatory doors, "then you can sprawl out on the sofa with the view of the grounds and listen to something better than my questions."

He chuckled again. As he pushed open the conservatory door for her, he said, "I do not mind your questions. I find you have a unique perspective on the most common of things."

"Like what?"

He smiled but did not answer. When the door shut behind them, it became clear Miss Middleton was not practicing. Murdock continued toward the sofa she had recommended. "You do know I was not referring to prayer," he explained. "No *prey*, no pay means that there is no income without a prize to take. The lieutenant, for instance, relies on being assigned to a good captain and a capable ship. Prize money is the only way to make any real income in the Navy."

"I see," said Sophie thinking. "You meant prey as in... well, as in... prisoners?"

Murdock shrugged. "Targets, I suppose, but as prisoner is a better way to end it all."

"Oh. So Perlmutter is not happy to be back in England then?"

"Not very much," said Murdock with a sharp intake of breath as he dropped down to sit. "Shore leave is half pay."

She almost sat beside him, but crossed the rug and sat in Billingham's favorite tufted chair instead.

"He made some good money in the Indies. I came to know him there through a good childhood friend, Mr. Cottle." He stopped speaking and locked his jaw shut.

Sophie waited. She remembered what Billingham had said about a lost friend named Cottle, but she did not want to ask more. Finally, she prompted him, "I remember you wore a black band on your arm when you first came to Pembroke."

"Yes," said the captain, "it was for him. William Cottle became my best mate when we were boys. He was a lively, cheerful, and ambitious friend. It was his idea to take to sea. I was fortunate to have some means from my family, but not a great deal because of my father's... Well, I had little in the way of family fortune because of my father's problems with finances."

"Oh," said Sophie, assuming the rest of it. "So, you joined the Navy then?"

"For a brief time, from midshipman to lieutenant, but my father wouldn't have it." Murdock licked his lips, talking with more earnestness than she had ever seen. "I took my earnings, what little inheritance I had, and bought a ship to commandeer myself with William's encouragement. I soon realized... Well, to be frank as I know I can be with you, Miss Crestwood..."

He fell quiet, then looking back up said, "I did not see that shipping sugar was any different than shipping slaves, for it all comes off their backs. So, being acquainted with Perlmutter and a great many others at sea, I decided to cast in my lot with Cottle and give up trading for something less immoral and more profitable."

Sophie frowned.

"I had a letter of marque," he explained.

"Oh. A letter; like permission. You were a—"

"A privateer."

"Oh, I see," she said, somewhat bemused. "Lady Mary did mention it to me." She thought how Papa did not always speak of privateering with compliments, but it was far better than piracy. "I do not think that is so bad," she remarked with some relief.

He laughed with warmth, and his eyes twinkled. "You do not? I didn't know it was questionable. "

"I'm sure it's not," she said. "Only... well... some may feel that way here, but I don't." She fell silent, unsure of what to say for surely he knew—had heard—what others said of him.

"You did not think I was of blacker salt, did you?"

She looked up at him and half-smiled. "I knew it could not be true."

"Ah," he said, now fully amused. "You heard then, that my income for Pembroke has been brought in by other means."

She took a deep breath. "Some say you are a pirate, Captain Murdock. I mean, you did arrive with no announcement and no introductions, and well, you do keep to yourself and your servants are, um... rustic." She stopped herself.

He gazed at her in fascination. "I did not know you yourself thought such a thing, Miss Crestwood. I must say I'm impressed."

"Impressed? Why?"

"You certainly did not seem to consider it might put you in danger. It did not stop you from making my acquaintance."

"You mean from wandering about your property?" she joked.

He smiled along with her. "No. I only meant you were a fair judge of character and gave me the opportunity, at the very least, to make your acquaintance without any fear of danger."

"Oh, I never believed it," she said with a toss of her chin. "It was an exciting idea at the first, but..." She would not bring her father into it, or Jack.

"It is not romantic at all." Murdock's gaze shifted toward the rain streaming down the windows. It echoed around the room, good company for the course of their conversation.

"I would never," he told her between raindrops, "take advantage or pirate another vessel just for profit." His face fell, and she saw a bleak cloud of sadness in him.

"Privateering has its guidelines. It was pirates we were after that day when I was wounded. We were only in the service of our King; but it is right and true, Miss Crestwood, no prey, no pay."

"So, you sought out the enemy to serve your country," Sophie said with decisiveness, "and to make a living. I don't see how it is any different than the Navy."

"Nor did I," he said with a sigh, "other than it brought in a great deal more money. Unfortunately, ships of the line make the naval news far more than privateers. I am not surprised many do not know my name. In fact, now I'm glad they don't."

She waited for a few beats of her heart then queried, "Why did you leave, Captain Murdock? Why did you not stay if the Indies is the only home you ever knew?"

Murdock swung his gaze back to meet her stare. "It was Cottle; my only true friend and family. He did not survive the day. A sharp-shooter..." He looked at the floor and swallowed.

After a pause, he said, "The truth is, Miss Crestwood, I never felt at home there, not in all my days. The only comfort I found was at sea with the horizon in my glass, but it is all ruined now. I saw too much and when I lost... Well, I lost too much there to ever feel any attachment to it. I dreamt all my life of Pembroke, even when fishing with Cottle or playing games. My father spoke of it with his dying breath. The sea is not the only water running through my veins."

"You love it then, Pembroke; your fountains and lakes and streams?"

"The trees and the air and turn of the earth... yes," he said. "I do find there are a great many things to love anywhere in the world if you look closely enough."

"If it is not shadowed by tragic things," she finished for him. Sophie smiled in satisfaction. "The sea will always be there when you miss it, Captain Murdock, but not Pembroke. It needs you now, and how better it already looks since you have come home. I'm happy you came. I'm truly glad."

He watched her with a sincerity that looked affectionate to her; a soft smile that barely creased his lips, but made his eyes crinkle up around the edges. His attention made her hands tingle and her heart flutter like the rush of birds lifting off a rooftop in one great swoop.

"So am I, Miss Crestwood. There are things I will miss about St. Kitts to be sure, but I am satisfied here. Happy, indeed."

CHAPTER THIRTEEN

Tea with Lady Mary felt like a hurried affair. The ladies chattered so much, Sophie could not get in a word. She wasn't used to being talked over, though well used to Miss Banks by now, but Katherine and even the chaperones prattled away like excited chickens.

Lady Mary smiled at Sophie now and then and said, "Is your gown ready? Will you need more help to dress?"

She declined, and when the opportunity arose, crept out and hurried up the stairs to her room. Her gown was laid out on the bed, clean and pressed. The white muslin glowed in the dull light from the overcast skies outside the window. At least the rain had stopped. Impetuous, she pushed opened the window and let a draft in. It cooled the stuffy confines of the room.

The bright blue ribbon that would tie around the high waist of the French-style gown looked too simple. Anxious, Sophie let down her hair and began brushing it out. It would be re-pinned and curled again. The small gold cross given to her by her parents would hang from her neck on its thin chain. She studied the looking glass. Her neck was not too long she hoped, thinking of a long-necked goose. It was the last night at Oak Grove after all, and she must take a more active role in considering whom she would welcome calling on her at Leatherbury in the future.

She bit the inside of her lip. Her stomach twisted, realizing Mama and Papa would expect some kind of progress in making a match. She sighed. It had not been her intention or her focus since her arrival to Oak Grove; she had put it from her mind so that she might enjoy herself. What did she have to show for her time here but for the making of a few new acquaintances?

Devlin's attention in the maze came to mind, but she shook her head. He had called to her from the library once that morning, and she had joined him with secret reluctance to listen to Miss Banks teach them about the best tailors in London. Devlin was put out, or so he scolded her, that Sophie had spent too little time with them on such a dull day and made her promise him her first dance. She'd agreed, much to Katherine's long, unhappy stare. She could not refuse the gentleman although she could hardly meet his eye, and dear Katherine did not know how bold the man could be.

Finished with her *toilette* at last, Sophie made her way downstairs on time. Despite her concerns over the simplicity of her gown, she felt rather elegant when she entered the ballroom to dance. It was not the grand ballroom, but its smaller companion where they had put on the play. She did not mind. The etching in the floor's wood-work and the polished walls glowed in the aura of a hundred candles; more if she stretched her imagination. There was a modest quartet who would provide music, and that would be well enough for their small party.

Devlin was the first to join her side. "Miss Crestwood, I've never seen you look so lovely." He bowed, and she reciprocated, noting that Miss Banks and Katherine were already perched on a sofa pushed up against a wall with chaperones on either side of them. Miss Middle-ton had not arrived.

"You look very well," she returned.

He took her arm. "I understand you are to lead the first dance with Billingham, and you promised it to me." He pouted.

Sophie raised a brow in surprise. Billingham stood with his back to her, having a word with the musicians. What a fine host he was, but—"I don't recall promising him the first dance," she apologized.

"Ah," said Devlin in a grudging tone. He strolled alongside her in a wide circle around the room. Great oval mirrors in gilded frames helped brighten the fading evening light. "Lady Mary announced it only moments ago." He looked around, and Sophie did, too, but her ladyship must have stepped out before taking her seat to watch the young people dance.

"I see," said Sophie. "If her ladyship has requested the arrangement, then I must see it through."

"You should." Devlin smiled with the side of his mouth and leaned his head close to her. "She made it clear upon our arrival that her nephew may claim you first for anything if he desires."

Sophie blushed. "He is the host."

They passed Byers and Perlmutter standing around Murdock who was seated. His poor leg stretched out before him.

"See, we are all here and ready to dance," cried Devlin. He patted Sophie's hand on his arm.

She smiled at them each one, her eyes lingering on the captain. He inclined his chin and looked as if to speak to her but then looked away.

A sharp clap from the rear of the ballroom quieted the party. Lady Mary had returned and was ready to settle in her commanding chair that had been moved in among the sofas. It was far enough from the windows not to catch a chill but close enough to catch a little air where they had been left slightly open. She welcomed them and reminded them of the propriety she expected, wished her nephew congratulations on his inheritance of Oak Grove, and they all broke into applause.

Billingham bowed with affecting modesty. A few feet away from his aunt, he looked nonplussed, if not slightly embarrassed to be the center of attention. His gaze caught Sophie's, and he glanced toward the center of the ballroom. At the same moment, his aunt announced the first dance and that he and Sophie should lead it, so she pulled away from Devlin with a faint smile. He made a show of looking enormously disappointed which made the ladies on the far side of the room laugh.

Her new partner had just caught her hand when her mind wandered over to the musicians, and she wondered if Captain Murdock enjoyed hearing them. She looked his way when she did a quarter turn and found herself unable to decide. He was listening or appearing to do so, but watching her. His eyes, darkened by the room's growing shadows, focused on her with such intensity she could feel his gaze on the back of her neck when she turned around.

Billingham's searching gaze caught her eye, and she pressed her lips together and gave a small shrug of apology. She tried not to let her attention rest on the captain every time she moved his way. He might think she was staring, and why would she do such a thing? She knew he could not dance after all. He would have to sit and watch, something he had done too much of since he had come to England.

She sighed and forced herself to concentrate on the steps. Billingham's attempt at some sort of gravity made her grin, and then chuckle, and before the entire room was dancing she found herself laughing.

Devlin claimed her next, and then Perlmutter, who danced in a stiff, formal way. The officer stared a great deal when her gaze was elsewhere, which made her feel a bit unsettled. He was a quiet sort for a lieutenant, much like his friend.

"You dance very well," she told him when the quadrille was through.

"I've had much practice," Perlmutter confessed. He led her across the room to the chair where Captain Murdoch sat. Mr. Byers stood beside him, hands behind his back and rocking on his heels.

"You have a full card I suspect," joked Murdock when she settled beside him. "I'm sorry I cannot stand."

"Don't apologize to me," she answered. "Even if I dance with everyone here two times it will be more than enough."

"It's a small party though," said Mr. Byers. "We will run out of partners."

"You have only danced once, Mr. Byers," Sophie chided him.

Whatever immediate response came to his mind made him cough.

Murdock said, "He is not fond of dancing."

"Oh, I could not tell it with Miss Banks. You looked very well."

"Did I?" Byers said in a hopeful tone.

"You did." She smiled up at him with encouragement.

"She insisted."

The strings sang out across their bows. Sophie looked at Murdock. "You must not let anyone convince you to do such a thing. You need to relax."

"I've relaxed enough." He moved the cane beside the seating as his eyes glanced toward the musicians.

"Would you rather play?"

He arched a brow at her.

"I suppose you could do just as well or better." She beamed at him, proud to know of his great talent.

He leaned toward her and in a quiet voice, replied, "I do not like to perform, you recall."

"It's just us, a small circle of friends."

He frowned, and she realized he did not feel his new acquaintances worthy enough to be called "friends."

"I'm sorry then," she said in a hushed voice. She looked up and saw Byers watching them whisper. "I'm sorry?" she said, sitting upright.

"I said," repeated Mr. Byers, somewhat befuddled and reluctant now, "would you like to, I mean, may I have this next dance."

She had not noted the new melody. Mr. Billingham had Miss Banks by the arm, and Devlin had Katherine, too. Perlmutter was Miss Middleton's companion, and all of them were looking Sophie's way waiting for her to join them on the floor. She touched the captain's shoulder as she stood, resting her hand where his epaulettes would be if he were in uniform.

"I would be flattered," she said to Byers and waited for his arm. Before she took it, she told Murdock, "You must at least play for me. Promise me you will as soon as we are home."

He looked up, his gaze moving over her face and then down to her neck before returning to her eyes. "You have my word," he said. He seemed pleased.

Satisfied, she danced with enthusiasm with Byers, who made a good effort and beamed under her compliments. Then Billingham claimed his second dance with her, a reel, and it was faster and required a great deal more energy. It left her breathless and laughing.

He held her hands in his as the rest of the company clapped for the efforts of Oak Grove's hired musicians. Trays of meats and cheeses were brought in, and during the distraction, Billingham took Sophie's hand and led her out of the room. They accessed the great marble hall behind the rising staircase and glided through a small study with outside doors that made for an easy escape into the garden.

Sophie's heart began to patter in her chest with consternation when she realized he meant to escort her alone out into the summer night. It would look unseemly to others, although she suspected his aunt might look the other way. Her hands grew damp, and she wished she had not removed her gloves.

Billingham cleared his throat when they reached the steps that sloped down to the lawn. From her innocent observation of the moon overhead, Sophie glanced at him wondering if the festivities had overwhelmed him or if he felt ill.

"You are not one to leave a party," she observed.

He chuckled. "Oh, but I do when I can. Why do you think I spend so much time in the library?"

"To read?" She laughed at her own wit. "I thought it was cards and cigars that tired you, not music and dancing."

"I love a bit of everything, Miss Crestwood, but not too much. That is the challenge for me."

"I think you undertake such great effort to be agreeable it makes you tired."

"I'm not exhausted, though I do not sleep enough."

"No, I meant in here." She touched her heart. "Have you ever met anyone you disliked?" she teased.

He took a step down, leading her behind him into the grass. "I thought I would check on the explosives and the groundskeeper, and no," he admitted, "there are few people I find disagreeable."

They walked arm in arm. "The fireworks will be over the lake, will they not?"

"Yes, but I thought we'd take the long path."

She searched his face for an explanation then looked away, her mind whirling with questions. Pray he would not coax her into the maze like Devlin.

"Her ladyship has forbidden the maze tonight," she said in a rush, and he laughed. It echoed off the stone wall of the house that towered over them.

"I do not mean to make you uncomfortable, Miss Crestwood." He patted her arm. "I only wanted to have a word."

A tight knot in Sophie's chest softened, and she released a breath that came out as a sigh.

"You are relieved."

"Oh, no," Sophie said, embarrassed. "I did not know what was the matter."

"I meant nothing, dear friend; and you are a dear, just like Aunt said you would be. I am happy to make your acquaintance you must know, since we will be neighbors, though somewhat distant neighbors, someday."

"Yes," said Sophie, pleased at the idea. "Someday we shall."

"There was something I wanted to tell you. Something I do not wish to be overheard by the others. I trust you can keep a confidence."

"I will," said Sophie with all the sincerity of her heart. If Billingham wanted to share his secrets, she would be happy to let him talk. He did seem to carry a weight.

"Do tell me," she said with Crestwood curiosity. "Is it why you are so morose when I find you alone? Is it your inheritance and the responsibility of this great place? How it must burden you so."

Billingham lifted his chin and gazed at the indigo sky. "I suppose that is a part of it. It seems my aunt has not shared everything with you."

Sophie stared, a question forming on her lips.

"It's a girl. I mean a woman."

She felt her eyes widen in surprise.

"I mean," he stuttered, "there is a young lady in Sydenham."

When she did not respond because her mind ran wild with scandalous possibilities, he continued.

"You have heard of the Templetons?"

Sophie shook her head, stepping over a dark clump of grass that should have been weeded out of the lawn by now.

"Yes, an affluent family who are cousins of the Earl of Wilton. There is a daughter, a pretty thing name Helen. I met her in Town last year, quite by accident. She had just come out and her family is... Well, I can only say they want to do right by her and make a provincial arrangement."

"Oh," said Sophie, when he glanced at her like he wondered if she was listening at all. He could hardly speak fast enough to satisfy her.

"The thing is, Miss Crestwood, I like her immensely. She is a great beauty and sweet and kind and... blast it all," he laughed, "listen to me go on."

"No," Sophie urged, "please do go on." Her heart simmered with happiness. Henry Billingham was an adorable, lovely man, and that he should find someone felt just right.

"Why, she is pretty, and she laughs with me."

"Upon my word," Sophie replied, tripping over the gravel, for they had come around to the front of the great house now, "you are head over heels in love." She said it in a loud whisper like it was the most shocking secret ever. He stopped, and she covered her mouth to keep from giggling with delight.

He took both her hands in his and said with earnestness, "The truth of it is, I do not appear to be quite good enough for her family."

Sophie blinked. "What? You are heir to Oak Grove. It's a tremendous estate and comes with a great deal of income."

"I will not be Sir Henry," Billingham said in a despairing voice. "There is a duke, his son will inherit, and they are rich, Miss Crestwood, richer than me. They are so rich it would be foolish to continue my attentions since they seek a match with the Templetons."

"Bah," said Sophie at once, although she understood such things. It was the very reason she had been sent to Oak Grove. Her shoulders sank at her friend's predicament.

"My dear, Mr. Billingham," she said with sadness. "You have chosen a romance that surpasses the popular sensibility. I am sorry, you poor thing, the lady's family will not do likewise."

Sophie thought of her mama. "My mother was practical in her youth, and today she is, why, she is..." The heaviness in Sophie sank down into her heart.

"Miserable?"

She pulled her hands from Billingham's and gave a violent shake of her head. "No, she's not. Please don't say such a thing. My mama, she is just... melancholy at times. She reads. She's a great romantic in her heart now. It worked out after all."

Billingham's arms fell to his sides. "I am so dejected. I have made every effort to enjoy my aunt's house party in honor of the inheritance, but Miss Templeton will not leave my mind."

"Oh, Mr. Billingham," crooned Sophie. She wanted to throw her arms around him, but she patted his cheeks instead. "You must not give up. Until the final hour, if you truly love her as you say, then you must pursue her again and again. Be relentless."

"You romantic girl. They'll think me mad."

"What does it matter? People see what they want to see or hear what they want to hear, no matter what we do. It's better to sacrifice a little for true love than to settle only for sensibility."

"Do you think so?"

Yes, I do."

"I'm not sure my aunt would agree." He hesitated to say more.

Sophie waved her hand as if shooing away a fly. "I know what you mean. She is fond of me and matchmaking, too, but she would never force you or me to pretend something we do not feel."

"Then I have not hurt you? I haven't led you to hope there might be some formal attachment between us?"

"Oh, no," Sophie said. She smiled, studying his kind face in the moonbeams. "You are the perfect gentleman, Mr. Billingham, in every way, and any lady would be foolish to refuse you. I am only sorry I have not fallen madly in love with you."

She realized she meant it, and that she admired him, but with a genuine heart of friendship. "Why, I have two brothers I love more than anything, and you have come quite close to replacing them, if not joining them, in my heart."

"I am honored then," Billingham said with a grin, "to be counted among your family."

She reached for his hands and squeezed them.

He drew her close to him with a mischievous grin. "You must put in a good word to my aunt for Miss Templeton, meet her soon, and somehow convince her I am the catch of the day."

His words reminded Sophie of Jack and of home. "I will," she promised, hopping up and down in her damp slippers with joy at the possibilities in Billingham's future. "I will find a way."

He laughed with happiness and circled both his hands around her elbow, pulling her toward the door. "Come," he said, "let's go back to the dance before they discover we've disappeared."

They darted forward to the front entrance of the house but came to a halt when they found Captain Murdock and Perlmutter just outside the front door. Billingham waved to them as he pulled Sophie alongside him.

"Oh, Captain," he said with cheer, "have you come to see them set up the explosives?"

Murdock nodded with a quick jerk of his head. Perlmutter said, "We have been invited to help set it up or at least lend a hand."

"Good of you," Billingham noted. "I'm sure you both know more than a groundskeeper about how to make a blow."

Sophie, out of breath, nodded in agreement.

"I'm sure it will be something to see," Perlmutter approved. He inclined his head toward the view, "Over the lake and all."

"It will indeed. Excuse me," said Billingham, remembering his intention, "I must take Miss Crestwood inside." The gentlemen nodded, and Sophie turned up the corners of her mouth, hoping they did not wonder what great secrets she knew.

Captain Murdock's glowing gaze examined her as she passed him by. He looked about to speak, but he seemed once again unable or unwilling to find the words. With a clack of his cane on the gravel, he moved on to follow Perlmutter. The moment left her so unsettled that Sophie glanced back before being guided through the open door. The retreating silhouettes of the two men was the only glimpse she had before it shut at the butler's hand. If she thought the captain would look back, she was wrong.

THE FIRST EXPLOSION sounded like a cannon, a loud *whump* followed by a shower of golden raindrops. They fell in sprinkles over the lake. On blankets spread out across the front lawn, the party watched as amazing hot, fiery stars left colored streamers in the sky.

"Are you frightened?" Miss Banks called between blasts, and in the lantern light, Sophie shook her head *no*.

The grand finale lit up the entire property, bathing Oak Grove in light so brilliant one could see the grooves between the masonry. It reflected off the windows turning the midnight hour into day.

"Congratulations!" Sophie called out to Billingham over the great noise. He thanked her as the others cheered for him as well. The display ended too soon, but Sophie felt reluctant, tired as she was, to go to bed. Her things had been packed, and the next morning she would leave to go home. Katherine had not packed her things, and by the look of it, had no intention of leaving Devlin's side until propriety or Lady Mary dragged her from it.

The party drifted up the steps together and went back into the house where a final drink waited for them in the salon.

"I must say goodnight," Lady Mary said in a gruff voice, as Perlmutter and Murdock filed last into the room.

"We will be up soon," Billingham promised her. She hesitated and raked the young women over with a meaningful stare before departing with her maid. Sophie looked sideways at Katherine, and her friend's eyes narrowed with mischief.

"We are off, too," Sophie said in a quiet voice, but loud enough that Miss Banks and the others knew her intentions.

The chaperones were talking with great animation to Byers across the room. Whatever could be so entertaining after such a show she could not imagine. A yawn crept up into her throat, and Sophie covered her mouth less it escape.

Devlin left Billingham's side and crossed over to the ladies reclining with obvious fatigue on the sofas. "What did you think? Good show, yes?"

"It was," agreed Katherine, eyes sparkling.

"You have an impressive talent with gunpowder," Devlin declared to Perlmutter and Murdock.

Perlmutter stopped speaking and bowed. The captain, leaning on his cane, straightened himself. "We only assisted the groundskeeper," he told Devlin with an air of modesty.

Devlin shook his head. "I don't believe it. That was quite a display. Only a man capable of firing cannons and sweeping a forecastle could put on such an event."

Perlmutter's face flickered with an expression of interest. "You have been to sea, Mr. Devlin? I don't recall hearing so."

Devlin laughed. "No," he said, "I would never trade good earth for dirty, old, salt water and tar."

Murdock said nothing, but Sophie felt offended for him. "Some people prefer the sea," she piped up, "the horizon and its endless possibilities." She looked from Devlin to Murdock.

"For what?" leered Devlin, "the blazing sun, poor biscuit, and the likelihood of drowning? No, it's not for me. Not for a thousand pounds. Not for ten."

"It has its benefits, with good company," answered Murdock.

Devlin's mouth made a rude noise in a blast of air. "The only benefits, as you know, Captain Murdock, are a great deal of income with the right luck and a ship of poor sailors who can't defend themselves."

Sophie sucked in a sharp breath. All the chatter around her came to a stop. She could not help but look at Miss Banks. The girl wore a look of smug satisfaction on her face. Katherine nudged Sophie's leg with her own.

"I'm—I'm sure what Mr. Devlin means is... Well, with the right trade routes and a good crew, life at sea has its merits." Sophie made herself chuckle, but it sounded forced. She glanced at Billingham and pleaded in silence for him to change the subject.

"I think not," said Devlin. He reached down and patted Sophie on the shoulder like she was a child.

Billingham laughed in a loud burst then shook his head like their discourse was all in fun. "You've had too much brandy, Devlin," he said. He turned to Murdock. "I admire your career and your courage, too."

"Ha," said Devlin, and Sophie cringed. She glared at him.

"It's true," said Miss Banks. She looked at Murdock like he was a stranger who had stepped into the room uninvited. "It's widely known."

"What is widely known?" inquired Murdock, his tone patient and low.

Devlin leaned against the settee beside Sophie and crossed his arms. "Well," he interrupted, "that you are a blackguard, a buccaneer, and were thrown out of the Navy. And that you are richer than a king. How many ships did you take after all?"

Sophie jumped to her feet. "He was not," she said in a fierce pitch.

Murdock chuckled, unruffled.

Billingham said, "He was in the Navy, but he was not thrown out, were you, Captain?"

"I was not," he agreed. He looked amused at the lot of them.

"Went pirate then," muttered Miss Banks, and Sophie jerked her head to stare at her, tongue-tied.

Everyone studied Miss Banks. Her weighted version of truth sank into the fabric of the sofas and added flame to the flickering candles and dangling chandelier over their heads. It settled into the rugs beneath their feet like a bad smell, a death scent that can never be washed out of anything it touches. Primly, Miss Banks bobbed her head. "We all know it's true."

Sophie broke the hush the others would not challenge. "How dare you say such a thing." Anger brewed in the pit of her stomach. She had never felt such fury, not in all her life. Not at her parents. Not at her brothers. Not at another soul. "How dare you insult Captain Murdock, the heir of Pembroke."

Devlin gave a sharp, loud laugh, and it vibrated the room.

Billingham cleared his throat. "Now, ladies," he said. He tried to smile and hide the fact he was losing control of his guests.

Devlin shrugged as if no harm had been done. "She only speaks the truth, Miss Crestwood." He grinned at Murdock, but it was an insolent one. "Truly, I admire you, Captain. How did you do it? Get away with it, I mean?"

"Mr. Devlin," Sophie cried. She stamped her foot on the floor.

"What?" he said with innocence. "We are all friends here. Tell us," he taunted the captain, "are you in need of safe harbor or have you retired?"

All faces turned to Murdock. His expression remained blank. Sophie could tell he was thinking; planning something to say to make them all look like fools. The silence from him went on too long to bear.

She sank back into her seat and said in a brash voice, "It's all nonsense. It's not true, just shameful gossip." Sophie glared again at Miss Banks who she realized she disliked with a great intensity. "Captain Murdock has never done anything illegal or any such thing." She raised her head high and looked around the room challenging them all to say so again. "Why, he had a letter of marque. He is no pirate at all."

Billingham took a loud breath. "Perhaps we should—"

"Now Miss Crestwood, you hypocrite," scolded Miss Banks. "We only know it because of you."

Stung, Sophie's head reared back into the settee with a thump.

"Yes," Devlin agreed, "why, I did not even hear of Captain Murdock until I came to Higfield."

Sophie swiveled her head his direction, and a painful prick in her chest burned like fire.

"I was told," he continued, "his crew was killed off because of him, at least half of them." He licked his top lip.

Captain Murdock recoiled like he'd been punched. Sophie looked at Perlmutter. His face flinched with pain for his friend. Then he fired a look at Sophie that made her believe he did indeed think she was the source of all the rumors. No wonder he had avoided her so.

"You must not say such things," Sophie said with a desperate hitch in her chest, but she could not lay all the blame on Devlin, Billingham, or even her Papa.

Katherine chimed in, "Yes, it's true."

Sophie stared at her in amazement. "Katherine."

"It is true," Katherine insisted, raising one shoulder. She avoided Sophie's gaze and looked at Devlin instead. "You did so, Sophie. You told everyone there was a pirate at Pembroke." She swallowed and turned her gaze on Murdock. "It's no secret you lost your ship and Lieutenant Perlmutter's cousin. Not now."

She bit her lip, and Sophie looked on in horror as her once closest friend continued to defy Murdock with a critical stare.

"So," Miss Banks said in triumph, "the only reason we even know such things is because of you, Miss Crestwood." She huffed. "Gossip, indeed. I am not the Crestwood here."

"I never said, I mean, I didn't..." Sophie beseeched Murdock with a sincere gaze across the room to understand and believe in her. He stared back. His pale, glowing gaze cut into her. She whirled back to Miss Banks. "You imply my family is horrible and cruel, Miss Banks."

"Your father is a Crestwood, is he not?" The copper-headed girl gave a humorless chuckle.

Sophie slid to the edge of her seat. Her body burned with indignation. "You don't even know them."

"My father does." Miss Banks furrowed her wide nose in disdain. "Who could not? Anyone who wants to hear the latest tittle-tattle anyway. Do not think I'm surprised you are here, with Mr. Billingham to inherit. Your family is always to be found wherever there is an opportunity."

Sophie's mouth dropped open as she choked on her thoughts.

"My," said Billingham in a rush, "we should retire. It's been a long day, and Captain—" He stumbled over his attempt to speak and ran out of words.

Everyone turned their attention back to Captain Murdock. He stood stiffly beside the mantel with noble dignity. Touching his forehead in a queer salute, he bowed and spun on his heel. Sophie saw his cane leaning against the fireplace but hesitated to call out. He did not need it. He glided out, shoulders tall and back straight. Shadows in the room filled in the space of his retiring figure, making it appear like the dark had swallowed him up.

Katherine moaned as if the whole scene had been excruciating. Someone coughed.

Sophie rose to her feet in a slow motion and all heads flicked back her way. She glared at Miss Banks who leaned back on a pillow. Comfortable and satisfied, she stroked an ivory teacup in her rosy, plump hands.

"I could squeeze your throat until your eyes bulged." A casualty of Jack's influence and wretched expressions, the words slipped out of Sophie's mouth before she could stop them.

The chaperones in the room gasped in horror. Devlin chuckled. A fleeting glimpse at Billingham told her she had quite shocked him, too. Beside her, Katherine's hand brushed her arm, but she jerked away, not bothering to look at the traitor.

Sophie bent her knee deep in a curtsey, and told Billingham, "Thank you for the invitation to Oak Grove." She marched out of the room as fast as she could without running. Captain Murdock was nowhere to be seen.

CHAPTER FOURTEEN

Leatherbury looked much the same when the small carriage came to a bouncing stop. "Has it only been almost a month?" called Mama, as she rushed out with her arms spread wide. "Dear Sophie!" Mama's eyes shined with excitement and expectation, but Sophie's heart sank.

She climbed down and forced herself to smile back. Her feet felt like tree stumps. They had to be forced to move as she slipped into her mother's arms.

Mama embraced her then stepped back and looked her up and down. "Why, you look no different." She put a finger to her chin. "Maybe... no."

Sophie knew she wanted to hear the news; stories about who had been at Oak Grove and if anything romantic or mysterious had occurred. Sophie wagged her head back and forth. "A few weeks," she said in a meek voice. "What could happen in less than a month?"

Mama linked her arm through hers and led her toward the house. "A great many things. Now, I'm sure something of interest happened at that great place that you did not include in your letter."

Sophie wanted to go upstairs first. The ride home had lasted many long and hot hours. Margaret was already there with a tray of fruit and water, lingering to hear whatever gossip Sophie had to share. It all moved quite fast after the slow amble of the horses from one county to the next.

Dropping onto her bed, she sucked back a beleaguered sigh. The morning had been dismal when she first awoke. She'd found Oak

Grove quiet as a tomb. Katherine did not visit to discuss the night before, so Sophie took breakfast in her room, claiming to be ill, and asked to be informed as soon as her carriage arrived.

To be the center of reproach among her peers, both new and old, had been horrific. All she'd done was defend Captain Murdock, and it was the right thing to do, but her stomach churned in humiliation, hour after hour throughout the dragging night. She could not put the moment from her mind when Murdock stared at her in surprise.

The whole of them, even her very best friend, had accused her of being the source behind the public ridicule of the captain, and no one had come to her defense. Captain Murdock's gaze felt like a rain of fiery needles that pierced her from head to foot. The rush of smoldering heat to her cheeks must have reinforced the guilt. If she had dared look long enough into his eyes, she was sure she would have seen hurt; but he was too proud to show it, too proud to even question or accuse her in front of the others. He'd simply walked away.

Murdock truly believed she had started the rumors of his dark repute and passed on the personal details he'd shared with her in private. She clenched a handful of her traveling gown and looked up. Mama was watching.

"My goodness," Mama said at last, "you are fatigued. I expected you to bounce right out of the carriage and fly inside. Dear Sophie, what is the matter?"

"I... Why, I—"

Mama drew in a sharp breath. "You do have news. Now, I won't be shocked, my dear. Many things can happen in only a few days. Do tell me." She bit her bottom lip and clasped her hands in her lap.

Sophie forced the corners of her mouth to turn up but knew it would never reach her eyes. With great effort, she sat herself up in the bed. "It was a fine party," she said at last, "a very good time. I met Miss Banks and Miss Middleton as I wrote, and Mr. Devlin was there, and of course, the nephew, Mr. Billingham."

Mama nodded. "How did you find Mr. Billingham?" She held back a tentative smile.

Sophie cleared her throat. "He is becoming, cheerful, and amiable. Oh, Mama," said Sophie in a rush, "he is all a gentleman should be and—"

Mama's hand flew up to her mouth, but it did not cover the grin that stretched from one apple of her cheek to the other.

"Oh, no." Sophie shook her head. "He is... We are very good friends. We got on quite well." She made herself smile again, but it was difficult because her eyes wanted to water up with tears.

"Friends, then?" Mama dropped her hand. "Wonderful," she said with cheer, "that is a good start." She nodded her head in approval. "You make friends so easily, it's to be admired."

Sophie could not answer. Mama lowered her chin, raised her eyes, and stared with meaning. "You are not yourself though."

Sophie looked down at her lap.

"You did not enjoy the company? There was trouble amongst the ladies, the Miss Middleton? I have heard of her—young and feeble and desperate to make a crowning match to save her family's estate."

Sophie shook her head in swift refusal. "Mama, no, it's not like that at all. She is sweet and quiet; shy yes, but an intelligent girl and very well behaved. She was one of the only guests not to turn on Captain Murdock."

"He was there?"

"He was." Sophie smiled a small bit. "Lady Mary is fond of him as it turns out, and she invited him a few days after everyone else arrived."

Mama studied her. "I am amazed I did not know. You are just tired then, or is it something else?"

Sophie found she could not hide the burden bruising her heart.

"Oh, my dear," Mama gave a little laugh. "I think I understand."

"You do?"

"I would guess that you hoped for the attention of a particular friend, but it was not reciprocated?"

Sophie looked up. Her mother's smile sweetened her handsome countenance.

"My dear, if you were fond of someone at Oak Grove, and he did not return your affection, you must not be so low." Mama pressed her lips together and cast her eyes down to the floor. "It will... Well," she said, exasperated at her loss for words, "that is the way of things most of the time. All will turn out right in the end."

She raised a hand and set it on her heart. "Sometimes we fall head over heels, tumbly-wumbly, and it all comes to naught. You must not mind being crossed in love, my dear. It is better to get it out of the way, so you are ready to meet Fate when he comes riding in to sweep you off your feet."

Sophie smiled at the romantic idea and thought it better that Mama believed her heart had been broken rather than the family humiliated. It would do no good to complain that Captain Murdock was disappointed in her, either. "Yes, Mama," Sophie said with humility, "I know it is better that way."

"Sometimes you can't see the roses for the trees," Mama added.

"The forest for the trees," corrected Sophie before she could stop herself. "Sometimes we can't see the forest for the trees."

SOPHIE COULD NOT REMEMBER all of Papa's quizzing and her unfeeling replies the next morning. She did recall his excitement and approval of her description of Henry Billingham. There was gratitude for Mama; that she did not mention there had been nothing more than a pleasant friendship between them.

No one seemed to realize Captain Murdock had been at Oak Grove, not even Jack. He greeted her only when forced to and stared at his plate throughout the meal. When she said, "You have not missed me at all, have you?" he replied, "No," and went back to pouting. It hurt her far more than she would admit, and she stewed over his bleak mood until she put the candle out to sleep.

The morning sunshine that invaded her room the next day did not make her feel any better. Tangled in the blanket, she rolled over to put her back to the dawn. Jack seemed angry with her for leaving, although he had waved goodbye when she left and promised to knot all her bedcovers together while she was gone. She wondered if he would walk with her after breakfast. They could go to the pond and check the lines. Maybe she could tell him what had happened at Oak Grove.

Yes, Jack would understand. Sophie hugged herself. He would be as furious as she was that Devlin and Miss Banks would call Captain Murdock out. Jack would have defended him; there was no fending off her brother's tongue when he was in a rage. He would even defend her to Captain Murdock if she asked him to do it.

Sophie's chain of worry stopped short. She sat up with the covers sliding into a puddle on the floor. Her shoulder felt the warmth of the swelling sun. Why, she had not even defended herself. The captain had been gone long before she departed, and she had thought herself the next to leave. A footman lingering outside had said that Captain Murdock left before daybreak, right before the stars put out their light. The revelation surprised her, for she'd spied Perlmutter walking back from the stables after speaking with Lady Mary in her breakfast parlor. Murdock had been so offended he'd departed as soon as it was possible.

"I should go," Sophie said to her quiet, empty room. "I should go to Pembroke." She tumbled out of bed in a rush, her mind racing for an excuse to go walking so early. Breakfast was not yet simmering downstairs, or at least the aroma had yet to creep up to her quarters.

Sophie washed herself down with hard, swift strokes in the cool morning air. She brushed her straight, long hair, knotted it into a single braid and then pinned it up as neatly as she could with no help to guide her efforts. A good bonnet would cover it. She could hardly lace herself up, so she put on her most accessible underthings and then the yellow morning dress she had left behind. It was clean and waiting, draped over the chest at the foot of her bed. Margaret must have missed her a great deal to have her things set out so soon, and pressed too.

When Sophie made one final self-judgment in the looking glass, she thought she looked well enough—clean and flushed on the apples of her cheeks—not that she had pinched or colored them. Her twisting stomach and palpitating heart made her feel almost faint. She didn't have an enemy in the world she reckoned, not counting Miss Banks, so there was no cause to believe Captain Murdock thought her unkind. However, he must think her unaccountable, undependable, and untrustworthy. The very thought of it made her feel so ill she thought she would be sick.

After slipping her stocking-covered feet into her boots, she snatched her best bonnet, watched her reflection tie it handsomely under her chin, and crept down the stairs and out the kitchen door dodging sleepy servants.

A light mist hung in the air like a spider's web, almost imperceptible as the sun melted it away. Sophie tramped through damp grasses that grew higher and higher as the lawn drifted into the meadows. Wildflowers bloomed at the peak of their season; purple-petaled, happy things that shivered in the early breeze. Wearing dew drops, their fairy dance made them glisten like gems in the half-light.

Sophie looked back. Leatherbury looked like it was still asleep. She had forgotten her parasol and did not bring her shawl. She squinted toward the horizon. Yes, in the morning shadows waiting for the fully risen sun, Pembroke had endured the night. The chimneys and a snatch of roofline were etched into the distance view.

Captain Murdock had risen before dawn at Oak Grove most mornings. Maybe he would be out riding or wandering through the orchard to check his fruit trees and make sure Jack had not been in their branches again.

At the stile, she stopped to wipe a thin layer of dirt from her heels. She noted with disappointment, that two of the steps had been damaged. A wandering cow or some other heavy beast had crushed them in. She would have to be careful and climb straight over the wall without scraping her arms and legs.

Scuttling across the old rocks like a crab, Sophie scrambled to the ground. She put her hands on her hips and scanned the pasture. Gazing up at Pembroke, she decided to take the direct route to the stables. At least it would give her some purpose, and she could inquire if Jack was there, or if he had been there, or perhaps suggest if he appeared that he be sent home at once.

As she came up over the rise to the horses' stables, she saw two men pitching straw. Both stopped, and one pointed, and the pair watched her come, appearing to discuss the matter before she reached them.

Pushing back the thudding cadence building in her chest, she put one foot in front of the other until she approached them. One, she recognized from her previous visits to Pembroke. He removed his cap and bowed at her, eyes burning with some tacit annoyance.

"Hello," she said, glancing toward the house. "I know it's early, but is the captain home?"

The man glanced at his companion.

"I supposed if he is, he is hardly to breakfast," Sophie blathered. "Yes, you see, I happen to be an early riser, and I thought he might be out riding."

The man said nothing, sliding his gaze up and down her yellow gown.

She cleared her throat. "I'm sorry. I've wandered out too far. If he is not available, then..."

She hesitated. The other replied with a nervous air, "He did order, Miss Crestwood, only last night, that if you or yer brother should wander over here that we send you right back home at once. For your own safety, 'course."

"Yes," said Sophie with a rush of hot on her cheeks. "I understand."

The former silent man beside him, grimy and sweaty so early in the day said in a cold voice, "It's the Captain's orders, and your father's, too, if I be hearing right."

Sophie blinked; surprised he should know Papa did not want her wandering far from Leatherbury.

"Back over the wall you go, my lady." He motioned back toward whence she'd come.

The other pushed his arm down and scowled. To Sophie, he said, "I can walk you back."

"Oh, no." She gave a little laugh. "I know my way." She had walked home from Pembroke so many times she knew the path by heart now. She could never get lost.

Feeling somewhat abashed, Sophie made a beeline right back over the hill. Her legs felt tired, and she wondered at it for all the walking she had accomplished at Oak Grove. Her stomach clenched in painful knots with disappointment. So, she was not welcome now. It had not even been a week. She thought if she wanted she could retch up all the water she had drunk that morning. To be coolly dismissed from Pembroke was shameful.

She wanted to be angry with them for making her feel this way. Her eyes watered, but she clenched her jaws to force back a sob that had been in want of release for some time. It broke out in a sudden rush, making her cough as her eyes spilled over.

Sophie stopped so fast she tripped over her own feet. Her shoulders quivered, and she covered her mouth with chagrin as she caught her balance and righted herself. Put out, tossed off at Pembroke. Not even welcome by a—a pirate! Tears flowed, and she bolted off, hurrying back toward home with long steps despite the swish of skirts pulling at her sides.

Mama had been right. She felt something, and it was unreciprocated. Sophie swiped at a tear creeping down toward the corner of her mouth. She had not been half as wounded when her new friends had accused her of spreading lies, as burning as those accusations had felt. It was Captain Murdock's rejection she could not bear. His disappointment in the salon pierced her to the very center. To think he thought poorly of her—that she had betrayed him—made her want to die. She could not look back; she would not. Even if he was standing at the tallest window in Pembroke Hall watching her retreat, she would not allow him to see her crumble.

SO DISMAL WAS THE REMAINDER of her afternoon, Sophie could hardly endure supper and the continual pounding of questions about Oak Grove. Papa wanted to know if the Banks of Cheapside indeed had a spoiled, fat daughter and how plain was Miss Middleton, because he had heard all the Middleton girls were quite dull with nothing to recommend them but their bloodline. "Their estate is not a great deal more than Pembroke, but I understand it brings in no income at all."

"No capital carrots," said Mama with heartfelt sympathy.

Jack offered little other than to remark, "No sir," when asked if he found Sophie's description about the little parsonage exciting and would he like to visit it and see his future stake.

When Sophie could bear no more and think of no other replies that were more generous and fair, she asked about Richard, and it turned the conversation another way.

The rain came during the night and did not extinguish itself by dawn, so the next morning, Sophie sought out Jack and found him in the library where he now appeared to attend to his preparations for Harrow with steady regularity.

She closed the door behind her and dropped down onto the couch, smiling at him when he looked over his shoulder to see who had come in.

"You are quite dedicated now, I see. You must have been extremely bored while I was away."

His square shoulders raised then dropped. The quill in his hand scratched loud enough to hear over the *plip-plop* of raindrops just outside the window.

"I think you missed me after all," she teased again.

"There was no one here to distract them," he said meaning, she assumed, their parents.

"So they reeled you indoors and put you to work. Does the new tutor come?"

"Only once a week now. Margaret and the rest of them don't let me out of the house." He sounded like education was a cruel torture. "No matter anyhow. Your interference in my fighting lessons put a stop to my visits to Pembroke." Jack's words sounded curt and low.

"You'll be fourteen soon, Jack. Not much longer now."

"Until what? I rot in a parsonage under the nose of a shriveled, old woman?"

"Lady Mary is not shriveled." Sophie scrunched her face. "She's very kind in fact, and wise, too."

"If you say so."

"She won't be in your business at all," chirped Sophie with great effort, "and I daresay you'll love having so much land at your disposal." She curled up her legs and leaned back into the old couch. "They have a fine stocked lake, and streams and meadows, and grand old trees as wide as carriages."

He stiffened, like her words described something so barbaric he had to brace himself just to listen.

"Brother," she said and not without some desperation, "it is a good living. We should be grateful she is so mindful of us."

Jack spun about. "Is you thankful, Soph? Are you happy to be matched up with whatever long-nosed dandy she chooses for you?"

Stung, Sophie replied, "No, of course not. It's not like that at all. Why, we were just introduced, Mr. Billingham and I, and he was quite lovely after all."

"So," he said, his tone dull and gaze drooping to the floor, "you like him after all."

"Oh, no, not like that. He's a good fellow though, a true gentleman. I dare say you would like him immensely."

"I doubt it." Jack turned back to his book.

"He wasn't the only one there," she confided. "Mr. Devlin, you recall, he was there, and Mr. Billingham's good friend from school, a Lieutenant Perlmutter."

This seemed to pique Jack's interest. His finger quit its slow walk across the page where he followed word after word. He tilted his head, and she watched his coppery dark locks flutter.

"He's just returned from the Indies, Perlmutter," she said. "He's on shore leave and hoping for another post."

"A good post," Jack acknowledged. "Who was his last captain?"

"I don't know, but I do know his cousin sailed with Captain Murdock." As the words left her mouth, she realized Captain Murdock did not volunteer this information to everyone. Warmth flooded her cheeks with heat that felt like guilt.

"Did he? That's a good connection. What's his name?"

"Um... I believe it was a Mr. William Cottle, but to be honest, I should not spread it about. The man was a good friend, but he died."

Jack shrugged. "If he lost that good of a mate I suppose it would answer why he's so sad. He's not just wounded in the leg." He turned about again and jabbed his pen into the ink bottle, leaving Sophie amazed at his observation.

After a quiet pause, she said, "He was there, too. Captain Murdock. He came."

"To Oak Grove?" Jack pushed back his chair and joined her on the couch. He wrinkled his brows. "I thought he was away on business. Does Papa know?"

"No, and I do not think we should mention it, do you?"

Jack shook his head. "No, probably best. Did you dance with 'im?"

"We did not dance, but we spent a great deal of time together walking and talking. He's very thoughtful and easily amused, although he does not laugh loud or often. It's a charming, clever chuckle, he has. Oh, and then we spent a great deal of time in the conservatory. He loves music and did you know, he plays the—well, he plays an instrument himself. I find him pleasant and easy to spend time with; far easier than some people."

"Yes, I know."

"Papa is mistaken. Captain Murdock is good and fair, and he cares about people. Why, he practically saved my life when a heavy rod fell down on me." She looked around the room at the dusty old books because her brother was staring at her like she was a ghost. She felt her cheeks color when she confessed, "I like him a great deal."

Jack pressed his lips into a grim line then said, "That's your secret, Sophie, and I will keep it, but you must keep mine."

Curious, she scooted up from where she had fallen back into the cushion behind her. "What secret?" Apprehension flickered in her chest.

He stared like he was not sure he would tell her then finally said, "Only that I have no intention of being sent away to finish school or to become a clergyman."

Sophie released the breath she'd held in as a puff of air. "Oh, Jack. That's no secret at all. You have said as much since you could utter a word."

He licked his lips. "What I mean is, Sister, I have decided to make certain it don't happen."

She nodded, feeling sympathy for them both because of the expectations they carried on their young shoulders, especially after her time at Oak Grove. It seemed everyone else in the world had the luxury to pursue their own hopes and ambitions. "You must know I support you, Brother dear. I promise I will take your side as long as you don't make too shocking a scene."

This seemed to satisfy him. Whatever else spun about in his seasoning mind seemed to settle. Jack leaned back across from her and threw a leg up onto her lap—dirty, stained stocking and all."

CHAPTER FIFTEEN

The rain did not taper off for several days. Sophie found she had to wander about Leatherbury alone because Jack kept to himself in the library. He often withdrew to his room in private. It was not like him at all.

When the weather cleared, she fussed over the flowers in the garden. She could not help but be drawn to the creamy white blossoms of the Bengal roses. The garden was doing very well in the mid-summer heat, and although most everything else outdoors sopped with wet, the flowers seemed to drink it all up and flaunt their vivid colors.

She clipped back a bush with wilting blossoms. A few respectable blooms she decided would look handsome in the vestibule. Before she could carry them inside, carriage wheels crunched along the lane, and she squinted in the pale sunlight to see who might be out this morning. Pushing back the brim of her bonnet, she saw with surprise, a gig come around the curve in the road and pull up to the house.

Sophie stood, and the blossoms in her lap tumbled to the ground. A man leapt out of his seat to the ground with excessive energy then swung off his top hat. "Devlin," she breathed in surprise.

They had not parted Oak Grove as friends, and he had not apologized for insulting Captain Murdock. True, he probably felt he was protecting her and her family from someone with a dubious reputation, but that did not make it right to be so rude. Her mind spun with conflicting thoughts of clemency and censure as she gathered her things.

Margaret came sidling out across the courtyard as Sophie approached the front of the house. "A visitor to see you miss," she said with a large grin.

"Yes, I know," Sophie replied. She passed Margaret the basket of flowers, peeled off her stained gloves, and patted down her morning dress. She'd just passed through the front door when Papa called from his study, "See here, Sophie, we have a guest."

She rounded the door to her father's study and curtsied as Devlin jumped to his feet. His smile was genuine, his hair neatly coifed despite the open gig, and the cravat at his neck looked like it had been knotted with great care.

He bowed. "Miss Crestwood."

She remained where she stood, uncertain of his intentions. Had he come to warn Papa of Captain Murdock? Concern almost overwhelmed her.

"Mr. Devlin, whatever are you doing here? When I left you at Oak Grove, you were on your way back to Town to see your parents."

"I decided to stay with my aunt and uncle for some more time," he explained with a grin. He smiled with an air of mystery, and she wondered at it before realizing her father's cheeks looked as red as cherry tarts from excitement.

"Mr. Devlin," said Papa with much formality, "would like to speak with you. Alone."

"Oh," said Sophie with relief. She stopped herself from resting a hand on her heart. He had not mentioned Murdock after all. "Would you join me in the drawing room?"

Devlin bowed again. Papa smiled at her like a fox, and she gave him a curt shake of her head. If he knew Devlin had come to apologize for his behavior on the last evening at Oak Grove, if not for his behavior in the maze, he would be sorely disappointed.

Sophie smiled to herself as she led Devlin away, passing her Mama and Margaret in the hall.

"Mr. Devlin," said Mama with happiness, "you have come to call."

"I have."

"I'm happy to see you." She glanced at Sophie and smiled, a certain comprehension flooding her eyes, and Sophie almost giggled thinking it was Devlin her mama decided had made her daughter so melancholy of late.

Really, the thought of him did nothing to her at all. Devlin was pretty to look at and entertaining to hear, but after a time he really made one quite tired. In fact, he often made Sophie want to read or sew or do something to escape his constant performing. She looked heavenward as she passed her mother, to show her Devlin did not affect her at all. He was rather like a ticking timepiece that never stopped making noise.

In the drawing room, she dropped into her seat. He walked over to the fireplace and had a look at the brass candlesticks her grandmother had passed down to Mama. Then he rested an arm up on the mantle. He grinned at her, his teeth clean and gleaming.

"What are you about?" she asked with suspicion.

Her query made him laugh. With a fist on his hip, he replied, "You are so ever hard to fluster, Miss Crestwood. Are you not surprised to see me?"

"I think you know well enough that I should be perturbed." She crossed her arms around her waist and gave him a smug look. "You have come to apologize?"

"Me?" He touched his chest and opened his eyes like an innocent schoolboy. "Yes, yes, oh my. Let's see. I've offended your sensibilities." He glanced at the door. "First, I insulted you in the maze and then with our friend, Captain Murdock."

"He is your friend? I could not tell when you quizzed him so, and before the others, too."

Devlin raised a shoulder with impertinence. "I did not know it was any great secret, and I thought it would benefit you to know the truth."

"I already know the truth," Sophie answered in a firm tone, "as you have accused me."

"Yes, well, truth is relative, I suppose. What the captain had already informed you of I did not know. I thought he should clear it up for us all."

"For what purpose? To make him share the most intimate and painful details of a terrible ordeal, or to make me look like a fool for misconstruing who he was when he first arrived?"

"Oh," said Devlin, "I do not think he minds what you think of him."

Sophie frowned. "I'm sure he does, Mr. Devlin."

"Now, now," said Devlin, his tone taking a turn toward platitudes. He dropped his arm from the mantel and took a tentative step toward her, his eyes glazed with an odd intensity. "You must understand, Miss Crestwood, of course you see it now. I was only trying to protect you."

"From what?"

"His interest in you was clear."

"Interest?" Sophie laughed, though to her surprise the idea of such a possibility tweaked her heart. "Mr. Devlin," she continued, "we are nothing more than friendly acquaintances."

Devlin took another step forward then stopped, put his hands behind his back, and leaned on his heels. "As it should be, at least, that's how I intend for it to be now."

Sophie raised a brow. "Why is that? You are now concerned about my future?"

Devlin gave her a faint smile. "Is it not clear?"

"I don't understand."

He put a hand on his heart. "Miss Crestwood, if you insist I will say it again. I am madly in love with you and have nothing but the highest regard and affection for your family." It sounded like he was reciting lines from a play, but his tawny eyes radiated with sincerity.

This again? Sophie almost cried, but the seriousness on the man's face gave her pause. His words made her warm and uncomfortable.

"Mr. Devlin," she began and attempted a modest chuckle.

He interrupted her by dropping to one knee, and she sucked in a gasp.

"I have not come to offend you or to take advantage of you, Miss Crestwood; only to offer my heart and to plead... no, beg you, for your hand." He took a nervous breath, loud and trembly then reached for her fingers.

Frozen like an ice-covered twig, Sophie could not move. The dampness of his hand made her want to jerk away and wipe her palm off on her gown.

"Would you," he said in slow, precise words, "do me the honor of staying by my side for the rest of our lives?" It was so formal, so rehearsed, and so ludicrous she did not know how to respond.

Sophie swallowed. Her heart pounded in her chest, slow like a blacksmith's hammer. "I—I—"

Devlin nodded and smiled to encourage her on.

Her stomach churned with a primitive warning. "Mr. Devlin," she said, almost wheezing with anxiety, "I am flattered but must refuse."

The anticipation of her reply slipped from his face. It turned white under its flushed and damp state. He stared, shocked at her response, and the pain she felt for him made her want to pat his curled fists.

"I am so sorry," she said in the stunned silence. "I cannot accept the offer." She was sorry. She wasn't sure she understood why after how he had behaved.

"Miss Crestwood," Devlin said in disbelief, "we get on so well and have spent so much time together."

"Not that much time, Mr. Devlin."

"Your family," he said, looking around like they were there in the room, "they are so amiable, and they like me a great deal."

"Yes," said Sophie, half-smiling though not with cruelty, "you are very well liked here, Mr. Devlin. I am fond of you, but less so since you behaved less than proper toward me and my neighbor." Katherine's happy face came to her mind. "I do not have strong feelings for you, Mr. Devlin, and it would not do to accept your proposal when there are others who are mad for you."

Devlin drew back his head, incredulous. "Mad for me?"

"Yes," Sophie said, chuckling now. She stood and pulled him toward her to lift him off his feet. "Miss Blackburn, you know."

"Oh." His face did not regain its former cheer. "Miss Blackburn, your friend."

"Why, yes."

He scowled like he tasted something bitter. "Miss Crestwood, I can do far better than a clergyman's daughter." He laughed with disdain.

Sophie knew the laugh, and today it sounded just as sharp and cruel. "She likes you very much," she said, frowning at his cut.

"What is that to me?" He put a hand on his heart again, one that was cold and cunning in her mind. "Do you think you can do better?"

"What? No. I mean, Mr. Devlin that is an inappropriate question."

"Inappropriate?" He glared. Devlin did not look so handsome with his eyes narrowed, his face red, and his teeth bared. "I have given you my attention since I first came to Higfield, and you have returned them. Why, my dear, you even let me kiss you in the maze."

"I did not," Sophie hissed. If she weren't already on her feet she would have leaped to them. "You took advantage of me, Mr. Devlin, and I kept it to myself." She stared at the door willing Mama or even Margaret to interrupt them.

Devlin said, "If I should tell your Papa of your attention toward me, I'm sure he would agree we should be wed. It's a good match for us both, although it isn't my first choice."

"Not for me either." Sophie shook her head. She did not like him at all now. She was finished.

"Am I not good enough?" He sniffed. "Do you think I have nothing to overlook? Your father is a silly old fool, and your mother is hardly aware of anything that goes on around her. Your brother runs about the countryside like a gypsy instead of receiving a proper education. It's no wonder you are still single at one and twenty."

Offended, Sophie did not tamp down her temper. "My father worries every day what everyone thinks of our name, and my Mama is the sweetest, kindest mother one could ever wish for. And by the by, I'll have you know, I am just almost twenty. I would think, Mr. Devlin, that your proper education would include not insulting the family of your friends; especially those of your aunt and uncle."

At the mention of his relatives, Devlin's white cheeks flushed again, but his eyes dulled with malice. "I am here because of my aunt and uncle. You may be my uncle's special friends, but it doesn't mean you will be mine when his home falls to me."

"Well, I do hope that does not happen for a very long time." Sophie pointed at the door for him to go, but the blackguard was not finished.

"I would kiss you again, just to see if I could make you do it, but I think you very well would hold me to it and force me to the altar. God knows you might convince that filthy pirate over the hill to do something about it, or Billingham, too."

Sophie was so startled at his insult she could only stare. "I refused you."

"That won't do, although I am not the least bit tempted by you. You're quite a mild and dull girl no matter what everyone thinks, and your inheritance will not come close to superseding mine once my parents and relatives are dead."

"Dreadful!" They were the only words Sophie could find in her horrified mind.

"No matter. Should I not find anyone better to please my family, you will have to marry me anyway."

Sophie shook her head in denial.

"I'll simply tell them of our affair at Oak Grove beneath her lady-ship's very liberal eye."

"It's a lie." She clenched her fists to keep from slapping him.

He smiled like he'd just convinced her to take a bite out of the forbidden fruit. "I can be polite company for now, and I'm sure you will do the same. There's no need for anyone to know you encouraged me only to send me on my way. We'll speak again soon."

He pivoted on his heel and strode for the door, leaving her fuming and flushing and full of outrage. When he pulled it open, he tripped back into the room. Jack walked in, his face calm but eyes on fire. He shut the door behind him, and Sophie almost fainted with relief.

"Mr. Devlin," he said, so low that no one else in the house could eavesdrop. "I recognized your voice when I stepped too close to the door. In fact, I confess I decided to listen." His face blazed scarlet with disgust.

Sophie swallowed. She watched Devlin's back for any sign of re-gret, but his shoulders were held high. The dog was more than ten years Jack's senior.

Jack crossed his arms over his chest. "I insist you leave at once." He examined the taller man like he was of particular revulsion. "I order you never to set boots on Leatherbury's soil again or speak ill of my sister to anyone. If you think a pirate at Pembroke is a thing to fear, you don't know the wrath of a brother whose only sister is wrongfully shamed."

Sophie's mouth dropped in surprise.

In one swift movement, Jack swiped a long dagger from somewhere behind his back, and he jabbed it into the air. "Get out of my house, Mr. Devlin, before I have you run out of Higfield for the filthy cur you are."

With a startled jerk, Devlin sidestepped him. He stormed out of the room at almost a run, mumbling on his way out, "As if anyone would believe you. Mad boy." Within moments, the front door slammed.

Jack put the dagger away and gave Sophie a grim look. "Heaven and earth, Soph. Please tell me there won't be any more callers unless it's our Captain Murdock."

PAPA FLEW INTO A VEXED fit; certain Sophie had sent Devlin away. When he hinted she had refused his advances, Sophie replied only that they'd had a disagreement. Beside her, Jack said nothing, only glancing at her on occasion with pity in his eyes. "A wasted summer," Papa grumbled into his pudding. She excused herself and dashed upstairs to bed.

"Did you run off Mr. Devlin after all?"

Mama hurried to Sophie's room as soon as the house settled for the evening. She did so under the premise of tucking her into bed early, something she had not done in many years.

"He is not what he seems."

"I'm sorry to hear it but hope that it improves your opinion of Mr. Billingham."

Sophie smiled but with some regret. "Mama, Mr. Billingham and I are a great deal alike. We have the same temperament, but I think after a time we would find each other dull. It's not like that with, say, Captain Murdock though. We are very much opposed, but we do not quarrel. He is a very good listener, and I like to make him smile and laugh. He's intelligent, and his heart is—"

Mama looked surprised. "You have not been wandering around Pembroke again since your Papa forbade it, have you?"

Sophie took a deep breath. She would not tell. "Why, he was invited to Oak Grove, you remember, and of course I could not avoid him there."

Mama stared, and Sophie looked away until she thought of something to change the subject of their conversation.

She spent the following week in the garden when not reading beside Jack as he studied. Often, he would disappear upstairs without a word to her or anyone else. When she invited him on her walks he declined, and she did little to encourage him since Papa had barred him from fishing or hunting.

On more than one occasion, Sophie dawdled at the pond all by herself, sitting on a fallen log waiting for turtles to come up to breathe. She also watched the trees for any movement that meant the men at Pembroke were checking on animals or fences. Once, a rising cloud of birds rose in a cacophony over the trees, and she hurried to the stone wall to see who was out. No one was there, not even a gamekeeper to shoo her away.

As far as she could tell from her time outdoors, Captain Murdock did not wander about his side of the property that touched Leatherbury, and she wondered if he was cooped up indoors with his injured leg. The idea burdened her with guilt. If she had not been so clumsy, he would not have been hurt. She wanted to tell him how sorry she was again, and to have a word so that she could explain that she had not spread any of the ridiculous lies about him. She had only wondered about his reputation at the first.

On Tuesday, as she strolled back toward the house, she spied a lone girl standing in the garden. She recognized Katherine, and her heart sank. They had not left Oak Grove as friends either, although they had been dear to one another for many years. Katherine had not spoken to her since, not even on the Sabbath day after church, and Sophie had made sure to avoid any unpleasant conversations by leaving in haste.

Oak Grove had been a failure indeed.

Katherine saw her and raised a gloved hand, just slightly moving her fingers in a feeble wave. Sophie hitched up her skirts and walked toward the house. Katherine did not come to greet her, but stood waiting, her boots fixed to the ground. As she drew nearer, Sophie realized it was not a glove on her hand but a fistful of handkerchiefs. Katherine's chest hitched up and down with jerky heaves, and Sophie found her feet carrying her faster to cover the distance left between them.

"Katherine," Sophie called, forgetting everything that had transpired.

Katherine hiccupped, and her face collapsed into a morose frown before bursting into sobs. Her round, cherub cheeks were mottled with scarlet stains. Tears flowed in one rivulet after another. She held out her arms, and Sophie swept her up in a pitying embrace.

"What is it, my dear? Whatever is the matter?" She braced herself for dreadful news. Only news of the worst kind would make Katherine Blackburn cry. Sophie prayed the vicar and his wife were not hurt, or worse. She patted Katherine's back with mild impatience as she wallowed in a last gush of weeping.

"There now, do come inside. Shall I call Mama?"

Katherine pulled back enough so that Sophie could see into her swollen, pink eyes. "Did you not hear?" she said, her voice at a hysterical pitch. "Have you not heard the news?"

Sophie shook her head.

Katherine's face wrinkled up again. "It's true. My papa heard it from Mr. Porter himself."

Sophie's stomach sank. What had Devlin been up to now? Had he told everyone she had agreed to marry him?

"He's engaged!" Katherine threw her face into the crook of Sophie's neck and began to sob.

"No." Sophie hugged her with ferocity. "It's not true. I swear it is not."

"How can you know?" Katherine wailed between sniffles. "Have you seen her?"

"Seen who?"

"That horrible Miss Banks. She pretended to be my friend." Katherine began to moan, wetting Sophie's shoulder with more tears.

"Heaven and earth."

"Yes, it's true. My father knows it to be true."

"Well, my Papa has said nothing."

"Oh, Sophie, I know your papa always knows what's about firstly, but Mr. and Mrs. Porter came to supper last night, and I thought Devlin would come, but he did not. They told us themselves. He is in Cheapside with her family. She just accepted him this last week."

Sophie's mind whirled. "I am all astonished," she whispered, rubbing the back of Katherine's neck. "I know you were fond of him, Katherine. I'm so sorry."

"He loved me," she sniffled. She raised her head and with great earnestness said, "He told me he loved me, and I believed him."

"He said so?" Sophie was aghast. "The very words?"

Katherine nodded. A lone tear swelled over her bottom lashes and trailed down her cheek. She looked in despair; truly broken-hearted. She had really cared for him after all.

"George Devlin makes me sick."

"I believed him, Sophie. We spent a great deal of time together. There are things you do not know but..." Katherine glanced at Sophie with guilt.

Remembering the maze, Sophie's heart sank. "What did he do?"

Katherine lowered her eyes and looked away. "I did not always nap in the afternoons. I did not always join you in your room because I was with him."

Sophie raised her brows in surprise. "You were with Mr. Devlin."

Shamefaced, Katherine nodded in a slow motion. "We were exploring the servants' quarters, hidden rooms, and halls, and even the very top floor in the attic. Outside, well, I knew the maze so well because..." She sighed. "We spent a great deal of time in there, too."

Sophie did feel sick. "Oh, Katherine."

"Sophie, you mustn't think ill of me. I did no bad thing. I mean," Katherine frowned, and then her face wrinkled up again and the tears returned. "I was not well-behaved. I was not at all ladylike or... He told me he loved me madly, Sophie. He said we were a good match, with his inheritance and my old and respected family name." More tears spilled over. "He said I was pretty and clever and great fun."

Sophie closed her eyes in sympathy. She drew Katherine to her again. "You are pretty, Katherine, and clever and fun. I'm sorry the villain lied to you about his true intentions. What kind of man goes from girl to girl making the same compliments and taking the same privileges?"

Katherine jerked away, her eyes wide. "You think he did so with Miss Banks, too?"

"I would bet my bonnet; my very best one. I suspect Mr. Devlin is a coward and a flirt and has tricked us all."

"He never should have been invited to Oak Grove," said Katherine with violent indignity. "How can he be a good friend of that family?"

"His relatives are old friends of her ladyship. She knew a great many folks in Higfield when she was a girl. I do not think Billingham knew him well although they got on."

"Well, Mr. Billingham gets on with everyone, doesn't he? He's a gentleman." Katherine pouted. "I suppose even Captain Murdock acts like a gentleman; at least he did at Oak Grove."

"Yes," Sophie agreed. Both were fine gentlemen. She frowned at the ache in her chest. Murdock had avoided them all since Oak Grove. "It's a gift, I suppose, to be born with such natural charm. It's a pity Mr. Devlin doesn't use his talents with more honor."

Katherine settled her head back on Sophie's shoulder with a sigh. "I'm so sorry I did not stand by you and defend the captain. I didn't know what to do."

Sophie gave her a squeeze and chose to forgive. They stood in the warming sun for some time, wavering back and forth in a slow and silent dance until it grew too hot to stay outdoors.

PAPA CAME GROWLING into the drawing room two days later in search of Jack. Katherine's news caused such distraction at Leatherbury, it should have come as no surprise he disappeared.

"I did not see him in the library this morning," Sophie admitted, as she set down her sewing. Katherine had begged her forgiveness, and knowing Devlin, Sophie had to pardon her behavior under his influence. She promised Katherine she would come and stay for a spell and looked forward to it since they were friends again. Her pleasure at another adventure had diverted her from Jack's problems.

"He's probably in his room," she said. Papa did not leave but stood near the mantle staring out the window and scratching his head.

"He spends a great deal of time there," Mama agreed. "Shall I call for him?"

"No," said Papa. "Margaret and I already had a look. I have a letter from the headmaster at Harrow, but I will share it with him at supper." With a sharp jerk, he stomped away, and Sophie's heart thudded with concern.

"Perhaps he just stepped outside," she offered, "to see the dogs." She prayed he had not run off to the lake; or worse, to Pembroke. A tingle welled up in Sophie's heart, for a tiny part of her wanted him to have gone off to Pembroke. It would give her a reason to give chase.

She started to rise to her feet, but Mama said, "I will check his room again. He missed breakfast this morning, too. He may be feeling poorly."

Papa snorted as he left the drawing room. Sophie frowned. Of course, Jack felt poorly. He was clearly in depressed spirits. A boy his age should be outdoors on horseback or aboard a cutter learning his latitudes. Being restricted to a library and bedchamber was not the best activity for a lad with so much vigor and curiosity.

At tea when she mentioned him, Mama said he was not found in his room, and she had not looked outdoors, although Papa had sent someone to check the pond. Sophie raised her brows, surprised Jack would step foot outside again after he'd become so submissive. It wasn't until supper when his empty seat at the table could not go unnoticed that she asked if he'd come home. With a frown, Papa said he had not.

By nightfall, Papa called for the cart and a horse to be brought around, and Sophie stood at the window twisting the folds of her gown as she stared into the deepening darkness. Her father was going to Pembroke, she overheard, and she wondered if Mama had spoken to him about the captain's presence at Oak Grove.

A knot of apprehension and fear swelled up in her belly. If Jack had run away to Pembroke and the Captain let him in, her parents would never accept Murdock's company. A sheen of perspiration dampened her forehead. Sophie jumped when the front door slammed.

It seemed like Papa was gone forever. When Mama roused her from where she had fallen asleep on the settle, Sophie could not believe Papa had returned some two hours before with Jack nowhere to be found. Mama broke into quiet weeping, and Sophie felt paralyzed. Jack had made her keep his secret—that he would do something final to stop anyone from sending him to school or Oak Grove.

She did not sleep that night or much more the following day. It seemed her brother had disappeared with the summer rain showers and left no hint of when he would return. Old George took a horse into Town, and Papa sent messages to the Blackburns and Porters. It was not until another two days passed with no word, that Mama, frantic with worrying and half-dumb from no sleep, convinced him to send word to Oak Grove.

Sophie could only stand at the drawing room window and stare. She wished it looked west over Pembroke rather than along the lane that ran beside the house. If only she could speak with Mr. Billingham or beg Captain Murdock for a few minutes of his time. If she asked for their help, which was more than Papa was willing to do, she knew they would not hesitate to help find Jack.

She thought more resolutely of Murdock with each passing hour until she could no longer ignore the prompting to pull on her boots and bonnet. Jack was not lost. He was exactly where he wanted to be. Somehow, he had left Higfield and made his way to the coast. In her heart, she knew it to be true. Her brother had gone to sea, and the only man she trusted to help them was just over the pond beyond the dividing stone wall.

Sophie slunk out the kitchen door, tiptoed past the hens, and dodged Margaret behind the laundry fluttering in a small, sticky breeze. Moving through the trees at a quick pace, she found herself panting before she reached the wall. She scrambled over it and made a straight line for the front of Pembroke's façade. Her back grew damp and the back of her legs perspired down into her stockings.

No one was tending the gardens in the front of the house; it looked quiet and peaceful. Even as she raised a curled fist to knock, Sophie's gaze took in the scrubbed windows and stonework, and she smelled fresh paint. The door looked almost new. Perhaps it was. She did not recall what it had looked like before. Much of the ivy was gone, and the tangles of brush and weeds, too.

The slight butler, Mr. Sykes, opened the door, but his eyes glassed over as if he did not remember her.

"I must speak with Captain Murdock." Sophie tried to sound demanding, even as she struggled to unknot the bonnet ribbon under her chin.

Mr. Sykes stepped back, bowed slightly, and replied. "He is not available."

"Is he in?"

The servant's expression remained blank.

"Mr. Sykes, I am not here for tours or lessons. My brother is missing, and I must speak with the captain at once."

"Jack's not here." Murdock's voice came from the shadows, and Mr. Sykes widened the door so that Sophie could see him standing in the great hall. His cane was at his side. His hair hung loosely over his shirt. His lightly browned skin contrasted against the white muslin in the dim light. Sophie stared. He looked captivating in morning dress, relaxed and lazy even.

"Your father has already called. Jack has not been to Pembroke for some time."

Sophie took a breath. She managed to pull off her bonnet and held it to her chest like it would protect her. "He has run away and is nowhere to be found." She gave Captain Murdock her most pleading gaze, even as her teeth caught her bottom lip and bit down. He stared back.

"May I come in?"

After a pause, Murdock blinked and abandoned his examination of her. He motioned toward the drawing room with his cane, and Sophie hurried through the door, past Sykes who frowned at her.

Murdock remained where he stood, and she curtsied when she passed him to enter the room. He glanced at her, his face expressionless except for those green eyes. They looked cool and guarded. Despite that, being in his company again felt like coming home. She wanted to take his arm and tell him everything that had happened since they had last seen one another, but they had not parted amicably. They had not parted at all.

She swallowed again with anxiety as she moved to the royal looking settee. The bright room had not changed; it was still influentially Oriental with pieces of other worlds littered here and there—the statue of the little fat man, stone fishes, and colorful masks staring from the walls. She sunk down onto the couch and waited.

Captain Murdock murmured something to the servant outside then marched in, his boots striking the polished floors in perfect, balanced time to the swish of his cane. He relied on it a great deal again. The fall at Oak Grove had set him back indeed.

When he came to a stop, Murdock stood across from her with his back to the writing desk, blocking the view to the windows now covered in heavy curtains. He sighed like she had put him out entirely.

"When your father came to me last, it was the first I'd heard of your brother's foolishness. I've already spoken with the hermit that lives in the backwoods to the north. No one has seen him anywhere on the property or near the road."

Picking at her bonnet ribbons, for she could not bear to look him in the eye because of the impatience in his tone, Sophie told him, "Yes, Captain Murdock, I understand. Papa told me only this morning. However, Jack has been secretive of late, and the last confidence he shared with me was that he planned to ruin all chances of receiving the living at Oak Grove."

She waited for a pause then glanced up. Captain Murdock's eyes studied the neckline of her walking dress. She blinked away the threat of tears. "I know where he has gone; away to sea, just as he always said he would. You know him a fair bit. He is as good as his word, even if it's of the smallest consequence."

Murdock inclined his head, watchful, not concerned she was on the verge of bursting into feminine hysterics. "He disobeyed your father when he was told to keep to Leatherbury's grounds. Are you certain he is a follow through?"

Sophie nodded. "Oh yes, because he never promised Papa he would stay away. He will not give his word if he finds something disagreeable, just as he never committed to my parents he would take up the cloth. His heart has been set on a commission since he was born, and he's almost fourteen. Too late for most, but he's determined. If I could fly to Portsmouth I know I would find him there, begging a post, or even as a cabin boy despite his breeding." She shook her head in sadness. "It's close by, and he's been influenced by those who've left Higfield to do the very same thing. Even..." She glanced up again.

"My father? Myself?" Murdock smiled a little, but with derision. "I am hardly a tempting paragon of life at sea."

Sophie rose to her feet, her hands clutching her bonnet. "Oh, but you are," she said, and the watery eyes she'd fought won the battle. A small tear escaped and trailed down the side of her nose. "You are dignified and intelligent, and despite your injury, capable and strong."

"You have a high opinion of me," he said with frost in his tone.

She took a step forward, her heart humming in her chest. "Why, yes, I have almost always."

"Almost?"

"It's true we did not know what to expect when you first arrived, and Papa did hear whispers in Town." Sophie's cheeks flushed with remorse. Captain Murdock's gaze became more attentive although he did not say a word. She could not bear it. She took another step closer, wondering at the notion that came to her mind that she should throw herself at his feet.

"I did not tell lies about you, Captain Murdock. Upon my honor," she said in a trembling voice. "I did wonder about your reputation like everyone, and I confess I discussed it with Mr. Devlin on one occasion, but I do speak before I think a great deal of the time. Sometimes things just fall out of my mouth, but I have not spread the ridiculous gossip abroad of your activities in the Indies, nor did I share with anyone at Oak Grove the personal information you disclosed to me."

He watched her with apparent interest. "The truth is," she blurted out like a silly goose, "I never believed it from the start, not really. I wanted to like you, I did, and I – why, I..."

Sophie's cheeks flushed as her heart flipped over in her chest. The force of it almost made her sit down again. She cleared her throat and tried to endure his steady gaze. Almost choking on the words, she whispered, "Why, I do... like you." She glanced away, tormented by the embarrassment of it all. "A great deal."

She stared at the curtains and pretended she could see through them. Her legs trembled like she was cold, but she was hot, melting in her layers. The quiet felt excruciating, like a thousand eyes could

see into her mind; see into her most secret thoughts. There were
ideas she did not know were there; not until this very moment.

Finally, he ended her agony in a soft and mollified tone. "Miss
Crestwood, I will send a few men to the coast to see what they can
find."

Her legs almost buckled with gratitude. She met his look with
wet eyes. "I knew you would help us."

He looked away, gave a small cough, and said rather fast and with
forcefulness, "As far as your opinion of me, I must advise you to save
your regard for the likes of Mr. Devlin or Mr. Billingham. They are
far more suitable for your adulation."

Horrified and speechless, she stared at him with cheeks flaming.
He used his cane to whirl about and depart the room. Sophie wavered, feeling unsteady on her feet. Had she really spoken aloud the
admiring thoughts about him that crept into her mind when she was
all alone?"

CHAPTER SIXTEEN

Weeks passed. The glaring sun baked the countryside leaving crops thirsty for rain. Sophie kept indoors and accomplished little. In unpredictable moments, she would crumble into a tired heap of sniffles and tears, but only when no one else was about.

Katherine embraced her before the family departed the chapel each Sunday, but she did not visit them in their time of distress. Mama came downstairs for only a few hours a day. Her face looked pale, and her eyes were red like she slept little and cried often.

Sophie understood. The post arrived with an invitation from Lady Mary. She had decided to visit with friends in Bath and cool off in the dismal temperatures. Sophie begged her forgiveness that she could not join her. To refuse the lady was absurd and not done, but she knew in her heart Lady Mary would understand.

"She's getting older," Papa told Mama when he thought Sophie could not hear. "We must not let Jack ruin her chances."

As if he knew Sophie had declined a visit to Bath, Henry Billingham came to call when the weather began to turn. She led him to the modest drawing room after introducing her parents. They talked for a time and then she invited him to see her gardens when she could not bear her father's loud banter any longer. Despite the family circumstances and agony over Jack's whereabouts, Mr. Crestwood was beside himself with joy to have finally met Oak Grove's future heir.

Billingham was content to take a turn out of doors. "You seem unhappy, Mr. Billingham," Sophie asked when they were alone at last. He smiled in apology.

"You are very observant, Miss Crestwood, and correct."

"Do you miss Town, or do you miss Oak Grove?"

"I miss them both," he admitted, "but for different reasons. Bath is too crowded for me at times."

"When do you plan to return to Oak Grove?"

"Aunt would like me there for Michaelmas, and my parents, too." He glanced at her then returned to admiring the roses. "I daresay she will invite your family."

"That would be generous of her since I've already spent time there this summer."

"She likes you. I'm sure my parents will like you, too."

Sophie felt peculiar that he should mention she should meet his parents. "Lady Mary takes her role as your aunt very serious."

He nodded. "Indeed."

They came upon the old garden bench, and he slid onto it, bringing her down with him by a light touch on her elbow.

"I must be forthright, Miss Crestwood," he said at last. She looked at him, disquiet welling in her bosom. "It is true I was distracted in Bath. I'm anxious to return to Town."

"You miss your family," she guessed.

He sucked in his bottom lip. A sorrowful regret in his eyes made her speak out again. "You miss someone, don't you, Mr. Billingham?" Her mind raced. "It is not Miss Banks, I presume."

He smiled a little at her joke, but it did not reach his eyes. "No," he admitted. "It is not Miss Banks, nor is it sweet Miss Middleton although she has a lovely heart."

"You remember Miss Templeton whom I mentioned at Oak Grove?"

Sophie nodded, all the puzzling pieces of his distraction falling into place. "I must assume she was not in Bath."

"She was not. I called on her when I returned to Town after my time at Oak Grove. Her parents did not encourage me, but they allowed it."

Sophie clutched his arm. "I'm so happy for you," she said with sincerity. Even as she said it, a small puddle of disappointment formed in her chest, but she chose to ignore it, for it was not there because she loved him.

"She was polite and kind, but we only talked a little bit."

"I hope it will be the first of many visits. Did they invite you to dine?"

Mr. Billingham shook his head. "No, but just to be in her company cheered me a great deal, although we had little to discuss. I think she is more shy than I supposed, and I am a great deal older after all."

Sophie took a small breath and said, "I must be honest. As much as your aunt is hopeful that you and I should find one another engaging, and I do adore you, I'm far more concerned that we both find our own happiness even if it does not meet everyone else's expectations. If you still think of Miss Templeton, you must go back."

He laughed, and it sounded high and breathless at the same time. "I am so relieved, Miss Crestwood. Your opinion matters a great deal to me, for I am fond of you, too." He patted her hand. "I thank you for letting me confide in you." He hesitated then added, "I must ask you to keep my feelings private. Aunt is not against my calling on Miss Templeton, but she has determined in her own mind it will come to nothing, and I don't want to disappoint her."

"She made you go to Bath, didn't she?" Sophie grimaced.

Billingham licked his bottom lip. "She did, but she was happy that I should visit Leatherbury. I do not mind it, not at all."

"You may say so," said Sophie with a teasing smile, "but your thoughts have been elsewhere. I will not whisper a word of what we have discussed. You have my promise."

"You are the kindest girl."

"You must leave at once," Sophie told him. "My brother has stood up to everyone else's designs for him. If Miss Templeton is not in Bath, then you must return to Town and not leave again until your feelings are made clear."

He looked as if she'd promised him she could make all his dreams come true. "You're not offended by our conversation or my intentions?"

"Me?" Sophie chuckled. "Your happiness is my happiness. You must do this, or you will be miserable forever. Oak Grove does not need a melancholy master." She sniffed. "It's far too big a place to be miserable."

He smiled at her, cheeks glowing. "Your encouragement means everything. I do wish the same happiness for you, you must know."

"I'm sure it will come." Sophie tried to hide the doubt in her reassurance.

He took both her hands in his. "Do not feel rushed, Miss Crestwood. Who minds that you are one hundred and still single?"

"Mr. Billingham!"

He laughed. "I only mean your time will come. When you meet your destiny, you will know it."

"Aren't you a romantic? You sound like my mama. Does one always know right away?"

"You are a romantic, too, Miss Crestwood. More than you know. Why else would you encourage me to think only of myself and my heart?"

Sophie tried to think of why, but all that came to her mind was a picture of Captain Murdock. It made her heart burn, with surprise and something else she could not name. "If my heart belongs to who I think of most often, my dear friend, I'm afraid I will only be disappointed in the end."

He jerked his head back, and his eyes widened with interest. "Who do you think of most often, Miss Crestwood?"

Sophie pulled out of his grasp and put both hands on her cheeks. "No one really, Mr. Billingham, not anyone I can say."

He chuckled, and she pointed at the Bengal roses in the center of her garden. "Come let me show you these lovely white buds who are cousins to your roses at Oak Grove."

THE LETTER ARRIVED a day after Mr. Billingham called. Sophie and Mama trailed behind Papa as he strode into his study, breaking the seal along the way.

"It is from Lady Mary. She advised Captain Murdock she would be in Bath when he wrote he would look for your brother along the coast. She asked him to keep her informed."

Sophie's heart pulsed with anticipation. She squeezed her hands together until they hurt. Captain Murdock had left Pembroke to search for Jack himself!

Papa began to read the lines out loud: "*You might as well know your Jack was put on the books of a seventy-four. Pratt is the captain's name. He is a man of good reputation and capable at the helm.*"

At the mention of a seventy-four gun ship, Sophie's heart spiraled into her stomach. She found she could hardly breathe.

Papa raised the letter and said, "Murdock says he's enlisted and at nothing more than powder boy. A man with the press gang says he did right by him when he mentioned Pembroke and his connections."

"That is good then," Sophie said in a questioning tone. "He's on a safe ship."

Mama did not look so agreeable.

Papa looked grim. "That is the bad news. Murdock says the ship has been ordered to the blockade. There's action in the Channel with that filthy Frenchman, and they need a good third rate. It's likely your brother will see battle." He looked at Mama. "It will not be a romantic scene."

Sophie's throat gnarled into a tangled lump of fear. The news should be sent to Mr. Billingham, she thought. He would want to know.

Although she abhorred the idea of pity, Sophie admitted she did find comfort in Billingham's sympathies, which he returned in a letter addressed to her father. He informed them Lady Mary had made arrangements to return home from Bath.

Not a fortnight later, Sophie heard horses but ignored the approach of visitors. Let Papa manage them. It wasn't until she heard his shoes bounding up the stairs that her heart trembled in her chest. Visions of Captain Murdock came unbidden into her mind, and with him, Jack. She stood up just as Papa knocked then burst into the room.

Out of breath and with flushed cheeks, he said, "You have a visitor. A caller has come." The corners of his eyes tensed. He took a heaving gasp of air to collect himself. With a fist planted on his hip and his other hand holding up the wall, he added, "Do freshen up and come down."

Sophie glanced at herself in the small looking glass. She did not think she needed any rearrangement. Unless it was... well unless Murdock had returned. Perhaps he had news. Perhaps, maybe, he had forgiven her.

Papa stared. "I will tell you rather than keep you in suspense. It is Mr. Henry Billingham again. He has come all the way from Town in a fine coach and four."

Sophie let her shoulders relax. "Oh," she said, "only Billingham? Why, of course Papa, I will be right down."

He looked at her with an expression tainted in disappointment then let himself out. She chuckled, tucked a few loose hairs back behind her ears, and patted her cheeks. She looked well enough she supposed. Her morning dress was not her oldest, not that Billing-ham would mind it. Curiosity moved her along with more enthusi-asm than she had felt in many days. Jack's departure had left her dull.

When she walked into the drawing room, Billingham stood at the window. Mama sat in her chair near the unlit hearth. "There you are." Mama's eyes beamed with a contentment Sophie had not seen since Jack's disappearance. "Look who has come."

Billingham bowed at the waist, and smiling, Sophie dipped at the knee. "I am so glad you are here," she said with much earnestness.

He crossed the room and took her hands. "Aunt has called, and I must submit, but I took the roundabout way to see how you get on since your brother's news. Forgive me for coming again so soon."

"We're glad you did," Mama said. She invited him to stay for sup-per, and he agreed.

"Do come sit and talk with us." Sophie motioned toward the set-tle across from her.

Mama rose to her feet. "I have unfinished letters which need my immediate attention." Billingham bowed, and Mama smiled, glanc-ing at Sophie as she departed. She shut the drawing room door.

Sophie groaned. "You must know how welcome you are here. My parents are delighted you have come."

Flushing, Billingham replied, "I hope they are not as happy to see me go."

"Don't worry. They won't be."

He bit his lip, and she realized he had something to say.

"Tell me. I would guess you have news about Miss Templeton?"

He shook his head. "No. I'm afraid I've made no progress in our acquaintanceship. She does not seem to enjoy my company, and I'm beginning to feel foolish and desperate. I have not come to trouble you with it though; I have news from the Channel. First, Perlmutter informed me yesterday the packet ships are in. I thought perhaps you had heard more from Murdock, but I see I am far ahead of the mail. I wanted to make haste to inform you."

"We've only had the news from Lady Mary that I sent on to you."

Billingham swept his arm out like he wished to present her with something. "Captain Murdock is no longer in Portsmouth. Did you know? He's gone to sea."

Sophie felt her jaw sag.

"Yes, it's true. He has commandeered a sloop, though how he acquired it I do not know, especially with his injury. He's joined the fray on some agreement with a person at Whitehall. It is my thought he has gone to fetch your brother."

Sophie almost jumped to her feet. "In the middle of a war?"

"The good man is off to save another Crestwood. It is no wonder you have not heard from him directly."

Sophie clasped her hands and looked down. "I could not bear to meet his eye the last time we spoke. I'm amazed at his kindness and courage."

"He cannot be so easily offended by a few flighty accusations."

"I hardly know, but despite them, he has gone after my brother as if Jack were his very own family—all the time knowing he has been maligned by mine."

"Perhaps he has forgiven it."

"I can only think that he is fond of Jack or feels some responsibility," said Sophie.

Billingham chewed the corner of his lip, crossed one foot over the other, and stared at the heel of his boot. "He failed to save his dear lieutenant friend. Perhaps he needs to save someone. Do you know what I believe, Miss Crestwood? I think your pirate has a heart of gold."

Sophie allowed a tremulous smile to escape. It dropped from her lips at a cry from the hall.

"I thought I heard the door," said Billingham, rising from his seat.

Alarm grew in Sophie's heart over the raised voices from outside the room. She held her breath, straining to listen even as her guest pulled open the door. Billingham stepped back, his eyes wide and cheeks pale. From the look of it, she knew it was dreadful, yet she could not come to her feet.

He gazed at her then shook his head in deep sorrow. Before she could muster the courage to plead for an explanation, Margaret dashed into the room, crushing him against the wall with a thud. She fell wailing into a pile of skirts at Sophie's knees. Sophie could not move. She could not breathe. Her hands hung useless at her sides. When she said nothing, Billingham demanded, "Say it then."

Margaret looked up into Sophie's eyes. Her face was rosy and wet; her eyes round and fearful. "Jack," she sobbed, "Master Jack."

Sophie's chest caved in and her stomach rolled over and over. She opened her mouth and tried to speak, but only made a small noise.

"The ship has gone down," cried Margaret. "They blew it to pieces, those filthy frogs." She collapsed onto Sophie's lap and began to scream.

Sophie felt all sense leave her head. It drained like thick syrup down into her toes. All around her sobs and shrieks echoed through the house. She could not bear it. Billingham's arm came around her, and she fell onto his shoulder. She covered her ears and burrowed her face into it. The spinning in her mind became a wild whirlwind, and a sob broke free of the knot in her throat. It erupted into a strangled cry.

Margaret was pushed from her lap, and someone swept her up in their arms. She realized it was Billingham but could not care enough to feel shy. Instead, she cried through her fingers until he carried her up the stairs and set her down in bed. She rolled over to hide the uncontrollable tears falling one after the other with great coughing sobs. Pain folded her in half and cut into her like a butcher's knife.

LIFE, THAT HAD ONCE been so happy and carefree, now trickled by dark and damp with autumn rain. Mama refused to accept Jack's death. She waited like he might appear, sheepish to be discovered missing after wandering out into the woods.

With Michaelmas fast approaching, and much to do with the harvest, Papa insisted on a funeral without his son's remains. The date was set, and it would be held in the cold stone church where Mr. Blackburn gave his sermons and his daughter blushed and giggled.

Katherine did no such thing on that day but sat nearby Sophie. She held her hand tight whenever they had the opportunity to touch, and she walked with Sophie into the church behind Richard and his wife, making Sophie feel that she wasn't so alone. Lady Mary came in her carriage, not the least put out with Mama for refusing to have the service at Oak Grove. Henry Billingham was at his aunt's side.

Spattering rain and mummified leaves swirled outside the church windows, making sounds Sophie found more pleasant than Mr. Blackburn's words. She could not bear to listen. The ring Papa had given her with a lock of Jack's hair should have brought her some small comfort, but its meaning ran a steel spike through her soul. When Mama began to sob in the crowded chapel, Sophie's own tears could not be contained. She let them drip down her face all the day long, even until she was back up in her room safe from prying, sympathetic eyes.

Days later, supper still felt like a continuation of the service, although the visitors had all departed. Papa tried very hard to lighten the mood, by telling his wife and daughter what he had heard in the village about a new governess and her flighty ward.

Sophie could scarcely pay any attention to him at all. It felt like Jack had disappeared into a hole in the floor, and that Mama grew quieter and Papa only louder. She escaped to the drawing room after Papa complained they must not all retire so early to their beds. He did not attend them long, and when he finally left, Mama felt like conversing at last.

"You almost seemed content when Mr. Billingham last came to call."

Sophie forced a small smile. "Oh, Mama, I'm not sure how I feel about all that."

From the door, Papa cleared his throat and took a step back inside. Sophie felt herself flush, surprised and offended he had been standing just outside the room.

"You did not refuse Mr. Billingham, did you?" His tone was hard and desperate all at the same time. Sophie thought he might faint.

"No, Papa. He does not mean to court me. We are just friends. He only came to tell me that Captain Murdock had commandeered the sloop."

Papa's face reddened as if Billingham had caused all their troubles.

"Please don't be disappointed," she exclaimed.

He frowned. "Then I will worry for you."

"No," Mama said from across the room. She set her knitting down hard in her lap. "We must not worry, Mr. Crestwood. Sophie is practical and intelligent, and she will sort it all out on her own. "

Sophie smiled at Mama's faith-filled remarks. "I am happy enough," she said with a stronger voice. "I miss Jack desperately, it's true, and even Richard a little bit, but I am content to stay here with you and Papa at Leatherbury. Why, who would manage the trout lines?" she joked.

Papa wagged his head back and forth, his face dark like his mourning clothes then marched from the room. Sophie hesitated then turned back to Mama. "Any word from Captain Murdock?" she begged, thinking perhaps she had not been informed.

"No, my dear, we have not had word today." Mama gazed at her, both needles stopping their dance just as quickly as they had resumed it. "Not of any kind from Captain Murdock since..." She stared. "I imagine he will be home soon with more than enough to tell, and none I will be able to bear. Tell me, my dear. Do you think of him so often?"

Sophie looked away. The gleaming firelight warmed her dull heart, even from across the room. "I don't know how I shall ever get on without Jack," she said in a voice that broke into pieces. Fresh tears leaked from the corners of her tired, raw eyes. She swiped them away. In a trembling voice, she whispered, "With Richard gone and Katherine at home, I cannot bear to think I have to go on without seeing Captain Murdock either. I admire him a great deal."

From the corner, Mama breathed deep in the silence that fell between them. She began to rock in her seat as if it were a rocking chair. Her hands moved the knitting needles at a very fast pace. "I know it, Sophie," she said in the quiet. "If Captain Murdock returns, well, when he does, we will welcome him here if he ever wishes to call on you."

Sophie shook her head in one swift jerk, returning her gaze to the flames in the hearth. She did not want to discuss it. *He will not ask, Mama.*"

CHAPTER SEVENTEEN

A few nights later, footsteps into Sophie's room woke her, and she sat up in fright. Mama carried a single lit candle, fresh and long, fluttering like flapping wings in the wee morning hours. She looked almost ghostly.

"What is it?" Sophie said in alarm, as her mind recollected the events of the last month. Her heart sank when she remembered what she already knew. Jack was dead. She squinted in the dim light that cast a wide halo on the floor around Mama's feet. Boots. "Why are you dressed to go out?" Sophie slid over to the side of her bed. Her feet nosed around on the floor seeking her worn wool-lined slippers.

Mama looked serious, but there was purpose written across her face in the tight jaw and clenched lips. "A man from Pembroke has come with news. Captain Murdock has come home ill, and the housekeeper there has called for us."

Sophie felt her eyes widen.

"We have sent for Doctor Stephens, and Papa has called for the carriage. He is going to take me to Pembroke."

"Papa will let you go?"

Mama's chin went up. "He is our neighbor, the son of one of my oldest friends, and after all he has done? They carried him from ship to shore, and he insisted he be brought home."

"Home. Did he call it that?" Sophie stumbled to her feet, spinning this way and that, in search of something to pull over her nightdress. "I'm coming with you."

"I don't think he will allow it. Your papa, I mean."

281

"Convince him, Mama. I've been to Pembroke. They know me there. I'll sit with you until the doctor comes."

Mama hesitated. "I thought you would insist. Change quickly."

THE BLACKNESS OVERHEAD faded into a dark ashen grey by the time the horse trotted down the windswept drive of the old stone hall. Though stars over Pembroke began to go out, faint lights in the windows still glowed. Sophie shivered from within a wool pelisse she had pulled from her armoire. The mornings were quite cold now. It would be a short time until dawn when the doctor would come. What she and her mother could do she did not know, but she had sense enough to be as helpful or to stay out of the way if that was best.

Mr. Sykes met them at the door, opening it with a slight bow. He glanced at Sophie but said nothing. Three men lingered in the wood-paneled hall, looking with uncertainty toward the stairs. They were rumpled and dirty in stained breeches. One had a low cap with ribbons knotted at the back. The other, a grizzled beard and shirt with merry stripes that made him look gnomish.

They stopped speaking and clumsily bowed when Mama strode in with Sophie at her heels. She watched her mother tug off her bonnet and toss it into Sykes' hands. She then gave her attention to Mrs. Brooks, who stood wringing her hands on the lowest stair.

"It's the Captain," Mrs. Brooks stammered like she did not know they already knew. "I've been caring for him this many years, but I ain't ever seen him like this." She bit her lip and searched Sophie's face, her eyes darting between Sophie and Mrs. Crestwood. "We don't know no doctor but your physician, and I don't know what to do, but I knew Miss Crestwood would help so I sent for ye."

Mama lifted her hem and strode across the floor to the bottom step. "I've sent for the physician, now take me upstairs." She motioned to Sophie. "Come along, Sophie. You may wait outside his door until I tell you to come in."

Taking a deep breath, Sophie nodded. She felt Sykes' scowl and wished there was time to explain to him that she was not the shallow, catty girl she'd been made out to be, but there was no time. What Mrs. Brooks now thought of the Crestwoods, she did not know; she only saw the tired, awkward back with its heavy hump. Mrs. Brooks' head hung low like she felt crushed.

The fear in the house made Sophie tremble. She moved her feet without making a sound up the stairs. The heavy tapestries were now clean and familiar, although it seemed like it had been more than a year since she had seen them last. On the third floor, they went around the awkward corner of the addition and down the hall to the second bedroom on the left. She remembered the windows faced almost east, looking out over the pastures beyond the woods and toward Leatherbury. The realization brought her some small measure of comfort. Whatever might be the matter, Murdock could always look out and know who waited for him across the stone wall.

Mrs. Brooks went in with Mama right behind her. They shut the door, and Sophie waited, straining her ears to listen. She only heard the soft murmurs of feminine voices. To be this desperate to call on a Crestwood, Captain Murdock must be near dead. Her knees quivered. How long she stood there she wasn't sure, but Mrs. Brooks relieved her from the onset of madness by opening the door in a soft, sweeping motion.

"Your mum says you can go in," she said and stepped out of the way.

Sophie forced a small smile to show her appreciation and brushed past the woman, stepping up off the floor onto a thick, soft rug the color of red wine. Across from the fireplace and smoking chair she had seen before, the dark polished wood continued around the room, blocked only by a modest-sized bed with four solid posts.

Its curtains were drawn back. A still, dark form lay under a grey naval blanket. Captain Murdock.

Sophie could tell one leg was propped up because it was raised above the rest of him. She grimaced at the thought of the pain his knee must have caused him since falling at Oak Grove.

Mama wrung out a cloth from a porcelain basin on a small table beside the bed. She glanced over her shoulder and motioned to the other side of the bed toward a ladder-back chair. "Take Mrs. Brooks' seat," she said in a soft tone.

Sophie moved around the bed, stepping over a pile of dirty linens. Heavy scarlet fabric covered the windows to keep out the chill. A low burning fire and two lamps on either side of the mantel were the only light in the room besides the taper near the wash basin. Sophie sank into the chair and tugged off her pelisse.

She recognized the captain's features, but they were as sharp and angular as ever like he had grown thinner in a very short time. A gleam of perspiration shined across his forehead. His tawny streaked hair was unkempt around his face, a dark spot against the white pillow.

"What is the matter?" Sophie asked in a whisper. He looked feverish to be sure and trembled with chills.

"It's not catching," Mama said, "at least I don't believe so." She put a wet cloth on his forehead, and he jerked.

"He put himself out." Sophie watched his still eyelids. "It was too much too soon to go back to sea."

Mama sat down on the bed, taking care not to rattle it and stared at him, too. "Yes, he was not well to begin with, not fully, and now he has a fever so high he cannot wake. I think it is his knee."

Sophie put a hand to her mouth.

"He's a sailor," Mama went on. "There is nothing keeping them back from the tide when they make up their minds to go." She swallowed, and Sophie saw tears well up in her eyes.

"Was his father like that? Sir Edward?"

"Edward?" Mama grimaced. "Oh, no, not at first. He was content with Pembroke and Town. I daresay he did not like to get dirty much less look for a fight."

"Oh yes, he loved Town," said Sophie with a smile.

Mama looked up. "Lady Mary must have told you a great deal."

"Enough for me to know Captain Murdock is nothing like him, at least in that way."

"I must say you are right," agreed Mama. "More like his mother, I suppose, whoever she was, though Edward had a good heart."

Sophie bit down on her lip and studied Murdock's profile. "A gentle soul," she whispered.

"One with great courage to take on Edward Murdock," Mama added with a soft laugh.

"Do you think it's just exhaustion, and he needs rest?" Sophie asked. She wanted to hear words of comfort and nothing of a more serious nature.

Mama raised the blanket and looked underneath it. "We will have to wait and see what Doctor Stephens thinks. They say Murdock does cry out in his sleep and tries very hard to speak."

Sophie settled back against the hard support of the chair. She watched Murdock as Mama sat beside him reading when not readjusting his covers or wiping down his face. Once, he tossed his head back and forth on the pillow and forced his eyes to open, and Sophie smiled at him, but before she could stand up, he closed them again and drifted back into his feverish dream with a wrinkle on his brow.

IT WAS AN ENTIRE NIGHT and half of a day before Doctor Stephens came, and he seemed surprised to find Sophie sitting at Murdock's side with her Mama on the other.

"When you sent for me, I did not realize you would be here."

Mama raised her chin. "Captain Murdock is our neighbor and friend. Mr. Crestwood has given his permission since you have been needed elsewhere on matters more urgent. My husband will be up shortly this afternoon."

"Very good then," mumbled the physician, a bit put off at the usually reserved Mrs. Crestwood. Sophie smiled to herself, knowing he probably wondered that she did not have a book in her hand, but it slid from her face when he looked up from studying the patient.

The doctor stared at Sophie from under his woolly brows. "I must ask you to leave, Miss Crestwood." He lifted the blanket to see the swollen leg as Sophie rose. She did not wish to go and did not mind seeing the poor man's wounds, but Mama stood behind the doctor watching so Sophie presumed that she agreed.

Sophie left the room and waited outside the door. Stretching her legs, she walked up and down the hall, now bright from the clean, undraped windows. It was a great while before Doctor Stephens departed, and when he did, he did not acknowledge her wrapped in her shawl in the chilly October light. He stared ahead, eyes blank, and his lips set in a forbidding streak that made her chest feel tight.

She tiptoed through the open door. Mama had gone back to sponging cool water on the captain's forehead. She did not notice Sophie's return.

"What does the doctor say?"

Lost in her thoughts, Mama flinched at the interruption. "It is grave after all. He has an infection in his knee which inflames the leg. The fever has accompanied him home from the sea." She shook her head. "All those men, coughing and shivering together on overcrowded death boats."

Sophie thought of Jack but pushed away the picture of him ill and miserable so that she could bear his absence. She studied Captain Murdock. His face shined with wet heat. The tanned color of his cheeks had faded so much they were only flushed dark pink with fever now. Mama stopped her ministering and dropped down on the bed to sit beside him.

"His leg is very bad, Sophie. The doctor says it is time they take it, or he will die."

Sophie recoiled in horror. "Surely he just needs rest."

"He has had more time to heal than most men do," Mama said with a sigh. "It is a lingering injury that cannot go on any longer."

On the bedside table were new vials of medicine Sophie assumed Doctor Stephens had left behind. Her shoulders drooped. It was a helpless feeling to see a man she thought of as resilient unable to even raise his eyelids. What would he do when he awoke half a man? Already his soul was broken by the loss of his treasured friend. He'd lost his mother, father, and home in the Indies, too. His health and the stones of Pembroke were all he had left.

She took Murdock's palm in her hand and began to rub it gently. Tears brimmed in her eyes, but she blinked them away.

Mama set her hands on her hips and stretched her shoulders. "I must send word to Mr. Crestwood. I'll send up Mrs. Brooks."

Sophie watched over the captain with such concentration she did not notice her mother leave. Shadows crept out of the corners of the room. The glow behind the heavy curtains faded. Noting the chill and that the fire had dwindled down, she pulled up the covers around the captain's still frame. He had calmed down after a time. The doctor's visit had agitated him.

Sophie took the quiet opportunity to study his leg, now propped up higher than it was before and draped with more sheets. She knew little about his injury, other than it had ruined his career and cost the lives of those around him. "What happened?" she said and searched his face, but he did not answer.

He turned his head toward her, and she felt a small squeeze on her hand.

"I'm here," she whispered.

She did not dare breathe for a few seconds, watching for any sign that he might wake up, but he didn't. Eventually, the room grew dark, and though she heard her mama come in, she found she could not lift her head from off the bed where she had dropped off to nap. The back of Murdock's hand rested against her cheek, so she would know from the warmth of it that he still lived.

BIRDS, WHISPERS, AND other morning sounds roused her from where she had dozed off in the unforgiving chair. Murdock seemed more aware now, but uncomfortable. He mumbled something as she rubbed her eyes, and his arm flailed out, slapping the bed before falling limp. From the chair near the mantel, Mama raised herself to her feet.

Sophie scooted to the edge of her seat and reached for his fist. His hot, damp fingers curled around hers. He opened his eyes with enormous effort and looked around the room until he saw her. Sophie saw the recognition, and her heart burned in her chest when he whispered her name.

He was handsome, gentle, calm, and brave, even near death. How she loved him, she realized, but he did not love her and now death loomed between them.

She moved close, turning her head to let him know he could speak.

"Howard," he whispered in a choked voice. She looked back at him and gave a little shake of her head to show that she did not understand. He sighed and closed his eyes.

Mama bent over them. "Drink this, Captain. Come now, you must." He opened his eyes again. With great effort, he rubbed his lips together then swallowed from the cup she put to his chin. After struggling to take the sip of water, he said in a hoarse voice to Sophie, "Mr. Howard has your brother."

The glass in Mama's hand tilted to one side and water spilled out onto the blanket covering the captain's chest. Sophie looked at Mama's pale face and back to Murdock, who must have been babbling in his fever. She stood up in a movement so swift the chair scraped over the floor behind her.

"Come now," she said, leaning over him, "you'll frighten my mother." She took the cup from Mama and patted Captain Murdock on the shoulder. He raised his head and gazed up at her with clear eyes. "Mr. Howard has Jack."

His head dropped back on the pillow, and his eyes fell shut. On the other side of the bed, Mama covered her mouth with both hands and sank to her knees on the floor. Sophie could not think what to do with the thunder of her own heartbeat raging between her ears. The bedroom door groaned open, and Mrs. Brooks tiptoed in.

"Mr. Howard has Jack," Sophie repeated in a trembling voice. She knew it was true. She knew it by the way Murdock had looked at her. It was his gaze, his passionate and knowing gaze that probed her eyes when he spoke.

The tray in Mrs. Brooks' hands wobbled so much the dishes on it clattered. "We ain't heard from Mr. Howard. He ain't come back."

Mama jumped to her feet. "Who's Mr. Howard?"

"The cook," said Sophie and servant at the same time.

"We must send word back to Portsmouth," Sophie said with growing confidence. "Call Mr. Sykes. Someone will know something. Someone must!"

LEATHERBURY WAS IN an uproar. Not a panicked, thundering, black storm, but a clattering, giggling, tearful dance. The servants chattered like squirrels, and Papa flitted back and forth from room to room with letters, orders, and dogs at his heels. Mama and Mar-

garet aired out Jack's room, and Sophie skipped between the library
and the drawing room, watching messengers that came and went.

Although the joy in her heart felt boundless, a lingering pain nib-
bled away at the happiness. She knew Captain Murdock was being
prepared for surgery. Doctor Stephens had sent for a peer, a ship's
surgeon, with more experience in the kind of treatment Murdock
needed. The doctor had also insisted, along with Mrs. Brooks, that
the Crestwoods return home and wait for their son.

His people, Sophie knew, would take care of their captain, but
the knowledge gave her little peace. She felt she should be there, that
she belonged there, and in some odd way that Captain Murdock was
as much hers as he was Pembroke's. If only he had not injured himself at Oak Grove or become ill in the Channel. He had sacrificed
what remained of his health to bring Jack home. He would always be
whole in Sophie's eyes. To Jack, he would be a hero forever.

Lady Mary's admiral friend found Mr. Howard before Papa's in-
quirers and only her stern admonition for patience kept the whole
family from cramming into the carriage and driving like lunatics for
the coast. The cook, Mr. Howard, had been discovered at Newhaven,
staying with a fisherman who had taken in a few refugees into his
humble home. Two men and a child were survivors of a shipwreck;
and Mr. Howard, the kindly cook and seaman acting for Captain
Murdock, had sent word only to his superior and not the Crestwood
family.

Captain Murdock became too ill to communicate the news, and
those who carried him home either had not known or they hurried
back to port thinking others would pass it along.

"To think, I did not know," Mrs. Brooks cried. She'd apologized
with great feeling for the delay, explaining that in their concern for
the captain, any particulars had been assumed or forgotten.

Mr. Howard was provided with resources from Leatherbury, and the family expected Jack home at any moment. Between Pembroke and Leatherbury, Doctor Stephens was sure to be kept on his feet.

A carriage turned into the drive, and Sophie leaped up from her mending of Jack's stockings. He'd left the torn ones behind. She caught her breath in disappointment, for she should have known by the heavy sound of it that it was a great coach. Lady Mary's carriage pulled up with a great clatter of horse hoofs. Sophie threw off her disappointment and found herself smiling when Mr. Billingham jumped out before the footman could open the door.

Papa raced to the courtyard ahead of everyone else in the house. "Mr. Billingham."

Behind Mama, Sophie dipped at the knee, unable to hold back her happiness. She had so much to share. Billingham abandoned his cordial bow to her parents and strode toward her, arms outstretched. Then aware of himself and the others, he dropped them back to his sides.

"My lovely Miss Crestwood!" He beamed so wide his cheeks glowed. "Happy news!"

Sophie clapped. "Yes. We expect him any day."

With the help of a footman, Lady Mary scaled down from the coach in a huff. Her nephew had bolted out before her, and she had almost been forgotten.

"Do come in," begged Mama.

Sophie realized with a blush she'd forgotten all about Lady Mary. They sailed into the drawing room as a throng of happy bodies. Mama nodded at Lady Mary's every word, and Papa dashed about to make the most comfortable seat for their dearest friend.

"It's been a great many years since I've felt such relief," Lady Mary said with a smile. Her blue eyes sparkled like forget-me-not blossoms in the brightness of the late morning. "Although I know Jack may not be pleased to see his former patroness, I'm overjoyed to see him come home." Her mouth quivered at the corners to hold back a smile.

Sophie clasped her hands to her heart. "He may be happier to see you than we know. After such a dreadful adventure..."

From the window where he'd situated himself, Billingham said, "He was lucky to survive at all. They say she went down fast, but a coxswain tossed him into a small skip, and he was able to get away in the confusion. Another ship fished them out, the—"

"The *Buttercup*," finished Sophie. "She was coming to the rescue and was too late, but not too late to pick up Jack and those other poor men. Mr. Howard says Captain Murdock intercepted them when he heard the *Buttercup* had found survivors.

Billingham frowned. "How he convinced them to release Jack I'll never know. He is enlisted now."

Papa spoke up. "Captain Murdock did us a great service, although I suspect your ladyship had much to do with it." He looked at Lady Mary and dropped his eyes in humble gratitude.

Sophie acknowledged Lady Mary's secretive look with a nod. To think the lady and Captain Murdock had set about without hesitation to do everything they could to save her foolish brother.

"You know a great deal," said Billingham to Sophie.

She looked up. "Mrs. Brooks has been able to learn some of the news, for Mr. Howard is on his way back with a few of the captain's men. Jack, we are assured, is with them."

"I can hardly wait," said Mama from a corner of the room. She looked spent just from listening to the conversation.

"Would you like to take a turn out in the garden?" Billingham asked Sophie. She shook her head in agreement and left the room for her things, noticing that Lady Mary's gaze followed her out.

"We're going out," Sophie explained to them all when she returned. "You should, while the weather is fair," said Mama with a faint smile. The women turned back to Papa and continued their discussion.

She buttoned up her spencer, and Billingham helped her with a shawl before they ambled out the front door into a late, fine October day. A cold breeze billowed the treetops under a golden harvest sun. Sophie took a deep breath as Billingham caught up her arm in his own, and they stomped together over a rust-colored carpet of brittle leaves that crunched at every step.

"I can hardly remember Michaelmas," Sophie said, without taking her eyes from the sky, "yet it will be Christmas soon."

Beside her, Billingham chuckled. "It's still weeks away, although with your brother missing, I can imagine you could not think of anything else."

"I must say," said Sophie, leaning into him as she stepped from the drive into the grass, "this has not been one of our happiest years." She glanced at her companion and turned up one side of her mouth in a churlish look.

"Don't be sad, Miss Crestwood." Billingham's aetherial blue eyes sought to comfort her in his cheerful way. She squeezed his arm back. He added, "Some times are good, some times are not, but always there is hope, and with heaven's blessing, little miracles."

"Yes, Jack is a testament to that," Sophie agreed.

They reached a copse of trees, and he took her hand. "Come, sweet friend, let me tell you of a little miracle I am hoping for myself."

Sophie followed him under the patchwork canopy. The worn path that led to the pond and off through the woods toward the stone wall reminded her of Jack. Leatherbury was so much his place, she realized. As much as he wanted to flee this land for open water, it was marked with the memories of his exploits and adventures.

A strong breeze rustled the surviving leaves overhead. Billingham stopped and faced her. "I have been at Oak Grove the past few weeks. Between the estate and keeping abreast of news of your brother and Captain Murdock, I found myself overwhelmed, or so I supposed."

"It's reasonable, Mr. Billingham. I imagine you have been troubled with Miss Templeton, too?"

He shook his head *no*, and Sophie inclined her head in question.

Billingham explained: "I've had a great deal of time to reflect, even when quite occupied. I've found my feelings have changed, or at least I've sorted them out."

"You are going to let her go?" Sophie understood. She knew how hard that could be. "You certainly will not be censured by me for withdrawing your attentions from the lady."

Billingham's mouth curled up into a weak smile. "Thank you." He brought her gloved hands to his lips and brushed them with a kiss.

Sophie found she needed to clear her throat. "You are so serious, Mr. Billingham, and here we are delirious with our happy news."

"I have something more to tell you, and I hope you will think it happy news."

"Oh?"

He dropped their clasped hands but did not let go. "It's me. I was stubborn when I came to Oak Grove. I knew I'd been given a prodigious opportunity in inheriting such a sizable estate, but I could not make peace with the fact I would be matched up with someone of my relatives' choosing."

Sophie nodded. "I understand completely." Then she blushed, realizing he had been her parents' greatest hope.

He touched her cheek. "Perhaps we were too hasty to rebel against our families' wishes."

"What do you mean?"

A slice of sunlight cut through the thinning foliage above their heads. It lit the ground around them. It soaked through Sophie's bonnet and warmed her crown despite the cool air.

"What I mean is—" Billingham cleared his throat and coughed. "Sorry. What I mean is, Miss Crestwood, you and I are more than amiable, and we get on so well that I..."

The view over Billingham's shoulder began to spin a little bit like someone was turning Sophie on a spindle.

"What I mean is," began Billingham for a third time, "I was far more fascinated with Miss Templeton's looks than her character. You far outrank her when it comes to sensibility and kindness. I think of you all the time and miss our conversations when we're apart. Truth be told, you are just as lovely a girl as I've ever seen; inside and out."

Sophie's heart bloomed at the compliment. She smiled so wide she felt her eyes scrunch at the corners. *If only Captain Murdock thought such things*, a silent voice whispered to her heart. She forced a laugh. "You always say the best things, Mr. Billingham."

He stared at her and swallowed so loud she saw the knot in his throat bob then he dropped to his knee. Above her, the clouds and all their weight seemed to crash down on Sophie's shoulders.

"Miss Crestwood," Billingham said in a hoarse whisper, "I find I have come to admire and love you, so much so I am certain I will not find another half as dear. Would you do me the honor of being more than a friend and companion? Would you consider being my wife?"

The weight of her body sank into her heels. Sophie felt certain she would drop into the earth. She held onto Billingham's grip for support.

Her thoughts flew about and hit the walls of her mind like a trapped bird. It all made perfect sense. Sophie Crestwood was not quite silly enough to find a husband in Town when she came out her first season. She had flirted with the idea of the Duncan boy, and there were other gentlemen who caught her eye, but they were never as interested in her once they knew her family.

The words of Devlin seared her heart. Her father was a gossip; her mother lost in books. Perhaps Sophie knew it all along. Perhaps she knew she was safe from the practical and opportune matches because of her parents' peculiarities and ambitions.

Her heart sank into her feet, too. It was the thing that had put off Murdock, to be sure. The very man who was not respected in Highfield because of his own father and murky repute, a man of mood and passion, did not want her. Billingham did. Despite it all, Billingham admired and esteemed her.

She swallowed. Dear Mr. Billingham. He was as adorable as a puppy, and thoughtful and generous, too. Then there was Oak Grove, that great estate. Sophie took a deep breath. The gentleman before her was all kindness, waiting with infinite patience, an angel compared to that devil, Devlin.

The sounds of life at Leatherbury echoed on the wind. Jack. What would he do? She closed her eyes, and they filled with tears beneath their lids. Jack had chased his dreams and nearly been killed for it. Foolish boy. Now, after Oak Grove's house party, she had finally won a proper and honest proposal. It was her greatest wish and her family's dearest hope. She squeezed Billingham's hand.

"I'd be honored," she replied in a whisper. Her heart swelled with hope and faith that he really loved her. "I'd be happy to be your wife. I say yes."

She could not raise her eyes to meet his, so great was her fear that she might spy Pembroke over the distant trees.

CHAPTER EIGHTEEN

Jack arrived home less than a week after Mr. Billingham's proposal. The wagon rattling past the house sounded much like any other, but as the horse slowed its pace, Sophie and Mama were drawn to the window with flickering flames of hope in their hearts.

Margaret, outside pulling late vegetables from the garden, was the first to spy him. Her shrill cry almost sent Sophie through the drawing room window.

"Jack!" Sophie called. She tried to wave but gave up when the familiar form of her brother was crushed by Margaret after the driver helped him to the ground.

Sophie dashed out the front door. A stout man with large forearms she assumed to be Mr. Howard clumped down to the ground from the wagon looking much pleased with himself. "Jack," she said in a choked voice, and tears poured from her eyes in shameless joy.

Mama reached him first. His chapped face hung over her shoulder, and Sophie realized he was not standing straight up; he was taller, his hair longer, and his cheekbones no longer carried the round bloom of childhood.

"How you have grown." Sophie clapped in delight. Mama released Jack just enough for him to reach out to Sophie, and she threw her arms around him and squeezed. A sob worked its way free, but she laughed it away.

Jack patted her back and mumbled something in her ear. She drew away and put her hands on either side of his face. "I am so happy you are here. You would not believe what we endured."

He gave a curt nod, and she saw remorse in his dark, green eyes. "I'm happy to be home," he admitted.

Mama drew him back into her embrace, and Margaret snatched his hand and put it to her cheek. There was no stealing him away. Sophie glanced back over her shoulder and saw Papa. He waited behind them with his arms folded and eyes watered with tears.

"Papa," said Jack, pushing away from the women and making a small bow. He cleared his throat, and Sophie held her breath. Mama stared and after a moment's silence, Mr. Crestwood held out his arms. "Come here, boy."

Jack stumbled forward, and the two men embraced while the ladies of Leatherbury cried in their handkerchiefs.

THEY PACED THE GROUNDS of Leatherbury in the late mornings, sometimes sitting on the wall, sometimes walking up to Pembroke's gardens and examining the fading roses that looked well-tended under Pembroke's new gardener. It had been a week since the naval surgeon arrived from London to remove Captain Murdock's leg; a physician with battle experience who came highly recommended.

The days they waited to see the captain felt eternal; like a cruel purgatory where Sophie and Jack could only peer up at the covered windows of the stone hall and wait for news. From what Sophie could glean, and Jack knew more than she, the captain was alert and resting, but in no state to entertain visitors.

During this time, Jack told Sophie about his adventures in the Channel fighting the French. He'd seen a great deal; her brother was changed forever. Sometimes, he would hesitate as if catching himself from saying too much, but he had witnessed violence and death, and Sophie knew it had affected him a great deal.

"You are fortunate to be in one piece, Jack. What shock and grief you gave us, and yet you speak like you are only here to visit for a time."

Jack angled himself to face her. He stretched his now long legs across the wall then he leaned back on his arms and looked up into the bright autumn sun. "I'm on the books now, my dear. Once I've recovered enough, I will have to go back."

"No," Sophie shook her head. "Lady Mary has offered to intercede and have it undone. You can go on to Harrow School now, for a time anyway."

"I'm almost fourteen," said Jack. "I'm wasting my time studying to be a clergyman when I know I won't ever finish at Oxford. Besides, Lady Mary cannot undo the Navy."

Sophie sighed and studied the small, soft hairs that had erupted onto his once smooth face. "You are lucky Papa has agreed to let you go. If it weren't for Mama—our mother of all people—who insisted you recover and be let to do what your heart commands, I'm sure he'd have you locked in the attic."

"I've climbed down off the roof hundreds of times."

Sophie laughed. "Please, don't tell me such things. I can only hope it helped you keep your footing in the shrouds."

Jack smiled back. He waved one of his boots back and forth, and she reached out and caught it by the toe.

"It's not all bad, Sophie. The gentle toss and sway of a ship is a glorious motion, and the water meets the sky in the most perfect line everywhere you look. The sun and the moon and the stars, well, I've never seen them better." He sighed. "It's a beautiful thing, and I can hardly wait to see the Indies. They say the water is as blue as it is green, and the sand is as white as angel wings."

"Your grammar is much improved," Sophie observed.

He shrugged. "I figure I should speak more like an officer than a bilge rat. I did show the boys a thing or two about manners; thanks to you and Mama."

"If you at least washed your face and combed your hair, you did us proud."

"That I did." Jack looked up the pasture hill toward Pembroke.

"I was happy there when things were peaceful, and I want to go back. It's truly what I want to do, and it's honorable. I can be a midshipman then a lieutenant and who knows," he jerked his head toward Pembroke, "maybe a captain someday."

Sophie's smile faded when she joined his gaze on Pembroke. "I don't know what Captain Murdock was like before he came to Pembroke, but I know the death of his friend affected him a great deal. What he will be like now with his mobility encumbered and his future in question, I can only imagine. I would never want that for you."

Jack scrunched his brows. "Oh, I've seen men with one leg, even men missing hands and arms. He'll do alright. It was the disease in his knee keeping him down all along anyway."

"He seemed to be growing content here before he took a turn; bringing Pembroke back to life and meeting Lady Mary, and Mr. Billingham, too, of course."

Jack snorted. "Your betrothed?"

She glanced at him. "You will have no reason not to find Billingham amiable."

"I cannot see you loving that big old house at Oak Grove. It's like a castle and far too empty for someone like you who has to chatter on to anyone who'll listen."

"Jack," scolded Sophie with a laugh. "I don't talk all that much, do I?"

He pursed his lips and narrowed his eyes. "Why do you think I go so far away?"

She blew out a breath of loud air in disagreement. "We get on well, and Oak Grove is a beautiful estate. I can hardly believe my good fortune."

"Mama and Papa are happy."

"I think so, though relieved is more like it."

"I can't say I am, but it's your life to live." Jack gave another shrug.

Sophie frowned. "What else would you have me do?"

"I thought you might stay at Leatherbury when Richard comes or even make a living up there." Jack motioned toward Pembroke with his chin.

Sophie widened her eyes. "At Pembroke? You think I would do better to set my sights on Pembroke Hall?" She tried not to blush. There was no reason for him to know she had once harbored such hopes, and worse, unrequited feelings for Captain Murdock.

Those sentiments were still there when she let herself feel them, but it only hurt when she did so. She tried not to think about it. "Henry Billingham is fond of me, as is his aunt. I like him a great deal; he's a true gentleman. Besides, his parents have consented despite my bringing much less to the marriage, and Mama and Papa are more than satisfied."

"So, you dare not refuse."

Sophie waved her hand to shoo away his question.

The grass of Pembroke was a dry yellow-green, and the distant trees paraded orange and red leaves. The early winter beauty contradicted the sad condition of the estate's heir. No one had signaled to them that the captain could see them now. Mr. Billingham had come and gone two times to Leatherbury since the surgery. There was a great deal of discussion of what needed to be done to prepare for the wedding.

Sophie knew her engagement to be a good situation. Billingham often found things to talk about besides his reservations about the

Oak Grove inheritance, like a new joke or a fun story about Devlin and his new bride, Mrs. India Devlin.

It pained Sophie she did not feel the mad rush of romantic feelings she thought she would for a husband, but she did love him with a deep and tender feeling. It was better this way, she knew, than to continue searching or waiting for some other gentleman who might never change his mind about her.

THREE WEEKS AFTER WHAT Sophie imagined was a ghastly surgery, word came to Leatherbury that the Captain was well enough to see Mrs. Crestwood. Like Sophie, she was anxious to check on the health of her now beloved neighbor. If Mama did not secretly admire him before, she now took delight in announcing herself as his friend and advisor, if not second to Lady Mary and her support.

Sophie and Jack joined their mother in the carriage and rode up for a formal visit. When they arrived, Mrs. Brooks walked them to the upstairs wing. She let them into the room, and they found Captain Murdock reclined on a pile of pillows. His eyes were closed as if trying to block out the light. His face had lost its pinched look, and he did seem to be comfortable.

Mama swept across the room, fell to her knees, and touched his arm. Sophie stood motionless at the foot of the bed. She tried to avoid looking at the empty space under the blankets where his leg should have been.

Jack, very matter of fact, looked down, and when Murdock opened his eyes he saluted him. "I'm back, don't you know. Did you miss me?"

Murdock gave him a slow, lazy smile. His gazed roved around the room, taking in Mama at his left and then stopped to rest on Sophie. He stared and swallowed.

"Captain Murdock is on a strict regimen of medicine," Mrs. Brooks said in a loud voice like everyone was hard of hearing. "Laudanum and some other potions, too." Stepping up to whisper in Sophie's ear, she added, "He's still silly at times. Yesterday he would only speak in Portuguese."

"Oh," said Sophie, realizing the man did look a bit too content for a person who had endured the loss of a limb.

"He don't even speak Portuguese," said Mrs. Brooks. "He just told me that's what it was."

Sophie stifled a giggle. Captain Murdock grinned back. The deep indentation in his cheek made an appearance. The dimple made him look young and charming.

"I'm doing much better," he said. The smile lingered on his face. He reached over and patted Mama's hand on his arm. "You are kind to visit with me here in this dusty, old place."

"Of course we would," said Mama. "I'm pleased you remember me. We have no intention of leaving you here to recover all alone."

Sophie glanced at Mrs. Brooks and added, "We mean except for your nurse, Mrs. Brooks, and your men, we thought you needed your neighbors here, too."

His eyes lit up. "You're very handsome," he said in a congenial voice.

Jack snickered. Sophie blushed. Mama gave a little laugh. "Oh, Captain, you take a great deal of medicine to stay comfortable. We will forgive whatever you might say."

"Yes, we will," Sophie blurted. She took a deep breath and set her shoulders back. She was practically married, or soon to be anyway. There was no use in behaving like he made her uncomfortable; not even for propriety's sake. "We are your friends and neighbors, and we owe you a debt for saving Jack."

"Yes, Jack," agreed the Captain. He closed his eyes, but the faint smile lingered on his face. "Jack is home. I am home. Mrs. Brooks is home, too, with her lumpy lobscouse pudding."

Jack drew in a breath, and Sophie caught his eye and shook her head. It'd not do to be giggling over the poor man when he could hardly think straight while in such confinement.

"We'll sit with you awhile," Mama promised him. She touched his forehead and brushed a few strands of hair away. "Then Jack will come, then Sophie. We'll all take turns," she looked over to Mrs. Brooks, "if it's acceptable to you."

The woman smiled in satisfaction. "See here, Captain, look at all your house. We ain't alone in this old place after all, and it ain't dusty no more neither."

SOPHIE SAT AT HIS BEDSIDE often, but Captain Murdock did not always acknowledge she was there. Mrs. Brooks brought in platters of food cooked up by Mr. Howard, more than any two people could ever eat. Murdock would only take a little soup and bread anyway.

Some days his mind was clear, and they sat in comfortable silence. She would ask him how he felt, and he would answer every day a little better. Sometimes she would describe the changes on Pembroke's grounds; the seasonal transformation he could not see from the window while in his bed.

The weather only warmed up in the afternoons, and Sophie took every opportunity to pull back the curtains and read a bit from his books on travel or botany of which he would listen with great intensity. Other times he would talk about his home in St. Kitts, and she'd listen quietly, imagining the white sand and rolling green hilltops that peaked over the sea.

One day, a week after the doctor permitted visitors, she thought Murdock was asleep, and so she busied herself studying his profile rather than stitching the sampler in her lap. When he opened his eyes and found her watching, he said in a quiet voice, "I understand you are engaged now."

It caught her off guard, and she could not think how to respond for a time. "Yes, to Mr. Billingham," she said at last in a stutter that made her blush.

Captain Murdock offered her a small smile. "I wonder why no one has told me sooner. It is a good match. I admire him very much."

"Do you?" Sophie leaned forward in her chair. "We do get on well."

"So your mother says."

"Yes, it's not difficult. He is cheerful and kind. He makes me laugh, and I'm amazed at his vitality."

"Yes, always going and doing and thinking, that one."

"It's true, but he's not always so relentless. He can be thoughtful or even overwhelmed when much is on his mind. We've had some very good talks."

The captain nodded. "That's important."

"Yes, we do talk a great deal. I mean, he talks well." She laughed at herself. "I suppose I do too much talking most of the time, but I'm more aware of it now since Jack pointed it out."

Captain Murdock caught his breath and used his arms to pull himself up. Sophie took the opportunity to arrange the pillows behind him then she sat beside him on the bed. "Do you think I talk too much, Captain?"

He smiled at her. "No, I enjoy our conversations, Miss Crestwood. You're just as cheerful as Mr. Billingham, but a good deal more in earnest. I must add, unlike some ladies, you do not talk about silly things, and you listen well, too."

Sophie smiled. "Thank you." His compliments satisfied her. "You will be better by Christmas then and come to the engagement party?" Her mind tried to work out how he would get about.

Captain Murdock gave her an agreeable look. "I'm going to be fitted with a false leg, you recall. They have wooden cores, but some are hinged with locking knees. It will be made special in London at a place that makes them for the wounded and the lame."

"Oh yes," said Sophie, remembering Jack's words, "so you will be able to get out then. Why, that's very good. Nelson did not have his arm, and he did well enough."

"Yes, I know it. Though I'm afraid I will never be without my blasted cane with the cut so high, it will serve me well enough to get around."

"Don't forget your horse," Sophie reminded him.

"I have not. With luck, my full health will return, and I will be my old self and better to ride him again."

"Your old self?" Sophie smiled at him, tenderness swelling up in her heart. "I would like to meet your old self."

Murdock wrinkled his forehead. "I'm sure you have met my old self at one time or another."

"You mean when I first set foot on your precious grounds," she teased, "and you ordered me right back over the wall."

Murdock gave an innocent lift of his shoulder. "I meant when I was fencing with your brother in the stables I suppose; or when we were at Oak Grove, and you kept me company."

Sophie gave a little shake of her head. "Oh, that old crowd. They weren't very kind to you."

He grimaced. "Word gets around. I blamed myself for Cottle's death in St. Kitts, and I lingered in my dark mood when I came to Pembroke. I do know I had my own part in it—the rumors." Murdock pulled the blanket up around himself to busy his hands. "I also know you were not the source of gossip at Oak Grove. Perlmutter made it known to me that Mr. Devlin liked to talk about my reputation endlessly. At first, he thought it came from you, as Devlin implied it did, but his true colors soon became clear."

Sophie made a face. "I admit it took me some time to see him for what he was, and I was too forbearing. I'm sorry he took it upon himself to be so rude and to stir up painful memories of your dearest friend."

"I am responsible for losing Cottle, but he was right there with me. He knew the risks, and we never disagreed." Murdock hushed and searched the cloudless sky out his window. Sophie waited.

He licked his lip. "We decided to pursue a bigger ship that day; a French buccaneer with no small reputation and more guns. We had more men, or so we thought. I'm afraid I was over confident, and in the excitement allowed Cottle to encourage me to choose an action with far more risk than we should have undertaken. We had done so well that season I suppose I thought we were unstoppable."

Captain Murdock paused. He looked at Sophie with sad eyes. They were paler than usual. "No man is indomitable. I suppose I thought my father so weak and myself so much stronger that I could not lose."

"Too much success?" Sophie reached over and touched his arm.

"I don't quite know," Murdock said in a whisper. "I was blessed, it's true, but I was too ambitious for my own good."

"That could happen to anyone. I'm sorry you were wounded on top of it all."

"Yes, I took a hit in the knee, but I was spared. Cottle..."

"I think he was here that day; when they did the surgery. I remember thinking I was dead or mad, but for the life of me I could swear now Will was standing by my side holding my hand, and I saw my father, too." Murdock glanced at her to see if she believed him.

Sophie's eyes brimmed with tears at the warm feeling that settled over the room. "I knew this place was haunted," she said with a joking wink.

Murdock grinned. "My father may have loved and missed this estate, but I have decided to leave my ghosts in St. Kitts, Miss Crestwood. I knew, I mean, I know now, I have a great deal more to learn about life, and there is much to do here at Pembroke before this old house chases me away.

MAMA CAJOLED HER OFTEN to rest, although some evenings Sophie did not feel comfortable even in her own bed. There was a great deal of wedding plans to see to and fittings in Guildford for a new wardrobe that she would take with her to Oak Grove.

She could hardly think of moving there with all the changes at Leatherbury. At night, she worried about a time when Captain Murdock might leave someday. He had promised to restore Pembroke to its former glory, but she imagined it would be reclaimed by the thistle and ivy if he ever went back to sea. The stone wall which had been repaired again would crumble away as moss took it over, and the trees between Leatherbury and her neighbor would thicken back into an impenetrable barrier until this part of her life was a long-forgotten memory.

Jack was satisfied to learn he'd been transferred to a new ship of the line, one of which he was on the books as a young midshipman. He came highly recommended by Lady Mary's good friend at Whitehall, and of course, there was Captain Murdock's word.

Autumn brought on so many changes, Sophie did not allow herself to feel surprised about the many stares at church over her engagement to the heir of Oak Grove. There were no longer glances of pity for the grieving Crestwoods. Rather, there were long looks at the stubborn Master Jack, who did not look the least bit sorrowful he had caused his own funeral. Quiet whispers about the ladies of Leatherbury tending to the sinister master of Pembroke like he was one of their own made for puzzled brows, too.

Katherine, deciding to be loyal on the matter, hung onto Sophie's hand and her every word. She was beside herself to be the best friend of the future mistress of Oak Grove and would even speak in defense of Captain Murdock if someone made mention of him in a questionable way.

Papa took it all in stride. He spoke of nothing but visiting Oak Grove when his own daughter was running the great estate. His hair had turned white, losing its silver shine to a cool, frosty shade, and his wiry locks curled around his forehead in little piglet tails. He had forgiven Sir Edward's reputation and past romance with Mama. He'd forgotten Murdock's questionable arrival to Higfield and in fact, defended the captain with violent enthusiasm whenever someone doubted the Murdock name. After all, the heir of Pembroke, who had gone to war to save a Crestwood, could not be a pirate. He told all who would listen.

Settled in a rocker after her Sunday nap, Sophie heard with satisfaction the clip-clop of Mr. Billingham's horses and dropped her dull book to gaze out the window. She wrapped a shawl around her shoulders to battle the cold air seeping through the glass panes. The sky hinted at an early snowfall. She grimaced at the thought that her engagement party might be cancelled due to weather. Worse, it could turn into days of grueling hours of entertaining snowbound visitors that would exhaust Mama and Margaret.

She watched Mr. Billingham hurry to the house and rushed to greet him. His smile widened in surprise when she opened the door.

"You are getting doors now?" he teased. "Where is Margaret?"

Sophie laughed as she curtsied. "Dusting and polishing in mad preparation for your party, Mr. Billingham. We cannot spare an extra hand, not even to answer a door."

"We have time yet," he exclaimed, reaching for her hand. He brought it up to his lips. His eyes danced with his good nature, even though a chilling wind swept into the house along with him.

"Come." Sophie led him to the drawing room and blazing fire. He took a seat beside her and tucked a blanket around his lap.

"You are still certain you wish to hold it here?" he asked her.

Margaret dashed in and offered to make him coffee. The strong, cozy smell of it drifted from the kitchen.

"Yes, Mama agrees there is no reason to put you out at Oak Grove, and besides," said Sophie, "it's closer for Captain Murdock here. It will be his first real outing since his surgery."

"Ah, yes," said Billingham, sitting back to get more comfortable. "I called on him earlier today. It is mornings when he is in his best spirits my aunt tells me."

"Yes," Sophie agreed. "Lady Mary has been to visit and buoyed him up a great deal. I think he was quite honored."

"He's looking forward to doing business with one of her investors, I understand."

"Something like it," Sophie said, wrinkling her forehead to recall. "I do know he is going to let out some of Pembroke's land for hunting like used to be done."

"Hunts, hmm," said Billingham. "Very traditional of him, I must say, and I know he is clever with finances." He looked at Sophie. "He's a brave man, but better with figures than futtocks."

Sophie's mouth dropped a little in surprise at his censure. "He was a brilliant captain and very successful privateer."

"Yes. It's true. I suppose he just got in over his head a bit like we all do. He will do well at Pembroke, I'd wager, if he settles for good." Billingham looked around the modest drawing room. "Are you certain you do not mind a crowd in this small place? We would have a great deal more room at Oak Grove, and I could be of more assistance."

Sophie chuckled. "Lady Mary has your ear, I see."

"She is all about parties," admitted Billingham. "I am overcome by details between her and my mother."

"I'm sure your mother is very kind."

"She is happy to be introduced to you at last. I'm sorry it could not be sooner."

"It's no matter," said Sophie. "We've had a great deal of distraction this year at Leatherbury."

Billingham nodded in agreement. "I'll let you choose whether or not to move our party to Oak Grove. I only want to make things easy for you. Murdock can ride in my carriage if it pleases him. He could ride with us there."

"I suppose," relented Sophie. She looked over the drawing room. Leaving Leatherbury to become a bride would be, in some ways, a sad day. "If it pleases you," she said at last, "it would ease the burden on my family here."

Billingham smiled with happiness. "Then stop your dusting and polishing at once, Miss Crestwood. You shall celebrate your engagement at Oak Grove whether it snows or not.

MR. BILLINGHAM STAYED late into the evening, then he rode back to Pembroke to sleep through the night as Captain Murdock's guest. A day later, he stopped for a time to see the Crestwoods once more, and then he left Higfield for good.

Sophie kept busy with list after list of things she must send to Oak Grove before Christmas. She exchanged letters with Lady Mary, agreeing on flowers and ribbons to decorate the salon. Both thought it must not be too Christmas-like.

Sophie waited until Thursday when it warmed up a little to walk to Pembroke. A brand-new stile had been built over the wall that made it easier to manage crossing between the pastures. She found

Captain Murdock in a winged back chair beside a fire in his modest study. His violin rested on his lap.

"How are you?" Sophie breezed into the room, recently refurbished in shades of gold, with a basket of fresh bread from Leatherbury's kitchen on her arm. The captain was gazing into the flames dancing in the hearth, but he motioned for her to sit.

"Well enough to see I need a new string for my bow," he answered, waving it back and forth. His words were loud and a bit more cheerful than the thoughtful look on his face.

"I interrupted your reflections," she said, rather than ask him why he looked so serious.

After a small hesitation, he replied, "You did not. I am always happy to see you here."

"You don't mind? I know it's a bit untoward coming without Jack or Mama."

"We are good neighbors now," he answered.

She settled in the chair next to him, balancing the basket on her knee. "Mama sent bread."

"She's too generous. We manage well enough here."

"It's true," she said. She smirked, teasing him. "You know I cannot rest if I'm worried Mr. Howard will wander off or Mrs. Brooks fall asleep and forget to bring you your supper."

Murdock glanced down at his half-leg covered by robes. "I manage well enough," he repeated, but it echoed with some surrender Sophie knew she would never understand.

"Mr. Billingham says you're troubled about how you will get on outside of Pembroke even with a new leg."

Murdock shifted in his chair, raising one shoulder in a shrug. "I thought I was half a man when I came to Higfield; no family, no ship, my home in St. Kitts sold off, and of course knowing my ambition cost Cottle his life." He shook his head slow and with sadness then looked back at Sophie. "Now I truly am."

"Oh, Captain," said Sophie, waving away his lament as if he had only misplaced a book, "you are not half a man, or you'd only have one eye and one arm." She narrowed her eyes, thinking. "And half a brain."

"You are miserable with compliments."

Sophie giggled. "I am sorry, but I won't pity you. It is too easy to do that for one's self."

He grimaced, and she worried she'd gone too far in her rebuke.

"I don't mean to make light of this great change in your life. I know you are in pain at times." She looked past him, over his shoulder, and out the window to the front lawn of Pembroke.

Murdock cleared his throat and picked up the violin. As he tucked it under his chin he said, "In many ways, I feel much better. The infection is gone. Your brother is home." He rubbed the bow across the strings, and the violin sang. After a few measures, he continued, "Then there is you, Miss Crestwood, who has your arrangement with Mr. Billingham. Everything is as is should be."

"Is everything as it should be here?" Sophie set the basket on the floor and sat back in the chair across from her admirable friend. She studied his chiseled cheeks that were no longer pale and sharp from illness.

He let the violin drop back to his lap. "I have a great deal of projects to concern myself with during the winter months, and I have ambitious plans for the gardens."

"The rose garden, too?" Delight washed over Sophie as she pictured it spreading from the house to the roadside.

"Yes," he said, "I'm going to expand it."

"You shall have clippings from Leatherbury," she promised him.

He nodded at her generosity.

"Did you know," she added, "that Lady Mary will allow me to use some of her greenhouse roses at the engagement supper?"

"They will look fine, I'm sure."

Sophie smiled, pleased that he agreed.

He chuckled. "You are more like your mother than you know, and your father, too, a small bit."

Sophie ducked her head. Her cheeks warmed at the memory of Papa's hurtful gossip. "If you mean that I speak far too much about other people, I know I do at times, and you are right."

"No," he said in a gentle tone. "That is not what I meant at all. Only that you are sensible but with fine taste. I have always admired how you give your opinion, yet you do so with restraint. You are mindful of others, and your concern is genuine. That is a rare gift these days."

She glanced up, happy he thought so well of her. "I used to think I had nothing in common with any of my family. You are a part of us now in a way, and you and I share many interests, like gardening, music, and walking or riding outdoors."

"We do not seem to mind the same people, either."

"I'm sure we have the same tastes when it comes to company. That we already know. Will you come to Oak Grove then? I know it is much further away."

Instead of answering, Murdock raised the violin again and played a sweet melody. Sophie sighed at his hesitation, but the peaceful sounds of the music calmed her anxiety. She reclined her head and relaxed her shoulders, sinking further into the chair.

At the final note, Murdock gave a sigh. Even playing a few minutes tired him out. "You should play at my party," murmured Sophie. "I am no musician, but I love it so." Her eyes almost closed.

"I will not be able to attend."

"What?" Sophie's eyes flew open.

"I said, I regret that I will not be able to be there." Murdock leaned over and set the instrument on the floor. He straightened and patted down the blanket on his leg. "It's just too far and the weather too cold now."

"Captain," Sophie contended, "it's not a full day's ride, and Mr. Billingham will send a carriage if your own is not serviceable."

He rubbed his lips together and shifted his gaze to the fire. "As happy as I am for you, Miss Crestwood, I do not think it wise I leave Pembroke."

A lump in Sophie's throat made her want to cough. She could not endure the idea of family, friends, and new relatives at Oak Grove with no Captain Murdock. "I know you do not sing or dance or like to lead every conversation," she said, "but your calm nature will keep us all... Well, I won't be happy if you're not there." Her eyes brimmed over with tears. "Neither will Jack." She crossed her arms over herself and willed him to look at her rather than into the fire.

"I'm sorry to disappoint you," he said in a soft tone, but he seemed more relieved than regretful. "I'm sure you will hardly notice my absence in all the excitement."

"That's not true," said Sophie. "I'm hardly excited anyway." She bit her tongue, both surprised and sorrowful that she would say such a thing. "Not that I'm not happy," she stuttered.

The room felt warm and airless. No. She was not excited at all to be married to her good friend, Henry Billingham. Sophie stared into the fire, hoping the heat on her hot face would camouflage the terrible thoughts swirling in her mind.

Murdock glanced at her without a word then his gaze went back to the fire. She sat with an uneasy sensation in her stomach, trying to pretend she did not really think what she had said and that there was not a dark and traitorous secret buried in her heart. It had always been there; her admiration for Captain Murdock had not gone away. She'd just decided to ignore it. It was more practical than ruining their happy acquaintanceship.

The lump in her throat felt like a walnut. Heaven and earth. She had strong feelings for the serious, handsome man beside her, but was marrying someone else instead. She forgot to breathe and gave a little hiccup, much to her embarrassment.

"You're alright?"

She nodded, not moving her eyes from the grey cinders where she had followed his stare.

Murdock saved her from the awkward and confusing admission by picking up the violin from the floor and playing a cheerful piece that sounded like men tromping up and down a deck. Sophie imagined sailors swinging each other around by the arms, elated to be off to sea with a horizon as the only limit to their freedom and adventures.

CHAPTER NINETEEN

One last look at the tall looking glass showed a pale girl in a stunning celestial blue gown. To compensate for its short sleeves, a white crape wrap draped around her shoulders. It was trimmed with lace and held together by a dainty chain of pearls at her throat. Betsy had curled Sophie's hair to frame her cheeks and tied a pretty Grecian scarf around her head, tucking small, white rosebuds in the back.

Sophie could not breathe quite right. She seemed unable to take in the air she needed and would have complained her stays were too tight, but everyone had left her alone. She studied her deep brown eyes. They may have been cow-like as Miss Banks had once said, but for certain, she looked like a frightened deer.

They would be waiting for her downstairs: Mr. Billingham, his parents, the mistress of Oak Grove, and all of Sophie's family and friends. Her heart thudded in a sick, unsteady beat. She closed her eyes and tried to square her shoulders. Now was the time to be brave. Without waiting for Papa or Mama to escort her down, she forced herself to put one dainty blue slipper in front of the other and appreciate the moment as the most celebrated guest at Oak Grove.

Angelic strings from the harp pealed through the slightly open door to the conservatory when she reached the stairs. Sophie hesitated with her hand on the railing. Everyone was downstairs, or so she thought, but the romantic trill from the tight strings sounded like a wistful memory. Her heart sank.

Devlin, she realized, had come after all, and brought his musical, mean wife. Sophie braced herself to face Miss Banks, now Mrs. Devlin, and pushed the door open far enough to peek through the crack.

A lanky man stood with his back to her, his jacket as dark as evergreen boughs. Trim brown hair, with streaks of gold and copper, fell over his collar. Sophie knew the solid set shoulders; her heart jumped in her chest, though she could not believe it. Not until he moved a slight bit, and his hand came down on top of the polished dragon head, and he struggled for balance.

Sophie slipped inside.

"Captain Murdock?" She did not want to break the spell the harp had cast over the room, so she spoke in a whisper.

He looked over his shoulder. She stared, first at his handsome, familiar face then at his trim waistcoat and slim trousers. They were long, blousing out over the tops of his boots, and showed no stocking. It felt like a dream. He was here, standing, and on both legs. She did not realize her eyes were creased in confusion until a smile passed over his face, and he laughed under his breath.

"You look as surprised to see me as I am to see you," he said.

Sophie put a hand on her chest, pressing it down to calm the thundering gallop in her heart. "I don't understand. You're standing."

Murdock looked down. He tilted himself to the side, raised the cane, and tapped his leg below his knee. It made a knocking sound. "New limb."

"Oh," Sophie said, embarrassed that she had not put it together. "You have your new leg, and you've come after all. You look quite normal."

"Yes," said Murdock. He did not seem to mind explaining. "It pains me after some time, but I could not disappoint you, so Doctor Stephens let me out and about as soon as he felt it was safe."

"I'm happy to see you," Sophie said, with an overwhelming rush of joy and affection. She crossed the room and held out her hands to him.

"I'm a bit wobbly," he warned. He took her by the hand and raised it to his lips, kissing the back of it.

It seemed he did so without thinking of it, but for Sophie, it set off a series of heated flashes in her cheeks and stomach. He dropped his hand as soon as he realized what he'd done.

"Pardon," he murmured. He leaned back onto the cane.

Sophie stared at the floor. "You're here, and it's wonderful. That's all that matters. Do they know downstairs?"

"Not everyone, no. I was almost to the salon, but I remembered I needed something from here." He motioned toward the violin case resting in the corner. "Lady Mary said I may borrow her bow, but I was tempted to play with her harp first."

Sophie clasped her hands together and raised them to her chin. "You are going to perform?"

"Of course, my dear, but on my violin, not the harp."

"Murdock," she said, dropping his title, "you do know how much this pleases me."

He dropped his chin in a curt nod. "That is why I came."

"You did? For me?"

She smiled so hard she felt it, but a little piece of her heart twisted until it hurt. Whispers of doubt flickered in her mind. Why had she come to Oak Grove?

"I wish I was as brave as Jack," she blurted. She put her fingers to her mouth to cover up the words.

Murdock smiled, his eyes crinkling around the corners. "You are brave, Miss Crestwood," he answered in a soft tone. "Are you searching for more compliments, before you walk downstairs and into your future?"

"Is this what you felt like when you left St. Kitts?"

Murdock shifted his weight, and Sophie reached for his arm and led him forward to sit on the red sofa.

"Tell me please," she whispered, dropping down beside him.

He looked at her; their faces so close she could see the slight curl of his lower lashes.

"You are going to wrinkle that brilliant gown," he said in a thick voice.

She could not tear her eyes away from his riveting stare. "You have never even noticed a bonnet, and now you are worried about my gown?"

"It's beautiful. You're beautiful, as lovely as I have ever seen you, besides the day... I mean when..."

Sophie gazed back into his eyes. Her heart danced with his every kind word, but her mind chided her to remember that she was over-due in the salon.

"The first time I saw you at Pembroke, that wall—" He stopped, pressed his lips together, and gave a little smile. "It was a boundary in more ways than one." His eyes shimmered as he studied her.

She could not keep the corners of her mouth from curling up. Warmth cascaded over her head and shoulders.

He took a deep breath and said in a soft voice, "I left St. Kitts fueled by hope that I would find a place where I belonged just as my father wished; and yes, I was afraid."

Sophie's head wavered in an understanding nod. "He hoped you might love it here as he once did."

"Yes, as did my mother. Her name was Constance Hamilton. She was from a family with Northumberland roots. Her widowed father brought her to the Indies to marry a cousin, but she met my father instead. I will always miss her and mourn that she died while I was just a boy. She talked about England with great affection."

"You've never spoken of her." Sophie reached for Murdock's hand. "I'm happy your father found someone else, and that he loved you despite his weaknesses."

Murdock nodded his thanks. "My father's habits, his grief over losing two lovers, and his discontent with English politics, made him a poor and inattentive parent. I cherished him though. Nothing will ever take his place or the place of my dear island home, but the tide is not so far from Higfield, and if I am not content in the gardens I can find my way to the seashore."

"Or stables," added Sophie, "fencing with the most willing local boy brave enough to take you on."

He smiled. "A one-legged man," he said with a shrug.

"I have never known you to have two good legs and have loved you just the same."

"Do you?" Murdock asked in a quiet voice, and he cast his gaze to the floor just as Sophie remembered where she was and why.

With burning cheeks, she shook her head. "I do." Her eyes filled with tears, and they spilled over as she looked away. Why must she speak her true mind at the most inappropriate of times?

In one swift, honest acknowledgment she now felt sad. Everything was all wrong, and once again she had put them in a terrible and awkward position. Captain Murdock had already made it clear she should not esteem him so.

She stood up in a rush. He came up off the couch at the same time, like she'd cried out, and reached for her arm to pull her close and keep her from leaving. His soft fingertips brushed her tears away.

"Don't cry," he ordered. His tone changed to a firm and resolute timbre. "What will they think when I take you downstairs." He looked past her toward the violin case. "We are late," he said but did not move.

Sophie could not move either. The grief in her soul made her want to be pulled through a hole in the floor. Everyone had what they wished for but her. She would not have Leatherbury. She would not have Pembroke. She would not have Captain Murdock.

An unseen chill moved through the room. She put the back of her hand—the hand he had kissed—over her mouth and released a sob as her chest sank. Before she could sniffle or feel mortified at her emotional exhibition, a strong arm went around her waist. Captain Murdock crushed her to him, and she found her face nestled in the center of his perfectly tied cravat.

"I don't want to get married," she choked out. "I love... I like... I do admire Mr. Billingham so, but—" She began to cry, horrified to expose such delicate and private feelings before him, but there was no one else to tell. She caught her breath, sniffled, and broke back down again. Murdock said nothing but embraced her, rubbing her arms and stroking her back.

"I did say you were the bravest girl I knew."

Sophie heard him swallow. He was very warm, radiating heat like stones in the summer sun. She raised her head. Murdock must advise her what to do.

"Jack would tell me to run away," she croaked. "My parents would have me do the sensible thing and become the mistress of this great estate. What say you, Edward Murdock?"

He looked down at her, his gaze probing. "What does your heart tell you to do, Sophie Crestwood?" His voice was a whisper.

She closed her eyes and took a deep, full breath. Her heart had been screaming the truth at her all along. She looked. Murdock's face was somehow closer, near enough for his nose to brush the end of hers. She glanced at his mouth and the little dip above his lip. There was a shadow with the faintest hint of a mustache. The room around them whirled by, and she clung to him so that she did not fall. Her lashes fluttered, and when she gathered the courage to glance up through them again, his eyes were low and watchful. She dared not breathe. Then, with the smallest movement, his mouth moved toward hers, until it rested softly on her trembling lips. She closed her eyes and kissed him back.

THEY WALKED ARM IN arm down the grand staircase, only to find Mama pacing the black and white marble tiles like an expectant father. When she looked up, Sophie tried to smile, but Mama's deep frown made her stomach tremble.

"Captain Murdock, we were not expecting you," Mama said, although she did not look surprised to see him bobbling down the stairs. It took a great deal of concentration for him to move down each step with his false leg, so he held on to Sophie's arm even as he replied, "I had a change of heart and sent word to Lady Mary."

"Did you?"

He bowed to her when he reached the polished floor. Mama lifted her chin, but her gaze raked him up and down before gliding over to study Sophie's face.

"I needed something from upstairs," explained Murdock.

"I see." Mama did see. Something. Sophie tried to hide her guilt, but it was difficult because her entire body buzzed with sweet elation. The top of her head felt like it could float up to the ceiling.

Captain Murdock blinked and made a great show of innocence, but Sophie worried since she could see through it, so could Mama. He had a much better bluffing face at cards.

Mrs. Crestwood stared. "I'd like to speak to my daughter alone, please."

"Of course," Murdock told her, trying to sound agreeable. He hesitated like he might inform her Sophie had changed her mind about the engagement.

And that he'd kissed her.

And now, Billingham might decide to blow his other leg off.

Sophie put her fingertips to her temples as he shuffled down the hall with a serious parting glance in her direction. He'd apologized for his impropriety, and she had begged him not to. He also assured her he would support her no matter how severe the backlash for breaking her commitment to the heir of Oak Grove; he had, after all, been Jack's greatest champion.

Sophie realized that Mama still watched her. Not her gown, but her cheeks and eyes, like she was trying to see something in Sophie that could not be hidden.

"What?" she asked, although it came out in a whimper. In only moments she would have to break Henry Billingham's heart, or at least disappoint him.

Mama pursed her lips and looked worried. "I am just come down from checking on you in your room. Only you were not there, and so I came back." Her serious gaze bore into Sophie's soul. "You left the music room door ajar, my dear."

A bolt of mortification struck Sophie with so much shame she thought she would melt into a puddle of disgrace on the floor. She could not speak.

In a soft voice, Mama said, "Kissing the pirate from Pembroke in Lady Mary's conservatory, while her nephew waits for you at your engagement party, is not quite the proper etiquette."

Sophie could not lift her gaze from her own slippers, so heavy was her regret. "It was not appropriate," whispered Sophie, "but not deliberate either, I swear to you."

"Romantic, yes, proper, no. This is not a novel, my darling girl."

Sophie nodded with downcast eyes.

"More like the on dits column," said an imperious voice.

Sophie dared not look up at the sound of Lady Mary's words, although she jerked in surprise. A searing wave of humiliation washed over her from head to toe. She was certain her cheeks looked as purple as wine. She peeked up at Mama and could have sworn her mother's lips were twitching to fight back a smile.

In a rustle of silk, Lady Mary came around the staircase. Sophie forced herself to turn about in a slow and prim manner and drop a deep curtsey.

The lady put her hands on her sharp hips that protruded from beneath her tight stays. "Have you finally made up your mind?" Her tone sounded layered with sadness and good humor.

Sophie bit her lip.

"Well, Miss Crestwood, I did not expect you to say yes to my nephew in the first place; you being so thorough in your decisions. Of course, I was delighted, and I dare say you both would have been content and done very well, however—" Lady Mary exhaled with a sharp sigh. "Your mother isn't the only woman who fell for an heir of Pembroke. The whole wretched family has a history of crushing dreams and leaving hearts in splinters; but they are a loyal, devoted sort once they are in love."

Sophie lifted her head in surprise.

"I've just had a word with Captain Murdock," Lady Mary explained. She shifted her scrutiny to the ceiling for an instant as if questioning heaven's way of things. "You are very fortunate I once swooned over Murdock's grandfather and find myself terribly fond of Edward's son; almost as fond as my Henry. Elsewise Sophie, I fear I may have turned the both of you out onto the front stoop never to see you again."

THE SNOW DID NOT COME. In the stables, Henry Billingham stood straight with boots together. Sophie found him the next morning. She could only assume he meant to ride off and escape the tension hanging in the halls of Oak Grove that would linger until the Crestwoods made their penitent leave.

Sophie stared at his shadow on the ground. She'd hid in her room the night before to avoid the awkwardness that would ensue when Lady Mary cancelled the engagement. In her room in the blue wing, the entire night blurred by as Sophie planned what she would say to Billingham when she could gather the courage to look him in the face. As she struggled to collect her thoughts, he spoke first.

"I know we are good friends," he said in the hush, "and I know I did not make any great effort to pursue you—"

"Don't," Sophie said in a whisper. The word came out strangled and gruff. She could not bear to tell him her soul ached only for the company and affection of Pembroke's master.

"I admire you far more than you know; far more than I knew. Please." Billingham held out a gloved hand. It seemed all the wealth and privilege in the world lay in the palm of it.

She found the courage to look up and meet his regard, then she smiled with as much tenderness as she could find in her heart. "I do admire you, Mr. Billingham, very much. You are one of the greatest friends I have been so lucky to find." Her throat clenched at the anxiety in his stare. "We shall be good friends always, I just know it."

He laughed, a short barking guffaw, and his shoulders drooped. It broke the spell between them. "I understand," he said in a croak, and then he laughed at the tightness in his voice. Sadness smeared his features.

Sophie could not bear his reddening cheeks. "I am sorry to have shamed you; to make it seem I've used you ill."

"What man does not truly care for a woman that he does not want her to be happy? That is what I love about you. You know your own mind; or at least when you do, you own up to it."

She shook her head in modesty.

"I knew it when you spoke out in defense of Murdock this summer." Billingham managed to smile. "You are a true lady, and I wish you every joy."

A runaway tear escaped the corner of Sophie's eye and trailed with great speed down her cheek. The silence between them felt strange; the sounds of animals moving around like a cacophony.

"It's him, isn't it?"

She did not have to question Billingham's meaning, for she knew it, and she knew he knew that she did. "My friend," she said with a forced chuckle, "if I am to be true to myself I suppose I am to expect some regret in my future. It may be that I am left disappointed."

"Oh?" Billingham gave her a small, teasing look. "Don't be so certain, my dear girl. If you are brave enough to look honestly into your own heart and live by it, I'm sure you will have your happy ending when all is said and done." He winked at her, and Sophie's brows rose with a slight smile at his hopeful forecast.

AS SOPHIE HUNG THE mistletoe in a prominent place in the drawing room, she wondered what Christmas was like on the other side of the equator. Snow had arrived weeks before, limiting her time outdoors. It did not deter Captain Murdock, who rode down on his bay often to visit with the Crestwoods. He was fascinated by the white blankets of snowflakes, despite the freezing weather and his handicap, and said he should never want to spend another Christmas sweating under the equatorial sun.

Sophie separated candlesticks to each end of the mantel, pleased to see Margaret had dusted well. Thoughts drifting back to Murdock, she suspected his leg pained him a great deal; more than he let on. Doctor Stephens had told Papa the captain would heal with time, although he would always need some medicine or another to reduce the shadowy aches and sharp twinges of the amputated nerves.

He seemed quite cheerful for such grey and bracing weather, and his commanding presence added an additional layer of comfort to Leatherbury. Alone with Sophie, he discussed a more permanent situation between them. She knew what her family expected of him; of them both, since ending her engagement with Billingham, but he was in no mad rush to force her to any commitment just because of the inconvenient timing of their hearts.

"If you keep moving the room around, I shall never be able to re-member where I put my knitting," Mama chided as she slipped in.

Sophie stepped back and smiled at her management of the pretty things over the fireplace. "Do you mind that I pulled back the cur-tains? I know it lets in a bit of chill, but the sunshine strikes the glass, too, and it's not been out for three whole days."

"I suppose not," murmured Mama. She settled in her chair and reached for a wool blanket.

Sophie hurried over and helped smooth it over her lap. She said, "I believe Captain Murdock will call today. He has news about his friend, Perlmutter, in the Caribbean."

"Oh yes," Mama agreed, "a Master and Commander. It does sound impressive, does it not?"

"Yes," said Sophie, "to Jack especially."

"Ha," Mama returned, "we will see how he endures the full glory of the sun and gritty, invasive sand in his every crevice."

Sophie laughed. "He will not mind it, Mama. He used to roll around in the mud just to feel it squish."

Mama pretended to sigh. "Really, the both of you. I'll be grey as a gander by the time that boy makes lieutenant." She gave a quick shake of her head in surrender. "Every young man I knew who went away to sea never came back home. Then there was Sir Edward."

"Captain Murdock has come home," Sophie insisted.

"His father must have been beside himself to have his firstborn sign on to the Navy."

Sophie nodded. "He was, but there was little choice."

"Yes, Edward always did like to drink a great deal, but most gen-tlemen do."

"You know him so much better than you ever let on. Why, I heard you tell Murdock last week you once outshot his father in a contest."

"Archery," Mama answered with wide, innocent eyes.

Sophie studied her mother's face. "You were deeply in love with Sir Edward, weren't you, Mama?"

Mama put the knitting down and looked her in the eye. "Very much so, but of course, Lady Mary has told you all about that I presume."

"She did say you were fond of him and that he broke a great deal of many hearts."

"Yes," Mama said, showing no remorse, "and one of them was mine."

"You found, Papa though."

"I did."

Sophie bit her lip. "Are you sorry?"

She waited without breathing, her cheeks growing warm. It all made perfect sense. She had known it in some quiet way but had not realized it. Sweet, romantic Mama had loved Sir Edward Murdock, and when he could not return the depths of her affection, she settled on a reasonably good alternative.

"I do love your father," Mama reassured her. "I confess I have my moments, but I made a wise choice, and I've been blessed with three wonderful children who have grown up to be intelligent, kind, and brave.

Sophie clasped her hands in her lap and studied her fingernails. "Do you understand why I could not accept Mr. Billingham?"

Mama nodded. "I do, and I certainly would expect it should Murdock return your affection."

Sophie smiled. "I didn't know he did. It took him awhile to come around, I think."

"I doubt he had to come around at all, sweet girl. He is a bit older than you and has regrets, not to mention the indignity of Sir Edward's last days, and the estate here so grown over and forgotten."

"All's well," said Sophie with a happy sigh. "He has moved past that now, and he's almost a hero all the way to London after what he did for Jack. I'm sure he'll always have sad memories of Mr. Cottle, and I daresay struggle with having one good leg instead of two, but he has settled into Pembroke and come to love it as much as we do."

"He loves you, too," Mama said with a wink.

Sophie blushed. "He has said as much, and he does show it in many ways—but his ways."

SEVERAL DAYS AFTER Christmas, a violin drew out the remaining notes of Handel. Sophie sank with contentment into the cushions of the French settle in Pembroke's drawing room. Mama, Katherine, and Mrs. Porter clapped with fervency. Across the room, Papa whispered to Doctor Stephens but gave the captain a bow to show appreciation for his talent.

"That was the loveliest piece ever," Sophie decided. "I don't wonder that your Mama made you learn to play such a fine instrument."

Captain Murdock dropped into his chair with a bit of an awkward plop. He swung out his false leg in front of him, a forethought that Sophie knew made it possible for him to stand up before anyone gave a thought to his limitations.

His right leg was stronger than ever and did a great deal of the work, so much so he complained he would soon have one giant trunk of a leg and a skinny stick for the other. The idea of it made her laugh, and she giggled when she wrote about it to Jack who would take it far more seriously than she.

"You have such a gift," Katherine said. She gave Murdock her most sincere study. "If I practiced my pianoforte twice as much as I do now, I would never be half so good as you, sir."

Murdock gave her a small smile that kept him from disagreeing or offering the compliments she wished for, and he glanced at Sophie with some amusement. "I promised Miss Crestwood at Oak Grove I would perform. Now—" he motioned toward a window with a slant of his head.

Katherine clapped her hands together, just as the echo of jingling bells could be heard from the drive. "Is it time? I'm so eager. I haven't been sleigh-riding in over two years." She looked around the room and found her mother. "May I?"

From her relaxed position beside Mrs. Porter, Mrs. Blackburn nodded her approval.

Sophie rose with enthusiasm, eager to take the captain's arm. Only she and Katherine could be convinced to venture out into such cold weather with him. There were mounds of cloaks and muffs waiting for them in the hall, but she would endure the layers to take a sleigh ride. She could not wait to glide across the glazed roads of Higfield in Pembroke's new sleigh. Not to mention, be snuggled up under warm animal furs with her best friend and beloved on either side.

Once they were dressed for the weather, a new footman with a peculiar earring dangling like a pendulum from his ear, led them through the door. Sophie grinned at his mutters about the freezing weather as he tucked her into the horsehair seat and swaddled her in blankets.

"Where is Katherine?" she wondered aloud as Captain Murdock was helped in beside her. He did not reply but moved close enough to pass his arm through hers. She peered past him and saw only Mama, who stood at the window watching them from inside.

The coachman cracked his whip, and Sophie cried out, "Katherine!" just as the sleigh began to skate across the silvery, white powder on the ground. She stretched to see over Murdock's shoulder and found him grinning at her. His teeth glowed in the light of a waning, yet almost full moon.

"It's all well and good," he said in a smooth voice. "She had a change of mind and decided to see the repairs on the old green-house."

Sophie pulled her head back in surprise. "At night in the cold?"

"It's not so cold in there, and Mr. Jarvis has promised to walk her out."

"Well," said Sophie with a frown, "I do not know about that. We hardly know Mr. Jarvis, other than he lived near you in St. Kitts, and why is he here again?"

Murdock shrugged, still smiling although it became wily. "I recommended the weather."

"Ha-ha," laughed Sophie, but then she felt shy. "We are alone then."

"Yes," said Murdock, "except for the driver." His hand found her gloved fingers under the mounds of furs. "Your parents will not mind. I especially asked your Mama."

"She would agree to anything you asked of her, and it's no secret she turns a liberal eye." Sophie gave a small toss of her head and would have shaken her finger at him, but it was too cold to lift one out even with them covered up.

Murdock snorted in laughter. "I'm only glad your brother is not here. He'd either be begging me to drive or slinging frozen walnuts at me for leaving him behind."

"Would you leave him behind, too?" Sophie teased. "I thought you liked him a great deal more than me."

"It depends on whom is wielding the weapon—the sword or the sneeze."

Sophie gasped then laughed. "I haven't sneezed in a very long time at Pembroke. It's all dusted up now, except the attic, which Mrs. Brooks says is your project next spring."

"Yes," mused the captain, "there is a great deal of furniture and trunks to sift through. It's not something I look forward to, digging into old and derelict things."

"I quite like old and derelict things," Sophie said with a grin. "You never know what you might find at Pembroke."

"Yes, we know, my dear."

Captain Murdock met her admiring gaze then turned to watch the road ahead, rubbing Sophie's thumb with his own, making her wish she had not worn gloves despite the cold. She sighed with happiness and looked up into a clear sky, shining with a thousand stars. "To think he sees the same moon," she whispered.

Murdock looked up, too, and Sophie dropped her head onto his shoulder. She did not mind that Katherine had not come after all.

"I'm sure your brother is missing home in his own way, but he'll do well for now."

"Thanks to you."

Murdock cleared his throat. He took a deep breath then said in a rush of words, "I am, in fact, quite happy he's not here." As he spoke, Sophie watched his words change into a cloudy mist that hung in the air.

"Why is that?"

"Because it would be awkward to propose to the young lady of Leatherbury with her brother hanging over my shoulder."

Sophie meant to laugh at the picture of Jack squeezing his face between their cheeks, but something Murdock said made it freeze like ice in her throat. She raised her head from his shoulder and peered into his bright eyes that glowed beneath a heavy beaver hat.

He smiled at her in the moonlight, a small, shy look that allowed just a trace of his dimple to form a hollow in his cheek. It made her heart drop into her stomach. He squeezed her hand.

"Would you marry me, Miss Crestwood, my dear, sweet girl?"

She gasped and laughed at the same time. "Yes," she whispered with a tight throat that could not hold back the tears. He squeezed her hand, and she thought he might kiss her by the look of affection in his eyes.

Gazing at her under the light of winter's twinkling stars, Murdock confessed in his dry way, "I would have walked you to the wall where we first met and taken a proper knee to propose, but I only have one good one."

Another chuckle escaped from Sophie's happiness. Her eyes overflowed with wet amusement and joy. "You do not have to take a knee, Captain Murdock." She laughed through her tears. "And by the by," she reminded him, "the wall is not the boundary of our estates." She lowered her voice to mimic his even tone, "but the low-lying stream several yards beyond the grove—to where you once chased my brother!"

EPILOGUE

Sophie Murdock, mistress of Pembroke Hall, loved her family. She felt there could be nothing more advantageous than having a father who knew everything about everyone; for he was an endless source of information she could turn to while ignoring the tittle and tattle around the village. Of course, she took her papa's news with a grain of salt, and never, as she swore to him, repeated it to anyone else.

As for her mother, Sophie appreciated her deep imagination and propensity for romance. She had encouraged her only daughter to marry a reputed pirate after all; for even an honest buccaneer in the family mattered little if he was loved and loved them back.

The pirate of Pembroke himself was a man whom almost everyone now admired. Captain Murdock had saved one of their own and brought life back to the crumbling walls of the oldest manor house in the county. Along with its forests and fields, Pembroke's gardens blossomed with roses once again, and the hunts in distant memories were revived.

And Jack, dear Jack. Sophie's brother, Fifth Lieutenant Crestwood, sent them all the best stories and gifts from Antigua where he was happily posted. It was just a day's sail away from a magical little island called St. Kitts; a place Captain Murdock promised to take his wife someday, should she ever find herself in want of pirates or adventure.

THE END

ABOUT THE AUTHOR

Danielle Thorne writes historical and contemporary romance from south of Atlanta, Georgia. Married for thirty years to the same fellow, she's the mother of four boys, two daughters-in-law, and she has two grandbabies. There are also cats involved.

Danielle is a graduate of BYU-Idaho. Besides writing pursuits, she's active in her church and community. Free time is filled with books, movies, too much yardwork, and not enough wandering the country or cruising the beautiful, blue seas. She's worked as an editor for Solstice and Desert Breeze Publishing and is the author of non-fiction for young adults.

She can be found on most social media platforms. Her first book with Harlequin's Love Inspired line will be out July 2020.

Find out more about Danielle's love of Jane Austen, pirates, and all things historical and romantic at www.daniellethorne.com

Made in the USA
Las Vegas, NV
25 July 2021